Katie Flynn is the pen name of the much-loved writer, Judy Turner, who published over ninety novels in her lifetime. Judy's unique stories were inspired by hearing family recollections of life in Liverpool during the early twentieth century, and her books went on to sell more than eight million copies. Judy passed away in January 2019, aged 82.

The legacy of Katie Flynn lives on through her daughter, Holly Flynn, who continues to write under the Katie Flynn name. Holly worked as an assistant to her mother for many years and together they co-authored a number of Katie Flynn novels, including *Christmas at Tuppenny Corner*.

Holly lives in the north east of Wales with her husband Simon and their two children. When she's not writing she enjoys walking her two lurchers, Sparky and Snoopy, in the surrounding countryside, and cooking forbidden foods such as pies, cakes and puddings! She looks forward to sharing many more Katie Flynn stories, which she and her mother devised together, with readers in the years to come.

A Mother's Love

KATIE FLYNN

arrow books

1 3 5 7 9 10 8 6 4 2

Arrow Books
20 Vauxhall Bridge Road
London SW1V 2SA

Arrow Books is part of the Penguin Random House group
of companies whose addresses can be found at
global.penguinrandomhouse.com.

Penguin
Random House
UK

First published in Great Britain by Century in 2019
First published in paperback by Arrow Books in 2019

www.penguin.co.uk

A CIP catalogue record for this book is available from the British
Library.

ISBN 9781784755256

Typeset in 11/14 pt Palatino LT Pro
by Integra Software Services Pvt. Ltd, Pondicherry

Printed and bound in Great Britain by Clays Ltd, Elcograf S.p.A.

MIX
Paper from
responsible sources
FSC
www.fsc.org
FSC® C018179

Penguin Random House is committed to a
sustainable future for our business, our readers
and our planet. This book is made from Forest
Stewardship Council® certified paper.

Acknowledgements

Thanks to Liz Dodds and her extensive knowledge on the Avro Lancaster, also to the Lincolnshire Heritage Aviation Society and their virtual tour of the magnificent Just Jane.

To the brave boys of Bomber Command

Prologue

Spring 1940

A small group had gathered around the open grave in Walton Cemetery. Pulling up the collar on her mother's old woollen coat, Ellie Lancton clasped the ends tightly together as the sharp bite of the March wind tried to penetrate the nape of her neck.

The priest's voice blended into the background as Ellie, tears trickling down her face, mulled over the events which had led to her mother's untimely death. Winter was always the hardest time of year for those who lived in the courts, and the beginning of 1940 had proved to be one of the worst on record. Millie Lancton had started off with a cough just after Christmas, and for a time it had looked as though that was all it was, but as February neared its end there was no denying that her condition had worsened.

'You know I don't like wasting good money on doctors ...' Millie had begun, only to break off into a bout of coughing which left her chest heaving as she fought to regain her breath. 'It's money what we need to pay the rent, or buy fuel for the fire, or food. Them's more important than cough medicine, so don't go spendin' it on what ain't necessary.'

Ellie had frowned at her mother. 'You're just like Gran used to be, God rest her soul – stubborn as an ox!' Taking her mother's limp hand in her own, she had looked imploringly into her eyes. 'Please let me call Dr Cotter, Mam. You're pale as linen and you've not been able to get out of bed for over a week. If I'm wrong and makin' a mountain out of a molehill, it'll be worth the shilling just to hear him say that I'm worryin' over nowt.'

Ellie's mother had opened her mouth to argue, but once again the dreadful cough had snatched her words. She had waved a weak hand in the direction of the door. 'I'm in no position to argue, or to stop you, for that matter. Do what you see fit.'

Smiling thankfully, Ellie had descended the steep stairs two at a time before her mother could change her mind. Her feet barely touching the cobbles, she had dashed across the court and within a minute or so she was racing down the Scotland Road. When she reached the doctor's house, she pounded the large brass knocker repeatedly until the doctor himself swung the door open.

Taking his coat from the peg behind the door, he reached down for his bag as he listened to Ellie's worries, a look of grave concern etched across his thin face. 'Your mother never would listen to reason,' he said impatiently. 'She must know pneumonia's been sweeping through the courts, yet she's still bothered about the expense. I'd wager she only let you come and get me now because she's too weak to argue.'

Ellie pulled an apologetic face. 'I did try before, but you're right, of course. She only listened this time 'cos she's got no choice.'

Passing Ellie his bag, Dr Cotter slid his arm into the sleeve of his coat. 'Bearing in mind it's only fifteen years since I brought you into this world, young Ellie, it beggars belief that you've more sense than your mother.'

When they reached the small house in Lavender Court, Ellie led the way up the steep wooden staircase to the room her mother rented. Entering the room behind her, the doctor looked sternly at Millie and wagged a reproving finger. 'Never mind scowlin', Millie Lancton; you're lucky your Ellie had enough sense to fetch me. It's not often the child has more sense than the mother. How could you be so silly?'

Leaving him to tend to her mother, Ellie backed out of the room and sat at the top of the wooden staircase with her hands palm down beneath her bottom. From inside the room she could hear Dr Cotter ordering her mother to 'take a deep breath' just as the door to the room at the bottom of the staircase opened and Sid Crowther, the landlord of Lavender Court, poked his head round the corner.

'Can't you get your mam to shurrup? I'm sick to death of hearin' her hackin' her guts up night and day. I barely got no kip last night, and I expect tonight'll be the same. There's plenty of folk what's interested in that room, and I dare say I wouldn't have to listen to any o' them coughin' all night long.'

Fearing eviction, Ellie spoke hastily. 'It's not as if she does it on purpose. Besides, Dr Cotter's in there now; he'll soon get her right as rain—' She jumped as the door beside her swung open and the doctor looked out.

'I've finished examing your mother,' he said. 'You'd better come in.'

Unsurprised, Ellie heard the door of the landlord's room clicking shut behind him. Typical, she thought to herself. The loathsome man was always quick to bully the women of the court, but as soon as a man appeared on the scene he was never slow to scuttle off.

Dr Cotter stood beside Millie's bed. 'I've told your mother that she needs hospital treatment. I'm certain she's got pneumonia, and it could get worse.' Looking at Ellie over the top of his round spectacles, he rolled his eyes. 'She's refusing to go to hospital; reckons she'll die if we admit her. Try to talk some sense into her, will you?'

Ellie crossed the small room and sat down on the thin blanket that covered the straw mattress. Clasping her mother's frail hand, she looked at her with pleading eyes. 'Mam, you've gorra go in. I promise I'll come and see you all I can, but please listen to the doctor. You can't stay here, not in this … this …' She waved a vague hand around the soot-coated walls streaked with condensation, the frost-laced window and the bare floorboards which were riddled with woodworm and mould. 'You've gorra go, Mam. Hospitals are warm and dry, and they've got medicine. You'll get better there …'

Back at the graveside the sound of a woman quietly clearing her throat brought Ellie back to the present. Raising her eyes, she looked into the anxious face of her neighbour, Mrs Burgess, who in turn looked

4

pointedly towards the head of the grave. Ellie glanced around the sea of expectant faces until her eyes met the priest's. He nodded encouragingly at her. 'I believe you have something ...'

Stepping forward, she gently pulled the sprig of lavender from her pocket, pressed it to her lips, then held it over the top of her mother's coffin. Opening her fingers, she whispered, 'Goodbye, Mam,' and let the dried flower fall. It was too much. Her shoulders began to shake and the tears coursed down her cheeks. She felt a heavy arm place itself around her shoulders and glanced up to see Mrs Burgess staring fixedly at the person whose arm it was. Twisting her head to follow the older woman's gaze, she saw that it was Sid Crowther.

Ellie could understand the older woman's dislike of their landlord, who was known for having a short fuse when it came to his tenants, but since her mother's demise his attitude towards Ellie had changed. Instead of hassling her for rent as he had when her mother had been ill, he hardly ever broached the subject, and on the few occasions when he had he had been far more relaxed and considerate.

'Your mam were allus a month in advance with the rent, so you've got that saving grace if you should need it, and if in future you should find yourself running a bit short o' time or money I'm sure we can come to some kind of arrangement.'

Ellie, who had half expected to be thrown out into the street, had been thoroughly relieved by the landlord's empathy, and had said as much when she had paid a visit to Mrs Burgess later that day. 'He said that

5

I were fine for now, and I weren't to worry, 'cos in future he'd give me extra time if I should need it.'

The older woman had looked sharply at Ellie. 'Are you sure those were his exact words?'

Ellie shrugged. 'As good as. He said me mam were a month ahead with her rent, so I've got some breathin' space.'

Mrs Burgess had laid a reassuring hand on Ellie's arm. 'If you ever need help, or if he turns on you—' She raised a finger as Ellie opened her mouth to interrupt. 'I only said if. You know what he can be like, so just you be careful, and make sure you come to me.'

Ellie nodded. 'Thanks, Mrs B, and I promise, if I can't find the rent or if he starts, you'll be the first to know.'

The older woman had nodded decidedly. No one ever spoke out directly against the landlord's methods when it came to making sure he got his rent on time, but there were always rumours, unexplained black eyes, and looks of fear whenever his name was mentioned, and as far as Mrs Burgess was concerned there was never any smoke without fire.

Now, the priest placed his Bible under his arm and walked over to Ellie. His face was stern as his eyes met the landlord's, and he nodded curtly. 'Mr Crowther.' His features softened as he turned his gaze on Ellie. 'If you should ever want to talk about anything, you know where to find me. My door is always open.'

Nodding, Ellie cringed as she felt Sid Crowther's hold tighteen. 'Same applies,' he said gruffly. 'If you ever need a shoulder to cry on—' He was interrupted by Mrs Burgess, who had linked her arm through Ellie's and was pulling her away.

'She's plenty of shoulders to cry on, although I'm sure it's nice of you to offer, Mr Crowther,' the old woman said firmly, her lips pursed, before turning to the priest and giving a small nod. 'Lovely service.'

Ellie felt Sid's arm tense on her back, but Mrs Burgess continued to pull and reluctantly, Ellie thought, Sid released his grip. For a moment the three of them stood in silence before Sid, touching the peak of his cap, spoke brusquely. 'I dare say I shall see you later, Ellie, and don't forget you know where to find me if you need owt.' He marched stiffly off in the direction of the cemetery gates.

Mrs Burgess gave a contemptuous sniff. 'If you take my advice that's one offer you should pass up.' She glanced sideways at Ellie. 'You all right, dear? I must say I thought it were a lovely service. Millie would've liked the hymns you chose.'

As they walked along the gravel path Ellie nodded towards one of the gravestones. 'That's what me mam should've had, summat grand like that, then everyone would know who she was and that she was someone special, and well loved.' She looked over her shoulder. 'Not stuck in the corner, with not so much as a cross to mark where she lies, forgotten and out of the way where no one ever goes.'

Mrs Burgess patted Ellie's ungloved hand. 'She were someone special – still is in our hearts – and you don't need no headstone to tell folk so. She'll never be forgot, your mam won't, not by the likes of us at any rate.'

7

Ellie smiled gratefully at the other woman. 'Thanks for comin', Mrs B. It means a lot havin' you here. I wish Arla could've come, but her auntie's been taken ill, so she had to go with her mam to help nurse her. I don't know if I could've coped if you hadn't been able to make it either.'

Mrs Burgess smiled reassuringly. 'You would have, You know. You've your mam's spirit.' She glanced approvingly at Ellie's thick black coat. 'That were your mam's, weren't it?'

Ellie nodded as she fingered the thick collar. 'It was her only winter one, which was why she always insisted I wore it if the weather turned bad. Probably why she got pneumonia in the first place.'

Mrs Burgess wagged a reproving finger. 'None of that talk, young lady. No one is to blame for your mam's passin'. It were a bad mix between that wicked winter we 'ad and the damp in those bloody rooms we live in.' She shook her head regretfully. 'They should've been condemned years back, the lot of 'em; should've knocked the lot down an' started afresh.'

Ellie nodded ruefully. 'Me mam always said the best thing about Lavender Court was its name. It was her favourite flower was lavender.'

Mrs Burgess looked at Ellie. 'Have you got anythin' other than that coat to remember her by? Any photos, perhaps?'

Ellie nodded. 'A couple. We keep 'em in a tin box under the floorboards, so's they don't suffer with the damp.'

The older woman pulled a locket out from round her neck. 'I gorra picture of my Arnie in 'ere.' She flicked it open and showed Ellie the miniature photograph of a cheerful-looking man with a bushy walrus moustache. 'If you got a locket you could put a picture of your mam in it.'

Ellie nodded thoughtfully. 'I'd have to save up to buy one, of course, then have one of the photos resized, and I dare say that wouldn't be cheap ...' She looked across at Mrs Burgess's weathered face, and the kind blue eyes that sparkled hopefully up at her. 'It's a grand idea, Mrs B, just the sort of thing I need at the moment, summat positive to think about.'

Mrs Burgess beamed. 'I know we've already talked about rent, but have you got any other money to be gettin' along with, to buy food and so on?'

Ellie nodded. 'I'm workin' for Mr Wong on the Scottie, and I took Mam's other laundry job on when she were too ill to do the work and Mrs Wardle reckons I've done as good a job as she did, so she's happy to keep me on as well.'

The old lady smiled approvingly. 'The apple didn't fall too far from the tree when it comes to you and your mam, did it? She were allus a hard worker and never shied from her responsibilities, and you're just the same. Peas in a pod, that's what you two are. Were.'

Ellie nodded. 'There's no sense in dwellin' on if onlys; you've got to get on with things. Put your best foot forward and keep smilin', that's what me mam always used to say.'

'Aye, an' she were right there, and whilst you've already proved you're more than capable of lookin' after yerself, tonight you're goin' to have your tea at mine. It's only blind scouse, but I like to think I mek a

9

good job of it. After that you can try and get your head down for a bit. It's been a tough day and I dare say your mind won't want you to rest when you turn in, but you'll have to try your best. There's no sense wanderin' round like a dead dog tryin' to do a good job of the laundry. And remember, if you need help with anythin', I'm allus here to lend a hand. She were a good friend to me were your mam, and I'd like to think she can rest in peace knowin' I'm keepin' an eye on things. After all, you don't need anythin' else goin' wrong.'

Ellie's bottom lip trembled and she wondered how, after the loss of her mother whom she loved so dearly, anything could possibly be worse, but instead of voicing her thoughts she said, 'Thanks, Mrs B. I could do with a bit of company tonight.'

Chapter One

Ellie raced along the jigger, her bare feet sliding painfully over the rain-soaked cobbles, her hair smeared to her face by a mixture of rain, sweat and blood. There was a flash of lightning, followed closely by the booming rumble of thunder. Clutching her coat and boots to her chest as she ran, she reached the end of the jigger before turning on to Blenheim Street, not daring to check for signs of pursuit as she raced on. Despite the lashing rain there were still people about and she was halfway up Limekiln Lane when she narrowly missed a collision with a courting couple.

''Ere, Dora, look out. It's Wee Willy Winky,' the man guffawed.

His girlfriend giggled, nodding her head towards Ellie's departing figure as she called after her, 'I've 'eard of sleepwalkin' before, but never sleep runnin'.'

Yelling a brief 'Sorry' over her shoulder, Ellie continued to run until she came to a covered doorway at the end of a row of shops. Panting hard, she ducked into the doorway and waited for a moment or two before risking a peep down the road. To her relief there was no sign of a pursuer. Placing her boots on the ground, she winced as she shoved her wet feet into the dry leather. Why on earth had the young man called her Wee Willy Winky? A sheet of lightning illuminated the shop doorway. To her horror a ghostly white figure stood before her in the shop's window. Stifling a scream, she hastily began to pull the sleeve of her coat over her arm, noting out of the corner of her eye as she did so that one of the spectre's arms disappeared. Another flash of lightning brought Ellie to a realisation. In her haste to escape Lavender Court she had forgotten that she was still in her nightie. She shook her head ruefully. 'That's what happens when you let your imagination run wild, Ellie Lancton. You're jumping at your own reflection now. No wonder that chap called you Wee Willy Winky,' she murmured.

With her coat buttoned up, Ellie peered cautiously round the shop doorway, and finding the coast to be clear she stepped out on to the street, only this time she continued at a more leisurely pace. She was heading towards the house of her best friend, Arla Winthorpe. She won't mind me coming round in the middle of the night, Ellie reassured herself, especially when she knows what's happened. Shoving her hands into her pockets, she ducked her head against the wind and reflected on the evening's events which had brought her to this point.

It had been nearly two months since the passing of her mother, and whilst Ellie had managed to pay the rent every week, her payments were nearly always a day or so late.

'Sorry, Mr Crowther. I know I owe you the money and I promise you'll get it, but Mrs Wardle, the one I do laundry for, well she says she's still waitin' to be paid by the folk what give her the laundry, and she reckons she can't afford to pay me till she's been paid herself, you see.' Ellie had looked nervously at her landlord. 'I did tell her I owed you the rent, and she said she would definitely pay me tomorrer, or the day after at the very latest. Sorry.'

Sid stood, arms folded, glaring. 'And how's that meant to be my problem? You're the one who owes the rent and you should make sure you get it to me on time. I don't care how you do it, just make sure you do. No one I know lives rent free, and even if they do they sure as hell don't do it my 'ouses, not when I've bills of me own to pay.'

Heading out into the court, he had slammed the front door behind him whilst Ellie retreated to her room and padded over to the window. Her heart sank as she watched her landlord enter the Cock and Bull public house. He was already in a bad mood, but throwing alcohol into the mix would be like pouring petrol on to an already blazing fire.

Turning from the window, she went to the small cupboard which she used to store food and cutlery, and pulled out a rather stale end of bread which she managed to half cut, half tear into two pieces. She glanced round the bare cupboard, wishing there was a small jar of dripping or jam in there, and put one of the pieces back on the shelf before biting down into the other and beginning to chew.

When war had first been declared, Ellie had asked her mother if she might leave school and get a job working in one of the munitions factories, but her mother had been against the idea.

'You ain't leavin' school, so there's no point in arguin'. Get your certificate first and then you can get a better job; only stands to reason.' Seeing the disappointment on Ellie's face, she had softened. 'I know you want to do your bit, but you'd be better off waitin' till you're sixteen. That way you can apply for one of the services, then you'd get a proper job, like one of them secretaries what do the shorthand and type stuff up – you know the sort of thing. Summat that'll set you up for life. You won't get that if you work in a munitions factory, even if you don't get blown up first.'

This conversation had taken place one Saturday whilst Ellie helped her mother scrub sheets in Mr Wong's Chinese Laundry. One of the women working opposite them had voiced her opinion.

'Our Reenie works in the Royal Ordnance factory in Kirkby and she's turned as yeller as a daffodil. It don't come off neither, no matter how hard she scrubs. You don't want to work in the one in Fazakerley neither. That poor Billy from Maple Court will never be the same again, not since the accident.'

Ellie had sighed. She knew they were right, but she would not turn sixteen until the following December, which was over a year away.

When her mother had died Ellie had reconsidered applying for one of the factory jobs, which would bring better wages and regular work. It meant she wouldn't have to worry over such things as rent, but it would also mean going against her mother's wishes, and that was something Ellie could not bring herself to do, no matter how hard the going got. She already felt guilty about having left school immediately after Millie's death, but that had been necessary and she knew her mother would have understood.

She drew the threadbare curtains closed and padded over to the washstand, dipped her flannel into the ice-cold water, then took a deep breath and gingerly drew the flannel swiftly across her face and hands. Shivering from her brief wash, she pulled her thick nightie over her head, then laid her clothes on top of her bed and climbed carefully between the sheets.

Curling up into a ball, she blew on her hands as she rubbed them together. They were halfway through spring, and even though the weather outside was mild the inside of the glass window was laced with frost and the room itself was icy cold.

'These bloody courts want knockin' down,' Mr Rogers, one of Ellie's oldest neighbours, had commented as they queued for the water pump which stood beside the privies.

Mr Turnbull had nodded his head in agreement. 'I reckon they should shoot the bugger who built 'em in the first place,' he tutted disapprovingly. 'Who in their right mind would build houses what was always in the shade? Stands to reason they'll allus be damp and mouldy. My missis is hackin' up summat awful, mornin', noon and night. And fancy stickin' the water pump next to the lavvy. It's a wonder we ain't all got cholera, especially when the bogs get bunged up.' Behind him there had been a general mumur of agreement.

Ellie turned her thoughts back to the problem of the overdue rent and how her landlord had reverted from the understanding man who had told her not to worry to the surly man who claimed he had been mistaken about her mother's payments.

'Dunno 'ow it 'appened, but I were wrong about your mam being a month's rent in advance, I noticed it when I were checkin' through me books, so you see you ain't got the time I thought you had.' His furtive glances and shifty stance had left Ellie in no doubt that the man was lying, but she had no proof. Sid insisted on keeping everyone's rent book in his room, so he could easily change any entries previously made. Asking to see her mother's book would be a waste of time.

It was shortly after this revelation that he had started hassling her for the money, making vicious, spiteful remarks if she was late with payments. So far, however, she had never been subjected to his violent temper. She had heard from her neighbours that he was known to fly into blind drunken rages, smashing windows or kicking in doors; then the next day, when he had sobered up, he would demand payment for the damage, reasoning that if they had paid on time in the first place he would never had got so angry. Of course it was unfair, but you were given two choices: pay or leave.

Ellie froze as she heard someone shouting outside, then relaxed again as she recognised the voice of an ARP warden ordering someone to 'put that light out'. It was Arthur Byrnes, Archie Byrnes's father, who lived in the same court as Arla. Ellie smiled as she remembered the last time she had seen Archie. She had gone to visit Arla and the two girls had been chatting whilst Arla waited for the privy.

'One pump and two lavvies between ten houses ain't enough!' Arla had said, as she hopped from one foot to the other. She had hammered her fist on the wooden door of the toilet. 'Archie Byrnes, you've been in there for the last five minutes, and you know full well the other one's busted. Stop bein' selfish and get your backside out here. Some of us is bustin'.'

'Sod off!' had come the reply from behind the wooden door. 'I told you already, I can't go wi' you standin' there with yer ear pressed to the door listenin'.'

Arla had rolled her eyes. 'I have not got my ear pressed to the door. Who wants to hear that?' She had turned to Ellie. 'When we join the WAAF it won't be like this. They'll have proper fassi – fassilli – lavvies, and more than one, no doubt.' She had grimaced at Ellie as she tried to stop nature taking its course. 'Remember when Miss Siege came back into school to show us her uniform? It was really smart; much nicer than anythin' we got. I think it'd really suit me.'

There was a rattling noise followed by the sound of rushing water and Archie Byrnes opened the toilet door. Wafting a hand in front of his face, he had winked at the girls. 'I'd give it a minute or three if I were you. I reckon this 'un's on its way out an' all.' Walking past Arla, he had grinned mischievously. 'They won't let you in the WAAF, not till you've got rid of them nits.'

Arla had balled her hand into a fist, ready to give Archie a good thump, but nature was calling, in fact it was yelling at her to get into the lavatory, so instead she had stuck out her tongue. 'I 'aven't got nits, Archie

Byrnes, but if I did it'd be you what give'm me in the first place.'

Lying as still as she could so as not to come into contact with parts of the sheets not yet warmed by her body, Ellie grimaced as a sheet of lightning penetrated one of the many holes in the curtains. She slid out of her bed and trotted across the cold floorboards to pick up her wash towel and hang it over the top of the curtains. From outside there came the sound of male voices. Pulling the towel delicately to one side, she peered through the gap, and watched as a couple of men, neither of whom was Sid, stumbled their way down the road. With a bit of luck, she thought, he'll be as drunk as a lord by the time he comes out, and at least that way he'll be too tired to pick a fight. She had been about to turn away when the pub door had swung open again and another man had left the pub. Her stomach lurched unpleasantly. This time it was Sid, and judging by the way he was holding on to the lamppost for support he was very drunk indeed. Ellie's brow wrinkled as she tried to make out what he was doing, until, to her disgust, she realised he was relieving himself against the lamppost. 'No better than a dog,' she had muttered, shaking her head reprovingly, and then Sid had tilted his head back and stared straight into her room. Their eyes had locked momentarily before Ellie let the towel fall. Chastising herself for being caught spying, she had climbed back into the small bed and pulled the mixture of sheet and clothes up around her ears, closing her eyes and praying that Sid had been too drunk to focus. There was another flash of lightning and she waited for the inevitable clap of thunder, then jumped as it boomed loudly before rumbling into the distance. The front door slammed shut and she held her breath, her heart sinking as she heard Sid mount the stairs. She lay motionless as the door to her room creaked open. Taking a deep breath she listened intently, but the only thing she could hear was the beating of her heart, which seemed to grow louder and louder until she felt sure he must be able to hear it. She had been wishing him far away when, to her relief, she heard the bedroom door click shut. Letting her breath out in a big whoosh, she was about to turn over when a voice from beside her bed broke the silence.

'Spyin' on me, were ya?' Sid had hiccuped, the foul odour of alchol filling the room. Lying still, Ellie was wondering whether she should pretend to be asleep when Sid gave the leg of the bed a vicious kick, causing it to scrape across the floor. 'Don't ignore me, you bloody tart,' he slurred. 'I seen you tryin' to tek a peek at me ... me manhood.' Grabbing her roughly by the shoulder, he turned her over.

Ellie had rubbed her eyes in a pretence of waking. 'S-s-sorry,' she stammered. 'I was asleep ... what did you say?'

Swaying, he leaned down in front of her until their noses were inches apart. 'Now then, you mustn't be coy. I seen you through the winder.' He screwed up his eyes in an effort to focus. 'Fancy a bit o' me, do ya?'

Despite her fear Ellie had eyed him in horror. 'You're old enough to be my dad ...' she had begun, but Sid, clearly offended by her statement, leaned back and struck her with the back of his hand. Blood spurted from her nose.

'You cheeky, ungrateful … who's been lookin' after you since your ma died, eh? Kept a roof over yer 'ead, promised to keep you on?'

Ellie had clasped her sleeve to her nose to stem the flow of blood. Wiping a few drops from his cheek, Sid placed his hands on her knees and leaned unsteadily forward. Staring hard into her face, he raised a hand, but this time instead of striking her he smoothed her hair back.

'Now I come to think of it, it's not such a bad idea is that. You're allus havin' trouble payin' the rent, and I remember you sayin' we could work summat out if you had difficulties, and I agreed. So the way I see it, two birds with one stone …' He dropped his gaze to her chest. 'You know, I ain't noticed till now, but youse ain't a child no more, are ya?' Ellie clutched the neck of her nightie as Sid pressed his mouth close to her ear. 'You keep me satisfied, and I reckon we can turn a blind eye to the rent …' As he spoke, he gripped hold of her nightgown with one hand whilst the other fumbled with the crotch of his trousers.

Fearing the worst, Ellie had balled her hand into a fist and punched him as hard as she could. As both hands flew to his nose, his trousers dropped to his ankles and he sprawled backwards, unable to keep his balance. He fell to the floor with a thud, his head knocking into the legs of the washstand as he went, and the ewer teetered briefly on the edge before plummeting towards his thick skull.

Leaping to her feet, she had looked down at her agressor. His eyes were shut and the broken ewer lay in pieces over his cut and bloodied face. Without further hesitation, she had grabbed her coat and boots and descended the stairs two at a time before heading into the stormy night.

Dodging to one side as the mud cascaded back down towards her, Ellie took careful aim with another handful of dirt just as a rather annoyed and sleepy-looking Arla lifted the sash window and squinted down at her.

'Bugger off, you little sod, else I'll report you to …' She paused briefly. 'Ellie? Hang on a mo.'

Within a few seconds Arla appeared at the front door. Standing aside, she placed a finger to her lips and ushered her friend in. 'We can talk in my room. Go quietly – I don't want to wake me mam and dad.'

Closing the bedroom door silently behind her, she whispered, 'I thought you was Willy Johnson from down the court. His mam lets him stay out till all hours and he's a habit o' wakin' folk up whenever he gets bored.' Turning to face Ellie, she gave a small shriek and clapped a hand over her mouth. 'What happened? Are you all right? Do you know you're covered in blood?' She pointed to the bed. 'Sit down, and I'll fetch a cloth to clean you up. Just make sure you don't sit on our Sally.'

Ellie looked at the double bed which contained all three of Arla's sisters, and carefully positioned herself on the edge. Arla dipped a flannel into the bowl and began to carefully wipe the concoction of blood, mud, sweat and tears from Ellie's face. 'So come on, what's happened?' she repeated.

21

Taking a deep breath, Ellie told Arla about Sid, his repulsive suggestion, and the ewer. 'Mrs B warned me about him. She told me to be careful, said I should go to her if I ever needed help. I think she suspected summat like this might happen.' She looked at Arla through tear-brimmed eyes. 'All I wanted was for him to leave me alone, but instead he's flat out on my bedroom floor, covered in blood. If he's dead the scuffers'll blame me.' She covered her face with her hands. 'It's not fair, Arla. I didn't do anything wrong. I just wanted him to go away.'

Kneeling down, Arla rubbed Ellie's shoulder with a comforting hand. 'Don't go worryin' about the likes of Sid Crowther. It'd take a lot more than a ewer to kill him off. You said he was drunk, so you've more than likely just knocked him out.'

There was a snort from one of the occupants of the bed. 'No one would give two figs if you had killed him. Everyone hates him, and once they find out what he's done to you—'

Ellie turned sharply. 'You mustn't tell anyone. You know what folk can be like – he's bound to twist things, make it look as if it was all my fault, or I'd led him on somehow. I'd be so ashamed.'

Sitting up on one elbow, Sally gazed into Ellie's frightened eyes. 'No one who knows you would ever think such a thing, Ellie luv, and you've nowt to be ashamed of either. It's him who should be ashamed, not that he will be, of course, but you needn't worry. If you don't want me to say owt I promise my lips are sealed.' Looking round the dimly lit room, she frowned. 'Where's your clothes?'

Ellie looked down at her nightie. 'I'm afraid this is it.' She let out a small groan. 'I've just remembered. All my money, the photos of me mam, everything I own is back in Lavender Court, so like it or not I'm goin' to have to go back at some stage.'

Arla jutted her chin forward in a determined fashion. 'You're not goin' anywhere near that foul beast of a man. I'll go for you.'

'Sidney Crowther would hit you as soon as Ellie,' Arla's older sister informed her brusquely. 'Why don't you go and see Connor Murray? I bet he's as tall as Sid.' Sally lay back down in the bed and yawned sleepily before adding, 'We all know Sid's a coward when it comes to confronting men, and I know wild horses wouldn't stop Connor if he knew Sid'd hit either of you.'

Ellie looked uncertain. 'I don't want to go getting Connor involved. He may be tall but he's a lot younger than Sid, so Sid might well hit him. Besides, I don't want to tell anyone about ... about what happened.'

'You don't have to go into all the ins and outs, just tell him the first bit, how Sid hit you and you hit him back. You can leave the middle bit out.' She smiled reassuringly at Ellie. 'You're goin' to have to tell folk summat, luv, 'cos you're right about one thing: Sid'll want to get his version across first and it won't be the real one. So you're better tellin' folk the truth before he gets a chance to muddy the waters, as it were.'

Ellie nodded. 'I'll go and see Connor first thing, but in the meantime is it all right if I kip here, just for tonight?'

Throwing back the blanket, Sally shifted over. 'Course it is, but you'll have to get in here with the rest of us. There won't be much room, but with a bit of luck you'll not fall out too many times.'

The girls had only been in bed a few hours when the air raid siren wailed across the night sky. As they headed for the shelter of the school in Bond Street, Arla reassured Ellie that she wouldn't look out of place, as everyone was still in their nightwear with coats or dressing gowns hastily thrown over the top; nor would anyone question her presence. The people who lived in the courts were known for their hopsitality, and Arla's parents did not raise a single brow when they saw Ellie tucked up next to Arla on one of the wooden benches.

''Ello, Ellie! I didn't know you was sleepin' over. Budge up, won't you, love?' Mrs Winthorpe joined them on the bench, while her husband, a cheery-looking man with a dark-stubbled chin, squinted down at Ellie.

''Ow's it goin', queen? Good job the missis woke me up; I thought Moanin' Minnie were more thunder.'

When Ellie woke some time later it was to find Betty Winthorpe kneeling in front of her, a look of concern on her face. 'You're all right, Ellie luv, you've just had a bit of a nightmare, that's all. You sounded real scared.' She glanced up at Arla. 'The all-clear's sounded, so I think it's best if you take Ellie back to ours and sort her some brekker out. Me and your dad'll see if anyone wants help in the city before we come back. I heard a couple of explosions, but let's hope there was no one inside when they hit.'

24

On the way back to the court Arla explained to Ellie that she had been shouting out in her sleep. 'You was shouting "Bugger off, you filthy devil" at the top of your lungs. I managed to convince Mam that you must have been shouting at the Luftwaffe; she did look a bit doubtful at first but I think she believed me in the end.' Entering the room in which they slept, Ellie filled the kettle whilst Arla fished some bread and jam from the storage cupboard. 'Do you want me to see if I can get summat to fit you, or will you be all right with that old coat of your mam's over the top of your nightie?'

'It's still a bit too big for me, so folk shouldn't be able to see what I've got on underneath. Besides, if Connor's home it shouldn't be too long before I can get my own clothes.'

'Right you are. We'll head off as soon as we've drunk our tea. I know it's still early, but with luck we can catch him before he goes off with his mates.'

Ellie and Arla had first met Connor at the youth club on Latimer Street, when Robert Green, a bully of a boy, had decided to cause trouble. It had been a couple of weeks before Christmas and Ellie had been making paper chains to decorate the room when Robert had snatched them out of her hands and begun wrapping them around her.

'Paper chains is for little kids,' he had sneered. 'I reckon you're slow, an' they give you this to do' cos you're too thick to do owt else.' His eyes shone malevolently as he started to pull the chains tight around her.

Hearing the paper start to tear, Ellie had held her breath. 'Pack it in, Robert. These are for the Christmas party. Surely even you look forward to Christmas?'

Robert had snorted. 'In this dump? Not with you and all the other dunces—' He had flinched as a hand slapped down hard on his shoulder. 'Gerroff or I'll punch your lights out,' he had started, releasing his grip on the paper chains and spinning round. He stopped abruptly as his eyes settled on the tall dark lad who had come up behind him. 'Oh, I didn't realise it were you. I were only 'avin a bit of fun.'

The newcomer had raised an eyebrow. 'I don't think she finds your idea of fun very amusing, so it'd be best all round if you ran along.'

They could hear Robert muttering under his breath as he walked stiffly away from them. 'Run along? Who the hell does he think he's tellin' to run along? It's a good job I kept my temper, that's all I can say …'

Ellie had smiled shyly at the other boy. 'Thanks for that. I've complained about him loads of times, a few of us have, but they just tell us to ignore him because he'll soon get bored.'

Connor held out a hand. 'I'm Connor Murray.'

Shaking the proffered hand, Ellie smiled at her saviour. 'I'm Ellie Lancton. Nice to meet you, Connor, and thanks again for gettin' rid of Robert. I don't recall seein' you around here before, but he seemed to recognise you.'

Connor had placed his hands in his trouser pockets. 'My family's not long moved here from Bootle. Me and Robert go to the same school, and someone in my class suggested I might like to pop down here and make new friends.'

Now, as the two girls approached the large terraced house on Bevington Street, Arla turned to Ellie. 'Do

26

you think we might be too early? You don't suppose they're still in bed, do you? It is the weekend, after all.'

Ellie, who was doing her best to hide her nightie under her coat, slid behind her friend. 'You should've said summat before we got here. I can't go hangin' about. What if people see me standin' 'ere in me nightie?'

A voice spoke from behind them. 'Why are you still in your nightie?'

Ellie jumped, knocking Arla against the front door. 'Connor!' Ellie hissed, whilst trying to stifle a giggle. 'You nearly sent me to an early grave.'

'Well, you nearly sent me straight through the flamin' door,' Arla said crossly, rubbing her forehead.

'So how come you two are up and about so early?' Connor said. He pointed accusingly at Ellie. 'And go on – why are you still in your nightie?'

Ellie shushed him. 'Can we talk somewhere else? I don't fancy discussin' the whys and wherefores on your front doorstep.'

Connor looked intrigued. 'We can talk in the kitchen.' He gestured for the two girls to go ahead of him. 'You needn't worry, there's no one in. Mam and Dad have gone into the city, and me brothers are down the rec playing footy. I was there too, but I forgot the money I owe Lofty for his old boots, so I had to come back for it.' Entering the small kitchen, he invited the girls to sit down. 'Well?' he said, his gaze settling on Ellie. 'Spill the beans, as they say.'

Taking a deep breath, she told Connor the whole story, ending, 'It was a gut reaction. I only hit him;

the rest was an accident.' She looked pleadingly at Connor. 'You don't think I could've killed him, do you?'

Connor pushed his thick fringe of dark hair back from his forehead and shrugged. 'I wouldn't have thought so. I reckon Arla's right: if he was really drunk, he probably passed out when he hit his head. There's only one way to be sure and that's to go back and see for yourself, only if he catches you there'll be hell to pay.' He pulled a face. 'The way I see it, you've got a double dilemma. First you have to get your things out. No problem there; I'll help you with that one.' Sitting upright, he puffed out his chest. 'I don't think Sid would be stupid enough to take me on. I'm younger and fitter than he is, after all. And second, no matter what the outcome, I think it'd be best if you kept your head down for a bit, just till the dust settles. I've got an uncle who rents a farm near Oxton. He's always look-ing for extra help, so you'd be doing each other a favour, if you see what I mean.' He paused, waiting for her response, but when none came he added, 'I'm sug-gesting you go and live on my uncle's farm for a bit. What d'you reckon?'

Ellie stared at Connor, hardly daring to believe that he had just offered her the opportunity to leave the courts and work on a farm, with fresh air and lots of animals – maybe even horses – and it was still a few moments before she found her tongue. 'I reckon yes, yes, and yes again!' She clapped her hands together. 'But are you sure, Connor? Perhaps your uncle has enough workers, or maybe he won't want me. I don't know anything about farms.'

Connor raised his brows. 'Course he'll want you. Who wouldn't want an Ellie in their lives? Besides, I'm his favourite nephew. If I say you're good enough, that'll do for him.'

A thought occurred to her. 'Connor Murray, you're a marvel, and I really appreciate the offer, but won't your uncle wonder why I need to go there? We all know Sid's a pig of a man, but I do owe him rent, and even if I didn't I still couldn't afford to pay your uncle.'

Connor shook his head. 'It's not as if you weren't intending to pay Sid, you were, so if anything my uncle'll be impressed you managed to keep your head above water for so long, especially under the circumstances. And you needn't worry about paying him rent: your hard graft'll cover any living expenses.' He glanced at the clock on the mantel. 'I've got to go and give Lofty his money before he sells his boots to someone else. How about we meet at Lavender Court early tomorrow morning?'

Ellie looked downcast. 'Tomorrow? But what am I meant to do in the meantime?'

Arla cut in. 'I'll lend you summat. With four of us girls – five counting you – all wearing each other's stuff half the time I doubt mam will even notice. I'll explain you're gonna be stayin for a couple of nights, and that should buy you enough time to get yourself sorted.'

Ellie beamed at her friends. 'You two are the bestest pals a girl could wish for. I'm so lucky to have you.'

Connor gave her a friendly wink. 'Any time, chuck.' Glancing at the clock, he stood up. 'Sorry, girls, but I'm gonna have to turf you out. I'll be at Lavender

Court for six o'clock tomorrow, Ellie. See if you can borrow a scarf or summat so's you can hide your face a bit. That way if Sid is around he won't recognise you.'

Walking cautiously towards Lavender Court, Ellie wrapped the scarf that she had borrowed from Arla's mother around her face. She peered at the figure that was leaning against the wall of the Cock and Bull. Straightening up, Connor walked towards her. 'Sid went out a couple of minutes before you got here, so the coast is clear, but even so we'd best be quick.' He grinned. 'I must say, he didn't look too good. His face was covered in cuts.'

Ellie breathed a sigh of relief. 'At least I ain't goin' to get done for murder. Let's get a move on and get my stuff out of there before he comes back.' Sliding her hand through the letterbox, Ellie gave a satisfied smile as she felt the weight of the key on the other end of the string. 'You'd think he'd have had the sense to move it in case I came back,' she said, fitting it into the lock.

'He probably thought you'd be too scared to come back. Just goes to show what he knows.' Connor grinned.

Ellie locked the door behind them and pointed towards the stairs. 'Up there,' she whispered.

Connor raised his brows. 'Why are you whispering? I told you I saw him leave.'

Ellie giggled. 'I'm as nervous as a turkey on Christmas Eve.' Gingerly, she pushed open the door to her room. The ewer still lay in pieces on the floor, along with a great deal of dried blood.

Connor gave a low whistle as he picked up some of the broken ewer. 'Blimey, queen, I see what you mean. It's a chunky old thing to have smashed over your head.'

Ellie nodded as she started to lift up the loose floorboard that hid her purse. 'My old school satchel is hangin' up behind the door. Can you empty all the books out, except for *National Velvet* and *Black Beauty*? They belong to my old teacher, Miss Siege. She lent them to me before she joined the WAAF.'

Connor retrieved the satchel whilst Ellie rooted around beneath the floorboard. Placing her few possessions in the bag, she took one last look round the small room before swinging the satchel on to her shoulders and jerking a thumb towards the stairs. 'I'll get changed at Arla's. No point in stayin' here any longer than we have to.'

At the foot of the staircase Ellie stopped abruptly, causing Connor to cannon into the back of her.

'Steady on …' he began, but Ellie was pointing at the key which was dancing on the end of its string as it slid up the door towards the letterbox.

'It's him,' she whispered. Grabbing Connor's wrist, she shouldered the door into Sid's room and was surprised to find it gave way with ease. She pulled Connor in behind her just as the key disappeared through the letterbox with a snapping sound.

Putting a finger to her lips she pointed towards the small window. 'Quick, through there,' she mouthed. Connor lifted the sash and they disappeared through its aperture just as a bewildered-looking Sid entered the room.

'What the hell?' he bellowed.

Thinking on her feet, Ellie ran to the front door and pulled up the string. Locking the door, she yanked the key, snapping the string, just as Sid's body barrelled into the wood. The pair leapt back, watching the door handle bounce wildly as Sid tried to force it open. He gave an enraged howl. 'Open the bloody door,' he roared. 'You're as bad as your bloody mam, you dirty, murderous, thievin' tart—'

'Don't you dare talk about my mam like that.' Ellie, her fists clenched by her sides, stared at the wooden door. Her words cut through the air like a hot knife through butter. 'She were ten times the person you are, Sid Crowther. She were the kindest, most caring person in the world. If it weren't for your stinkin' house she'd most probably still be alive today.'

The thumping ceased and Connor pointed to the sash window, where Sid's face, red with rage, was beginning to turn purple as he tried to force his shoulders through the frame. 'There's nowt wrong wi' these houses, and if you don't wanna foller your ma to an early grave you'd best mek sure I never see your face around here again.'

Watching the bully of a man as he struggled to get to her, Ellie's fear left her. She strode forward, and leaned down until her eyes were on the same level as her former landlord's. 'You're nowt but a dirty, fat old man, and I'd rather be dead than come anywhere near you again, Sidney Crowther. The day me mam moved into this pit were the worst day of her life, and one day,' she lowered her voice, 'one day you'll get your comeuppance and I hope to God I'm there to see it when you do.'

Connor pulled at her elbow. 'C'mon, queen,' he said urgently. 'We'd best get goin' before all his yellin' attracts the scuffers.'

Trembling with rage, Ellie nodded. 'I'm not runnin' this time, though,' she said as they headed across the court. 'I'm leavin' with my head held high.' She glanced towards the house where Mrs Burgess lived and saw the old woman, a worried frown on her face, standing in the doorway. 'Don't worry about me, Mrs B, I'm goin' to be just fine from now on.' A broad gappy smile of relief appeared on the old woman's face, and she gave Ellie an approving nod.

The two friends walked in silence until they reached the end of Arla's road. 'It's true, you know,' Ellie said quietly. 'Those courts need demolishin'. They're filthy, and there's rats everywhere.'

Connor nodded. 'I know. Everyone does. Sid Crowther's an ignorant pig and one day he'll get his just deserts.'

Ellie raised a warning eyebrow. 'Not from you, Connor Murray. I don't want you gettin' into trouble over that lowlife. You and Arla are the only family I've got. At least, you feel like my family.'

Connor tousled the top of her hair. 'Don't you worry about me, queen, I've more sense than to do time because of that poor excuse for a man.'

'Are you comin' in to Arla's, just to say hello?'

He shook his head. 'I was thinkin' of goin' to Paddy's Market to see if they've got any rotten tomatoes. If Sid's still stuck in the window I could charge the kids a penny a throw, probably make a bob or two.'

Ellie laughed. 'I reckon you'd make a small fortune.' Standing on tiptoe, she gave Connor a peck on the cheek, then clapped a hand to her forehead as a thought struck her. 'I completely forgot to ask! Have you spoken to your uncle yet?'

Connor nodded. 'He's ready for you any time, so I said we'd go there tomorrow. My cousin'll meet us off the bus.'

Swinging her satchel off her shoulders, Ellie pulled out her purse and tipped the contents into the palm of her hand to show Connor. 'Will that be enough? To get me to the farm, I mean?'

He closed her fingers over the loose change. 'Don't you go worryin' about money. I took the liberty of visitin' Mrs Wardle, explained how her tardiness had got you into a rare bit of trouble, and that a business-woman of her standin' couldn't afford to be accused of swindlin' workers, so ...' He opened the palm of his hand to reveal several coins. 'I told her, and the people at Mr Wong's too, that you wouldn't be available for a while, so you mustn't worry about that either.'

Ellie flung her arms around his neck. 'Thanks, Connor you're a real pal, and one of these days I'll find a way to repay you.'

Blushing, he tipped the money into her hand. 'It's no more than you deserve. You've gone through enough this year; it's about time you had a bit of good luck, and I think the farm's just the place to start.'

She smiled gratefully. 'I can't wait to meet your uncle. Does he have any horses?'

Connor laughed. 'Yes, and pigs and cows! I know how much you love animals, so you should fit right in.'

'You're right there, but horses are my favourite. The only one I get to see round here is Billy, the old carthorse that pulls Mr Spooner's milk wagon.' She smiled reminiscently. 'He's got big fluffy feet and a long nose, and he wears these things on his ears in the summer to stop the flies annoyin' him.'

Connor chuckled. 'And what does Billy look like?'

Ellie punched him playfully on the arm. 'You know full well I was talkin' about Billy,' she said, although she couldn't help giggling as a picture of Mr Spooner with big fluffy feet, a long nose and big ears formed in her mind. She linked arms with Connor. 'Night before last I thought my whole world were coming to an end, but thanks to me two bezzies my life's finally taken a turn for the better.'

Chapter Two

Standing with her back to the Mersey, Ellie blinked at the magnificent stone statues that adorned the top of the Liver Buildings. She pointed upwards. 'Is that Bella or Bertie? I can never remember which is which.'

Connor squinted at the copper statue with its huge wings stretched out as if it was about to take flight. 'That's Bella. She's lookin' out to sea, searchin' for handsome sailors comin' into dock.' He turned and indicated the other statue. 'The one facin' the city is Bertie. He's lookin' to see if the pubs are open.'

Ellie sighed blissfully. 'Wouldn't it be wonderful if you could sit on their backs and fly out to sea?'

Connor feigned shock. 'But if that were to happen the city would fall! Don't you know anything?'

Ellie nodded. 'Of course! That's why they're chained to the domes, just in case they should spring to life and leave.'

Connor's green eyes twinkled. 'Silly, really. After all, if a thirteen-foot statue came to life I think we'd have a bit more than the city falling to worry about. I've seen the mess seagulls make ... Ah, it looks as though they're ready for us to board.'

Chuckling, Ellie linked her arm through his and they handed over their tickets. Once aboard, Ellie headed for the railing and leaned against it. Shading her eyes with one hand she watched similar-sized vessels coming into dock. 'It must be wonderful to own a ship and go to all sorts of strange and exotic lands.'

'Not with a war on it mustn't. Think of all the mines and U-boats. I think I'd rather keep both feet on dry land, thank you very much.'

Ellie turned sharply. 'I hadn't thought of that! There's no danger of us hitting a mine, is there?'

Connor shook his head. 'The authorities are checking the Mersey all the time. They'd know if there was anything lurking in the water.' He pointed towards the brown paper bag that Ellie carried and raised his brow hopefully. 'Did you say that Arla's mam had given you some grub for the journey?'

Ellie chuckled. 'Connor Murray, we've not even left the harbour.' Fishing around inside the packet she pulled out a couple of jam sandwiches, one of which she handed to Connor. 'You'd think we was goin' to Timbuktu with all the food Arla's mam and yours gave us. Just as well with your appetite.'

Connor patted his stomach. 'An empty sack won't stand up, and it won't take long to get through this little lot. Let's have a look and see what we've got.'

Ellie counted the items off on her fingers. 'Two jam sandwiches, two Spam rolls, two fairy cakes, four scones and a bottle of ginger beer.'

Connor frowned. 'I'll need fresh supplies for the journey home tomorrow, but if I know Auntie Aileen, she won't let a growing lad go hungry.'

'Do you ever think of anything else—' Ellie began before a loud blast from the ferry's horn drowned out the rest of her sentence. 'Dear God, I nigh on left me own skin then!' she said, much to Connor's amusement. 'I forgot they did that.'

The ship's engines roared into life and Ellie watched the waves break against the side of the ferry, trying to remember how long it had been since she last made this journey. Her mother had taken a rare day off work and treated her to a day at New Brighton. Millie, who hated being cold, had cautiously dipped her feet into the water.

'Crikey,' she had gasped as the icy water lapped around her bare ankles. 'If I stay in here too long I'll be blue!'

The water temperature, on the other hand, did not perturb Ellie, who swam out happily, turning on to her back and calling back to her mother, 'It's a lot colder'n the Scaldy, but it's a lot cleaner too.'

'You're like one of them mermaids. But you mustn't stay in too long else you'll be like a cube of ice.'

On their way home they had bought fish and chips to eat on the ferry. Breathing in now, she tried to remember the scent of that long gone fish supper.

'Penny for them?'

'Hmm?'

'Penny for your thoughts. You've been lookin' across that water with a big old smile on your face ever since we left the Pier, so what's made you so happy?'

'Oh, you know, just thinkin' of the old days when me and Mam used to cross the Mersey,' Ellie said. 'I never dreamt I'd be comin' over the water with you one day, nor that I'd be so pleased to get away from Liverpool. It feels odd that I should be so happy to leave a place that's meant so much to me.'

'You've had a bad time of late. It's only natural you should want to get away for a bit.'

Ellie watched as the tobacco warehouse and its chimneys grew smaller whilst the town of Birkenhead grew larger. 'It's not just that. Ever since she died it doesn't really feel like home any more.'

Connor shrugged. 'My dad always says that life's a journey, and we have to think carefully about which path we choose.' He smiled at Ellie. 'Looks like you're about to start on the second part of your journey, chuck. Workin' on the farm is about a million miles away from life in the city, so I hope it'll help you decide which way you want to go next ... Oh, look out, we're comin' into dock.'

Ellie felt her tummy lurch with anticipation. So this was it, the start of her new life. Holding firmly on to the ship's rail, she prepared for the slight bump as the ferry joined the dockside, and turned her thoughts to the conversation she had had with Arla earlier that morning.

'We are still goin' to join up, ain't we? Only if we go together there's a good chance we'll get the same postin'. Life'll be a lot easier if I've got me bezzie by me side. I know you're gonna be sixteen before me, but I'm only a month after you, and ... oh, please say you'll not join before me,' Arla pleaded.

Ellie had smiled reassuringly. 'As if I'd join up without me bezzie! You just make sure that you're up and dressed ready for the off, and in the meantime I promise to write whenever I can, so stop worryin' your head.'

Her knuckles whitened as the ship bumped against the side of the dock. If Connor's right about life being a journey, what will happen if I decide I don't want to join the services, she thought. What if my journey puts me on a different path from the one Arla intends to travel?

Connor interrupted her thoughts. 'Come on.' Taking her by the hand, he led her down the ramp and on to the dockside. 'The bus stop is just over there. Of course, there aren't so many running now, what with the war an' all, but we shouldn't have to wait more than an hour at the most.' He studied the timetable. 'We need the number 3. Accordin' to this it should be along in fifteen minutes or so, then once we're on it'll be about forty-five minutes before we get to Oxton. Aidan said he'd pick us up at around five o'clock, so ...' he glanced at the small watch on his wrist, 'that should be about right.'

Ellie sat on the small wooden bench and pulled out the bottle of ginger beer. 'Fancy a swig?' she said.

Taking the bottle he uncorked the top. 'D'you reckon Sid's still stuck in that window?'

Ellie giggled. 'Could you imagine? My mam would've laughed fit to burst if she'd seen the look on his face. I thought he was goin' to pop like a balloon the way he carried on.'

'Serve him right if he had, especially after all the nasty stuff he were sayin' about you and your mam.' He offered the bottle to Ellie, who shook her head. 'I hope he's still stuck in that window and I hope the Nazis—'

Ellie shot him a warning look. 'I don't like him any more than you do, but you shouldn't go wishing that lot to target dear old Liverpool.'

Connor pulled a face. 'I wasn't. I was wishin' for them to hit him, and his stinkin' court. Get everyone else out first, use his big red face as a target and then ... BOOM!'

Ellie stifled a giggle. 'Two birds with one stone. Connor, when you were talkin' about journeys earlier, it made me think, do you know what path you're goin' to take? D'you reckon you'll join up?'

Connor nodded enthusiastically. 'Too right! Soon as I'm eighteen I'm off to the RAF. Don't get me wrong, there's nowt wrong wi' the Navy nor the army, but all the girls want to date a pilot. Don't ask me why, but I believe it's summat to do wi' the uniform, so when I'm not up in the clouds fightin' for me country I'll be fendin' off the ladies ... well, it just can't come soon enough is all I can say. Only don't mention it to me mam. She'll only worry.'

Ellie's heart sank. Whilst none of the services was thought to be a safe option, being a pilot was considered to be one of the most dangerous choices and she could see why Connor's mother was so concerned.

He sat down on the bench beside her. 'I saw your face just now when I mentioned the RAF, but you mustn't worry about me, Ellie. I'll be one of the lucky ones. I'll be up there in the clouds, swoopin, duckin' and divin' out of the Luftwaffe's way, then turnin' round and shootin' the blighter in the rear.'

Ellie forced a smile. 'If anyone can send Jerry off with his tail between his legs, then I've no doubt it's you.

Did you say our bus was the number 3? I think this is it comin' now.'

The green and cream double-decker chugged slowly to a halt alongside them. Getting to her feet, Ellie swung her satchel on to her shoulder.

Connor pointed to the upper deck. 'Come on, you can see for miles from the top.'

They had just managed to sit down when the bus lurched forward. Glancing at his wristwatch Connor raised his brow. 'He's a couple of minutes early. Still, I can't see anyone running.'

An elderly conductor appeared at the top of the stair-well, one weathered hand gripping tightly on to the rail whilst the other tried to keep his cap from falling off his head. Ellie resisted the urge to leap to her feet as the doddering old man weaved his way unsteadily down the aisle towards them. 'Fares please,' he said, half falling, half sitting in the seat in front of them. Ellie opened her mouth to reply, then looked helplessly at Connor. 'Gosh, I've just realised I don't know where I'm goin'!'

The conductor gave Connor a wry smile. 'Wimmin! Never mind, little lady, I 'spect your boyfriend 'ere knows where you're headed for.'

Ellie furrowed her brow. 'He's not my boyfriend, and I should jolly well hope he does know where he's goin' 'cos it's his uncle's farm.'

''S not my fault you dunno where you's goin'.' Sniffing, the conductor turned to Connor. 'Where to?'

'Oxton, please. I'll pay for us both—' he was beginning, but Ellie cut him off mid-sentence.

42

'If I've enough I shall pay the fares, thank you very much.' She addressed the conductor through pursed lips. 'Two tickets for Oxton, please!'

The conductor reeled off the tickets and tottered back up the aisle, muttering as he did so, 'I'm sure as I don't care who pays for the fare as long as someone does.'

Connor's mouth twisted as he tried to hide his amusement. 'I heard you and Arla talkin' about joining the services together?'

Ellie nodded. 'Why?'

'After seeing the way you put that conductor in his place, I reckon you'll make corporal in no time. In fact, it wouldn't surprise me if you ended up in charge of your own regiment.'

The bus had travelled down what seemed to be an endless maze of country lanes with high hedgerows before finally stopping at a small village green.

Connor yawned. 'This is where we get off.'

Ellie brushed the crumbs from her dress on to the palm of her hand. 'Can you see your cousin any-where?'

Connor laughed and pointed to where a young man sat in the driver's seat of a pony cart. 'Bit hard to miss him, wouldn't you say?'

Ellie's mouth dropped open and the delight on her face was clear to see. 'Oh, Connor, is that him? Are we really goin' for a ride in a cart?'

Connor grunted as he stretched his arms and legs. 'We ain't goin' to walk along at the back of him, if that's what you were thinkin'. How else did you think we

43

were goin' to get to the farm? I did tell you he was comin' to meet us.'

Ellie nodded vigorously, and as they walked up the aisle of the bus she kept her eyes fixed on the ride that awaited them. 'I know, but I thought he was comin' to meet us on foot and we were gonna walk to the farm.'

Connor chuckled. 'You don't know Aidan, do you? I thought I might have mentioned him in the past, but all will soon become clear.'

The two friends got off the bus and headed towards Aidan, who was waving merrily at Connor. 'Come on, kid, get a move on. I told me da that we'd be back for supper.' He rolled his eyes dramatically. 'Mam said they wasn't to start eatin' till we get back, so he's chompin' at the bit.'

As Connor swung Ellie's satchel up towards his cousin, he showed Ellie how to get on to the cart. 'One foot on the step and then ... heave!' he said, giving her a hefty shove from the rear. Landing in Aidan's lap she blushed hotly, and mumbled a quick apology as she scrambled back off his knees and sat down on the wooden seat beside him. Indignantly, she turned to Connor. 'Steady on. You nearly sent me over the other side!'

''S not my fault you're lighter than a feather!' Connor retorted, sitting down beside her.

Smiling, Aidan held out a hand. 'Hello, Ellie. I'm only guessing that you're Ellie, of course, and that our Connor here hasn't a whole host of women wantin' to flee the city?'

Shaking his hand, Ellie felt her blush racing towards her hairline, which seemed to amuse Aidan, whose lips curled behind his beard. 'Don't worry, queen, I was havin' you on.' He looked across her to Connor. 'How's things wi' you, coz? Me da says you'll be stoppin' the night?'

Connor nodded. 'Just to make sure Ellie settles in okay. And to see you all, of course.'

'Of course!' Aidan laughed. He clicked his tongue and the brown pony started to walk forward.

Ellie's stomach gave a small lurch, but the smile that spread across her face left no one in any doubt as to how she was feeling. She addressed Aidan without moving her gaze from the pony's back. 'What's the pony's name?'

'Pony. We've only got the one so we thought it wasn't worth while tryin' to think up a name for him.' He chuckled at Ellie's reproving face. 'Blimey, you're an easy one to tease. His name's Spud.' He wagged a finger at Ellie. 'Don't look at me like that. It was me da's fault. He asked me little sister Cassie to name him when she was helping Mam to peel potatoes in the kitchen, and she said she wanted to call him Potato because he looked like one: round, brown and covered in dirt. I told me da there was no way I was goin' into Coin Meadow and shoutin' for a potato, so we compromised and called him Spud instead.' He gazed wistfully at Spud's back. 'It could've been worse. We could've been mucking out.'

Ellie stifled a giggle, and Aidan smiled. 'If you think that's funny, wait till you get introduced to the rest of the animals that Cassie was allowed to name.'

She looked fondly at the small pony as he plodded methodically down the lane. 'If I had been allowed to name him I'd have called him Winnie, because he reminds me of a fluffy teddy bear.'

Aidan shook his head. 'It must be a girl thing, calling animals by soft names.' He looked at Ellie, who was pulling her sleeves down over her wrists. 'Are you cold?'

'Just a little bit. I reckon it's after being in that warm bus—' She broke off as Aidan passed her the reins.

'Hang on to these a mo',' he instructed. 'I've gorra blanket in the back somewhere.'

Stunned by his actions, Ellie held the reins in a rigid grip whilst Aidan turned round on his seat and started to root about in the back of the cart. Connor started to laugh. 'You should see the look on our Ellie's face. Her eyes are as big as a couple of saucers.'

Turning back, Aidan spread a thick patchwork blanket over her knees. 'There you go, snug as a bug.' He took the reins back and started to whistle a soft tune.

Ellie peered curiously at him from the corner of her eye. He had the same piercing green eyes and black curly hair as Connor, but that was where the resemblance stopped. Unlike his cousin, who was clean cut and well presented, Aidan had allowed his hair to grow into a thick bushy mop; his beard, if you could call it that, was thin and patchy; and whilst his skin appeared tanned she wondered after a glance at his stained overalls whether it was, in fact, just dirty.

She glanced at Connor, who, to her dismay, had seen the way she had eyed his cousin. He gave her a large wink and leaned towards her. 'Like peas in a pod, aren't we?'

Ellie blushed. 'There's certainly some family resemblances.'

'What?' said Connor. 'Are you tellin' me I look like Worzel Gummidge?'

'Connor! Don't be so rude,' Ellie chided him.

'Don't worry yourself, queen; he's only jealous. What I lack in looks I make up for in brains.' Aidan chuckled. 'Looks of a scarecrow, brains of a genius, that's me. After all, what farmer in his right mind dresses in his Sunday best to work the land?'

As they rounded the corner Spud's little hooves picked up speed and Aidan's attention was redirected towards the madly trotting pony. 'Little beggar,' he said as he pulled gently on the reins. 'Can't get the blighter to budge half the time, but as soon as he smells his hay he thinks he's a racehorse!'

Looking ahead, Ellie saw a large wooden farm gate, and as they got closer Aidan pulled Spud to a stop. 'Connor, be a pal ...'

Jumping down from the cart, Connor opened the gate, and without waiting for instruction Spud walked forward.

Ellie stared in awe as a large stone house with deep-set windows and a thatched roof came slowly into view. A climbing rose of palest pink crept its way around most of the windows, and bees leisurely made their way from one flower to the next. A wisp of smoke trickled lazily out of one of the chimneys. The cobbled yard they were crossing was enclosed by stone stables on two sides.

'It's beautiful,' she breathed. 'I bet it's at least three times the size of Lavender Court ...'

One of the stables had a net full of hay tied up on a ring outside the doorway. Spud strode determinedly towards it, only stopping when his lips were close enough to pull the hay out.

Aidan shook his head and chuckled. 'Typical pony, always thinkin' of his stomach!' Placing the reins by his feet, he rummaged underneath the seat. 'Aha, found you,' he said as he pulled out what appeared to be a large stick.

Ellie's eyes rounded as Connor helped her down from the cart. 'What on earth are you going to do with that?'

'I'm not goin' to beat Spud with it, don't worry. Blimey, I know some farmers think that kind of thing's acceptable, but not us Murrays.' He paused. 'Didn't Connor tell you?'

Ellie shook her head. 'Tell me what?'

He raised his brows. 'That I'm a cripple.'

Ellie gasped at the words. 'No. I mean, I – I ...'

Seeing her discomfort, his face softened. 'Sorry, Ellie. I was only joking. Well, partly anyway.'

Ellie turned to Connor, her brows raised in the hope that he might say something to break the awkward silence. He smiled ruefully. 'Sorry. It didn't cross my mind to say owt. I've known Aidan all my life and I never think of him as bein' any different from the rest of us.'

Aidan laughed. 'I wish they saw me that way down at the recruiting office.'

'Which of the services have you applied for?' asked Ellie innocently.

Aidan clambered awkwardly to the ground and turned to face her. 'None of them. They wouldn't let me, though I tried to get into the RAF. Our grand-daddy flew in the last lot and he taught me a lot about the controls, so I know you have to use your legs, but I know I could manage if only they'd give me a chance.'

'If you really want to do it then you must keep trying, although I must admit I think you and your cousin are mad for wanting to go up in one of those aeroplanes. If it were me I'd be scared senseless. I'd far rather keep both feet on the ground, and I must say, given the choice between working on the farm or risking all in the clouds, I'd choose the farm every time.' She patted Spud's rump as she spoke, then hastily removed her hand. 'He won't kick me, will he?'

Aidan laughed. 'Spud? Nah, he's too lazy to kick anyone. It's just about all we can do to make him put one foot in front of the other when he's in the cart.' Taking his stick, he walked round to the pony's head. 'Would you like to give him an apple? He'll be your friend for life if you do; they're his favourite.'

Ellie nodded eagerly. 'You're ever so lucky to have a pony. I love horses. My dream has always been to ride a big white horse on Seaforth Sands.'

Aidan patted Spud's neck. 'You're not her colour, pal, but we could always paint you, I s'pose …'

Forgetting that she had only met Aidan half an hour or so ago, Ellie made a playful swipe towards her host. 'Don't you dare. He's beautiful just the way he is.' She placed a hand on top of Spud's back. 'I know he's only small, but that's a good thing because it wouldn't hurt so much if I were to fall off.'

'She's calling you short now, pal,' Connor pitched in, winking at Ellie. 'Mebbe we could make him some really thick horseshoes. You know, to raise him up a bit?'

'Crikey, what is this? Pick on Ellie day?' Ellie laughed as she chased after Connor, who had dodged out of the way of her flailing arm. Running backwards, Connor collided with a thickset man.

'Steady on … oh, it's you. I might've known.' The man tousled the top of Connor's head with one beefy hand, then turned his attention to Ellie. 'Well! I'm guessing you must be Ellie? I'm Connor's Uncle Kieran.' He grasped Ellie's hand in his, giving it a firm shake as he did so. 'Now what's all this runnin' around, and why's that pony still got his tack on?'

Aidan gave his father a wry smile. 'She knows his name's Spud.'

The older man rolled his eyes. 'Your sister's never allowed to name anythin' again, not even her own kids when she has 'em.' He grasped one of the shafts and nodded his head towards Aidan, who took hold of the other side. 'Ready?' Together the two men freed Spud from his burden; then, taking the shafts in either hand, Connor's uncle pushed the cart across the cobbled yard into a large stone-built shed.

Ellie's jaw dropped as she watched him effortlessly guiding the cart through the aperture. 'You don't need Spud. I reckon your dad could've pulled us home.'

Aidan burst into laughter. 'You're right there. When we were kids he used to take us for rides around the yard. It might look heavy, but if a cart's well balanced it's easy to pull. That way you don't put too much of a strain on the horse's back.'

Ellie listened enviously. How she would have loved a childhood like Aidan's, with ponies and a father who took you for rides around the yard. She had never known her own father, who had left before she was born.

She recalled the day she and her mother had discussed her father's whereabouts. She and Millie had been in Mr Wong's when Sybil Herd, a schoolfriend of Ellie's, had burst into the laundry, looking for her mother.

'Mam! It's Dad! He said to come and tell you to leave the washing where it is. He's got the promotion and we're moving to London. He says you'll never have to do laundry again. You'll have someone to do it for you from now on.'

Ellie had watched enviously as the pair had left the building, and then grimaced as she went back to scrubbing the sheets. 'I wish my dad would come and take me away so I didn't have to do laundry again.'

'Well he won't, will he, because he doesn't know you exist!' her mother had snapped. 'It's not my fault he beggared off before I could tell him I were pregnant with you.'

Ellie dunked the large white sheet into the hot water. 'What I don't get is how a man can leave his wife just like that without even lettin' her know where he was going?'

Ellie heard a ripple of sniggers from the other women. Looking up to see what had amused them, she saw nothing but a sea of lowered heads. She looked back to her mother, who had gone scarlet.

'Never mind that,' Millie had hissed, her eyes never leaving the sheet which she was scrubbing with ferocity. 'Get on wi' that sheet. There's a couple o' stains on there which will need a lot o' soap an' elbow grease to shift 'em.'

At the time nothing more had been said, but at home that evening, with gossip being so rife amongst the court dwellers, her mother had decided to tell Ellie the whole story.

'Your father was what they call a charmer. He was real handsome, and all the women admired him.' She had sighed reminiscently. 'When we was courtin' he used to take me on the overhead railway to Seaforth Sands and buy us a fish supper. We'd take it down to the beach and eat it watchin' the tide come in. It were so romantic, Ellie. He'd tell me as how I were the only girl in the world for him, and that one day he would take me far away from the courts and we would live a life of luxury in a big house, where I would be the one payin' for someone to do my laundry, and I'd never have to work a day in me life again. I were in love, so of course I believed every word he said, and he truly believed that he loved me with all his heart and would never do anything to hurt me. It all seemed to be too good to be true, and of course it was.' She put an arm around her daughter's shoulders and gave them a squeeze. 'He did love me, but he were only sayin' that stuff 'cos he knew it was what I wanted to hear. He knew if he laid it on thick I'd give in and let him have his way wi' me before we got wed, and of course I did.' She heaved a sigh. 'I were young, foolish, and willing to believe just about anything if it meant I got out of the courts. It were the first time I'd ever been with a man and I caught straight away.'

Ellie had frowned up at her mother. 'Caught what?'

Millie had laughed. 'It means I got pregnant.' Dropping her arm from Ellie's shoulders, she clasped her daughter's hand in her own. 'Soon as I realised I were pregnant I went to see him, but he'd gone to seek his fortune, and the rest you know.'

'It's not really his fault, though, is it?' said Ellie. 'Like you said, he didn't know you were pregnant with me. If he had I'm sure he'd have come back and given you the life you dreamt of.'

Sighing, Millie stroked Ellie's hair back from her face. 'Of course he would. He'd have loved you an' all, but like most things in life it's not that simple.'

A voice from beside her ear caused Ellie to jump. 'Oi, dilly daydream! You comin' in or what?' Connor smiled curiously at her. 'You off wi' the fairies again?'

Shaking her head, she yawned. 'I don't know about you, but we spent the small hours down the shelter again, and those wooden benches are not easy to sleep on, 'specially when everyone around you is chattin' or singin' and Arla's dad snores summat rotten.'

Connor chuckled. 'You've not seen our Anderson shelter, have you? It's at the bottom of our yard. Dad kitted it out with mattresses, pillows and blankets, so when we hear the siren we just swap our beds for the cosy ones in the shelter. I must admit I slept like a log.' He looked around him. 'We needn't worry about

Moanin' Minnie tonight. It's a lot quieter in the country-side, you know.'

Aidan, who had been taking the tack off Spud, pulled an old leather head collar over the pony's ears and turned to Ellie. 'Fancy takin' Spud up to Coin Meadow with us?'

Ellie nodded. 'Yes please. Is that where he lives?' She looked down at her boots. 'Is it very muddy? I'm afraid I don't have any wellies.'

Aidan laughed. 'Not to worry. You can sit on Spud on the way there, and young Connor can give you a piggy back on the way home.'

Ellie's mouth hung open in disbelief. 'You mean for me to actually ride him? To sit on his back and every-thing?' Her eyes dancing, she turned to Connor. 'Is that okay with you? The piggy back, I mean?'

Connor eyed her critically. 'You can't weigh more than a few stone soakin' wet. I doubt I'll even notice the extra weight.' He nodded his head towards the farmhouse. 'When Auntie Aileen starts feedin' you, you'll soon fill out.'

Aidan grinned. 'Aye, and if you don't believe us, tek a look at me da.'

'I 'eard that, you cheeky beggar! Just you tek Spud back an' then you can come an' introduce our guest to your mam,' Aidan's father hollered from across the yard.

Chuckling, Aidan turned to Ellie. 'You ready?'

Ellie nodded, then gave a small gasp as Aidan lifted her clean off her feet and gently placed her on the pony's back. 'You can hold on to his mane if you want,' he said as they set off.

Ellie wound one hand in Spud's mane and stroked his withers with the other. Watching her host from under her lashes as he led the pony up the grassy path to his field, she marvelled at the way he had so easily lifted her on to Spud's back. He may have a limp, but other than that he seems very strong, Ellie thought to herself. I know I'm not heavy, but he damned near lifted me up to his chest to get me on to Spud's back and he's not even out of breath.

To her disappointment, the distance to Coin Meadow was only short. Aidan scooped Ellie from the pony's back and placed her carefully on a patch of grass whilst he opened the gate.

Spud whinnied as he trotted into the field, before collapsing to the ground and rolling enthusiastically. Closing the gate, Aidan tutted. 'Little blighter. He'll be caked in mud now. He's allus the same: can't stand bein' clean.'

Ellie giggled. 'He sounds like some of the boys I used to go to school with. Oh—' She stopped talking as two magnificent draught horses trotted towards the pony. 'So that's why he whinnied. He was calling them over.'

'Meet Samson and Hercules. You'd not think it, but Spud's the boss,' Aidan said, a look of admiration crossing his face.

'Do you ride them?' Ellie asked hopefully.

'Sometimes, but we mainly use them for all the heavy jobs around the farm: pullin' ploughs, shiftin' fallen trees after a storm, collectin' the harvest … you know the sort of thing.'

Leaning on the gate, Connor called out, 'She's ditched you already, little feller.'

Ellie looked appalled. 'Don't be so awful, Connor Murray. I'd never ditch Spud, he's too sweet.'

Connor chuckled. 'You can't fool me, Ellie Lancton. I know one of your favourite books is *National Velvet*.'

Ellie smiled as she watched Spud get to his feet and shake himself violently. 'I always wanted to be Velvet Brown.'

Connor smiled smugly. 'Precisely, but I can't see Spud jumping anything, let alone entering the National, unless they let him limbo ...'

Ellie giggled as she imagined herself on Spud's back, dodging the high fences as the graceful racehorses soared overhead. 'You're mean to me you are, Connor Murray. Spud too, come to that.'

Connor turned his back towards her. 'Come on, queen, jump aboard.'

When they had returned from Coin Meadow – so called, Ellie was told, because there had been a pot of old Roman coins unearthed there many years ago – the boys had given her a tour of the farm, starting with the field just down from Spud's, where the cows grazed. 'I'll teach you how to milk,' Aidan said. 'It's difficult at first but you'll soon get the hang of it.' Next she had been introduced to the small drift of pigs, whose ears intrigued her.

'How can they see with their ears hanging over their eyes like that?'

'Don't you worry about their ability to see,' Aidan snorted. 'If you jumped in with them I can guarantee you'd be surrounded by hungry, squealing pigs before you could say knife.'

On their way to the farmhouse, Aidan pointed to the hens milling around the yard. 'We just put them away for the night so's the fox doesn't get them; they've got their own hen house in the orchard. That's where we grow all our apples, pears and damson plums. Me mam makes delicious jam out of the plums, and she uses the pears and apples in pies and crumbles.' Aidan smacked his lips at the very thought.

Ellie pointed to a tractor that was parked near the orchard. 'You said earlier on that you use Samson and Hercules for all the heavy jobs around the farm. Why don't you use the tractor?'

Aidan glanced at Connor. 'Now, we don't use the tractor because of diesel rationing, but in truth we haven't used it since the accident.'

Ellie frowned. 'Why? What happened?'

Aidan led the way to the house, speaking to Ellie over his shoulder. 'It was just after me tenth birthday and we'd been hard at it all day. The harvest is always a race against time and everyone's always in a rush. I was runnin' out of one of the barns 'cos Lady, our collie, had started to give birth to her litter o' pups. I was too excited to think straight, and—' He clapped his hands together, causing Ellie to jump. 'Straight into the tractor and under the wheels.' He patted his leg. 'That's how this happened.'

Ellie slowly pulled her hand away from her mouth. 'Oh, Aidan, that's awful. You're lucky you weren't killed.'

Aidan nodded. 'Me da took me straight to hospital, but some of my thigh bone had been crushed beyond repair. They did what they could but it's left me with one leg shorter than the other, which is why I limp a little.' He ran his hand through his hair. 'To make matters worse it was Da who was driving the tractor at the time of the accident, so he blames himself. I told him over and over that I was the one to blame for not looking where I was going, but he wouldn't have it. So we only ever use the tractor now if it's totally necessary.'

Connor wiped his feet on the welcome mat outside the kitchen door. 'Farming can be really dangerous, not just the tractors but some of the tools they use for harvest, but you needn't worry, Ellie. I know our Aidan'll take good care of you.'

When they entered the large room with its low-beamed ceiling, Connor's Auntie Aileen gave a cry of delight as she laid eyes on Ellie. 'Here she is, our new farmhand! Come on in, Ellie dear. Leave your boots by the door, there's a good girl. I'm just about to dish up, so if you'd like to wash your hands in the sink – Connor'll show you where – you can take a seat and we can all have us suppers.'

Sitting at the table, Ellie thought she must have answered a hundred questions before a plateful of delicious-smelling food was placed in front of her. When she took the first spoonful, she was surprised to find that it was real scouse and not blind, as she had been expecting, and she said as much. 'The scouse is lovely. It's a real treat to have meat ... I've not had proper scouse for ages. Me mam couldn't afford it.'

Auntie Aileen smiled sympathetically. 'Bless your heart, child, I'm glad you like it. Farming is hard work so we make sure our men are full.' Her gaze travelled down Ellie's frail form. 'You're already startin' on the back burner, so to speak, so I'll mek sure you get a bit extra so's you can catch up to the rest of us.' Pointedly, she turned her eyes to Uncle Kieran's large stomach.

Following her gaze, Connor stifled a chuckle. 'Bloomin' 'eck, Auntie Aileen, you'll never get our Ellie to catch up wi' Uncle Kieran, not in a year of Sundays!'

Even though the plateful of food had been bigger than anything Ellie had ever been offered, she polished it off with ease and found it was all she could do to stop herself from licking it clean. Not expecting anything else, she was about to ask her host if she could help with the dishes when Auntie Aileen asked if anyone wanted pudding. There was a rumble of yeses.

'Would you like a hand, Mrs Murray?' Ellie asked.

The older woman smiled appreciatively. 'No formalities in this house. You've two choices, you can call me either Auntie Aileen or just plain Aileen. Pick your poison.'

Ellie smiled gratefully. 'Auntie Aileen, would you like a hand with the dishes?'

'That's better! You can take this lot over to the sink, and then when we've all finished eatin' you can help me wash up whilst the men check on the animals. That way we can have a bit of a chat and get to know each other a little better.' As she spoke she opened the oven door and a glorious smell of cooked apples filled the air. Scooping the crumble into a row of bowls, she lifted a saucepan from the Aga and raised her brow. 'Custard, anyone?'

It was not long before everyone had finished, and as the men trooped towards the back door Ellie joined her hostess by the sink. The older woman nodded to some tea towels that were draped over the oven rail. 'Take one of them, and as you dry I'll show you where everything lives.'

Nodding happily, Ellie took the warm cotton towel from its place and watched as Connor, Aidan and Uncle Kieran picked up their wellies, which were neatly lined up on some newspaper. Mr Murray pointed at a pair set off to one side from the others. 'You can use them, Ellie. They used to be our Cassie's, only she don't need 'em any more, not where she's gone.'

Ellie stood in dismay as she watched the men leave the kitchen. What had Mr Murray meant when he had said that Cassie wouldn't need the boots any more, *not where she's gone*? She looked hesitantly at Auntie Aileen. 'I hope you don't mind my askin', but what did he mean about Cassie?'

Mrs Murray smiled, and a wreath of wrinkles formed around her eyes. Looking at her, Ellie thought her to be considerably older than her own mother had been when she died. 'I'm not with you, chuck. What did you want to know about our Cassie?'

Ellie took a deep breath. 'When Mr Murray – I mean Uncle Kieran – said that she wouldn't be needing her wellies any more ...'

Mrs Murray burst into laughter. 'Oh, bless you, you thought she was ...' She waved a dismissive hand. 'Oh, sweetheart, she's not dead, she's in the Wrens.'

Confused, Ellie spoke her thoughts. 'But Aidan said that his little sister Cassie had named Spud ...'

Auntie Aileen emptied the sink of its water and absentmindedly wiped her hands on a tea towel whilst nodding her understanding. 'Now I see! Aidan and Cassie are twins, but because he was born before her – only by a minute, mind – he likes to tease her by calling her his little sister. Is that clearer?'

Ellie nodded. 'Lots.' She cast an eye around the kitchen. 'Is there anything else I can do? Wipe the table down, sweep the floor …?'

'You sit down whilst I wipe the table.' Auntie Aileen glanced at her. 'I don't expect you to tell me why you're here, but if you ever want to talk I'm always willing to lend an ear if that's what's required. Our Connor's a good boy, and we know he'd never bring trouble to our house, so you're welcome to stay as long as you need.' She rinsed the cloth, then began wiping the table with large circular motions. 'With most of the young men off to war we've been left short-handed, so your help's much appreciated, 'specially with harvest approachin'.' She placed the cloth on the table and reached across to lift Ellie's hands and examine her palms. For a moment Ellie wondered whether the older woman might be reading them, and was getting quite hopeful until, with a smile of satisfaction, Auntie Aileen released her and commented, 'You've calluses, and your skin's tough. That's the sign of a hard worker, and just as well, as farming's not easy …'

'I do washing for people, and I work for Mr Wong who owns one of the Chinese laundries.' She hesitated. 'I've not done anything bad or unlawful.'

Auntie Aileen had finished wiping the table, and settled into a chair across from Ellie's. 'Our Connor says your mam's passed on?'

Ellie nodded. She opened her mouth to speak, to explain about the pneumonia, but the words stuck in her throat, and as her eyes met the older woman's she felt tears trickling down her cheeks.

There was a scraping noise as Auntie Aileen took the chair next to Ellie. She gently pushed Ellie's hair back behind her ears and handed her a hanky from her apron pocket, and Ellie noticed the comforting scent of lavender, which her mother had always used. 'You must miss your mother so much, especially when life becomes a tough row to hoe ...'

Ellie nodded. 'She wasn't just me mam, she were everything to me. We worked together, we lived together, she always made sure there was enough to eat, and with her gone I'm all on me tod. I've got no other family, you see, apart from Arla, who's like a sister and me best pal, and Connor, who I think of as a brother.' She looked into Auntie Aileen's kind eyes, blue like her mother's. 'I couldn't pay the rent because Mrs Wardle couldn't give me what I was owed, and ...'

When Ellie had finished her story Auntie Aileen shook her head fiercely. 'Beast of a man!' she said, her face reddening. 'How *could* he? To take advantage in the most despicable way ... and of a child ...' She tried to smile. 'Well, one thing's certain, alanna, you did the right thing by goin' to our Connor, and he done the right thing by bringin' you here.' She shook her head again, this time in disbelief. 'It's not often I'm at a loss for words, but this one's got me beat. Connor said you was worried about payin' your way here, but believe me, by the time you've mucked out the pigs and cows, and fed the chooks, and done the milkin', you'll realise that's more than payment enough.'

A frown creased Ellie's brow. 'Chooks? I don't remember Aidan showing me any chooks.'

Auntie Aileen laughed. 'Sorry. It's my pet name for the hens.' She smiled warmly at Ellie and clapped her hands on to her knees. 'Now, I think you'd better be gettin' some sleep. You've not slept properly for three nights that I know of, and like I say, farm work is hard goin'. You come wi' me an' I'll show you to your room.'

Collecting her satchel from behind the kitchen door, Ellie followed her host up a set of narrow wooden stairs.

'I've put you in the room next to our Cassie's. It's at the back of the house so the noise of the farm shouldn't disturb you too much.'

Entering the room, Ellie placed her satchel on the wooden bed opposite the small deep-set window. The blackout blinds had already been drawn and Auntie Aileen lit the oil lamp from the one she carried. She indicated the two-drawer chest that stood at the side of Ellie's bed. 'You can pop your clothes in there, and if you want hot water, come down to the kitchen in the morning before breakfast. There's always a saucepan or the kettle on the boil. You know about blackout blinds, so no need to explain them.' She cast an eye around the room, then, satisfied, she raised a brow at Ellie. 'Any questions?'

Ellie shook her head, then changed her mind and nodded. 'What time shall I get up? I'm really lookin' forward to workin' with the animals and I don't want to sleep in and miss out on anything.'

Her hostess nodded approvingly. 'Not to worry. I'll wake you up in plenty of time, so if that's all, I'll let you get into bed. Goodnight, alanna.'

Ellie smiled. 'Me mam used to call me that. It's good to hear it again.'

Auntie Aileen chuckled. 'Irish roots, no doubt,' she said.

Ellie nodded. She had only known the Murrays a matter of hours, yet she already felt at ease in their company. As the older woman left, closing the door softly behind her, Ellie looked around at her cosy room, then wandered over to the chest and opened the top drawer. She looked at a small bag inside. Picking it up, she immediately smelled the scent of lavender, and smiled to herself. She might be a long way from Liverpool, but in her heart she was home.

Bitterly regretting having not asked her hosts where the air raid shelter was, Ellie clattered down the stairs, raising the alarm as she went. When she reached the bottom she looked around the dark kitchen. It was deserted. Where was everybody? Surely they had not left her in the house on her own? She was about to go into the yard when a bleary-eyed Aidan stumbled through the door from the hall. 'What's all the racket?' he said, rubbing his eyes.

'Air raid siren; didn't you hear it? Where's everyone else? Where should we go?' Ellie clutched her night-gown tightly around her.

Aidan frowned. 'I didn't hear owt. Are you sure?' He looked up at her, an expression of confusion in his eyes.

'Hang on a mo, we don't have an air raid siren out here. You can't have heard it.'

His father came into the kitchen, tightening the belt on his robe and then running his fingers through tousled hair. 'Whassup? What you doin'? It's the middle of the night!'

Outside, the cockerel announced his presence, causing Ellie to jump six inches and Uncle Kieran to retract his earlier statement. 'Okay, so it's not the middle of the night. It just feels as if it is.'

Ellie looked awkwardly at the two men. 'I'm so sorry. I thought I heard Moaning Minnie sounding off, but I think it might have been that ... that ... what *was* that?'

Aidan gave a tired chuckle. 'That was our cockerel, and just so you know, he does that every morning at dawn, or before, or whenever he feels like it, in fact, and the bugger doesn't shut up until he has the whole farm up.'

'What do you call him?' Ellie asked.

'Depends what time of day he gets us up, but mostly we call him Eric,' Aidan said with a yawn.

As Connor and his aunt entered the kitchen Ellie found her cheeks growing hot with embarrassment. Apologising for disturbing everyone's sleep, she asked what the drill was for a real air raid.

'Put your head between your knees and kiss your ar—' Uncle Kieran had begun when Auntie Aileen cut in, her voice shrill.

'Kieran Murray! I'll not have any of that language in my kitchen!' She turned to Ellie, who was looking confused, whilst the boys stifled their laughter. 'I may as well start warming the water through now, as we'll be getting up in the next half-hour or so.' She filled a large kettle from the tap. 'If you come with me, Ellie, I've got a heap of our Cassie's old clothes in a trunk on the top landin'. There's woollies, skirts, dresses, shirts, an' trousers for doin' the farm work in, and you're welcome to try on and use whatever fits you. I dare say you haven't got much of your own and Cassie's grown out of most of it, so anything that fits you're welcome to keep. Come along now, and by the time we come back down the water'll be ready.'

Chapter Three

'That's it!' Aidan cried triumphantly. 'I said you'd get it eventually, and you have, you clever girl!'

Ellie was delighted. She had been on the farm for a little over a month and she was enjoying every minute of it. The Murrays had welcomed her with open arms and it wasn't long before she felt like a member of the family. She didn't regard her tasks on the farm as real work; they were a pleasure not a chore, and she very much enjoyed the early mornings when she was always first downstairs, with the kettle on and the porridge simmering before Auntie Aileen appeared.

Before Connor had gone home he and Aidan had tried to teach Ellie how to milk, but no matter in which manner she pulled the teats she couldn't extract a single drop, although she had become adept at dodging angry hooves.

Now, with the milk hissing into the pail, Ellie could not have been more pleased with herself. 'It's working. I can't believe I'm doing it!'

Aidan smiled down at his new assistant. Whether she knew it or not, Ellie had been a godsend to the farm, and not just because she helped with the work.

With all his friends and workmates gone to war, Aidan missed having someone his own age around the place, and he found himself appreciating Ellie's company as much as her help. What was more, he could see by her transformation that she too was enjoying the benefits of her move to Oxton, thriving for the first time in her life on a good diet and clean air.

When she had first arrived at the farm Aidan's mother had not been slow to remark on the condition of their house guest. 'She's as skinny as a rake and her hair's drab and lifeless, and she's that pale you'd think she were about to drop dead any minute. I'm tellin' you now, she's arrived at this farm a little girl, alone and weak, and if it's the last thing I do I'm gonna make sure she leaves here a healthy, happy, strong young woman.'

True to her word, his mother had started the very next morning by asking Ellie if she would like a haircut. 'Nothin' fancy, just a couple of inches should do the trick. I reckon it's been a while since you last had it done?'

Fingering the ends of her hair, Ellie tried to remember when she had in fact last had it cut, and thought it must have been before her mother died. Nodding her agreement, Auntie Aileen guided her towards the kitchen sink. 'Wash first, then trim; it's easier that way. I'll warn you now I rinse with cold water. It's good for the scalp, so try not to holler like Aidan.'

Several freezing minutes and one haircut later the older woman had stood back to admire her work. 'You've got beautiful curly hair, alanna, although you'd never have known it before.'

Taking the proffered mirror, Ellie admired her new look. She tilted her head from left to right, then back again, her hair swinging like a curtain around her cheeks, and she smelled the rose-scented soap which had been used to wash it. Her gaze locked with the one in the mirror, and for a brief second it was like looking into her mother's almond-shaped eyes, only her own were hazel not blue.

And it hadn't stopped with the haircut, Aidan thought as he watched Ellie continuing to milk. She had flesh on her bones now, and was starting to develop curves; the pale complexion had been replaced by a healthy glow, and her eyes sparkled.

Sitting up, she patted the cow's leg. 'That's you finished, Clara. Let's see what you've managed.' She squealed with delight and held the pail out to Aidan. 'It's at least a quarter full. Isn't she clever?'

Aidan nodded. 'Yes, she is. Annabelle's next. Let's see how you manage her.'

Annabelle, it seemed, did not wish to be as cooperative as Clara, and proceeded to try to kick the pail over as soon as she heard the hiss of milk. However, Ellie had watched Aidan milking often enough to be familiar with her tricks, and whipped it out of the way before any harm could be done.

By the time Ellie had finished milking the last cow she no longer doubted her abilities, and she revelled in this newfound confidence. With the cows back in the pasture Aidan closed the gate firmly behind them and turned to her with a smile. 'I don't need to ask how you feel after your first successful milking session; the grin on your face is answer enough. But how are you finding life on the farm in general?'

'I love it,' said Ellie. 'In fact I can't think of a time in my life when I've been happier. I just wish me mam could see me. It's her I get my passion for horses from, and I know she would have loved to ride in the cart.'

'You must miss her an awful lot ... Do you miss your friends too?' he asked hesitantly.

Ellie nodded. 'I've only got two friends that I'm really close to, and that's Arla and Connor, and to be honest they're more like a sister and brother to me. I'm going to write to them both later and let them know about the milking. Connor will be thrilled. He saw how hopeless I was to begin with, and he knows how much I hate it when I can't get the hang of something.'

Aidan raised an enquiring eyebrow. 'Have you known Connor for a long time? I can't say as I ever remember him mentioning you before.'

'A few years. We met when he saved me from a nasty bully. He was my knight in shining armour.'

Aidan was surprised to feel his cheeks grow hot. He found himself wishing that he had been the one to save Ellie from the bully, the one she saw as a knight in shining armour. How unfair, he thought irritably, that Connor, who had so little interest in her that he had neglected to mention her for years, was described in such a favourable manner.

Walking back down the grassy lane, Aidan chastised himself for getting angry with his cousin. It wasn't Connor's fault that Ellie had described him so; besides, she had also described him as like a brother, so she obviously did not see him in a romantic light.

Ellie's voice cut across his thoughts. 'Are you all right? Only you look a bit red and blotchy … do you want to stop for a minute?'

Aidan shook his head and turned his face away. 'Come on, little milk maiden. It's time to release the hens and see if they've managed to lay us a golden egg.'

When the Liverpool Murrays entered the farmhouse kitchen just before supper on Christmas Eve, Connor took one look at Ellie before releasing a low whistle. 'Blimey, you look a bit different from the last time I saw you!'

Connor's mother stood staring for a moment or two before she clapped a hand to her mouth. 'Ellie Lancton! Well I never … just look at you.' She turned to her sister-in-law. 'Aileen Murray, you've worked wonders with that cookin' of yours. I've never seen the child lookin' so healthy.'

Ellie glowed under the admiring glances as the new arrivals subjected her to a volley of questions and compliments. When she had first arrived at the farm in May she had sometimes found the kindly curiosity of Auntie Aileen and Uncle Keiran a little uncomfortable, but a lot had changed since then, and she had not seen her old friends for a long time, so she revelled in the attention, answering their questions with pleasure and relaying stories of her experiences on the farm, until Connor brought the inquisition to an end by asking, 'Have you ridden the bull yet?'

His mother held up a hand. 'That will do, Connor Murray. This poor girl hasn't had a chance to catch her breath since we arrived.' She looked kindly at Ellie.

'From what you've said, and from what you wrote to Connor, you're doing your mam proud, chuck.'

Beaming under such praise, Ellie looked round for Aidan, her cheeks growing crimson when she spied him leaning against the wall on the far side of the kitchen, watching her with interest. 'I do hope so, but Aidan's the one who really deserves the compliment. He's the one who's taught me all I know.'

Mrs Murray looked proudly at her nephew. 'He's a good lad, and a brilliant farmer. Well done, both of you.'

Ellie, who had not been looking forward to her first Christmas without her mother, soon discovered that she should not have doubted the Murrays. They took her mind off her loss by spending the evening playing charades as well as a lot of different board games, one of which greatly intrigued Ellie, who had never heard of chess before. Uncle Kieran had challenged Aidan to a game and Ellie watched in fascination as the two men sat at opposite sides of the table, their heads bent in thought as each tried to outwit the other.

The kitchen clock was approaching midnight by the time the pair had finished their second game, and Ellie, who by this time had memorised the moves of all the pieces, was just about to ask if she might try when Uncle Kieran scooped the little carved figures back into their box and picked up the board. 'Christmas or not, come mornin' the pigs and hens'll still want feedin', and the cows'll need milkin', so I think it's time we all went to our beds.' He turned to his brother's family. 'Not that I expect our guests to do any of the work, of course.'

'I don't mind helping in the morning. Me and Ellie can milk the cows if you like,' Connor volunteered. 'That way the rest of you can have a lie-in whilst she shows me how much she's improved since I last saw her.'

Aidan glared at him. 'Thanks for the offer, but Ellie and me have got a routine goin' an' I reckon the two of us'll be quicker if we're left to get on wi' things our way.'

'How about if I help Ellie with her side of the work and then, when the two of us have done, we can come and help you? It'll give me and Ellie a chance for a catch-up. Surely two pairs of hands are better than one?' Connor suggested.

Aidan appeared to consider, then shrugged his shoulders. 'If you insist on helping you'd best make sure you're up betimes. I don't want you dragging your feet and slowing us down.'

'Aidan!' Auntie Aileen scolded. 'Don't be so rude! If someone offers you a helping hand you accept it gratefully.' She turned to her sister-in-law. 'I think it's all the excitement of Christmas.'

'Mam!' snapped Aidan. 'I'm not a child.' He turned apologetically to Connor. 'Sorry if I was a bit abrupt. I didn't mean to be, it's just that we've an awful lot to do in the morning before we can relax and enjoy the day. I just wanted to get it done as quickly as possible.'

Shrugging, Connor smiled, but Ellie could see that her friend had been confused by his cousin's outburst. 'Don't worry, I won't hold anyone up. I may be a bit rusty, but it won't take me long to get the hang of things again.'

When Ellie awoke the next morning it was to find that snow was falling thick and fast. She, Connor and Aidan had already breakfasted and were about to step into the cold when Auntie Aileen entered the kitchen. 'Merry Christmas, kids. Are you comin' or goin'?'

'Just leaving to do the feeding and milking, Mam. It shouldn't take more than an hour or so between the three of us,' Aidan said, his hand resting on the kitchen door handle.

Auntie Aileen pointed to the stockings that hung over the Aga. 'I hope no one's had a sneaky peak at their prezzies whilst I've been sleepin'?'

Aidan rolled his eyes. 'How many times, Mam? We're not kids any more. I'm sure we can wait until we've finished the morning's work before opening our presents.' As he opened the kitchen door an icy blast swept into the warm kitchen, bringing a flurry of snow with it.

'Out you go!' Auntie Ailene shrieked as she pulled her dressing gown tightly closed. 'And make sure you shut that door properly after you.'

Outside the wind whipped fiercely around them, picking up the snow which had already lain and settling it into drifts against the farm buildings. 'I'll do the pigs,' Aidan shouted, 'then the hens, but they shouldn't take more than a few minutes because I shan't turn them out, not in this weather! When I've finished I'll come and give you two a hand.'

Ellie opened her mouth to reply then shut it quickly as the whirling snow caught her breath. Nodding, she ran to the cowshed, and once she and Connor were inside she bolted the large metal door shut.

'I like snow, but only when it's finishing snowing, if you know what I mean,' she said as she placed a halter

74

around the nearest cow's head. 'I'll fetch the pail and stool whilst you tie Dave up.' Dave was another of Cassie's victims.

Connor shook the snow off his jacket. 'You mean you prefer it deep and crisp and even, like in the carol.'

Ellie placed the stool down and positioned the bucket below Dave's laden udder. As the milk hissed into the pail she smiled up at Connor. 'Well? What do you think? I told you I'd got the hang of things good and proper.'

Connor gave an approving smile. 'From city girl to milkmaid in little more than six months. I'm impressed. You've obviously taken to farming like a duck to water, but then I guessed you would.' He leaned against Dave's rump. 'I saw Arla a couple of days ago. She wanted me to ask you about your plans for joining up. She reckons from your last letter you sounded so happy on the farm that she feared you might've changed your mind.'

Ellie's smile faded. 'Oh no, that's not the case at all! I mean, she's right that I do love it here, but not enough to stay. I'm still plannin' on joinin' up in January. When you go home you can tell her from me that come her sixteenth I'll be round her house ready to go down the recruiting office just as we planned.' She pulled the pail of milk from under the cow and handed it to Connor. 'I didn't realise she thought I wanted to stay on the farm. I'm going to write to her later this evening to thank her for the Christmas present you brought, whatever it is, so I'll reassure her that my intentions haven't changed.'

Connor grinned. 'That'll be grand – you joining up I mean – 'cos then all three of us'll be in the services. I've been accepted into the RAF.'

Ellie broke off from the milking. 'You kept that quiet! When did all this happen?'

'I got my papers a week ago. Only don't go talking about it in front of Mam.'

Ellie's eyes rounded. 'You mean she doesn't know?'

'Course she knows, but that doesn't mean to say she's happy about it. I'll be going to the training camp in West Kirby on the third of January.'

She placed the pail under Bella's teats. 'But both your brothers have joined up. What's so different about you doing it?'

Connor shook his head. 'Because I'm the last to go. She still sees me as the baby and I think she hoped to keep me at home. To be honest, she's not been thrilled about the others going, but she couldn't do anything to stop them, whereas I still needed Dad's permission, so things have been a little tense as I'm sure you can imagine. I can't so much as mention the war; if I do she tells me to "hush my noise" or "get to my room", so Dad and me thought it best just to keep shtum.'

Ellie grimaced. 'Your poor mam. You can't blame her for bein' scared. Have you heard from your brothers?'

Connor nodded. 'Regularly. They both say the same thing: it's hard work, but someone's got to do it.'

Ellie finished milking Bella and waited whilst Connor slipped the collar over Amy's neck. Ellie patted the cow's leg in a friendly manner. 'Come on, girl, soon have you done.' As the milk hissed rhythmically into the pail Ellie kept her eyes lowered. 'You promise me you'll take care of yourself?'

'Are you talking to me or Amy?'

Ellie shot him a withering look. 'You, not that you deserve it ...'

'Of course I'll look after meself. What've I always said?'

'That you'll dodge out of the way and shoot the beggars in the rear, but it's not a game,' Ellie said, her voice hollow.

Kneeling down beside her he placed an arm around her shoulders. 'Come on, queen. I know you're worried, but I promise you I'm not treating this as a game. I just don't see the point in getting all het up about something I haven't even started yet.'

She stopped milking Amy and turned to face him, their noses no more than a few inches apart. 'You're a good lad, Connor Murray, one of the best, and I'm sure you'll make a brilliant pilot. Just don't go pulling no heroics.'

Connor had opened his mouth to reply when he was interrupted by a sharp cough coming from outside the shed. Turning, they saw Aidan, who was resting both arms on top of the metal door. 'Hope I'm not disturbing owt. I wanted to ask Connor if he wouldn't mind helping me with the pigs. That blooming Dotty's hunkered down in the corner and is refusing to budge.'

'We weren't ... I were just ... Connor's joined the RAF,' Ellie gabbled.

Aidan shook his head dismissively. 'No need for explanations, and I know about Connor joining up.

I can't deny I'm a tad jealous. I'd give anythin' to be given the chance.'

Ellie looked at Aidan and could not help noticing the furtive glance he shot towards Connor from underneath his lashes. In the hope that she might lighten the mood, she asked, 'When was the last time you tried joining up? If it was a while back things might've changed. And if you did get in you and Connor might be posted together, and you might even end up in the same part of the country as me and Arla if we get accepted.'

Aidan appeared confused. 'You and Arla? Accepted into what?'

Ellie giggled. 'Into one of the services, you goose! Surely your dad mentioned it when I first arrived?'

Aidan shook his head. 'When was all this decided?'

'Before I left Liverpool,' she said. 'Me and Arla, my best pal, we're goin' to join the WAAF. I told your dad when I got here that it wouldn't be for long, just until my pal turned sixteen in January.'

Aidan opened the door to the shed and beckoned Connor. 'Well, that's that settled. I'm not going to be left out of all the fun and games. Soon as winter's over I'm off down that recruiting office and come what may I shall join the RAF. It's got to be easier than moving that stubborn pig!'

Chapter Four

New Year's Day 1941

Ellie looked out of her bedroom window and was delighted to see that it had snowed heavily again during the night and the farmyard had been transformed into a winter paradise. She had not seen snow this thick since Christmas, and with time running out before she left for Liverpool she had begun to think that the wintry weather had left for good and that the ride through the snowy woods that Aidan had promised for today might never happen.

Clattering down the stairs, she entered the kitchen to find Aidan already waiting for her at the breakfast table.

'Blimey, you're keen!' he chuckled, as she started gulping down her porridge in large spoonfuls. He eyed her critically. 'You're going to need a lot more than that to keep you warm.' He nodded to a chair by the Aga. On it there was a thick woollen overcoat and what looked like some large woollen socks, warming by the oven. Walking to the door, he shoved his feet into his wellington boots. 'When you've drunk your tea get that lot on, and we can be off. I got Hercules in earlier and gave him a bit of a brush, so there's not much to do save tacking up. I'll do that whilst you finish here.'

Ellie nodded as she scraped the last morsels of porridge from around the bowl's edge.

In the stable Aidan placed the bridle over Hercules' head and fastened the throat lash. 'Fancy a bit of fun?' he asked, as the hot breath of the horse clouded the stall.

'Yes please!' Ellie said, unlatching the stable door.

Aidan chuckled. 'I was talking to him, but I suppose it applies to you too.' He pushed the door open and led the gentle giant out into the snow.

Ellie frowned. 'You've forgotten his saddle! Do you want me to go and get it?'

He raised an eyebrow and grinned. 'No thank you, no need for saddles today. We're going to be riding bareback, for two reasons: for one thing it's jolly uncomfortable to ride two up when there's a sodding big saddle in between you, and for another you get the benefit of Hercules' warmth and thick coat.'

Ellie looked doubtful. 'Are you sure? Remember, I've only ever ridden Spud before.'

Aidan beckoned her to stand beside him. 'You'll be fine, alanna. You can hold on to Hercules, and I'll hold on to you. Now bend your knee so's I can give you a leg-up.'

Ellie obeyed and found herself being hoisted swiftly on to Hercules' broad back. She looked around for a small wall or something similar for Aidan to stand on, and gave a small squeal of surprise when he effortlessly swung himself up behind her.

Putting his arms around her, he grasped the reins, and with a click of his tongue he ordered the big gelding to walk on.

As they rode along the track that led to the woods, Ellie felt as if she could burst with happiness. The snow was at least six inches deep, and yet Hercules traversed it with ease, lifting each heavy feathered leg high and thudding the hoof down with a soft crump. A light breeze had come into play and Ellie pushed her fingers into the horse's thick mane. Aidan leaned forward so that his cheek brushed lightly against hers and whispered into her ear, 'If we keep our voices down we might see some foxes and maybe a rabbit or two, so stay as quiet as you can.' As he spoke a buzzard flew silently just above their heads before settling on a tree branch further up the lane. Looking down, Ellie could see pawprints in the snow, and wondered which creature had made them. She turned to ask Aidan and he leaned forward again to hear her whisper, and she noticed the familiar scent of Pears soap. She pointed at the prints. 'Who left those?'

'Rabbit,' he said softly. 'You can tell because the two front paws are close together, and the back legs wider apart.'

Ellie nodded. When Aidan had leaned forward his arms had tightened gently around her and she had felt an unfamiliar yet rather delightful tingling feeling throughout her body, so that she found herself wishing to spot more pawprints just in order to experience the same sensation, and was disappointed when she saw none.

She was glad that Aidan appeared unaware of her secret delight as he gently guided the big horse into the woods. She stared in wonder at the towering fir trees, their mighty branches weighted low to the ground with their burdens of snow, one of which would occasionally slide to the ground with a soft thud. Keeping her voice low, she whispered, 'Aidan, it's so beautiful. The trees look as if someone's poured icing sugar on them. I can see why you wanted to bring me here.'

She felt the muscles in his chest move as he leaned forward once more. 'There's something magical about it, isn't there? When Connor was really little we used to come into the woods whenever it snowed and look for Toad, Badger and Mole. He thought they might be easier to find if we could follow their prints.' He paused, and she felt his chin brush against her cheek. 'Have you read *The Wind in the Willows*?'

Ellie relaxed in his embrace. 'It's one of my favourite books, and I must say this is just the sort of place you could imagine them living in, isn't it? Do these woods lead to the river?'

Aidan nodded. 'I remember Connor thinking he'd found Toad's caravan when he spied a dim yellow light on the banks of the river.' He chuckled softly. 'He nearly scared that poacher half to death when he yelled "I've found him" at the top of his voice.'

Forgetting to be quiet, Ellie giggled. 'What did the poacher do?'

'First he fell in the river, because he'd been leaning down whilst using the light to attract the fish, and when he managed to get out he took off like a hare! And our Connor started wailing because he was disappointed that it wasn't Toad Hall. He couldn't have given a damn about the poacher.' They had reached a track through the centre of the woods and Aidan rested his chin on Ellie's shoulder, his breath tickling her ear as he whispered, 'Fancy a canter?'

'Hmmm?' she said vaguely. She had heard his question, but she had been distracted by the delicious shiver that enveloped her body once more.

'I said do you fancy a canter?'

Ellie nodded doubtfully. 'I'd love to, but I've never cantered before. What if I come off? It's a bit further to fall than from Spud.'

She felt Aidan's warm breath against her cheek again as he whispered, 'I won't let you fall, alanna. You'll be grand, I promise.'

Taking a deep breath, she nodded eagerly. Aidan clicked his tongue and Ellie felt him squeeze the horse between his legs. Hercules broke into a brief trot before starting to canter steadily up the track.

Uncertainty and fear forgotten, Ellie called back excitedly, 'He's just like a rocking horse.' Looking at the track ahead, she spotted a thick branch that must have broken off under the weight of the snow. 'Aidan, look out!' she yelled, but instead of reining the horse back Aidan urged him on.

'Hold on, alanna, and don't worry, I promise I won't let you fall.' Hercules lifted his front legs high above the branch and they sailed over the top, landing neatly on the other side, and Ellie gave a whoop of joy.

When they reached the top of the path Aidan slowed the horse to a walk. Leaning forward, he pulled her hair back from her face, and, seeing the sparkle in her eyes, he smiled. 'No need to ask you whether you enjoyed that, then.'

Ellie breathed out happily. 'Can we do it again one day? Perhaps when I come back on leave?'

Aidan frowned. 'With a bit of luck I won't be here.' He paused. 'That is to say, I'll be in the RAF, but we could always come back together.'

Ellie smiled dreamily. 'I'd like that very much.'

'Although of course you don't have to join up. You could always stay here on the farm.'

Ellie let out a small groan. 'Don't tempt me. I find the thought of leaving hard enough as it is.'

He smiled. 'Good. I wouldn't like to think you found it easy. Don't forget, you still have time to change your mind.'

She laughed. 'Stop it! Tell you what, how about I have a go with the reins? What do you think? We're not far from home, and I think I'll be fine if Hercules doesn't mind plodding.'

She heard a resigned sigh behind her, and he held his hands up for her to take the reins. 'I'll still have to hold on to summat, though,' he said. He slid his strong arms round her waist and clasped both hands tightly in front of her.

There was a brief pause before Ellie spoke. 'Fine,' she gulped, her voice just above a whisper. Her waist was tingling under his touch and as her heart began to beat faster she found herself wishing he would slide gently to the ground, taking her with him, and kiss her.

Instead, he released his grip and tousled the top of her hair. 'Look at you, kiddo! Is there nothing you can't turn your hand to? You remind me a lot of our Cassie.

She's a natural with the animals too.' He chuckled. 'We used to ride two up like this to take the hay to the other horses in the field. We had a few more then, mind you. You'd get on well, the two of you. She loves horses as much as you do.'

Ellie cursed inwardly. What a fool you are, Ellie Lancton, daydreaming about kissing him when all he sees in you is a replacement for his sister, just as you see Connor as an older brother. Don't start falling for someone who's not interested, or you'll end up like your mam, broken-hearted and alone. She breathed out heavily. Perhaps it was all for the best. After all, what would Arla say if she turned up with Aidan in tow? Her friend had her sights on the two of them marrying officers, not some farmer with bushy black hair and clothes fit for a scarecrow.

'She's coming home! I know she said she would, but I didn't think she really meant it.' Arla flourished the paper at her father. 'My days are numbered in these courts. She's kept her word and will be coming for my birthday so's we can join up together!' She looked across the table to where her father sat draining a cup of tea. 'Where's Mam?'

He shrugged. 'In the lavvy?'

Running out of the kitchen, Arla made her way to the privies at the top of the court and banged enthusiastically on the door. 'Mam! Are you in there? Only I've had a letter from our Ellie.'

There was a cough of acknowledgement from behind the closed door. Beaming, Arla began to read the letter aloud.

'Dear Arla, Guess who's coming to see you on your six-teenth birthday? That's right ... me! I can't wait to see you, it's been such a long time, and I've so much to tell you. I bet you won't recognise me – Connor's mam didn't. I've put on a few pounds but all for the better according to the Mur-rays. Gosh, I've missed you so much and we're going to have such fun in the WAAF, just as we planned. Have you seen Archie? Only Connor reckons he's joining the army or something similar ...' Arla snorted. 'I wish he'd join up and bugger off quick. Least then I could get some peace round here.' She giggled. 'That was me sayin' that, not our Ellie.'

There was the sound of a chain being pulled, fol-lowed by the rushing of water. Seeing the latch lift, Arla stood back from the doorway, grinning with excitement. She moved forward to hug her mother, only to recoil with horror. 'Archie bloody Byrnes! Why didn't you tell me it were you in there and not me mam?'

Archie smirked. 'I hadn't got a paper and to be fair it's a bit hard to see in the dark, so it was nice to have someone readin' to me.'

Arla pursed her lips. 'But that information weren't for your ears.' She sniffed uncertainly. 'What's this about you joinin' the army? Not that I believe it for a second, of course.'

Archie pretended to look hurt. 'That's not very nice, I must say. And for your information I have signed up. I'm just waitin' for me papers.'

Arla looked at the boy, a range of emotions swirling inside her as she struggled to find her tongue. Archie Byrnes might have been one of the most annoying people living in Harebell Court – he certainly seemed to go out of his way to get on Arla's nerves – but he was also one of the kindest. He'd always help out if you needed a hand, and he wouldn't stand for any nonsense off the kids who lived in the posher houses. He'd given one of them a good thump once when they'd made fun of Arla for living in a court. She tried to imagine him in army uniform. He was older than her, but he had what her mother referred to as 'boyish good looks', meaning that he looked a lot younger than his years. He was not much taller than Arla herself and rather skinny; certainly not like the men she'd seen marching down the streets towards the recruiting office.

'Cat got your tongue?' he said, folding his arms across his chest.

'You're just a boy.' The words left her lips in a whisper.

Archie frowned his annoyance. 'No I'm not. I'm older'n you.' But then, looking into Arla's tear-brimmed eyes, he held out a hand. 'What's up? I was only havin' a laugh before.'

'I didn't mean it,' she said, before turning and running back to her house.

Archie stared after her retreating figure as he tried to work out what on earth had just happened. She had called him a boy, and he had pointed out that he was older than her. What was wrong with that? It was only the truth, after all. Shaking his head, he stuffed his hands into his pockets and strolled back to his own house. Closing the front door, he looked across to Arla's. As far as he was concerned, Arla spent most of her life pouting and scolding him for one prank or another. He'd have thought she'd be pleased to see the back of him; heck, she'd even said so when she'd thought she was speaking to her mother. Shrugging, he closed the door behind him. He'd never understand girls like Arla if he lived to be a hundred.

Back in her own home, Arla found her mother sitting at the table, darning one of her stockings. 'There you are,' said Arla, sniffing back the tears. 'Why couldn't you have been here ten minutes ago?'

'Why, what happened ten minutes ago?' Mrs Winthorpe looked up from her work. 'Arla! What's happened? why are you cryin'?'

Arla shook her head dismissively. 'Don't worry, there's nowt wrong. I were just bein' silly.' She put the letter down in front of her mother. 'I've had a letter from Ellie. She says she's comin' home for my birthday so that we can join up together, and you know what that means. We'll be able to learn a trade, marry an officer, and get out of these courts, that's what that means!'

Mrs Winthorpe looked up from her darning again. 'I know you're keen to get out of the courts, but there's worse things in life than livin' round here. Life in the services won't be easy, you know. It'll be hard work with little thanks and less pay, so don't you go thinkin' it's gonna be one long picnic.'

Arla leaned over the small kitchen table and hugged her mother. 'Don't worry, Mam, I know it won't be easy, but it'll be worth it in the end. Besides, I'll have me partner in crime wi' me. We'll have such a hoot.'

Mrs Winthorpe placed her darning down on the table and looked curiously at her daughter. 'Considering that your bezzie who you ain't seen in an age is coming home, why were you cryin'? They didn't look like happy tears to me.'

Arla lowered her eyes. 'I've been talkin' to Archie Byrnes ...'

'Ah! That explains the tears,' Mrs Winthorpe said wisely. 'Honestly, you two seem to take great joy in teasing each other to desperation. What's he said this time?'

Arla's bottom lip trembled. 'He's joined the army, Mam. I know we fight like cat 'n' dog, and I know that I'm always complainin' about him, and he can be a right pain in the neck, but ...'

Getting up from the table, Betty Winthorpe stroked her daughter's hair back from her face. 'I know, I know,' she soothed. 'He may get on your wick and drive you potty half the time, but that doesn't mean you don't like him.'

Arla nodded. 'He's gorra big gob with a heart to match, but there's norra bad bone in his body. He's always jokin' around and messin' about, but he's not tough like some of them others what have joined up. They'll make ground beef out of him.'

Her mother fished around in her apron pocket for a hanky, and handed it to her. ''Ere, 'ave a good blow,' she instructed. 'And as for Archie Byrnes, you just 'ave to 'ope he's one of the lucky ones. From what I hear they're tekkin' young lads on for them ack-ack batteries at the minute. If he winds up on one of them it's got to be a damned sight safer than it is on the front line.'

Arla brightened. 'Do you think? He wouldn't have to go overseas then, would he? Oh, I do hope you're right, Mam.'

Betty smiled reassuringly. 'You know Archie. Wherever he goes he'll land on his feet. He's got the gift of the gab, that one.'

Arla giggled. 'I know, and you're right. If anyone can look after themselves it's him. I'm glad Ellie mentioned it in her letter, else I might not've found out until after he'd left.'

Her mother looked at her quizzically. 'If Ellie's coming for your birthday, that means she's going to be here the day after tomorrow.'

Arla squealed with delight. 'Can she stay, Mam? Until we get called up, I mean?'

Mr Winthorpe, who had been keeping quiet whilst his wife and daughter sorted out Archie's future, placed his newspaper on the table. 'Don't see why not. It'd be good to have another body about the place; it's been quiet as the grave round here since your sisters all left.' He half raised his paper. 'Just before we completely leave the subject of boys joining the services, don't forget, Arla luv, that I was Archie's age in the first lot, and I'm still alive, aren't I? So try not to worry too much. Your mam's right: boys like Archie often come out of these things unscathed.'

'Didn't stop me worryin' half to death, mind,' Mrs Winthorpe said. 'That's what happens when you care for someone. You just have to try and put it to the back of your mind, chuck.' She picked up a small jar from the mantel. 'In the meantime we've a guest arrivin' the day after tomorrer, so we'd best get some extras in. Come on, Arla luv, we've shoppin' to do.'

Spud drew to a halt beside the bus stop, and Aidan rested the reins on the seat between himself and Ellie.

'Are you sure this is what you want to do? It's been fun having you on the farm, and you know you'd be more than welcome to stay on for as long as you wanted.'

Ellie had been dreading the moment when she had to say goodbye to the Murrays. She loved her life on the farm, and in truth she would be happy to stay there for the rest of her life, but that idea was inconceivable. Unless she were to marry Aidan, she had no real future at Springdale, so to try to make a life there would prove fruitless. No, Ellie knew she had to put her best foot forward and start the next part of her journey. I can't stay here just to keep Aidan from getting lonely. I need to earn my own money so I can stand on my own two feet and look after myself. That's what my mam would've done.

She had already discussed her decision with Aidan earlier that week when the two of them had been fetching animal feed from the village.

'I know how much you love the farm, and I think it's a shame that you feel you have to leave when there's really no need. I'd like to think you saw us as family,' Aidan had said as she helped him to load the heavy sacks of feed on to the hay wain.

'I do, and being with you all has been wonderful, but the longer I stay the more I'll become reliant on you and your parents, and that was never the deal. Besides, you know I promised Arla that we'd join up together.' She'd looked into his face and saw the disappointment there. 'I promise to come back whenever I have leave – as long as that's all right, of course ...'

He had smiled reluctantly. 'You know full well it's all right with us, and if you ever want to reconsider ...'

'You'll be the first to know,' Ellie had said.

Now, she looked into the depths of Aidan's green eyes. Feeling tears begin to form, she jumped down from the cart and swung her satchel over her shoulder. 'I promise to write and let you know where I am, and what I'm up to.'

Aidan nodded, began to speak, cleared his throat and tried again. 'Make sure you do, and who knows, if I get lucky I'll soon be in the RAF myself.' He looked into her upturned face, his eyes connecting with hers for a moment, then with a click of his tongue he focused on Spud's ears. 'I never say goodbye, so I'll just say t.t.f.n.' Spud obediently walked forward and Aidan turned him round in the direction of home. He called out over his shoulder, and through the sound of Spud's hooves hitting the ground she heard: 'Take care, alanna.'

Ellie waved but said nothing, afraid that her voice would give her innermost feelings away. She watched as Spud trotted down the road, and smiled through her tears. She would miss them both – miss them all – terribly.

'Look at that queue! I dunno about you but I thought there'd only be a handful of us,' Arla said, her voice filled with disappointment as she and Ellie joined the end of the line that wound round the town hall. 'My tummy's doin' somersaults at the thought o' signin' up. I can't wait to see which of the services we'll be goin' into. I hope it's the WAAF, then we might see Connor and all them handsome, brave pilots ... I'm gonna marry me one o' them if we get in the WAAF.'

The girl in front of them snorted. 'Not only are you delusional if you think a pilot would want to marry the likes of you, but also you've picked the wrong day. They're takin' on for the ATS today, so there won't be no pilots up for grabs.'

The girl she was with giggled. 'Not unless you shoot one of 'em down by accident.'

Ellie frowned. 'Women aren't allowed to fire guns, everyone knows that, so I don't know what you're flappin' your gums about.'

Neither girl responded, but the one behind them in the queue leaned forward. 'It's for the ack-ack batteries. You're right about the gun thing, but they want women to operate the instruments. You'll have to work with men as well as women; I think they call them "mixed batteries". Mr Churchill's daughter's already in one, I believe.'

Arla looked thoroughly deflated. 'You must be joking. Have you seen the ATS uniform? An' I don't fancy workin' with a bunch of soldiers. I wanted a proper job, you know, like drivin' or talkin' to the pilots over the radio, or …'

'I believe the batteries will have officers as well as sergeants and corporals in them, and as there'll only be twelve in a section—' the other woman began, clearly realising Arla's priorities when it came to choosing a career in the services.

'Only twelve, you say?' Arla cut in. She looked hopefully at Ellie. 'What d'you reckon?'

'I think you should go for it,' the girl in front of them chimed in nastily. 'The odds would be far better for someone like you.'

Ellie held up a hand as Arla's face flushed angrily. 'Now, now, girls, for all we know we may end up on the same battery, so let's play nicely, shall we?'

As they talked, the line in front of them had been getting smaller, and the girl who had made the comment about shooting a pilot down was next to be seen.

The fat sergeant who sat behind the table spoke gruffly. 'Name and papers.'

'Tilly Jarvis, and here's my papers.'

Heaving a sigh, the sergeant took one look before passing them back to her. 'Not old enough. Come back in two years.'

Tilly stood for a moment, her mouth gaping, but the sergeant was gesturing her to move away so that he might see the next in line. Arla gave Tilly a sarcastic smile as she walked past and hissed out of the corner of her mouth, 'The ATS ain't for little girls, you know.'

Tilly glowered but stood to one side, waiting for her friend, who had taken her place in front of the table. 'Evelyn Maddox.' She stared at a point just to the left of the sergeant's ear.

He looked up. 'Fair enough, you're in. Go home and wait for your papers to arrive.'

As Evelyn turned to leave the line she smirked at Ellie and Arla. 'You're wastin' your time. They aren't lookin' for girls like you.'

Ellie, who was next in line, turned crimson as she handed over her papers. Behind her she could hear Tilly protesting at the unfairness of it all as she and Evelyn walked towards the door of the hall. The sergeant looked at the papers, heaved a sigh and handed them back. 'Too young. I may as well be a gramophone record, 'cos that's all I seem to be sayin' today.'

Ellie, looking at the papers in her hand, frowned. 'But I'm sixteen. It says so here, see?'

The sergeant, who was not having a good day, gave her a withering look. 'I know how old you are – I can read, you know – and sixteen's too young for gun sites. If you wanna come back another day and try your luck wi' one of the other services that's up to you.' He held his hand up for Arla's papers, and was not surprised when she shook her head and, grabbing Ellie's elbow, guided her out of the hall and on to the pavement.

'Now what?' She demanded.' I'm not goin' to wait another two years, nor am I goin' through the humiliation of bein' turned down again.'

Ellie wrinkled her brow. 'You never went through any humiliation. You never even showed him your papers,' she pointed out.

'Precisely! I knew what were comin'. So what are we to do?'

Pulling a face, Ellie shrugged. 'I'm not hangin' around waitin' for them to start takin' Waafs on again. It could be months, for all we know, so the way I see it there's only one thing we can do, and that's to change the date of birth on our papers, wait for that sergeant to go on his break, and then try our luck with whoever comes to replace him. Just keep your fingers crossed that he doesn't look too carefully.'

Arla gave a mirthless laugh, but then, staring hard at her friend, her eyes rounded. 'You mean you really intend to do it? What if we get found out?'

'That's a risk we're goin' to have to take. Besides, I don't see why not. From what I hear a lot of people change their date of birth on their papers, so why shouldn't we? Besides, I can't go back to Springdale Farm. It wouldn't be fair.'

Arla shrugged. 'Well, we can't do it here; someone might see us. Let's go to the Corner Caff. We can share a bun and a glass of lemonade whilst you forge our documents.'

'Why should I be the one to do it? You're just as capable as me—'

'It was your suggestion,' Arla interrupted. 'Besides, you've much better writing than me, so it only makes sense.'

'You make it sound as if I'm some kind of forgery expert,' Ellie said as the pair made their way to the café. 'I thought you'd be more disappointed that we wouldn't be joining the WAAF. You did say you thought the ATS uniform was horrible, and I agree with you that air force blue would suit your eyes much better, but from my point of view the green will go very nicely with my copper hair, don't you think?'

'I'm lucky. Blonde goes with anything.' Arla smiled.

Ellie eyed her friend suspiciously. 'That didn't really answer my question, did it? You were dead set on joinin' the WAAF, so how come you're not throwin' a hissy fit? What do you know that I don't, Arla Winthorpe?'

Arla's cheeks were tinged with pink. 'Nothing. I just think we might know a few more folk in the ATS than we would in the WAAF. It's probably more suited to girls like us.'

Ellie, who had known Arla since they were toddlers, was not buying this for a second. 'Who do you know in the ATS, Arla? Connor's in the RAF, but I don't think we know anyone in the ...' She paused, and eyed her friend shrewdly. 'Which of the services has Archie Byrnes joined? I seem to remember Connor mentioned he was applying to the army.'

Arla avoided meeting Ellie's gaze. 'I'm really not sure. I think he said it was the army, but who knows with that one? I'd be surprised if they took him; he's too short and skinny, if you ask me.'

Ellie pushed open the door to the café. She knew that Arla had set her sights far higher than a boy who lived in the courts, yet there was something about her attitude towards the ATS that did not feel right. She had been far too easily swayed. A familiar image of Arla and Archie formed in her mind. They were standing toe to toe, a furious-looking Arla shouting at Archie whilst he grinned infuriatingly back at her. Ellie chuckled. Whatever the reason for Arla's change of heart, it could have nothing to do with Archie.

Sitting down at a table far from the window and the prying eyes of passers-by, Ellie swung her satchel on to her lap and rummaged around until she found a small pencil. She smoothed out her papers and slowly and carefully, her tongue licking her upper lip as she concentrated on the task in hand, turned the four on her birth date to a two. Sitting back to admire her efforts, she turned the paper round so that Arla might inspect her handiwork.

Arla nodded her head approvingly. ''Ere, that's not bad, not bad at all.' She pulled her own papers from out of her pocket. 'Now do mine.'

Ellie frowned doubtfully. 'Can't you do yours? Changing a five to a three should be much easier than a four to a two.'

'But I'm useless at things like this,' Arla said pleadingly. 'Besides, you've had a bit of practice doin' yours, so it only makes sense.'

Sighing, Ellie pulled the paper towards her and had begun to change Arla's date of birth when a voice behind them caused her to jump.

'Guess I weren't the only little girl to apply for the ATS today, then.'

Turning, they saw the girl who had been turned away before them by the sergeant in the town hall.

Arla's cheeks flushed pink and her mouth hung open as she tried to think of a suitably damning retort, but Tilly continued, 'Relax; you're not the only one who's gorra pencil, y'know.'

She handed her paper to Ellie, who smiled. 'Pretty good effort. I see you're the same as me, and were born in 1924 or should I say 1922?'

Arla, who did not like the manner in which Tilly's companion had addressed them, did not wish to strike up a friendship. 'Well, you mustn't let us keep you ...'

Tilly ignored her. 'Why don't we all go back together? We can wait till that fat old sergeant is out of the way and when the next feller comes along we can say we're pals, and stick up for each other if he starts a fuss over our papers.'

Ellie nodded, but Arla nudged her foot sharply under the table. 'Well, me and Ellie *are* pals. Why don't you go back with that mate of yours, 'cos we don't need anyone else.'

Tilly raised her brows at Ellie. 'She's gone, hasn't she, 'cos she got in. They say there's strength in numbers, so I reckon the more of us who stick together the better. What do you reckon ... sorry, what's your name?'

'Ellie,' Ellie said, holding out a hand. 'And if we're goin' to be pals it's best if we get to know a bit about each other first, so this is Arla ...'

'Hello,' Arla said sulkily. 'Although I still don't see why ...'

After shaking Ellie's hand, Tilly extended her own to Arla. 'Look, I'm sorry if I were a bit of a cow earlier, only I were nervous about gerrin' in. I knew you had to be eighteen to be on the ack-acks, but someone told me they never really look at your papers so I thought I could bluff my way through. Can we call it pax?'

Conceding defeat, Arla shook the proffered hand. 'Looks like you two've already made up your minds, so I s'pose I'd best foller suit.'

Grinning, Tilly pulled up a chair. 'How long d'you reckon it'll be before that sergeant beggars off for his break?'

Ellie shrugged. 'Probably best if we try in about an hour or so. That way we'll have time to get our stories straight. Agreed?'

Arla and Tilly nodded, and the girls spent the next hour sharing a cheese and pickle sandwich as well as a pot of tea. When it came time to leave, they all knew a lot more about each other.

The long queue that had stretched around the town hall had dissipated. Tilly peered round the door. 'He's gone,' she hissed. 'There's a young lad there now.'

She beckoned for the other two to follow her lead as she strode towards the table. 'Afternoon,' she said, placing her papers on the desk in front of the corporal.

He picked them up and glanced at them, then looked at Ellie and Arla, who were standing on either side of Tilly. 'Comin' in threes now, are ya?' he said, laying Tilly's papers down and holding his hands out for Ellie's and Arla's. They dutifully handed them over and Ellie, who had seen the frightened expression on Arla's face, feared the corporal might notice it too. If he does, she thought anxiously, our goose will be well and truly cooked.

One by one, the young man behind the desk glanced disinterestedly at the documents in front of him, copied the details into a book, and handed them back. The girls exchanged furtive glances. Why isn't he telling us we've been accepted? thought Ellie. Perhaps he's spotted our changes and is going to report us.

After a moment, the corporal looked up at the girls, a confused expression on his face. 'Well? What are you waitin' for?'

Swallowing hard, Ellie spoke first. 'What happens now?'

'You go home and wait for your papers. What did you expect? A fanfare and a gold medal?'

Turning as one, the three girls were heading for the door at a brisk pace when a voice called out from behind them, causing them to freeze on the spot. 'Don't forget your fathers'll have to sign permission.'

Outside the hall, Ellie, Arla and Tilly started to giggle.

'I thought we'd had it when he called out,' Arla jabbered excitedly. 'I thought he were gonna say there'd been a mistake.'

'Me too. And after all that worry over whether they'd notice we'd changed our birth dates, he never even looked. Pity he wasn't on duty earlier on, then we wouldn't have had to go through all this bother,' said Tilly.

But Ellie was more concerned with his last statement. 'I haven't got a father to sign my papers. D'you think I should've told him?'

Arla shook her head vehemently. 'No. Besides, how will he know who's signed your papers? It could be anyone.'

'Oh, yeah.' Ellie chuckled. 'I hadn't thought of that. Heck, I wouldn't know me dad even if I fell over him.'

Looking confused, Tilly raised her brows, but Arla shook her head. 'Too long a story. Save it for another time.' A thought struck her. 'How old was your pal, the one who got in?'

'Evelyn? Same as us, sixteen, but all she has to do is bat those long lashes of hers at the fellers an' they're putty in her hand. I reckon that's why he let her in.'

Arla pulled a face. 'Typical!' She glanced at Ellie. 'We'd best be off, tell me mam what's happened an' that, but it'd be grand if we all went to the same training camp.'

Tilly chuckled. 'Fingers crossed. Although you might not say that once you get to know Evie.'

'Sounds ominous. Why do you say that?' Arla said inquisitively.

'Let's just say she finds making new friends rather difficult. People often take her the wrong way, and I can understand why.' She sighed resignedly. 'When I was rude to you earlier on it was because I was nervous, but Evie's like that all the time. It's not because she's a wrong 'un, it's just ...' She shrugged her shoulders. 'Like your dad, Ellie, it'd take too long to explain now, so best keep it for another day. Besides, I'd best be going too. Let's hope we'll meet again in a week or so.'

The girls waved goodbye as Tilly ran for her bus. 'What do you make of that? She doesn't sound very keen on her own pal, does she?' said Arla.

Ellie chewed her lip thoughtfully. 'On the other hand, she didn't exactly stick up for us when her pal was being rude in the recruitment office, so maybe she's used to it.'

Arla put an arm round Ellie's shoulders. 'I dunno; I reckon that Evie's one to watch. But never mind them – this time next week we could be rubbin' shoulders with officers.' She sighed happily. 'One of them might be my future hubby.'

Ellie chuckled. 'I see you've still got your priorities straight.'

'Ooo, I'd never let me priorities slip. Morals maybe, even me principles, but never me priorities,' said Arla with a wink.

Ellie, clad in thick navy blue trousers and a dark duffel coat, cautiously poked her head round the corner of Lavender Court. The familiar foul smell of stale air mixed with the odour of the privies wafted unpleasantly into her nostrils. Pinching her nose, she lowered her head and made straight for Number 6, home to

Mrs Burgess and her daughter, and knocked perfunctorily on the door.

After a moment there came the sound of approaching footsteps, the door opened an inch and a suspicious eye appeared in the gap. 'Ellie!' Mrs Burgess exclaimed, before opening the door further and ushering her guest inside. The old woman admired Ellie with an approving eye. 'You're lookin' good, chuck, but what on earth are you doin' back 'ere? You know Sid's tellin' everyone that you robbed him of his rent and belted him over the noggin with a rare china vase ...' She snorted contemptuously. 'Not that anyone'd believe that, o' course: you'd never steal nowt off no one, and the only rare thing Sid's got is that skin complaint of his.'

Ellie giggled. 'Mrs B, you're a tonic, and I've missed you; that's why I thought I'd come and pay you a visit. I may hate Sid, but I'm not frightened of him, and no matter what I still consider Lavender Court to be my home. Even if I never live here again, it's where I grew up, all me memories of me mam are here, and I'll always care for the folk that live here, so I thought I'd pop by and see how everyone was doin'.'

'Just like your mam, allus thinkin' of others.' Mrs Burgess gave Ellie a gappy grin. 'Come and sit down. I'll put the kettle on and you can tell me where you've been all this time. I must admit, there's been all sorts of rumours flying about and people've been real worried about you. We all know Sid can be a vicious bugger at times, and word was goin' round that he might have killed you, only I didn't believe it, 'cos if he had, he wouldn't still be fumin' and shoutin' the odds about you leavin' the way you did; he'd be keepin' shtum instead.' She tapped the side of her nose knowingly. 'Besides, I've a pal or two live near the Winthorpes, and word 'as it you've been doin' a bit of farmin'.'

Ellie nodded eagerly, and began to tell the older woman all about her stay at Springdale Farm and the animals she had helped look after. Several questions and two cups of tea later, Ellie finished with how she and Arla had joined the ATS.

Mrs Burgess looked impressed. 'Our Ellie, milkin' a cow,' she breathed, 'and joinin' the ATS too.'

Ellie smiled. 'We're waitin' for our papers, so I'm stayin' with Arla till they arrive, although I'd appreciate it if you wouldn't mention it to anyone, just in case he comes round and starts giving the Winthorpes grief.'

Mrs Burgess nodded solemnly. 'I'll not say a word. You know you can trust me, Ellie.' Leaning across the table she clasped Ellie's hands in her own, and Ellie could see tears brimming in her bright blue eyes. 'I'm that proud of you, Ellie Lancton, and I know your mam would be too. If you ask me I reckon she's your guardian angel, makin' sure you come to no harm. She were allus a good 'un, your mam was; she was the only woman in these 'ere courts what ever stood up to Sid Crowther. She wouldn't tek none of his nonsense, so it were no surprise when you told him where to get off.' She looked up at Ellie from beneath thin lashes. 'I know it's none of my beeswax, and you can tell me to mind me own business if you like, I won't take offence, but ...' she licked her lips nervously before continuing, 'he didn't try and mek you do summat you didn't want to? I only ask because you wouldn't be the first one he'd tried to force himself on.'

Ellie stared blankly at Mrs Burgess, her cheeks reddening with anger. 'Who else did he try to do this to, and why didn't you tell me before?'

Mrs Burgess wrung her hands. 'I couldn't say owt because I didn't know for sure, else I'd have warned you. It were only when she 'eard about you 'ittin' him with the ewer and runnin' off that she told me all about it, asked me to make sure he hadn't touched you, but she said I mustn't tell no one else. She reckons it's too late to do anything about it 'cos it happened too long ago. I'm that ashamed, Ellie. Deep down I knew what he'd done at the time, and I did ask, only when she denied it I left it alone, and I shouldn't have. I should've dug deeper, got the truth.'

The tears trickled down Ellie's cheeks as she clutched the older woman's hands in her own. 'Not your Irene …?' Mrs Burgess hung her head and gave a feeble nod. Releasing her hands, Ellie cradled the older woman in her arms. 'Oh, Mrs B, I had no idea. If I'd known …'

Raising her head, the older woman smiled weakly at her. 'There's nowt you could've done, queen. I'm just glad he didn't force you too … he didn't, did he?'

Ellie shook her head reassuringly. 'No he didn't, but he did try, only I hit him hard, and the ewer smashed on his head, and that's how I got out. At the time I were frightened I'd killed him, but knowin' what I know now …'

Mrs Burgess smiled. 'You've got the same fightin' spirit as your mam. I wish our Irene had come to me, but she were frightened he'd evict us … so she let him …'

Ellie frowned. 'Why are you still here? How can you *stand* ...'

Mrs Burgess shrugged. 'Where am I meant to go? What with all the bombin' there's even less 'ouses round than there used to be. Besides, I couldn't afford anythin' bigger'n this. I would've gone to the scuffers only Irene told me not to. She said they'd say it weren't rape 'cos she gave consent.'

Ellie shook her head in disbelief. 'No she didn't; she gave in. There's a difference.'

The older woman held up a pacifying hand. 'I know that, and so do you, but the scuffers? They don't believe it when a woman walks in with two black eyes half the time.' She looked hopefully at Ellie. 'But after what you did? I bet that old git'll think twice before attackin' another gal, not after you clouted him over the 'ead with the ewer, an' serve the bastard right. I bet that's why he didn't chase after you, ain't it?'

Ellie raised her brows. 'He'd have had a job. It knocked him out cold. That's why I went to the Winthorpes'.'

Mrs Burgess nodded approvingly. 'Yes, and then you went to Connor Murray an' he took you to this Aidan of yours.' She smiled knowingly at Ellie. 'I take it you two are together?'

Ellie shook her head in astonishment. 'Gosh no, he's not interested in someone like me. He's applying for the RAF.'

The older woman looked surprised. 'Don't see what that's got to do with anything. If he's as smart as you seem to reckon, he'll know a good thing when he sees it.' She eyed her guest shrewdly. 'You wish he were yours, am I right?'

Ellie sat, her mouth gaping, whilst she tried to find any answer other than 'Of course I wish he was mine', but none came to mind. Instead she changed the subject. 'Did I tell you I was going to be on a gun site?'

Mrs Burgess laughed. 'Yes you did, dear, and now you've answered my question, I will tell you this. Don't waste time not mekkin' your feelin's plain, not in a time of war, 'cos you never know what's round the corner. Mark my words, Ellie Lancton, tell this feller how you feel, before some other woman comes along and takes him for her own.'

Ellie smiled. 'You don't understand, Mrs B, he's not interested in me. I'm five years younger than him. Besides, I've got more things on my mind at the moment than chasin' after a man who sees me as a little sister.' She got to her feet. 'It's been lovely seein' you again, and do pass my best on to everyone else, won't you?' She paused, then added, 'And tell Irene I'm askin' after her. What's she doing now?'

'She's joined Auxiliary Nurses, and she's doin' a grand job. When the war's over, she's hopin' to have enough money behind her to get us somewhere better to live than this dump.' She cast her eyes around the soot-blackened room. 'Just like you, I shan't miss this hovel, but I will miss the people what live here.' She patted Ellie's hand. 'God only knows I miss your mam. She had a tough time when your dad up and left, but she rallied and carried on as if nowt had happened. She were a rock your mam was, and she loved you

107

more than anything else in this world. That's why she wouldn't … do what he wanted and leave with 'im.'

Ellie looked confused. 'What are you talking about?'

'Your dad, of course. What did you think I were talkin' about?'

'I've no idea. Mam told me that Dad left before she told him she was pregnant.'

The old woman's wizened face flushed scarlet. 'Oh, I – I …' She paused briefly. 'I'm so sorry, queen, I didn't realise. I thought you knew.'

Ellie shook her head. 'But why would she lie?'

Mrs Burgess shrugged. 'P'raps she was worried you'd blame yourself, or think that he didn't love you.'

'So he knew she were pregnant, he just didn't want to have a baby, is that what you're tellin' me?'

Mrs Burgess nodded ruefully. 'That's about the size of it, but if truth be told he was only a kid himself, so he got frightened and took off.'

Ellie looked calmly into the worried features of her hostess and shrugged. 'That's no excuse. Me mam were younger'n him but she held on to me. She loved him, but she still chose me.'

'Shes always looked after you. Still does, I reckon.'

Ellie smiled appreciatively. 'It's a nice thought.' From outside there came the sound of the privy door being slammed shut. Ellie looked sharply at the older woman. 'Does Sid still live here?'

Mrs Burgess nodded. 'He's still in the room below your old 'un, and his temper's not improved, especially since he's lost half his tenants. All the young 'uns have joined up, so there's only us old folk left.' She held out a hand and started to tick the residents off on her fingers. 'There's old Pete Turnbull, Mr and Mrs Rogers, and me.' She held up four fingers. 'Four of us left is all, only o' course to mek things easier, they've all moved in wi' me. It meks more sense for us to split the rent between us.'

'I bet Sid doesn't like that! Where's he gettin' all his drinkin' money from now? Serves him right!' Ellie chuckled.

By the time Ellie left Lavender Court, dusk was starting to fall. It had been an interesting visit and Ellie had come away with a greater understanding of her own past. She did not feel anger towards her father for not wanting her, but she felt heartbreak and sorrow for the position he had put her mother in when he had asked her to choose between the two of them. How could anyone, she reflected, ask the person he loved to choose between himself and their baby? She shook her head. Men could not be trusted. A picture of Aidan and Connor appeared in her mind's eye. I can trust them, she decided, but only because they don't want anything from me except friendship. She thought back to Mrs B's proposal that Ellie should tell Aidan how she felt about him and determined that this would be an even bigger mistake now she understood the workings of the male mind. Keep them at arm's length, that's the best way, she concluded. Don't get involved and you can't get hurt.

Rounding the corner into Blenheim Street, she hummed 'I Wanna Be Loved By You', a song that her mother had often sung to her as a child. A man coming from the other direction had to skip hastily round her.

'Watch it!' he snarled.

Ellie's stomach lurched. It was Sid. With barely a moment's hesitation she walked on, her breathing quickening as the anger began to rise. Suddenly, she turend on her heel, and had began to walk briskly after him, her fists clenched by her sides, when she suddenly became aware of the soft scent of lavender. She stopped in mid-stride, and watched the beast of a man disappear round the corner. It would have been foolhardy to confront him; he was far bigger than she and would have no qualms about hitting a woman. Turning back, she looked to see where the scent had come from, but there was no greenery in sight, let alone a sprig of her mother's favourite flower. A faint smile forming on her lips, she jammed her hands deep into her pockets, and turned back in the direction of Bond Street. So Mrs B thinks me mam's watching over me as some sort of guardian angel. She thought of Sid, and how the distraction of the lavender scent had stopped her from making a grave mistake. Slowly, she nodded her head. Guardian angel or not, someone was looking out for her, and she was pretty sure she knew who.

Chapter Five

It was still dark as Ellie and Arla boarded the train for Preston. The cold winter frost sparkled like diamonds under the light of the moon, and, not knowing where Preston was, Ellie hoped the weather might be warmer there than it was in Liverpool. Taking her seat opposite Arla in an empty carriage, Ellie rubbed her sleeve on the window and peered at the people still boarding the train. It would not get light for at least another hour, but, as she said to Arla, it would be nice to see the sunrise.

'I used to love watching the sun come up after we'd finished milking. Me and Aidan would go to the top of Coin Meadow if there was a clear sky, and watch it from there.' She sighed wistfully.

Arla grimaced. 'I'd rather be in me bed. Do you reckon they'll make us get up before the crack of dawn? I bet they do. Probably have us doin' star jumps in the dark.'

Ellie chuckled. 'Not regretting your decision already, are you? Just think of all those lovely officers; that should make early-morning exercise more bearable.' Outside, the conductor waved his green flag and blew

111

his whistle loudly. She turned to Arla. 'No goin' back now. Looks like we're off, but at least we've got a nice roomy carriage to ourselves.'

But as the train drew out of the station, the door to the girls' compartment slid open and Ellie was disappointed to see that their roomy carriage was about to be crammed full of various servicemen and women. Even before any of the newcomers had a chance to sit down the carriage door slid back once more and yet more passengers entered, this time a grumpy old woman followed by two sullen-faced children.

Pushing past everyone else, the old woman sat down heavily in the seat one over from Arla's and slammed a weathered hand on the seat between them, snapping impatiently at the children. 'Stop muckin' around and gerrover 'ere afore some bugger teks your seat. And find summat to wipe your nose on, our Davey. It's mekkin' me feel woozy lookin' at that thing hangin' outta your snout!'

Ellie giggled as Arla, a look of horror on her face, scrunched up as close to the window as she could get. The Waaf who had been about to sit in the seat between her and the older woman looked relieved that she had not done so, and quickly sat down next to Ellie.

The old woman unfolded her arms. 'For goodness' sake, Davey ...' She rummaged around in a large canvas bag and produced what looked like an old grey flannel from its depths. ''Ere, use this, and mek sure you give it a good blow.'

The occupants of the carriage watched on as Davey, taking the flannel, blew his nose loudly. The door to the carriage slid open once more and two men in air force blue looked in briefly before deciding to move further down the corridor.

Arla, who would have much preferred to be seated next to any of the serviceman, looked gloomily at Ellie as Davey's little sister, who could not have been more than three, tried to squeeze into the nonexistent space between Arla and her brother and the two instantly started a tug of war over Davey's colouring book.

The journey to Preston involved several changes, and after suffering Davey and his little sister for the best part of an hour the girls quickly learned that being first in a carriage was not necessarily the best idea. It was far better, in fact, to be the last on and search for a carriage that was filled with servicemen, who would always give up their seats when young women appeard.

Stepping out on to the platform in Preston, the girls heard a sergeant shouting, 'All those for the barracks, over here if you will, and trotted towards him. 'We're for Preston,' Ellie said, trying to peer at his clipboard. 'I'm Ellie Lancton and this is my pal Arla Winthorpe.'

Holding his clipboard close to his chest, the sergeant scowled at them both. 'There's two trucks waitin' outside. Go and get yerselves on board either one, and be quick about it. I ain't got all day.'

Outside, the girls headed towards the first of the two large lorries. Ellie, who was used to climbing on to Spud's cart, boarded with ease, but Arla found it difficult to maintain what she considered to be a ladylike stance whilst lifting her leg on to the floor of the lorry. The driver of the vehicle, who had come round to give them a hand, chuckled at her efforts. 'Give it some welly, gal. We 'aven't got all day.'

Arla, red with exertion and embarrassment, scowled at him. 'I'm doin' me best, but these things weren't built for women wi' short legs, and this bloomin' snow's just makin' everything so slip— Gerroff!' Ellie smothered a giggle as Arla shot into view, the private's hands leaving her rump as she hastily smoothed her skirt back down. 'I was managin' fine on me own, thank you very much, and I don't remember askin' for no assistance neither.'

The man grinned. 'No problem. Always ready to lend a hand.'

Arla smiled sarcastically. 'If that's the case you can get up early and do all me exercises.' She looked gloomily round at the snow-covered forecourt. 'How long's it been snowin' 'ere? There's nowt back 'ome. I hope they got a burner where we'll be sleepin'.'

The driver raised his brow. 'Blimey, don't want much, do you? Still, with a pretty face like yours, at least I expect it is when you're not scowlin', you'll find a whole host of willing volunteers, includin' me, only I won't be tekkin' your jabs. I hates needles, and you'll be like a pincushion by the time the army have finished with you.'

Arla's smile faded and she absentmindedly rubbed the top of her arm. 'What do I need jabs for? There's nowt wrong wi' me. I'm as fit as a fiddle!'

'That's not the half of it. You're gonna have doctors and nurses proddin' and pokin' you till you're black 'n' blue. They'll check your 'air, your teeth,' he shuddered, 'and places you never knew you 'ad. It's like bein' one of them 'osses what runs the National.'

Arla, who did not believe a word of what the driver told them, smiled wryly. 'If that's the case then quite frankly I'm surprised you got in.'

Not seeing the irony in Arla's comment, he shrugged. 'They tek all sorts 'ere, so you're bound to pass. Once you're settled just you come an' see me, and if I'm not too busy I'll tek you out and show you the sights.'

'Private Struthers! Stop your incessant yapping and help this lot on. As soon as you're done you can move out.'

Private Struthers jumped to attention and threw his cigarette into the snow, burying it with the toe of his boot. 'Right you are, Sarge!' He turned to face the women who were slipping and sliding their way towards the rear of the lorry. 'C'mon, ladies, let's be 'avin' you.'

Closing the tailgate, he grinned at his passengers. 'A lorry full of lasses ... All those who get travel sick, sit down this end.' He slapped the side of the vehicle with the palm of his hand. 'It's a bit of a bumpy ride, especially for those of you who've never travelled in the back of a lorry before!'

The lorry lurched, bumped and swerved its way to the training camp which was, to the women's collective relief, a mercifully short distance away. Looking out of the back of the vehicle, Ellie could see the huge snowdrifts that lined the side of the road. She turned to Arla. 'You know you asked Private Struthers how long it'd been snowin'?' Arla nodded. 'Since last Christmas by the look of it. In Connor's last letter he said as how we'd be runnin' round the exercise yard every mornin', doin' press-ups and all sorts, not to mention marchin' till we got dizzy.' Ellie grimaced as a large lump of snow, too heavy for the branch on which it had gathered, slid on to the road behind them.

Arla glanced at her. 'Ever think you've made a mistake?'

It had been a whole week since they had begun their initial training and so far Ellie found she was quite enjoying army life, although she had to admit she wasn't so keen on the endless queues, or the intrusive medical examinations, which, just as Private Struthers had stated, had included what they called the free from infection inspection, which involved a thorough search of the scalp.

The girl in front of Ellie had cupped her hand over her mouth and hissed, 'If I had nits I'd die of shame, wouldn't you?'

Ellie had declined to answer. Having nits was considered to be a normal part of life for those who grew up in the courts. Mothers would spend hours combing through their children's hair in a bid to 'get rid of the little buggers'. You could always tell those who had fallen prey to an infestation, not just by the incessant scratching but by the cries and yelps of those who had inadvertently been stabbed by the unforgiving steel comb, or, worse still, had a knot ripped out by the over-enthusiastic groomer.

She had been given so many injections that she had quite forgotten what half of them were for, but none of these things was feared more by Ellie than the visit to the dentist. She could not remember the last time she had sat in the dreaded chair, and despite her pessimism was relieved to hear that she had been given the all clear.

They had queued for clothes, bedding and food, as well as making a trip to the store in order to purchase such things as soap, toothpaste and boot polish. Ellie had never owned so much stuff in all her life. Other women in her hut had grumbled at the stiff and unfashionable ATS uniform, but apart from the things she had borrowed from Cassie, the uniform was the best clothing Ellie had ever possessed.

When they first entered the hut, each girl had claimed either the top or the bottom of one of the twenty bunk beds. Arla had strolled over to the bed beneath Ellie's and held up a straw item. 'What are these cushions for?' she asked the room in general.

One of the girls giggled. 'They're not cushions. They're called biscuits and they're your mattress.' She was laying hers down on the hard base of her bed as she spoke. 'My sister's in the WAAF and she said they've got the same there. They're horrible to sleep on, 'specially when a bit of straw pokes through and stabs you.'

Arla shrugged. 'At least I won't have three others girls diggin' their sharp toenails into me whilst I'm tryin' to sleep.'

The girl who had spoken stopped laying her sheet down and turned to face Arla. 'Did you just say four of you slept in the same bed?' she asked incredulously.

117

Arla spread the biscuits on her bed and sat down. 'Five when Ellie comes round,' she said, prodding the bunk above her head with her fist.

Ellie leaned over the side. 'Pack it in! I don't reckon it would take much more than a sharp breeze to have this thing on the floor!'

The girl who had addressed Arla leaned forward, her hand outstretched. 'I'm Mary Dingle, from Norwich. You?'

'Arla,' said Arla, 'and her upstairs is Ellie. We're from Liverpool, and we've been bezzies all our lives.'

Mary smiled up at Ellie. 'Must be nice comin' in with a friend. I reckon it must get pretty lonely for some.' Lowering her voice, she added, 'I bet there'll be a few who get homesick, poor blighters.'

Ellie nodded. 'It's good comin' in with a pal, but 'cos I'm Lancton and she's Winthorpe we've been nowhere near each other most of the day.'

Mary frowned, then, as realisation dawned, she nodded. 'Of course, they do everything in alphabetical order here.' She yawned noisily. 'I'm whacked. I wonder what time lights out is, and reveille, come to that.'

'What's reveille?' Ellie slid from her bunk and sat next to Arla. 'Has Connor mentioned it in any of his letters? He hasn't to me.'

Arla opened her mouth to reply but Mary was already providing an answer. 'It's like an alarm call. They blow a trumpet, and when you hear it you're to get up and at 'em.'

At first the girls worried that they would forget their new routine, get an instruction wrong, or turn up late only to find they ought to be somewhere else, and in truth for the first couple of days this did happen quite regularly, but after a week of continually repeating the same routine things soon started to come naturally.

Every morning as reveille sounded, Ellie's feet would hit the floor before the last note died. Arla too would be standing up beside her bunk, ready for the day ahead. At first they'd had a few collisions, until Arla came up with the idea of getting out on opposite sides of the bed.

Both girls had expected training on gun sites to begin immediately and were disappointed to find that instead of learning how to work the instruments they spent their days peeling potatoes, cleaning the ablutions or scrubbing floors.

'I can see why they call 'em fatigues: it's all I can do to keep meself from fallin' asleep, they're that borin'. When are we goin' to start real army work?' Arla moaned to Ellie, as they stood next to a mountain of unpeeled potatoes. 'I can't see what any of this has to do with ack-acks, can you?'

Ellie tossed a freshly peeled potato on to the small pile beside her. 'I dare say they didn't ask us to join up so's we could spend the entire war peelin' spuds. They just want us to get into the swing of things first, get used to obeyin' orders an' that, no matter how borin' it may be.' She paused as she picked up a large dirt-encrusted potato and methodically began peeling it with the small army-issue knife. 'We're bound to start soon. Let's face it, there can't be that many spuds left in Britain.'

Unbeknown to the girls their corporal was standing by the door to the storeroom. 'I'll have you girls know that "real army work", as you put it, Private Winthorpe, *is* peelin' spuds and the like. An army can't march on an empty stomach, so don't you go thinkin' that jobs like these are beneath you.'

'I didn't mean to …' Arla began, but the corporal continued as if she hadn't spoken.

'But as you seem so keen to be getting on to a gun site you'll be glad to know that your training begins on Monday, although I wouldn't get too excited if I were you. You'll still be expected to peel the odd spud or two.'

The corporal was right about starting their training that Monday, but by the end of the first week, Arla had to admit that whilst peeling potatoes might be tedious it was a lot easier than learning all the different types of aircraft, as well as being subjected to any number of tests whilst having to answer what felt like an endless stream of questions.

'The next part of your training will take place in Aborfield,' the sergeant informed them, 'but not all of you will be going. Some will need to repeat this stage of training.'

Ellie and Arla waited with bated breath to see if they would be going to Aborfield, and were relieved to find they had passed. Arla sighed with relief. 'I couldn't stand doin' all them spuds again.'

'Mr Murray, I am telling you what I've told you the last three times you've been here: we have nothing for you at the moment, but should the RAF ever—'

Aidan cut across him. 'Should you ever need a cripple? Is that what you're trying to say?' Aidan leaned towards the sergeant, both hands palm down on the gnarled wooden surface of the table.

The sergeant's eyes darted wildly as he sought help from one of his colleagues, but it seemed that everyone else in the room either had gone momentarily deaf or was too busy to notice the unfolding scene. He looked up at Aidan, his eyes pleading for understanding. 'That is *not* what I am trying to say. It's just that we're ... we're ...'

Aidan stood up straight, folding his arms as he did so. 'You're what? Full?'

The sergeant ran his fingers through his hair. This was not going to be a good day. The young Irishman who was presently giving him grief had been coming in regularly over the past two weeks. Each day he came, he would park his scruffy-looking pony and cart below the steps of the town hall, an act that brought the sergeant no end of complaints from the general public as well as the council. Once inside he would brandish his papers and demand to be signed up, whilst outside his transport fouled the paving in the smartest part of town. The sergeant sighed miserably. It was true that the services took able-bodied people on first, and with good reason, for goodness' sake, he thought to himself. Even people with flat feet got turned away, and this chap appeared to have a lot worse than fallen arches. He opened his mouth to try to explain his reasons for the umpteenth time, but the Irish man refused to let him speak.

'Hundreds of others have already met their maker whilst doin' this job, yet here I am, willing to risk it all just to be in the RAF. Can't you understand that I don't want to be just a farmer? I want to be out there doin' my bit, flyin' a Spitfire, or a Lancaster, anything, as long as it means I get to have a go at Jerry. I'd be good at it, I know I would, but you won't even let me get my foot through the door, just because it's—' He broke off as an officer who had been standing nearby approached the desk.

Without saying a word he looked Aidan up and down, before resting his eyes on the stick that Aidan had laid across the table. He looked curiously back at Aidan. 'Name?'

For the first time in weeks, Aidan suddenly sensed the approach of a breakthrough. Normally it was he who was doing the talking, but this officer was looking at him as though he were a magistrate weighing up the charges. 'Aidan Murray, sir,' he said. Standing as straight as his legs would allow, he pulled off what he thought might pass as a salute.

The officer's eyes narrowed as he appeared to reach a decision. 'What's the matter with your legs?'

Aidan swallowed hard. In all the times he had come here, no one with any kind of authority had so much as acknowledged his presence. In that moment he knew that this could be his one and only shot at getting into the RAF, so he'd better make it good. He licked his lips nervously. 'Tractor, sir. Farming accident when I was ten years old. I've been left with one leg slightly shorter than the other, but there isn't a damned thing I can't do on our farm as well as any man, if not better. And I know about steerin' aeroplanes, and how you need to use your legs – my granddaddy fought in the first lot and he told me – and I know I could do it.'

The officer nodded his head thoughtfully. 'Any good in school? Did you get your higher, or are you just a farmer who—'

The words 'just a farmer' sparked a fire inside Aidan; nerves gone, he interrupted the officer's flow. 'As I told the sergeant, I am not *just* a farmer. And in answer to your other question, yes I did pass my higher. Did bloody well too, sir.'

The officer's lips curved slightly at the corners. 'I can hear that you're not *just* a farmer, and, despite that old nag of yours outside, I can see it too.'

Aidan was about to stand up for Spud when he realised what the officer's words implied. He searched for his next question, but the officer was still speaking, only this time he was addressing the sergeant. 'Crumpton, take this man's details and then pass them on to me.' Turning back to Aidan, he lifted the stick off the table and handed it over. 'As for you, Murray, when your papers arrive you're to come straight to me, understand? Captain Mathias. The instructions will be clear on the letter.' He glanced at Spud, who was just visible on the pavement outside, and added, 'And for God's sake, get that crapping machine off government property. When you're told where to report I suggest that you leave the pony at home and take the train instead.'

Reading the letter in front of him, Connor punched the air with glee, his fist accidentally connecting with the underside of the top bunk. There was an aggravated snort as an annoyed-looking face appeared above him. 'Bugger off, Connor. You know I hate it when you start messin'about like that. This bed's hardly safe as it is; a kid of two'd do a better job with matchsticks and sticky tape.'

'Aidan – the cousin I told you about – has been accepted into the RAF, and they're sending him for pilot training, can you believe it? We could end up in the same aircrew.'

The owner of the face gave a brief, sarcastic round of applause. 'Well, bully for you … or him … whichever. I'm sure you'll be very happy. Now if that's all, can I get on wi' writin' me own letters? Only after you knockin' me like that I'll have to start the last one again, 'cos I've got a bleedin' line goin' straight across the first page.'

There was the sound of ripping paper as Connor tore a sheet from his own pad and held it up. 'Sorry, Shorty. Here you go,' he said repentantly. 'It's just that they've turned him away so many times, 'cos of his leg, that I didn't think he'd ever get in. Heck, if I were him I'd've given up a long time ago. I wonder what made him reapply?'

Shorty shrugged and took the proffered sheet. 'Darned if I know … or care, for that matter. Ta for the paper.'

Connor read the letter again, and wondered if Ellie had heard about Aidan's success. He had been writing to her on a regular basis, and Arla too, and all in all their little group seemed to be doing quite well in the services. Both girls appeared to be enjoying their training and were going to a camp in Arborfield, wherever that was. Connor himself had remustered as an air gunner after being spotted by one of the officers when they had been playing cricket on the airfield one afternoon.

'You've got bloody good hand-eye coordination, lad. Have you ever shot a gun?'

Connor shook his head. 'Never seen a gun, never mind shot one.'

That afternoon the officer had taken him clay pigeon shooting, and Connor had proved to be a crack shot.

'Sorry, lad, I know you wanted to be an electrical engineer, but someone with that good an aim is more useful as aircrew.'

It was all Connor could do to stop himself whooping with joy. When he had first entered the RAF he had applied for pilot training, but having been rejected he had signed up to be an electrical engineer, something that his mother had approved of as it would give him a good job when the war was over. But being a gunner meant that Connor would get to go on sorties with bomber command, something he had always longed to do.

Now, the tip of his pencil hoverad over the pad. Did Ellie and Aidan correspond? He felt sure they must; he knew his cousin had a soft spot for Ellie and would be surprised if he had not at least attempted to contact her. But neither had mentioned the other in their letters, so ... *Dear Ellie* ...

Entering their barracks in Arborfield, both girls noticed the similarities between their new hut and the one they had just left.

'It's like déjà vu,' said Arla. 'Shall we keep to the same routine as we did in the last one? You on top and me below?'

Ellie, who had already begun spreading her biscuits in a row, nodded. 'Only as long as you stop giving the underside of my mattress a good shove just as I'm about to fall asleep. I know you think it's funny but it takes me ages to drop back off.'

With her bed made up and possessions safely stowed away, Ellie sat on her top bunk and glanced around the room at the rest of the girls, some of whom were still trooping in from various parts of the country. When she and Arla had arrived the NCO had advised them to get an early night: 'Reveille will sound at six-thirty and you've a full day of intensive training ahead, so it'll be better for you if you get plenty of sleep.'

Ellie was sure everyone would have received the same advice, but Arla was looking at the clock above the door. 'It's only half past eight, way too early to go to bed. How about we go and get summat to eat? I'm starvin' and it'll give us a chance to see where the NAAFI is and what it looks like,' she said, as Ellie slid down from the top bunk. 'Let's hope there's some decent fellers from the Royal Artillery in there, or are you savin' yerself for that Aidan you're allus bangin' on about?'

Ellie shook her head. 'I'm not savin' myself for any man, least of all Aidan. Besides, that's not why I applied for the ATS. I'm happy bein' single, thank you very much. And I don't bang on about him. It's just that I loved life on the farm and he was part of it.' Aidan, perched on top of Hercules, smiling broadly down at her ...

She had deliberately not told Arla about Aidan's accident, not because she feared her friend would make fun of him or be mean in any way, but because she knew that Arla thought they should both marry officers who could take them away from the slums of Liverpool. Ellie envisaged some of the officers she had seen since she had been in the ATS. All smartly turned out, all well presented. Then she thought of Aidan with his bushy black hair and raggedy old clothes. There was no doubt about it, Aidan was not the sort of man Arla had in mind when it came to marriage, and whilst his looks did not matter to Ellie, of course, she would be the first to admit that he was not what you might call typically handsome, although there was something about him that she found attractive.

Arla raised her eyebrows fleetingly. 'Blimey! Keep your hair on. If you want to sit on the shelf watching all the prime cuts being taken, that's your prerogative, but I don't intend to settle for scrag end.'

Ellie shrieked with laughter. 'You're not in the butcher's, Arla Winthorpe.'

Arla lifted her brow. 'Have you seen the way some of those women look at the men? It's like being at the farmers' market, only instead of bidding they're grabbin' what they can.'

Walking around a new station in the dark was not ideal when you had no idea where you were going, and the girls soon found they were back where they had started. 'It really will be time for bed by the time we've found the NAAFI,' groaned Ellie. 'I'm game for one more try but if we end up back here I'm callin' it a night.'

As it turned out, the NAAFI was not far from their hut, and they had already walked past it on their first expedition. Looking round the inside, Arla nodded to

127

Ellie. 'Looks the same as the one in Preston. Let's see if the food's any better.'

The only food left on offer was a rather stale cheese sandwich, which they cut in two and washed down with a mug of tea. 'I'll have nightmares tonight after eatin' that cheese,' Arla said ruefully. 'Give us a prod if I start screamin' in me sleep.'

Ellie rolled her eyes. 'It was your idea to come here—' She broke off as a familiar face entered the NAAFI. 'Struthers! Over here.'

Private Struthers nodded to the girls. 'Be right with you. I'm just gettin' a cuppa.'

When he sat down Ellie and Arla bombarded him with questions. 'What's it like here? Is there anywhere we can go dancing? Is there anyone to watch out for?'

Struthers laughed. 'You two caught on quick, didn't you? It's the same here as it is everywhere: you'll learn that as you move around the country. There are a few places you can go dancing off camp, but they hold a weekly one in the mess so if all else fails there's always that. As for anyone to watch out for, the usual bunch of shouting sergeants, officers and the like.'

'Are all the camps the same, then? Doesn't anything change?' Arla said, feeling a shade disappointed.

He shook his head. 'Sorry, but no. They do it intentionally, so it don't matter where they send you, see?' He pointed at their empty plate. 'The food don't get no better neither, before you ask.'

Arla pulled a face. 'Join the army and see the army,' she said sullenly.

'How come you're here, anyhow? Do you move from camp to camp same as us?' Ellie asked.

Struthers nodded. 'I go wherever I'm needed. I'm trained to do more than just the gun sites.' He winked at Arla. 'I'm versatile.'

Arla groaned. 'I knew I shouldn't have had that sandwich. I've got awful indigestion now.'

'Good old army food, there ain't nowt else quite like it – thank God. Tell you what, Winthorpe, how about I take you dancin' one evenin'? Not tonight, of course, but once you've settled in?'

Arla stared at him in disbelief. She wanted to say, 'But you're not an officer, or a sergeant, or even a corporal,' but looking into his hopeful expression she hadn't the heart. 'We'll see,' she managed rather lamely.

Ellie grinned like the Cheshire Cat all the way back to their hut. 'Who's got themselves a hot date with *Private* Struthers?' she teased.

'Pack it in!' Arla said glumly. 'My tummy's churnin' and I'm not in the mood.'

Ellie linked arms with her. 'Not going smoothly, your plan to join the army and marry an officer, is it? Still, we all have to start somewhere ...'

Arla giggled. 'Poor Struthers. He's a nice enough chap, but let's be fair, even if he was an officer ...'

'... he wouldn't have a chance, not with you at any rate. Not that I'm implyin' that you're bothered about the way a feller looks, but ...'

'... I do prefer them to have all their own teeth, and not be sufferin' from what looks like a severe bout of the measles,' Arla finished.

Ellie nodded. 'Poor Struthers indeed. I'm sure he'll grow out of the spotty stage. Most of us do.'

'He might be quite handsome under that lot, who knows? Personally I prefer my men to've gone through puberty.'

Laughing, Ellie shook her head. 'Listen to you, Arla Winthorpe. The way you carry on anyone'd think you were a woman of the world, not a young girl who hasn't had her first kiss.'

'Neither've you,' said Arla defensively.

Ellie chuckled. 'No, and I don't want to kiss anyone for a long time yet, man or boy.'

Arla raised her brows.'Not even Aidan?'

'Not even Aidan,' Ellie said, grateful for the dark night sky which hid her blushes. 'Besides, I think we've a bit more to worry about at the moment than kissing boys. From what the NCO said it's going to be all systems go from tomorrow onwards, so we'd best try and get us some sleep ... if we can after that awful sandwich.'

Arla looked down at the empty page. How was she meant to ask her mother if she had heard from Archie Byrnes without actually coming out and saying it? She knew from her mother's last letter that Archie had left the court, but not whether he had gone overseas or was, as Arla hoped, working on a gun site in England.

She tapped her pencil against her forehead. Perhaps she could ask her mother to ask Archie's mother for his whereabouts so that she might write to him? She stopped tapping the pencil against her forehead and tapped it against her chin instead. No, that would not do at all. It would be worse than asking after his well-being. She gazed vaguely around the room as she tried to come up with an idea. From the corner of her eye she saw two soldiers marching past the window, and smiled. She would say that she thought she might have seen Archie in Preston. Then she would ask if her mother knew whether he was in a camp nearby, and peshaps if she did not already know the answer she would ask Mrs Byrnes.

Arla gave a contented sniff. It was the perfect plan. No one would question her reason for asking about her adversary's whereabouts, and she would be able to stop worrying. Providing he's not been posted abroad, that is, Arla thought wretchedly. If he has then I'm going to worry myself sick. She bit the end of her pencil. Confound the dratted boy! Why did he have to run off and play soldiers? Surely he must realise that all he'd achieve would be to harry everyone who cared two hoots about him into an early grave? If she ever found out he'd left the country she'd give him a damned good dressing-down the next time they met, and a thick ear besides, she thought decidedly.

Setting pencil to paper, she put her plan into action.

Ellie smoothed out the page in front of her.

You were right, Ellie! After days of making a nuisance of myself down at the recruiting office they finally listened to me – well, Captain Mathias did at any rate. It's him I'm training under now. I just wanted to write to thank you for persuading me that I should keep trying. If it hadn't been for you I think I'd still be on the farm. Not that I'm saying there's anything wrong with farming, mind you. Although I'd wager it's less dangerous being on a gun site than it is dealing with our Blue.

Ellie chuckled as she read. Blue was a mean, bad-tempered bull, whose irritability was made worse by his being blind in one eye. If he didn't want to go somewhere then he quite simply didn't go. If you couldn't make him move by persuasion, usually a bucketful of his favourite food, you just had to hope he'd either give up or change his mind. Sneaking up on his blind side was never a good idea: his hearing had become acute and he could move quickly despite his size.

It had been late in the autumn and the Murrays, along with a few of the villagers, had just finished piling the hay into stooks when Aidan had asked Ellie if she would mind helping him move the cows from one pasture to another. Everything had been going well until Blue, halfway to the new pasture, had changed his mind about following the cows and had instead headed straight for the feed shed. Ellie and Aidan had waved their arms in a vain attempt to redirect him, but he was having none of it, and the cows, unsettled by the commotion, had bolted back into the old field. Pausing only to secure the gate behind them, Ellie and Aidan had run down to the shed where they found Blue happily munching the hens' corn.

'We've got to get him out,' Aidan had told Ellie. 'He'll eat the bloomin' lot, and it's not as if we can afford to just go out and buy a load more.'

At the time, Ellie had no experience with the large beast, as his fearsome reputation had led the Murrays to insist she should stay away from him. 'Me or Aidan can muck him out, get him in and all that,' Uncle Kieran had said. 'You just stick with the cows, our Ellie. They're no bother to anyone.'

Outside the shed she had asked Aidan whether it was men in particular that Blue objected to, or women as well.

'Damned if I know. Why?' he said.

'The chooks prefer women. They don't run away from me or your mam, but as soon as you or your dad stroll by ...' She had made flapping motions with her arms.

Aidan laughed. 'Perhaps they think you're one of them.'

Ellie had shot him a withering look. 'Well, I think it's worth a try. You never know, it might just be you and your dad he's taken against.' And with that, despite Aidan's protests, she had entered the shed. It was only when she was inside that she realised how enormous the bull was compared to the cows. To make matters worse, the shed in which he stood was not overly large, and there was very little room in there for the two of them. Rather than stay in the confined space for too long she had called back to Aidan. 'What do I do now?'

'Get out before he notices you!'

'Shall I grab him by the horns?'

'God, no! That would really upset him—' And then Ellie had emerged at top speed, heading for the cowshed, followed by a furious Blue.

'You shouldn't have done that, ' Aidan had told her later, when he found her sitting on top of the muck heap, fighting for breath as she tried to control her giggles, whilst Blue grazed on some old hay.

Ellie had grinned at him. 'It worked, didn't it?'

Now, Ellie turned her attention back to the letter. She couldn't help wondering what Aidan looked like in his flying uniform, and the image which she conjured up was not very flattering. The cap squished his hair out sideways, whilst his wispy beard hung over the collar of his jacket.

She looked across to Arla, who was chatting to the cook behind the counter. Ellie had enjoyed her time in Aborfield. Sergeant Briggs had proved to be firm yet fair, and according to other people around the station he was one of the best the army had to offer. With him at the helm, Section B – Ellie's section – would be the best trained recruits in the camp. Disappointingly, Arla had been placed in Section C, which was the first sign that the girls might not spend the war together. Standing at the board they had checked the lists two or three times.

'Why'd they have to go and separate us?' Arla had complained. 'We've come all this way together, I don't see why they have to go and shove a spanner in the works now.'

Ellie's brow had creased as she scanned the list for Section C, and she rested her forefinger on one of the names. 'Have you seen this?'

Arla had squinted at the list and then looked blankly back at Ellie. 'Archie Byrnes? Well, it can't be our Archie Byrnes. We'd have heard summat by now if it were.'

'Awww, is that how you describe me to your mates? As *your* Archie?'

Turning, Arla had hissed sharply, 'No I do *not*! Where the hell did you spring from, anyway? And how come we ain't seen hide nor hair of you till now?'

Archie's grin had widened. 'I'm what you might call a sight for sore eyes, ladies, and the reason you ain't seen me till now is 'cos we've been training on different camps. I've been sent over to replace one of your gels what's goin' home on account of not bein' suited to the job.' He raised his brows. 'To be fair, Arla luv, when I 'eard one of the gels had wimped out, I thought it must be you.'

Ellie had hidden her amusement behind the palm of her hand as she watched her friend rise to the bait.

'You cheeky little beggar! I've done bloomin' well on all me tests, passed with flyin' colours, haven't I, Ellie?' Without waiting for a reply, she continued, 'To think I was worried—' She broke off and folded her arms across her chest.

'Worried? Who was you worried about?' He had raised an inquisitive brow. 'Don't tell me you've been worryin' over your Archie.'

Arla had stamped a furious foot. 'Not on your life!' she had said, her voice becoming shrill. 'They only put you on a gun site 'cos if they'd stuck you behind a desk somewhere the smell would've driven all the others out!'

Archie had rubbed his chin thoughtfully, although Ellie suspected it was to hide his mirth. 'Good luck to those sharin' a gun site with me then, eh?'

Arla had nodded vigorously. 'Too bloody right,' she began, before realising that she would be one of them. She scowled at Archie and Ellie, who could not contain the giggles escaping their lips. She did not want to

135

laugh with them, because he had been so infuriating, but their laughter was infectious.

'Don't you worry about a thing, our Arla. I promise not to get under your feet or cramp your style. I dare say you've a whole host of officers lined up waitin' to take you out and about.'

Arla nodded curtly. 'Thank you.'

'And if anyone mentions a smell, I'll mek out it's me what smells and not you,' he said, dodging a badly aimed blow.

Despite her words, Ellie knew her friend was relieved to have Archie where she could keep an eye on him. He might be annoying, and Arla seemed to spend most of her time complaining about him in one way or another, but it was plain, to Ellie at any rate, that their relationship had become close over the years, and their arguments resembled those of sibling rivalry – annoying each other to within an inch of their lives, but woe betide anyone else who spoke ill of either.

Their time in Aborfield had been mostly spent in classrooms or learning how to operate the complex instruments which were used to work out the height and speed of approaching enemy aircraft so that gunners knew where to aim their shells. When Ellie had first clapped eyes on the predictor, an intimidating machine that bore a whole host of dials and switches, she thought she would never get the hang of it, but after some intense training sessions she soon understood the controls and was pleased when her instructor asked her to explain some of the intricacies to one of the other girls in her section. The height-finder –

which the sergeant referred to as a glorified pair of binoculars – was far simpler, and when everyone had worked out what went where and did what, they would spend days acting out the scenario of a raid, each trainee undertaking a different role, from taking the calls to raising the alarm, from spotting the aircraft to predicting where it would be when the shell exploded. Out of all these jobs Ellie liked spotting the aircraft the most. She was good at it and never called on an Allied plane. She found the act of scanning the skies through her binoculars as she hunted the enemy thrilling, and considered it to be one of the most important jobs she could do. After all, without the spotter no guns would be fired. For the first few days they had all suffered with sore throats from all the shouting they had to do. 'When you go to a real gun site, you have to shout as loud as you can in order to be heard above the chaos, and it is chaos,' Sergeant Briggs had told them. What with guns and shells being fired and the noise of the aircraft overhead, as well as the air raid siren, you'll have a job to make yourself understood, so I want to hear you roaring clear instructions as loud as you can so that everyone around you knows what's going on. We haven't time to be repeating things. Got it?'

'Yes, sir!' had been the collective barked response.

She had enjoyed this part of the training far more than the initial four weeks, when they had still been in the dreary depths of winter. It was, after all, far more pleasant to be working under bright blue skies, with birdsong in the background and the warmth of the spring sunshine on your back. With the evenings stretching out, the girls from her Nissen hut had taken the opportunity to explore the local area for dance halls and cinemas.

'You'll be living cheek by jowl, so it would be better if you not only worked together, but took time to get to know each other out of working hours too. That way you will become a far more efficient work engine,' had been the advice of Sergeant Briggs.

He had been right. They had moved on from being individuals working next to other people to being a team that acted as one. Ellie often wished that she was in the same section as Arla and Archie, but her fellow trainees proved to be likeable and fun, and it was interesting to work with girls from such a wide range of backgrounds.

The last part of Ellie's training would be starting in a few days' time in Weybourne. If you failed there, it was back to the beginning to retrain, something that was always in the back of Ellie's mind. She loved her job and could not imagine doing anything else. Even though she knew that being called to man her station would mean Britain was under attack, she could not wait to put all her training into action and help to defend her country from the Luftwaffe.

She was polishing the brass buttons on her jacket when Arla burst through the door of their hut with a look of dismay. 'I've just been told ... our section's off to Cornwall.'

Ellie felt as though someone had pulled the rug out from under her feet. She stared blankly into space before finding her voice. 'Cornwall? Why Cornwall? I thought we'd all be going to the same camp.'

'I asked if I could go with you now that that girl – Mabel, was it? – has had to go home to look after her sick mam, but they just shook their heads and said that would leave Section C one short, so I suggested I could swap with someone from Section B but Sarge just said there was no room in the army for sentimentality and they didn't like swapping members of sections unless it was absolutely necessary and that's why we all train in teams in the first place. But it's too late anyhow, 'cos we're leavin' tonight.'

Ellie put her polish down on the floor and clasped Arla's hands in her own. 'Perhaps we'll end up on the same placement together when we get posted. You never know your luck. We'll just have to keep our fingers crossed.'

Arla nodded wearily. 'We can always write to each other, and when we get a bit of leave we could meet up somewhere.'

Ellie smiled. 'That's the spirit! I know you won't be able to come to the dance tonight, but there's nowt stoppin' us goin' into town now and gettin' a sticky bun and a cuppa.'

A small smile appeared on Arla's lips. 'You payin'?'

Relieved that her friend's mood was improving, Ellie nodded. 'Course I am. It'll be my goodbye prezzie, and when we come back I'll help you get ready so there'll be enough time to see if there's any films playin' on camp before you leave.'

Arla gave Ellie's hand a squeeze. 'You're a good 'un, Ellie Lancton, and I ain't half goin' to miss you.'

Ellie nodded. 'It wasn't how we planned things, but I suppose deep down we must've always known

139

summat like this might happen, although it would've been grand to be together. Look on the bright side: at least you've got Archie.'

Arla giggled. 'I thought you were meant to be makin' me feel better, not worse. Come on. Sticky buns are calling!'

Chapter Six

'How do! Are you Aidan Murray?'

Aidan looked up from the letter he was writing. 'Morning, and yes, why?'

The man stepped forward, a broad grin on his face as he held out a hand. 'I'm Norbert Wiggins, Wiggy to my pals. I'm afraid we've had a bit of a leak in our room so they told me to come up here 'cos you've got a spare bed.'

Aidan nodded to one of the beds in the corner of the room. 'That one's free over there. What kind of leak?'

'Not the kind you eat.' wiggy chortled, and Aidan couldn't help thinking that he had probably told this joke more than once in the past hour or so. 'The sink tap had a bit of a drip, nothing major but annoying all the same. One of the lads decided he'd try and fix it.' Wiggy rolled his eyes. 'The tap was stuck fast, so he hit it with the spanner.' He gestured to his wet uniform. 'Next thing we know there's water squirtin' everywhere and no one can find the stop tap.'

Aidan nodded towards their bathroom. 'There's a towel in there if you need it.'

'Ta. As you can imagine, everything in our bathroom got soaked through.' Wiggy looked out of the hotel window. 'Coo, look at that view! If I'd've known I could change rooms for one with a sea view, I'd've broken the tap meself!'

Aidan chuckled. 'I must admit after Ludlow I thought they were pulling my leg when they said our new barracks was going to be a hotel, and when I saw this place for the first time I really thought someone was having a laugh at my expense.'

'Me too, especially with my luck. I've never been somewhere this grand in all my life – pardon the pun.'

Aidan smiled. 'That's probably why they named it The Grand.' He wrinkled his brow, something Wiggy had said sticking in his mind. 'What do you mean, "especially with my luck"?'

Wiggy placed his bag on the bed that Aidan had indicated. 'I've had nowt but bad luck ever since I signed on the dotted line. I got on the train to go to Lords and the bloomin' thing broke down. Twelve hours we were stuck on that line, no food or water, and to top it off the onboard lavvy broke. I thought that were bad enough, but after initial training, when we were on our way from Lords to Ludlow, the flamin' driver didn't know where he was goin'; not that he admitted it, of course. We got two flat tyres 'cos we'd ended up on some godforsaken back lane with potholes the size of your head, and when we got out of the truck we found some bugger had taken the spare. Not only that, but when we walked to the main road and flagged a car down we found out we were eighty miles in the wrong direction.' He puffed his cheeks out. 'I'm tellin' you now, if it weren't for bad luck I wouldn't have any at all.'

Aidan felt sorry for the crew who would be flying with Wiggy. 'Maybe your luck's changing. After all, you said yourself that you're in a better room now than the one you were in.'

Wiggy rubbed his chin thoughtfully. 'Aye, you're right there, but on the other hand we've got to pay for the tap to be fixed and the carpet to be sorted out, and I bet it weren't the cheap stuff, not in a place like this.'

'I don't see why you should have to fork out. It wasn't you who broke the tap.'

'Yes, well, I know I didn't hit the tap myself, but it was me what told him to do it, like,' Wiggy said sheepishly. He pointed at the letter Aidan was holding. 'I don't s'pose you got a spare piece of paper, by any chance? I wouldn't mind writin' to my Minnie, only of course mine got wet 'cos we were trying to stop the leak with anything and everything we had to hand.'

Nodding, Aidan handed him a spare sheet. 'Minnie your wife?'

Wiggy shook his head. 'Me girlfriend, or at least I think she is.'

Aidan raised a questioning brow. 'How do you mean, you think she is? Surely you know whether you're courtin' someone or not?'

Wiggy sat heavily on to his bed. 'I know I'm courtin' her; trouble is, accordin' to one of the old fellers in the Nag's Head, it looks as though I might not be the only feller she's courtin', if you follow my meaning.' He let out a soulful sigh. 'Bit of a popular girl is my Minnie.'

He jerked his head towards Aidan's letter. 'You seein' anyone special?'

Aidan nodded, then shrugged. 'Kind of, only it's a bit complicated.'

Wiggy looked interested. 'How so?'

'It's a long story.' Aidan would have stopped there, but Wiggy was insistent.

'We're going to be rooming together for the best part of five months, pal; you've plenty of time to tell it.'

Pushing his letter away reluctantly, Aidan turned to face him. 'I met her last spring, She was havin' a bit of bother back in Liverpool: her mam had died a couple of months before and she was finding it hard to pay the rent, so she came to work on my dad's farm. When she first arrived it was like having my sister Cassie back, but after a while ...' he shrugged his shoulders, 'she started to mean more to me.'

'Did you tell her?' said Wiggy, who was clearly intrigued.

'I wanted to, but I knew she intended to join the services so that she could prove to herself that she could cope on her own.'

'Ah,' Wiggy said knowingly. 'She can't be relyin' on a feller if she wants to cope on her own. I see your problem.'

'I just hope she doesn't prove she can cope on her own with someone else,' said Aidan. 'Working day and night with a bunch of fellers on the gun sites she might easily fall in love with one of them.'

Wiggy grimaced. 'Softly softly catchee monkey is all very well if you haven't got a whole heap of eager monkey-snatchers joinin' the chase.'

144

Aidan laughed. 'Thanks a lot, pal. That makes me feel a lot better.'

Wiggy held up an apologetic hand. 'Sorry, mate; I were just sayin' what you were thinkin', only I'm not very good at these things. Me mam always used to say I were about as subtle as a brick.'

'But you're right,' Aidan concluded. 'Whilst I'm giving her space and time some other bugger's waiting in the background to snatch her up.'

'So?' said Wiggy. 'Are you goin' to ask her to be your belle?'

Aidan heaved a sigh. 'I want to, but what if she turns me down?'

'Faint heart never won fair lady,' Wiggy pointed out.

'Only fools rush in?' Aidan countered.

Wiggy rolled his eyes. 'You can sit here and argue back and forth whilst someone else steals her out from under your nose.'

'If I am going to tell her how I feel it won't be in a letter. I'd rather do it face to face; that way I can see her reaction for myself and I'll know how she really feels towards me.'

'Fair enough.' Wiggy glanced at his wristwatch. 'Time for a drink?'

Aidan nodded. 'There's not a lot a glass of beer won't cure, especially when it comes to nervous suitors.'

Wiggy laughed. 'And what fair maiden doesn't love a suitor too drunk for words?'

Arriving in Weybourne, Ellie felt that she had finally taken charge of her own life. With no close friends or family nearby, she had no one but herself to rely on. It helped that she was now familiar and at ease with life in the army, and of course the camp set-up in Weybourne was much the same as everywhere else. As she entered the barracks she looked at the bunk beds and decided that this time she would have a bottom bunk. She wondered what Arla was doing right now and whether she would change too, or would stick to the same bed she had had all the way through their training till now.

As she laid the biscuits out she realised for the first time how very alone she felt. Normally Arla would be chattering away, making suggestions as to where they should go and what they should do before turning in. Ellie smiled. She'd be suggesting that they put their stuff away, made up their beds and then headed for the NAAFI to see whether there were any eligible stripes nearby. Ellie tried to thump some air into her pillow, then gave up. She was being silly. It wasn't as if she didn't know anyone in her new barracks – she had after all travelled here with the rest of her section – it was just—

A voice from behind her interrupted her thoughts. 'This one taken?'

Turning to see who had spoken, Ellie saw a tall girl with raven hair and pale skin pointing to the top bunk. Backing out from her bed, she held out her hand. 'Hi. I'm Ellie Lancton, and no, it's free if you want it.'

The other girl took Ellie's hand and shook it vigorously. 'Thanks. I'm Gwen, by the way, Gwen Jones. Are you in Section B?'

Ellie smiled. 'I am,' A thought occurred to her. 'Are you replacing Mabel?'

Gwen nodded. 'Are they a friendly lot in Section B?'

'They are, and it was a shame Mabel had to go, but don't worry: I'm sure you'll fit in well.'

'Good. It's a bit of a bind having to start all over again with a new section, but if they're friendly that's half the battle.' She scanned the room. 'Don't think I know any of this lot. D'you fancy goin' to get summat to eat?'

Ellie smiled. 'I don't see why not, thought I don't s'pose there'll be much choice this late in the day.' She paused. 'Where're you from? I don't recognise the accent.'

Gwen grinned. 'I'm from the Rhos in Wales. It's not far from Wrexham, which isn't far from Chester. Have you heard of it?'

Ellie nodded. 'I've heard of Chester, because it's not too far from Liverpool, which is where I'm from. I think I might have heard of Wrexham, but not ... where did you say?'

'Rhos. It's short for Rhosllanerchrugog, only most of the English find that a bit hard to say.'

Ellie giggled. 'I should think they do! I can certainly see why they've shortened it down a bit.' She looked into Gwen's dark brown eyes and came to the decision that she liked the new girl. 'Tell you what, how about I help you make up your bunk? It'll be less to do when we get back.'

'Sounds good to me.' Gwen placed the three biscuits in a line, whilst Ellie unfurled the sheets. She handed one side to Gwen and the two girls smoothed them over the mattress. 'Did you join up on your own, then?' Gwen asked, tucking her side in.

'No, I joined up with me bezzie.' Seeing the look of confusion on Gwen's face she added, 'That's what you call your best mate in Liverpool.'

Gwen looked round the room. 'She not here with you?'

Ellie shook her head. 'We were together right up till this point, then she got sent to Cornwall. She was in a different section to me, you see.'

'Tough luck! Still, at least you've got the rest of your section. It's a bit daunting coming into a whole new group of people who've already bonded, I can tell you, but if they're all as friendly as you, I dare say I'll get along fine.'

'How about you? Did you come in on your own?' Ellie asked, smoothing down the blanket on her side.

Gwen nodded. 'I live with me Auntie Flo and Uncle Nobby on a farm high up in the hills, so I don't have many friends, or at least not of me own age.'

'How come you live with them and not your mam and dad?' Ellie asked, adding hastily, 'Sorry, I hope I'm not being too nosy.'

Gwen shook her head. 'Me mam abandoned me when I was a few days old, left me in the porch of the local church and beggared off, never to be seen again.' She attempted to plump up the flat pillow. 'Me Auntie Flo were in charge of opening the church up that mornin', so she was the one who found me.' Folding her arms on the bed, she leaned her chin on the back of her hands. 'Cut a long story short, I stayed with me auntie and uncle whilst they looked for me real mam, but of course she didn't want to be found, so they couldn't trace her. I were due to go to an orphanage, but Auntie Flo and Uncle Nobby couldn't have kids of their own, so it was arranged for me to live with them.' She smiled happily.

Ellie eyed the other girl curiously. 'Weren't – aren't you angry? About bein' abandoned, I mean?'

Gwen pulled a complacent face. 'Nah, life's too short. Besides, I didn't do too badly out of it. I got to live on a farm, which is better than bein' with someone who don't want you. I'm not sayin' me mam were a bad person, just that she couldn't cope; she must've had some feelin's for me, otherwise she wouldn't have left me the locket.'

'What locket?'

Gwen fished around in her kitbag and produced a thin silver chain with an oval locket on the end of it, which she passed to Ellie. 'This 'un. Be careful when you open it. The catch is a bit iffy; that's why I don't wear it.' She watched whilst Ellie carefully opened the locket. 'We think the picture inside is me mam. After all, it'd be a bit queer if she left me a locket containing a picture of a stranger inside.'

Ellie squinted at the tiny photograph inside the locket, then studied Gwen's features. 'She does look a bit like you. Didn't anyone in the village recognise her from the photograph?'

Gwen shook her head. 'Nope. The coppers went from door to door, but she definitely weren't from the village, and none of the locals could remember seeing her before.'

Ellie closed the locket carefully and handed it back to Gwen. 'I wish I had summat like that to remember my mam by.'

Gwen raised her brows inquisitively. 'Is she …?' She hesitated.

Ellie nodded. 'She died last year. I have got a couple of photographs, but I don't know whether they'd be any good to put into a locket even if I had one.'

'Sorry to hear about your mam. Have you got the photos here?'

Ellie shook her head. 'I left them at me bezzie's house when we joined up, just in case anything happened to them. They're all I've got.'

'I'm sure you could get summat done. Does she look like you, your mam I mean?'

Ellie considered. 'I'd like to think so, and a lot of people do say we've the same smile.' She paused. 'Only she's got blue eyes and mine are hazel and she had brown hair and as you can see mine's more like copper, and hers was wavy and mine's more curly.'

'And your dad? Do you ever see him?'

Ellie gave a short burst of laughter. 'Wouldn't know him if I tripped over him! He did a runner before I was born, and from what I've heard – not from me mam, mind you; she never said a bad word against him – I wouldn't want to meet him either.'

Gwen walked to the end of the bed. 'Like peas in a pod, ain't we? No mam or dad left to speak of, and no relatives. Or at least I haven't.'

'Me neither,' Ellie confirmed. 'So you're right, we are like peas in a pod.' She smiled brightly at Gwen. 'Ready?'

The girls paused outside the door to their barracks. Standing on tiptoe, they looked at each building in turn before Ellie pointed to a long low hut not too far from the parade ground. 'NAAFI!' she said.

As they stepped through the door, Ellie took in the familiar surroundings that were more or less identical to those of her previous camps. 'Cup of tea?' she suggested.

'That'll do nicely, as long as it's not gnats' pee. I hate weak tea, don't you?'

Ellie giggled. 'Two mugs of tea, please, and ...' She peered at the stale-looking sandwiches before turning to Gwen. 'Want to share a cheese sarnie?'

Gwen shrugged her indifference. 'Can do, but that bread looks like it's got rigor mortis. It's all curled up at the edges.'

The cook glared at Gwen from behind the counter. 'You don't have to eat it if you don't want to. I don't know which la-di-da camp you've come from, but we're on a tight budget here.'

Looking at the cheese sandwich again, Gwen raised her brows. 'You can tell, I know the army's not exempt from rationing and they have the old waste not want not rule, but they'll be a man down if anyone eats that.'

The cook turned to Ellie. 'Did you say two mugs?' she said icily.

Ellie nodded and watched as the woman, grumbling her displeasure, poured tea into the mugs before placing them roughly down on the counter, causing the contents to spill over the rims.

'I think you upset her,' Ellie said as they chose a table.

'Few more days and they'll be able to use them sarnies as missiles,' Gwen said with a giggle, but then, looking in the direction of the door, she groaned. 'You've got to be kiddin' me. I thought I'd seen the last

151

of them two after basic trainin'.' She looked earnestly at Ellie. 'Please tell me they're not in our section!'

Ellie looked over her shoulder, then turned back to Gwen. 'D'you mean them two by the counter with their backs to us?'

Gwen nodded. 'The gruesome twosome. Evie and Tilly, although Tilly's not too bad when you get her on her own. But that Evie – oh damn.'

One of the girls whom Gwen had referred to had turned to face them, and now spoke loudly so that the whole room might hear. 'I thought we'd left all the rubbish behind, so what on earth is orphan Annie doin' here?'

Ellie thought the voice familiar, but could not quite place it. She turned to look at the speaker and nearly dropped her mug.

Shrieking, the speaker pointed an accusing finger. 'Oh my God! Orphan Annie's palled up with one of the slum sisters. Talk about birds of a feather! D'you remember her, Tilly? She's one of the ones from Liverpool.' She was nudging the other girl in the ribs whilst still pointing at Ellie. 'You – where's your mate? The one that thinks she's good enough to marry an officer?'

Her cheeks glowing, Ellie ignored the question and turned back to Gwen. 'As you can see, we've already met, and in answer to your question, no, they are definitely not in my section.'

'Oh dear, looks like I've offended someone.' Evie giggled. 'I would ask if her mate'd been successful, but no officer could be that desperate.'

'So have *you* managed to find the right one yet?' Gwen said, her tone heavy with sarcasm. 'Only I were thinkin' that if Ellie's mate needs any advice on how to date an officer she should come to you, 'cos you've had plenty of experience. In fact, you could even put her in touch with a few of your cast-offs. God only knows there's enough of 'em, all lickin' their wounds ...'

Evie's eyes flashed furiously. 'At least I can get a man,' she said haughtily. 'Come along, Tilly; there's a vile smell in here and I'm not referring to the food for once.'

The cook, who had been enjoying the sideshow, scowled angrily. 'Oi!' she began, but she was addressing the backs of Evie and Tilly as they strode towards the doors.

Ellie grinned at Gwen. 'Blimey! You soon put her in her place!'

'I know a thing or two about that girl Evie, and it's not pleasant. Like I said, Tilly's all right, and to be honest I don't know why she's hanging round with the likes of Evie. She could do so much better.'

Ellie nodded. 'She was a bit of a cow in Liverpool, but when Evie left my mate and I bumped into Tilly in a café. She came over and started chatting and we got along quite nicely. She said that Evie was all right once you got to know her, so perhaps that's why she sticks with her.' She sighed. 'I must admit, I did hope she'd say summat to defend Arla and me just now when Evie started being nasty, but she's obviously worried about upsetting her.'

'You've hit the nail on the head there. Evie's like the puppeteer and Tilly's her puppet. I've never seen Tilly stand up to her yet, not even when Evie's being nasty to her, and believe me she's got a spiteful tongue even when it comes to Tilly.'

Ellie frowned. 'There's got to be some reason why she doesn't just walk away. Perhaps she's got some sort of big dark secret she doesn't want anyone finding out about and Evie's holding it over her head.'

'Sounds plausible. Tell you what, next time Evie finds some poor sap to take her out we'll ask Tilly what the deal is. It's the only time they're ever apart.'

'Good idea. Now, let's drink this tea before it gets cold and go back to the barracks. I don't know about you, but I'm whacked.'

'What's up with you? Tilly! Slow down, for goodness' sake!'

Trotting to catch up, Evie grabbed her friend by the elbow and pulled her to a halt. 'Where's the fire?'

Tilly shook herself free from Evie's grip. 'Why d'you have to make enemies wherever we go? You promised me it'd be different here, you swore you'd behave, yet we've not even got the first day under our belts and you've already alienated two of the girls.'

'Oh, come on, play fair! You can't expect me to be friendly to the likes of Goofy Gwen and the queen of the courts?' Evie said, clearly exasperated.

'Gwen's not that bad. She speaks her mind, that's all, and that's why you don't like her, because she doesn't dress things up.'

Evie glowered. 'She practically called me a tart in there! How's that speaking the truth? It's nothing but pure jealousy.'

154

Tilly drew a deep breath. 'You started it, Evie. You always do. She was happy minding her own business, but you had to start calling her names.'

Sullen-faced, Evie looked at the toes of her shoes. 'I like to get in first, you know that. Always throw the first punch, be it physical or verbal. That's what my dad used to say and I still think he's right.'

Tilly shook her head. 'How on earth do you ever expect to make friends if you go round attacking people all the time?'

Evie raised her eyes to meet Tilly's. 'I made friends with you, didn't I? Besides, who wants to be friends with the likes of them? People'll avoid you like the plague if they think you're friends with people like them.'

'People like us, you mean?' Tilly said sharply.

Evie pointed an accusing finger in the direction of the NAAFI. 'I am not like them, and neither are you!'

'Maybe not once, but you are now,' Tilly said pragmatically.

'Never! You can take the girl out of Cheshire, but you can't take Cheshire out of the girl. You should remember that, Tilly Jarvis, and you've done a lot better for yourself since I came on the scene.'

Tilly frowned as she tried to work out exactly what in her life had improved since she had become friends with Evie, and could think of nothing. She began to walk in the direction of the barracks. 'I'm not going to stand here arguing with you all night, Evie Maddox. All I'm saying is can you please at least try to get along with folk, for my sake if nothing else?'

Evie patted Tilly's arm in a friendly manner. 'Of course I will, but do try to understand that if you don't set your sights a bit higher than …' she searched for a word which would not start another argument, 'you are at present, you'll never achieve everything you're capable of, and that's all I want for you, to see you do well and be happy.'

'I know, I just wish you'd think before speaking occasionally, and if you really don't like someone keep it to yourself,' said Tilly, relieved that the unpleasantries were over. She was not by nature a confrontational person, and took no pleasure in seeing others squirm under her friend's verbal onslaughts. She had hoped that mixing in with a whole lot of girls might improve Evie's attitude – she still hoped it would – but so far the evidence did not suggest a change would be coming any time soon.

She cast her mind back to a couple of days after Evie and her mother had arrived on the Scottie Road. Tilly had been standing with her mother whilst she scrubbed the front doorstep, and their neighbour, Mrs Armitage, was telling them about her sister who had come to stay.

'They used to 'ave it all: maids, money and a bloomin' mansion, least it was compared to my 'ouse, but 'er 'ubby got into trouble with the tax man. Owed 'em a fortune he did, and when he said he couldn't pay the tax took the lot off 'em, left 'em 'omeless and penniless. Even took 'im to jail, so o' course I said Val an' the kid could come and stay with me till they got back on their feet.' She pulled a sneering face. 'Not that 'er brat of a child thanks me for it, h'oh no, looks down her nose at me an' my food. I tell you straight, she'd 'ave the back of my 'and if she were mine and no mistake. Should've 'ad a damned good beltin' years ago, if you ask me.'

Evie's aunt had been speaking out of the corner of her mouth, a cigarette clenched firmly between her lips. Tilly had watched in fascination, wondering when the woman's ash would eventually fall on to her own beautifully scrubbed step.

Tilly had been intrigued by this tale of fancy living in a grand house with maids, and could not wait to meet their new neighbour. But their first encounter in the school playground had proved disappointing, and she realised that making friends with the newcomer was not going to be easy.

'I don't want to be your friend,' said Evie to one of their classmates who had been admiring her patent leather shoes. 'I don't belong in a place like this. Besides, I won't be here long. As soon as my father has sorted out that silly man's mistake I'll be back in Frodsham, far away from the likes of you.'

'Sooner the better!' snapped the girl. 'Stuck up cow! Them shoes are no good for round 'ere anyway. They'll be ruined before you can say knife.' One by one the circle of children who lived on the Scottie had disbanded, leaving Tilly and Evie standing in the middle of an ever-decreasing circle until just the two of them were left.

Tilly had approached Evie shyly. 'I 'eard your auntie sayin' your dad was in the nick. Is that true?'

Evie scowled. 'Don't you go spreading rumours about my father. You haven't the foggiest what you're on about.'

Tilly stood scraping the dirt and gravel across the stones with the toe of her shoe. 'It's true, then?'

Evie's face had softened. 'Please don't go telling the others. They'll get it all wrong, or start making stuff up.' She looked appealingly at Tilly. 'He's not a bad man. If anyone's bad it's the tax man.'

Tilly looked up from the pattern she had been making. 'My dad 'ates the tax man, he reckons he's a thievin' git, same as the landlord.' She considered for a moment. 'He don't like the scuffers neither.'

Evie smiled. 'There you are then! That proves it. Even your dad knows my dad's not a bad man, it's the tax man, and all the others.'

It had been a strange way to bond, but from that moment on, Evie had considered Tilly to be her friend, and the two girls had gone everywhere together. Tilly enjoyed Evie's company and found that the other girl treated her reasonably well, certainly better than she did everyone else. At first it had made Tilly feel special, but having Evie's friendship came at a price. Tilly's old friends had decreased in numbers since she had palled up with Evie.

Now, approaching the Nissen hut, Tilly wondered what it was exactly about Evie that had deserved her loyalty. It wasn't pity, or empathy, although it had been at first, of course, as they both had fathers who disliked the tax man. But then the rumours had started and Tilly had heard a different story. The family had been sitting round the table when her father entered the kitchen; slamming the morning's newspaper down on the table he had pointed an accusing finger at it. 'That bloody Maddox feller, the one whose wife and kiddy live next door, gambled the company's wages away. Diddled loads of hard workers out of their money he did! I 'ope they throw away the key.'

With housewives being the bloodline of all gossip it was not long before the news reached the local children, who had proved to be relentless in their taunting. Many of their parents worked for men just like Evie's father, and they had not taken kindly to the news.

If it had been Tilly who was on the receiving end of the bullying she would have run away, but Evie had stood strong. She had refused to believe the accusations against her father, instead accusing the government, the newspapers and the children of lying. This had all happened some years previously, but even though the taunting had stopped some time back, Evie had relished the idea of joining the ATS and leaving Liverpool.

Tilly too had hoped that starting a new life would be like turning over a new leaf for Evie, but so far this had not proved to be the case. Instead, her friend acted as though she was on a quest to prove that she was better than everyone else, and Tilly had begun to suspect that until Evie admitted that her father had been in the wrong, she would be forever fighting those around her.

Now, Evie linked arms with her only ally. 'It's been a long day, and I'm shattered. That's probably why I had a bit of a go at those two in the NAAFI. I'm sure things will seem a lot better after a good night's sleep.'

Tilly gave Evie's arm a squeeze. 'I know you don't mean to be mean, so let's start afresh tomorrow, see how we go from there. Agreed?'

Evie half smiled, half smirked. She had known she would win her friend round in the end. 'Agreed,' she said, returning the squeeze.

Arla frowned. 'When they said Cornwall I was hoping we'd be somewhere like Penzance on the south coast. I've never even heard of Bude!'

Archie gave her an admiring glance. 'Fancy you knowing where Penzance is. Just goes to show, you may look—'

'Don't you dare say I look ignorant, Archie Byrnes, or I'll give you a thick ear,' Arla warned him.

'Actually, I was going to say you may look as if you're half asleep in class, but you obviously aren't.'

She frowned her annoyance. 'I don't look half asleep ... do I?'

'When we were in school you used to stare out of the window a lot. At the time I thought you were day-dreaming,' Archie said reasonably. 'You're different here, though. You look as if you're listening more, as if you're interested in what he has to say.'

Arla raised a quizzical eyebrow. 'Watch me a lot in class, do you?'

Much to her surprise, Archie blushed. In all the years Arla had known him he had never shown any sign of embarrassment no matter what she had thrown at him. He gave his fingernails a thorough examination, then shrugged. 'Not really, just every now and then.'

Arla's mouth twitched in amusement at his discomfort. 'Still, I suppose watchin' me is better than lookin' at old Woody.'

Woody was the nickname of their new sergeant. 'They call him Woody 'cos he stands like some bugger's shoved a wooden rod up his ar—up his back. Walks like it too' had been the cook's explanation for the sergeant's nickname. As the kitchen was the main hub of every household, so was the NAAFI in every camp. It was the first port of call for most, where the kitchen staff would happily fill you in on any gossip going.

Archie chuckled. 'Do you reckon he knows what people call him? He must've wondered why a few of us chuckled when he started to pace the room.'

Arla shrugged. 'To be honest, I think he might be going a bit deaf too.'

'What?' said Archie, cupping a hand behind his ear.

'I said, I thought he might be going a bit—' Arla broke off and made a playful swipe towards him. 'Very funny,' she said, her mouth twitching as she tried to hide her amusement. 'Anyway, as I was saying, I don't think he could hear people laughing, which is probably just as well.'

This conversation had taken place as they walked along one of the footpaths which followed the coast. Reaching a bench, Archie gestured towards it. 'Fancy a break?'

Arla nodded. 'It's a good view from here, but not what I was hoping for.'

He sat down beside her. 'Why? What were you hoping to see?'

Blushing, Arla held up a warning finger. 'Don't you laugh if I'm wrong, but I thought we might be able to see France if we were a bit further south.'

He raised his brow in surprise. 'Oh! I don't know whether you can or not, but it'd be a strange thing if you could, wouldn't it?'

She tilted her head inquisitively. 'Why?'

'Well, the thought of being able to see them but not help them, I s'pose,' Archie said. 'You know they're all over there doing their bit for freedom, but you can't actually join them.'

Arla shivered, and Archie removed his jacket and offered it to her. 'You cold, chuck?'

She shook her head. 'It were just a shiver runnin' down my spine at the thought of what you said.' She gave a grim little smile. 'You're right. I hadn't thought of it like that.'

'Blimey,' Archie said, his brow shooting towards his hairline. 'I never thought I'd hear you say that.'

'What?'

'That I'm right,' he said with a chuckle.

She gave him a sidelong look from under her lashes. No matter how bad things were, Archie Byrnes could always make her laugh.

'Do you like it? Being on a battery, I mean?' she said.

'Me mam prefers me to be on ack-acks, rather than the front line,' he mused. 'I'm happy to be wherever I can do most good, although being here has its advantages.' He leaned his elbow against the back of the bench and rested his head on the palm of his hand to look at her.

Arla returned his gaze. Archie Byrnes was handsome in a cheeky-chappy kind of way. He had bright blue eyes, pronounced cheekbones and deep dimples; his hair was the colour of sand and whilst most of it was straight, the back of his hair formed into little curls above the nape of his neck. She smiled. 'I think I'd agree with you.'

'Ellie? Is that you? It's me, Aidan.'

Ellie smiled. His voice was faint and had a tinny quality, but it was unmistakable, and just hearing him made her tummy flutter.

'Course it's me, you goose! How many Ellie Lanctons do you think there are in Weybourne?' She giggled. 'You are *the* Aidan Murray, aren't you?'

'Ha ha, very funny! I can see the ATS hasn't changed you much. But tell me, how are you?'

'I'm doing well. I miss Arla awfully, but I've made a good friend called Gwen. She's from Wales, and she's been teaching me how to speak Welsh, so it's not just the ack-acks I'm learning about.' She gave an excited squeal. 'Saying that, we'll have finished our training in a couple of weeks so it'll be all systems go then. How's your training going? Have you been up in a plane yet?'

Aidan chuckled. 'You certainly sound as though you're enjoying yourself. As for me, I've done my initial training, and now I'm in Scarborough; will be for the next five months, doing my flight training. I've not been up yet, but hopefully I will be soon, providing I pass the next stage, of course.'

'Oh, you'll pass, no problem. Probably come top of your group, too,' she said with assurance.

'Thanks for the vote of confidence; I hope you're right. I've been chatting to Connor and he suggested we should try and get together if we can. What do you think? Have you any leave coming up?'

Ellie pulled a face. 'I wouldn't have thought so. Once we're trained they'll want us to experience a real site before they'll consider giving us any leave. You?'

'I wasn't going to ask until I knew what everyone else could do first,' Aidan admitted. 'Let me know as soon as you can get something and we'll try to meet up so that we can talk properly.'

Ellie frowned. 'What's wrong with talking like this?'

Aidan floundered for a moment or two before being interrupted by the operator telling him to replace the receiver so that the next person might take their turn.

'I'll have to go, Ellie, but it's been good to talk. Take care and speak to you soon. T.t.f.n.'

'T.t.f.n.' Ellie managed before hearing the click on the other end of the line. Replacing the receiver, she went back to her hut where she found Gwen lying on her bed, reading one of the many women's magazines that circulated the barracks. Seeing Ellie enter the room, she waved a greeting.

'So? How was he? Is he in the air yet?'

Ellie took her shoes off and sat down heavily on the bed beneath Gwen's. 'No. He's hoping to be soon, though.' She heaved a sigh. 'I'm pleased for him, I really am, but, well ...'

'You're worried that the Nazis' ack-acks will be doin' the same to Aidan as we are to the Luftwaffe,' Gwen said, her feet appearing over the edge of her bed.

Ellie nodded. 'I want him to be happy, and he is; I just wish he could have been happy stayin' on the farm. It's not as if he had to join up.'

Gwen slid off her bed and sat beside Ellie. 'We're always being told we're trained much better than their lot, so they're not as good as us, and let's face it, we're not that great. From what you've told me he's pretty savvy, so he'll know to fly high until the last minute, but we'll both keep our fingers crossed, just for good measure.' She groaned. 'Look out, here comes trouble.'

Evie and Tilly might not have been in the same section as Gwen and Ellie, but they did share the same barracks, and unfortunately for the girls their bunks were almost directly opposite their own. So now, when Evie sauntered casually across to join them, Ellie and Gwen exchanged wearied glances.

'Did I hear you right a moment ago? Did you say you had a pal who was going to become a pilot?'

Ellie nodded. 'What of it?' she said, expecting the other girl to say something sarcastic in reply, and was surprised when Evie continued to speak in a friendly manner.

'I think it's fabulous that you know someone in the RAF. You must be awfully proud; I know I would be.' She looked up from her fingernail inspection. 'Know him well, do you?'

Ellie shrugged. 'Relatively. I worked on his father's farm ...' she began, but fell silent when she remembered whom she was talking to. 'What's it to you, and why?'

Evie's eyes shone with interest. 'A landowner? Is it a big farm? I had no idea you liked animals; in fact, I thought someone told me you lived in the courts.' She shot an accusing glance in Tilly's direction before adding hastily, 'Not that there's anything wrong with that, of course.'

165

'I did use to live in the courts, but then I moved in with Aidan and—'

'Moved in?' Evie said. She sounded astonished. 'How very ... modern of you.'

Ellie scowled defensively. 'Not like that! I lived with the family whilst I helped out on the farm.'

Gwen shook her head. 'That just goes to show how your mind works, Evie Maddox. Not everyone would assume Ellie and Aidan were an item. In fact, they're more like brother and sister, so you can keep your filthy thoughts to yourself.'

'Oh, I am sorry,' said Evie, but Ellie had seen the glint in the other girl's eye and knew she had been delighted to hear that Ellie and Aidan were not courting. Evie tentatively patted Ellie's arm in what she obviously perceived to be a friendly manner. 'Tell you what, to show there's no hard feelings, how about you introduce me to your pilot friend? I've always been fascinated by the RAF and love anything to do with flying. I could buy you both a drink to say sorry properly.'

'Blimey, what would she want to go and do that to him for?' Gwen choked in disbelief. 'It'd be like feedin' Christians to the lions.'

There was a shriek of laughter from across the room. 'Shut your cakehole, Lizzie Tunstall,' Evie snapped, her eyes narrowing as she addressed Gwen. 'I know you think I'm a bit of a one when it comes to the fellers, but I can assure you you've got it all wrong. I just have a lot of male friends.' She stamped her foot angrily as yet another shriek echoed across the hut. 'Shut up, Lizzie.' Standing up, she clicked her fingers impatiently towards Tilly, who handed her her wash kit. 'Come on, Tilly, before I say summat I'll regret.'

The door swung shut behind the two girls and the room fell silent, apart from the occasional muffled snort from Lizzie. Ellie turned wide eyes to Gwen. 'How stupid does she think I am? As if I'd ever introduce her to anyone that I cared about!'

Gwen eyed Ellie inquisitively. 'Do you think Aidan would be interested in her?'

Ellie shook her head. 'Wouldn't matter if he was. He spends most of the day covered in manure from tending the animals and he has an old leg injury which he's a bit self-conscious about 'cos he walks a bit funny. Not her type at all. I can't see her fallin' for someone who looks like Worzel Gummidge with a limp, no matter how many stripes – or wings – they had, can you?' Ellie felt a hot flush rush to her cheeks at the thought of Evie fawning over Aidan.

Gwen shrugged. 'I think Evie'd go after just about any feller if it meant she got a bit of attention, especially when she thinks he's a pilot with a bit of land, so who knows? Mebbe a young feller what walks a bit funny isn't out of the question. Is he handsome?'

Ellie gazed at the brass buttons on her uniform jacket as she sought an answer. 'Not as handsome as his cousin Connor; he's the real looker. There is some resemblance, but most of Aidan is hidden beneath his scraggy beard. He's quite scruffy compared to Connor.'

Gwen smiled. 'Doesn't sound like her type at all, then. She likes 'em clean cut and well presented; she's not bothered about much else as long as they look decent.'

167

Ellie felt a wave of relief wash over her. She knew it was silly to be concerned that Aidan and Evie might get together: they weren't even in the same part of the country, let alone the same service, so the likelihood of their ever meeting was remote to say the least. Nevertheless, before she could stop it, a picture of Evie arm in arm with Aidan entered her mind. Evie was smiling, her eyes fixed on his mouth as she drew closer to him. Ellie shuddered, a sense of foreboding coming over her as she mentally compared herself to the other girl. Evie was very attractive, with sleek platinum curls that always looked pretty even on the windiest of days, or after a night's sleep. She had bright blue eyes and an enchanting smile, and as for her figure ... Ellie grimaced. When she and Arla had first tried their uniforms on she had admired Arla, whose cinched waist gave her an hourglass figure, but thought she herself resembled a runner bean in the green uniform. Evie was more like Arla, and Ellie found it hard to believe that Aidan, given the opportunity – and the full dazzling smile of a flirtatious Evie – would deny himself the chance to date someone so stunning. She looked across to Evie's empty bunk. There was only one way of ensuring the two never got together and that was to make sure they never met in the first place.

Connor spoke hurriedly into the receiver. 'Haven't got much time before I've got to be back in class, but I thought I'd let you know that they've selected me to be a gunner on a heavy bomber.'

'That's fantastic news, coz. Any idea where you'll be going?'

'Probably Lincoln way,' said Connor. 'That's what they reckon anyway, although it's still too early to say, but as soon as I'm qualified I'm going to see if I can wangle things so I can end up in your crew.'

Aidan laughed. 'Nice idea, but you'll be qualified before me, so you'll probably be terrifying some other poor soul!'

'Oi! Be nice to your favourite cousin.' Connor chuckled. 'Just think, the two Murray men, both in air force blue ... the girls won't stand a chance.'

'I'd've thought a good-looking fellow like you would've been snapped up ages ago,' said Aidan. 'You telling me you're still on the market?'

'Too many girls and not enough time,' said Connor. 'Besides, I'm waiting till I get my AG's wing. Might get myself a bit of a looker with that on my chest.'

Aidan rolled his eyes. 'I can see you're going to get me into all sorts of trouble if we end up on the same bomber.'

'I'll try my best ...' Connor began, only to be interrupted by someone calling his name in the background. 'Coming now,' he yelled. 'I've got to go, coz, but I'll give you a bell in a week or so.'

Aidan said goodbye then heard the click of Connor's receiver. He shook his head, a broad grin spreading across his face. He'll be like a dog with two tails if he gets to be a member of my aircrew, he thought cheerfully. God help us all.

*

169

Gwen held up the mirror so Ellie could examine her reflection. It seemed unfair that whilst she thought she needed all the help she could get to look even remotely attractive, which as she understood it was the sole purpose of make-up, even the smallest amount of the stuff seemed to make her look far worse. The slightest dab of mascara made her lashes clump together, giving a thick, heavy feel which made her rub her eyes so that the end result looked as though she had tried to smear the stuff on. Lipstick was a no–no, unless it was the faintest whisper, so, as Ellie quite rightly said, it was hardly worth the bother. Gwen on the other hand looked remarkable with the faintest touch of mascara, which set her doe-like eyes off a treat. A dab of rouge to her cheeks and lips, along with her raven hair, resulted in a resemblance to Snow White.

'Have you ever been to the circus, Gwen?' said Ellie as she turned her head from side to side so that she might see her full reflection.

Gwen shook her head. 'Waste of money, my uncle reckons. Why?'

Ellie screwed her lips up. 'You must have seen what a clown looks like?'

Gwen stopped holding the mirror up. 'For the umpteenth time, you do not look like a clown, Ellie Lancton, so stop saying you do.'

The girls were getting ready for their last night in Weybourne. The NAAFI was holding one of its many dances, and they intended to treat it as a sort of leaving party.

Before joining the ATS Ellie had never danced a single step, but now, nearly three months in, she could hold her own, even when it came to the more difficult ones such as the foxtrot. Dances were always a good excuse to get off camp for a bit, the only drawback being that the girls still had to wear the khaki uniform, with the hated brogues, and the cap that hid any attempt at a hairstyle. It was all right for the likes of Evie, Ellie thought bitterly, whose waspish waist was accentuated by a belted uniform, but for those such as Ellie it meant sitting around whilst the men chose girls in pretty frocks, with high heels and loose hair.

Now, she stood in front of her friend whilst Gwen straightened her cap and tie for her. 'I must say, I won't miss goin' through the woods to get to the village. I never knew tree roots could be so treacherous, especially in the dark.'

Gwen nodded. 'Stubbing toes on upturned roots does not a happy dancer make.' She and Ellie were looking forward to the evening. Tonight was not just their last night in Weybourne, it also heralded the end of their training, and everyone was in good humour, Everyone except Evie, that was.

Shuffling up the queue for tea and biscuits in the NAAFI, Gwen nodded in Evie's direction. 'I reckon she was hopin' to've got married and gone off to some cushy office job by now, I don't think she ever intended to go to a real gun site. Probably explains why she's got a bottom lip you could trip over, which reminds me – have you heard off that mate of yours, your bezzie, the one who was moved to Cornwall?'

Ellie looked surprised. 'You mean Arla? Whatever made you think of her?'

171

'Didn't Evie say summat about her wanting to marry an officer, so that she could get out of the courts? I just wondered if she'd had better luck than Evie.'

Ellie shook her head hastily. 'I hope you don't think Arla's like Evie, 'cos she's not. She might dream about meeting and marrying an officer, but only in the way that most girls dream of marrying their Prince Charming. She wouldn't go out of her way to bag one; she's not like that.'

'Sorry. I've obviously got hold of the wrong end of the stick. I should have known you wouldn't be friends with anyone like Evie. But I think you should have told Evie about your Aidan's gammy leg – that would have put her off.'

'I never said his leg was gammy,' Ellie said, clearly annoyed at the description.

Gwen placed an apologetic hand on Ellie's arm. 'Sorry. I'm makin' a right pig's ear out of this, aren't I? Let's start again. Has Arla told you where she's goin' yet?'

'Somewhere near Lincoln; she did tell me the name of the place but I've forgotten. It wouldn't help even if I remembered' cos I haven't got a clue where Lincoln is, save that it's miles away from Liverpool. Oh, I couldn't believe it when I heard we were being posted back to Liverpool. It'll be like going home.'

Her cheeks were still warm from Gwen's comment. I shouldn't have snapped at her, she thought guiltily. Especially because she's right: Evie *would* find Aidan's lameness off-putting. She turned apologetically to Gwen. 'Sorry for snapping at you just now. I shouldn't have done it.'

'Don't worry yourself, cariad. I think we're all a bit nervy about leavin' the safety of the trainin' ground and strikin' out for real. I know I wish we could have just one more week, I'd enjoy that.'

Ellie giggled. 'I don't think you're meant to enjoy yourself in the army.'

It was much later on that evening when the two girls returned to their hut for the final time. Settling into her bed, Ellie cast an eye around the room. She would miss Weybourne. It had been the final stage in her transformation, not only from trainee to operator, but also from girl to woman. She had left Springdale Farm in order to make her way in the world and achieve independence, and she had done it. Tomorrow would be the start of her new life as Ellie Lancton, gun site operator, dependent only on the others in her section to fight off the enemy. She sighed happily as she brought the blankets up around her cheeks. Goodbye, little Ellie, she thought to herself. You've done a grand job.

Chapter Seven

Standing on the parade ground, Ellie was grateful for the peaked cap which prevented the bright sunlight from blinding her. It was their final day and they would soon be heading for Liverpool. Ellie breathed in happily, the scent of the morning dew mixed with fresh grass cuttings filling her lungs. She loved this time of day. None of the big army vehicles had started belching their smelly exhaust fumes and the only noise to be heard was the voice of their sergeant as he barked out his orders.

Ellie found herself growing impatient as she waited for the sergeant to command the troops to fall out, and gazed across the yard to where D Section, including Evie and Tilly, were also standing at ease. It was just her luck, Ellie thought bitterly, that Sections B and D were to travel together to a gun site just outside the city. She had hoped that Evie would be moved to a different part of the country, and felt it was typical of the army, who had chosen to split her and Arla up, to lumber her with Evie.

Earlier that morning the two sections had gone to their final briefing. 'You'll be in Liverpool until the army see fit to move you elsewhere. As per your training, you will work, eat, sleep and live together, only this time when the alarm goes up, it will not be an exercise.' The commanding officer strode up and down the lines of desks in the classroom. 'I have confidence in every single one of you to carry out the job that you have been trained to do. So have faith in yourselves, and remember, you've been taught by the best in the land.' He paused momentarily, eyeing them with an air of pride. 'Good luck, everyone.'

Now, standing on the tarmac, Ellie heard the sergeant command the troops to fall out. She trotted over to Gwen. 'That's it! We're off to Liverpool!' She breathed out happily. 'I can't wait to get going. It seems like we've spent an eternity training. It's going to be good to get stuck in.' She linked arms with Gwen. 'You got everything ready for the off?'

Gwen nodded. 'Remind me to do summat about my locket when we go into the city, won't you? When I packed it earlier the damned thing opened without my noticing and me mam's photo fell on the floor. It was sheer luck that I saw it.'

Ellie followed her into the hut that had been their home for the past four weeks, where their kitbags stood waiting for collection. 'Will do,' she said. Counting to three, she heaved the sausage-shaped bag on to her shoulders before promptly dropping it to the floor. 'Blimey, how the fellers manage to carry these things on one shoulder I'll never know.' Leaning down, she picked the bag up, and cradled it between her arms. 'Ready?'

Gwen braced herself as she swung her own bag up on to her shoulder, then tottered precariously backwards into the bunk bed, which scraped noisily across the wooden floor. Chuckling, Ellie shook her head. 'I reckon they should get us one of them golf trolleys like what old Mr Burgess used to talk about. It'd make life a lot easier.'

'Ha! Since when've the army liked to make life easy for us? You'll be suggestin' proper mattresses next, and nice soft blankets instead of them awful itchy ones,' Gwen said. She took a final glance around the empty hut. 'Can't see that we've left anything behind. Let's go.'

As they approached the waiting trucks, Gwen turned hopefully to Ellie. 'Seeing as how we're goin' to be manning a real gun site, d'you reckon they really might give us proper mattresses and stuff? Perhaps they only use rubbish bedding for trainees. After all, how can they expect trained army personnel to get a good night's sleep on those awful things?'

Gunner Jones, who was responsible for driving the troops to their new destination, winked at Gwen. 'You could allus come an' snuggle up to me in my bed if you like. I'd make you forget all about—' He made a sharp grunting noise as Gwen's elbow connected with his ribs. 'Crikey, them's sharp elbows you got there! I were only 'avin' a laugh, Miss Crotchety,' he said, rubbing his ribs.

Gwen scowled at him. 'I am not crotchety, I just don't like improper suggestions. Some girls might be that way inclined' – she glanced meaningfully at Evie – 'but I'm not one of them.'

'When you've quite finished …' Ellie puffed as she struggled to hold her kitbag up to Gunner Jones.

He nodded absentmindedly. Grasping the bag in one hand, he swung it into the back with ease, muttering under his breath, 'Last time I offer to keep someone warm of a night.'

'Good,' said Gwen, who had sharper hearing than most.

When the last of the girls had climbed on board, Jonesy closed the tailgate then hopped into the driver's seat. Hearing the engine roar into life, the girls started to chat excitedly about their new destination.

'Lancton's from Liverpool, so if you want to know what's what and the best places to visit, she's the one to ask,' Gwen informed their fellow travellers.

Evie frowned her annoyance. 'Excuse me, but I'm from Liverpool too. Not originally, of course, but I've lived there a few years now, and if you want to know the better places to visit then I'm the one to come to.' She glanced sidelong at Ellie. 'Of course, if you're only interested in the more common parts of the city then she's your girl.'

Sensing the atmosphere, Gwen broke the silence. 'I've an idea. Why don't we all have a girls' night out? We could go dancing, or to the cinema, or … or …' She looked encouragingly at Ellie. 'What is there to do in Liverpool?'

Ellie, grateful for the chance to prove herself, leaned forward. 'Depends what you want, but Liverpool has it all, from Paddy's Market, where you can buy every-thing from cheap clothing and furniture, to Blacklers, where you could break the bank just by lookin' at all the beautiful, expensive jewellery. There are plenty of cinemas, theatres and dance halls as well as museums, cafés … You name it, we've got it, and of course being born in Liverpool I know all the best places to go.'

Evie gave a snort of contempt. 'As if the likes of you could afford to shop in places like Blacklers, and I bet you've never been to the theatre. You make it sound as though you lived the high life before you joined the ATS whereas we all know you came from the courts.' She shook her head. 'You seem to think you're some kind of Cinderella who joined the ATS to find your Prince Charming, but you're a bit old for fairy tales, I'm afraid.'

'That's a bit rich comin' from you,' Gwen retorted.

'What do you mean by that? I didn't grow up in the courts.'

'Mebbe not, but you're always on the hunt for a pot of gold with a man attached to it,' said Gwen.

One of the girls from deeper in the truck leaned forward. 'C'mon, girls, let's play nicely. I think Liverpool sounds great and I can't wait to have a good look round.'

Delilah Crompton, another girl from Ellie's section, clapped her hands together eagerly. 'I'm from Chester, which isn't far from Liverpool. It's easy to get to by train. I've been to Blacklers, and she's right: it's huge, and the stuff they've got in there is amazing. We've landed on our feet with this posting. I was worried we were goin' to get sent to somewhere on the east coast to defend the airfields, stuck out in the middle of nowhere without a shop or a cinema in sight … I can't believe we're lucky enough to be going to Liverpool.' She jiggled excitedly in her seat. 'I'll be able to go home and see my family.'

The rest of the journey passed pleasantly as the girls planned a shopping trip to the market in Great Charlotte Street.

'Posh shops are all very well,' Delilah had informed a scowling Evie, 'but we're in the army. None of us have that kind of money.' She had raised a single eyebrow. 'Not even you, if I'm any judge.'

Evie's cheeks had flushed red, but instead of speaking out to the contrary she narrowed her eyes and looked out of the back of the truck.

With Evie out of the conversation, Ellie continued. 'You need a whole evening for the cinema. They always show plenty of adverts before the newsreel, and a short film before the main feature. Then there's the cinema café; their fish and chips are legendary.'

'You couldn't afford an evening at the cinema,' 'Evie interjected,' 'let alone fish and chips, so how do you know what it's like?'

'If you know the right people you don't have to pay to go in,' Ellie began, but Evie interrupted once more.

'You mean you snuck in round the back with the rest of the rats.'

Ellie leaned forward in her seat. 'Arla's uncle works as a caretaker at the cinema, and he'd let us in for nowt as long as we agreed to help him tidy up afterwards. As an extra treat he'd take us for a chip supper, and sometimes, if there was any left over, the owner would chuck the fish in for free. So don't go tryin' to suggest that I don't pay my way, Evie Maddox, 'cos I do.'

Delilah shot Evie a withering glance. 'Take no notice, Ellie. Some people are always out to spoil sport. My brother and his mates used to sneak in round the back all the time. Lots of kids do.'

'Sneaking in sounds fun, but I don't think we'd get away with it, not in our uniforms,' said one of the girls.

Ellie smiled. Despite her attempts Evie hadn't managed to spoil the atmosphere. When they pulled up outside the gate to their new barracks, the guard on duty smiled curiously at the happy troop, all laughter and wide smiles.

'Blimey, where've you lot come from ... the pub?' he said as he closed the gate behind them.

'Nope, but that's where they're going, as soon as they get some time off,' Jonesy said as he made his way to the rear of the truck. 'Think they're coming to a holiday camp this lot do. You should've 'eard 'em on the way here. They've got big plans for the city, especially these two.' He waved a finger in the direction of Gwen and Ellie. 'You mark my words, you wanna keep a close eye on them. Don't take no nonsense, and make sure they don't come sneakin' back in after time.'

The guard chuckled. 'They wouldn't be the first, but I'll tell you summat for nowt; the sergeant – 'is name's Barton – is a stickler for the rules and he won't take no messin' about, norreven if your granny's died – and you're only allowed two of them, so think twice if you don't want to end up doin' fatigues for the whole time you're here.'

Jumping down from the back of the truck, Ellie laughed. 'Don't listen to Jonesy; he's pullin' your leg. But thanks for the heads-up on Barton. It's always good to know what's what when you reach a new camp. Talkin' of which, where are we headed?'

With a jerk of his head the guard indicated an approaching NCO. 'That's Corporal Caldecott, and if you think Barton's bad, she's worse.'

He stopped talking as Jonesy nudged him sharply in the ribs. 'Watch out ...'

The corporal drew to a halt in front of them. 'Section, 'shun!' she barked, her tone sharp.

Several kitbags dropped to the floor as they stood to attention. The guard silently withdrew into his box, whilst Jonesy surreptitiously took his place back behind the wheel of the truck. Like rain falling on a blackboard, the corporal's steely expression wiped the frivolity and mirth from the troops that stood before her. She was a slim woman, with dark hair all but hidden beneath her cap. Ellie looked hard at the corporal and was surprised to see a streak of silver hair amongst the black, peeking out from just below the crown of her cap. She examined the corporal's face. The other woman could not have been more than her mid-twenties, yet there was something about her which made her seem far older. Her eyes travelled along the ranks in a critical fashion and Ellie glanced sidelong at the guard sitting in his box. He was eyeing them sympathetically.

A large man in sergeant's uniform approached the assembled troop and stood alongside the corporal. 'So ... you're the Weybourne lot.' His eyes scanned the men and women before him, resting momentarily on Evie. 'I recognise some of you.' He turned to the corporal. 'Corporal Caldecott here will see to the women and the rest of you will come with me.'

Corporal Caldecott held up a clipboard and ordered Section B and Section D to get into line before marching them off across the camp, pointing out the parade ground, the NAAFI, the officers' mess and the ablutions as she went.

Standing outside the barracks, she turned to face them. 'Tomorrow morning reveille will be at six a.m. You have the rest of the day to get yourselves organised with any supplies you should need and so on before reporting for duty at eight p.m. You will then be taken to your first gun site, where you will remain for the next twelve hours. Any questions?'

Ellie waited for a response from one of her fellow gunners, and was relieved when none came.

'Fall out.' The corporal turned on her heel and marched off in the direction of the mess.

Gwen laid a hand on Ellie's arm and pulled her aside from the others. She lowered her voice to a whisper. 'That Barton chap is the one we did our initial training with. There was rumours about him and Evie; I don't know whether they were true or not, but he's married.'

Ellie raised her brow. 'But he's ... old. Well, compared to us he is. What is he, d'you reckon? Forty?' She grimaced. 'How could she? It'd be like kissin' your dad.'

Gwen nodded. 'They reckon that's why he was moved – y'know, because of all the rumours. I don't know whether his wife ever found out, or if there was anything to find out if it comes to that, but you know what they say: there's no smoke ...'

Entering the hut, Ellie eyed Evie, who was sitting on one of the beds, her head bent in whispered conversation with Tilly. The rest of the girls were talking about their new corporal. 'Do you reckon she ever cracks a smile? Even the fellers are scared of her.'

Delilah wrinkled her nose. 'There we were makin' plans to paint the town red, and what happens? We're landed with two of the most miserable so-and-sos in the army! Looks like we've had it easy up till now, girls.'

Evie broke away from her conversation with Tilly and smiled smugly at Delilah. 'That may be the case for you, but as they say, it's not what you know, it's who you know, and Sergeant Barton gave me my initial training.' She glared at two girls who appeared to be suffering from a sudden outburst of coughs and muffled laughter. 'You'll be laughin' on the other side of your face when I'm trippin' the light fantastic whilst you're peelin' spuds,' she snapped.

Gwen nudged Ellie. 'See?' she whispered. 'It's not just me that reckons there were summat fishy goin' on.'

Nodding, Ellie jerked her head in the direction of the door. 'C'mon, let's go for a nosy round the camp. I don't think I can stand seein' that smug smile on her face for much longer.' If Evie could kiss a man like Barton then Aidan would be fair game, she thought miserably.

Stepping out into the dusky evening, the girls decided to delay their plans for a look around camp until the next day. 'It's too dim to see properly. I reckon we visit the NAAFI and see what the gossip is,' Ellie suggested.

Ellie chuckled to herself. The NAAFI was identical to the one in Weybourne: same tables, same chairs, and probably the same type of food. She approached the girl who was on duty behind the counter. 'Two cups of tea, please, and ... what's left?'

The girl looked down at a trays in front of her. 'I've got mash and sausages ...' she peered into a tray to the side, 'and probably enough gravy for the two of you if you want it.'

Ellie and Gwen nodded their approval, and the cook dutifully doled the food on to two plates. 'You're new, ain't you? Do you know who your corporal is?'

'Caldecott,' Ellie said grimly.

The cook smiled sympathetically. 'She's not a bad stick, not really.'

Gwen looked hopefully at the cook. 'Some of the girls reckon that our escapades around Liverpool are goin' to be over before they even begin with her in charge. What do you think?'

Ellie cut in before the cook could answer. 'She can't stop us doin' what we want in our free time, not as long as we do our jobs properly and don't go makin' trouble for ourselves.'

The girl behind the counter nodded at Gwen. 'Your friend's right, and if I'm honest I don't think Caldecott wants to stop anyone havin' fun. She's a lot on her mind, and just gets a bit crotchety at times.' She glanced quizzically at them. 'Has anyone told you what happened?'

Ellie and Gwen exchanged glances. Judging by the tone of her voice, whatever it was, it did not sound good. Ellie shook her head. 'No, what?'

Glancing at the clock, the cook wiped her hands on her apron. 'Go and sit down and I'll bring your teas over … it was tea, wasn't it? Only I've finished me shift, so I may as well join you for a bit.'

Ellie and Gwen took a seat at the table nearest the counter and waited for the girl to join them. 'I'm Ann,' she said, placing three mugs of tea down on the table in front of them.

'I'm Ellie and this is Gwen,' said Ellie, and shuffled expectantly in her seat, eager for some kind of explanation. 'So? What's the goss?'

Taking a deep breath, Ann pulled a face. 'No one knows exactly what happened, 'cos none of us was there at the time, but you know what it's like in the army, there's no such thing as a secret, and word soon got round. Apparently her and her feller had a right old ding-dong. I don't know the ins and outs of the argument, but it was a real belter; so bad, in fact,' glancing around her, the cook leaned forward and lowered her voice to a whisper, 'that her kid took off, never to be heard from again. The army've done their best, but it was like tryin' to find a needle in a haystack.' She sat back. 'That's why she's so quick to snap. She's got enough on her plate wi'out a bunch of newcomers givin' her grief.'

Gwen nodded slowly. 'Poor Caldecott. No wonder she's short-tempered. You said it was like lookin' for a needle in a haystack?'

Ann nodded ruefully. 'It happened not long after the war started, so her kid would've been mixed up with hundreds, even thousands, of evacuees, all heading off in different directions, all starting new lives.'

'Surely someone somewhere must realise they've got an extra child?' Ellie said incredulously.

'If they have no one's said owt, an' it's been more'n a year now. That's why some folk reckon summat bad's happened.'

Ellie looked shocked. 'Like what?'

Ann shrugged. 'Who knows? Mebbe ran out into the street and got run over, or ran off to sea ...'

Ellie shook her head sadly. If anyone knew what it was like to be separated from their mother she did. 'That poor kid must be terrified. Some men can be pure evil. Fancy makin' your own child so miserable they'd rather be alone on the streets than safe at home with their mam.'

Gwen nodded thoughtfully. 'We'll have a word with the girls, make sure they don't go pokin' the wasps' nest.'

Ann swilled the tea around her cheeks before swallowing. 'Good. I can't imagine what Caldecott must be goin' through, but it must be heartbreaking.' She sniffed loudly as she placed her mug down on the table. 'Anyway, from what I hear you lot are on lates tomorrow, which may seem a bit harsh for your first posting, but at least it gives you a whole day to relax and find your way around.' Pushing her chair back, she picked up her mug and smiled at them. 'See you in the mornin'.'

Ellie nodded, her mouth full of mashed potato and sausage, and raised a thumb.

With Ann gone, Gwen said seriously, 'Blimey, what Delilah said about us havin' it easy before we got here was bang on the money! Poor old Caldecott. We should get back to the barracks and let the others know.'

'Did Ann say whether it was a boy or a girl what'd gone missing?'

'I don't think she knew, but what does it matter?'

Ellie shrugged. 'I suppose I've always thought of boys as being tougher than girls; able to look after themselves more. She didn't say how old the child was either, did she?'

Gwen shook her head. 'You just have to hope that someone like my aunt and uncle have found them and taken them in. At least that way they'll be safe.'

Back in the hut, Ellie and Gwen gathered the girls together and explained the tragic circumstances surrounding their new corporal. 'So you see,' Ellie concluded, 'she's had a rare time of it, and I think we should make allowances if she gets bad-tempered sometimes.'

There was a murmur of agreement, broken by a small, squat girl who was twisting her fingers round each other in an awkward fashion. 'I'm bound to do summat wrong, I always do. I wish we'd got that feller, that ... what was his name again?'

'Barton,' said Gwen, her voice muffled as she pulled her pyjamas over her head before swinging herself on to the bunk above Ellie's. 'And believe me you don't. He was in charge of us durin' initial trainin' and he's like a bear with a sore head at the best of times. Unless your name's Evie, of course. Then it's a different matter entirely.'

'Why, what's so special about her?'

Gwen opened her mouth to speak, but Ellie cut her off. 'Let's not say anything we can't take back. We don't want to be accused of starting any rumours.'

Once again Gwen opened her mouth, but before she could say anything the small squat girl pointed a comprehending finger at Ellie. 'Or maybe ...' she glanced around the assembled group of women, 'maybe they had a bit of a fling.' There was a choking sound as the two girls who had laughed before tried to keep their faces straight.

Gwen leaned over the side of her bunk, a self-satisfied smile forming on her lips as she looked at Ellie. 'And you were worried I might start a rumour,'she hissed.

Feeling the conversation was running away from her, Ellie held up a hand. 'That's not what I meant ... I never suggested ... he's a married man, so mind what you say. No one wants to spread a rumour which isn't true.'

'It's those bloomin' long lashes of hers,' the short girl muttered, ignoring her. 'I wish I 'ad lashes like that; I'd use 'em for all sorts. They work like magic on the fellers.'

Ellie gave up. Rumours were bound to spread no matter what she said or did. Scrambling into her own pyjamas, she smiled resignedly up at Gwen. 'I tried.'

Gwen giggled. 'Don't blame yourself for not stoppin' the gossip; There's people in here what worked Evie out in two minutes. Besides, a few of these girls did their initial trainin' with her, same as me, so you're goin' against the tide, so to speak.'

The door to the Nissen hut opened and there was a hushed silence as Evie and Tilly walked in. Evie stopped in her tracks and surveyed the room with a suspicious eye, then huffed irritably to herself as she headed for her bed. The girls, who until Evie's arrival had been happy to stand about gossiping, wandered off in dribs and drabs.

Ellie brought her blankets up around her ears and peeped at Tilly through her lashes. The girl was eyeing the occupants of the room with interest. She knows, Ellie thought, that we were talking about them before they came in and that's why it went so quiet. I do hope she doesn't think we were gossiping about her. It occurred to her that Tilly and Evie had not been party to the information regarding Caldecott. Sitting up on one elbow, she waited until she caught Tilly's eye and beckoned the other girl over.

Tilly looked back towards Evie before tiptoeing across to Ellie's bed. 'What's up?' she asked.

When Ellie had finished her explanation, she nodded towards Evie. 'Make sure you tell her, won't you? Not that I give two hoots about Evie gettin' into trouble, but I don't want the rest of us to suffer 'cos of her.'

Glancing over her shoulder, Tilly nodded. 'Will do.' She gave Ellie a half-smile. 'And thanks for lettin' me know. You didn't have to, and I would have understood if you had decided not to, but I do appreciate it.' She looked back at Evie before continuing, 'As I said before, she's not all bad, not when you get to know her. You just have to be patient.'

'Tilly! Are you turning in or what?' Evie said, her voice sharp.

Tilly grinned at Ellie. 'Very, *very* patient.'

Ellie watched as Tilly hushed her friend before speaking earnestly. Their conversation at an end, Tilly nodded to Ellie before climbing into the bunk above Evie's.

Pulling the blanket up once more, Ellie nodded to herself. She had been right about Tilly: the other girl wasn't nearly as bad as her friend. If I can get Tilly on side, then maybe, just maybe, we can persuade Evie to stop being so horrid to everyone. With this encouraging thought Ellie closed her eyes and fell to sleep.

Lying in her bunk, Gwen tried to sleep, but she could not shake Caldecott and the missing youngster from her thoughts. She tried to imagine what it must be like to know that you had a child out there somewhere, alone and scared. It was easier than she thought; in truth, she had often supposed it was how her own mother must have felt when she had given Gwen up. She had often wondered whether she had come back to look for her, maybe hidden behind the hedge opposite the church to see if she could catch a glimpse of the child she had once held as her own. It must be awful, Gwen supposed, not to know whether your own flesh and blood was safe and well, dead or alive. She screwed up her eyes in an effort to force herself to sleep, but the thought of a mother without her child, not knowing whether he or she was being looked after properly, or was involved in the war, would not leave her. Her eyes snapped open. What if her own mother was in the services? She could be in the WAAF, or the ATS for that matter. But how would Gwen know? She had no name to go by, just some fuzzy old picture in a broken locket.

Her heart began to pound and a solitary tear trickled down the side of her nose. My mother could be in this very room and I wouldn't know it. Another, more unpleasant thought crossed her mind. What if she was already dead? The Luftwaffe had bombed nearly every major city in the country from London to Cardiff, and if there was one thing she did know about her mother it was that she had not been local to the Rhos.

Gwen thumped her pillow with her fist in order to plump it up. It did no good to ponder the whys and wherefores; all it did was bring pain and misery. She should know: as a small child, she had spent many a night crying herself to sleep as she turned different scenarios over in her mind. She glanced towards the top of the hut where the corporal's bed was still empty. I hope my mother didn't suffer the same way as Caldecott. I hope she's alive and well and happy, and I'm sure she must feel the same about me. After all, she would never have chosen to leave me at a church if she didn't care.

Turning over, she wiped a tear from her cheek. She could not get angry with her mother. If she had to point a finger of blame it would be firmly directed at her father, whoever he might be, she thought bitterly. The proof was in the pudding when it came to the male of the species. Ellie's father had left her mother, Caldecott's child had run off because of the corporal's feller, and she would bet a pound to a penny that her own mother was in the same boat as the other two. After all, the photo in the locket was of a woman, and even though there was space on the other side there was no picture of a man. Besides, if her father had been involved her mother wouldn't have had to take such drastic measures to ensure her child's safety. A small smile formed on Gwen's lips. *My mam was like Ellie's, because whilst she could've put me in an orphanage she chose the church, because that's where I was most likely to end up with honest, loving, law-abiding parents.* She crossed her fingers under the sheets. *I hope Caldecott's child knows how much their mam loves them, knows that she spends every minute worryin' as to where they are, who they're with and what they're up to.* She nodded decidedly. With such deep love there comes a strong bond, and she felt sure it would pull the Caldecotts together like an invisible string, so they could be together, as a mother and child should.

Sitting on his bed, Aidan stared at the letters he had spread out on his mattress. There were eight bundles in total and five of them were from his parents. His mother wrote every day; she said it was to keep him up to date with all the happenings on the farm, but Aidan knew it was her way of filling the void he had left when he joined the RAF. He loved her for it, and even though each epistle was more or less the same as the last he still looked forward to reading them. The other three were split evenly between Connor, Connor's parents and Ellie. Aidan picked up the latest letter from Ellie and stared blankly at the page. He had read it four or five times, so practically knew it word for word. She was going to be based back in Liverpool: with the censor in mind she hadn't written those words, of course, but simply stated, *You'll never guess what, I'm going home! Don't know how long I'll be there, but it'll be grand to show the girls around.*

The news had come as a mixed blessing. Liverpool was a long way from Scarborough, so there would be no casual visits, but if he could get a forty-eight, or maybe longer, and Ellie could do the same, then the pair of them could go to his parents' farm and spend some time together. He drew a deep breath before slowly releasing it. The thought of spending time alone with Ellie on the farm was perfect, but it would come with drawbacks, the biggest of which would be saying goodbye. He loved his pilot training, and even though it would be a while before he got his wings he appreciated the time and effort Captain Mathias had given him since they met at the recruiting office. Aidan gazed out of the small, deep, stone-set window as he let the memories wash over him.

Upon receiving his letter he had gone straight to the captain, who had explained his reason for taking Aidan on. 'I've a son, Murray. His name's Andrew, and when he was a nipper he contracted the polio virus. It turned out to be a bad one, and for a while it looked as though we might lose him. Thank God, he pulled through, but it left him with muscles so weak and bones so fragile the doctors feared he might never walk again.' He stopped pacing the room and stared Aidan square in the eye. 'The day you walked into that town hall and started demanding a place in the RAF you reminded me of Andrew. You're very alike, the two of you, both physically and mentally. You see, despite the doctors' predictions our Andrew insisted we should try, and after many gruelling months he was finally able to walk, although like yourself he needs help sometimes. He manages his condition well, so that most people wouldn't ever know there was anything wrong, and that's because of his attitude.' He smiled approvingly at Aidan. 'Something else you've got in common.' He sat down on the opposite side of the desk. 'And that's why I thought you deserved a chance. If we'd listened to the doctors Andrew would probably be in a wheelchair, but we never gave up on him, because he wouldn't let us.' He looked under the desk at Aidan's legs. 'We had a chap like you flying a few years back. All it took to get him straight was a special built-up shoe so that his legs were evenly matched. It might not look pretty, but under your trousers no one will ever know, except yourself of course. I want you to go to my doctor, who will check you're fit enough before passing you on to a chiropodist who'll measure you up and order a special shoe for you. Any questions?'

Aidan had left the captain's office feeling as though he could conquer the world. The man genuinely believed in him, and had set the wheels in motion to get him into the air. After that initial meeting the rest of his time to date had been a whirlwind of tests, both physical and mental, as well as examinations which were designed to pick off those unfit for aircrew.

Aidan himself had breezed through the process, and had become the protégé of Captain Mathias, who was determined to see him succeed. Aidan was grateful, he truly was, but the thought of meeting Ellie again on home ground was as appealing as that of flying. He looked down at the hated built-up shoe. It was ugly, with its thick sole and heel moulded into the upper; it was heavy, and reminded him of the shoes he'd seen worn by the monster in the posters advertising the Frankenstein film, yet without it he couldn't fly the plane properly. He imagined turning up to see Ellie for the first time whilst wearing it. Even though it was almost totally hidden under his trousers, the fact that he walked with barely a trace of a limp would in itself draw the attention of those who knew him well, and they would want to see why. He grimaced. He could not, would not, show Ellie the shoe. He heard his mother's scolding tones in his head. 'Pride comes before a fall, our Aidan,' she would say, but he didn't care. Anything was better than letting Ellie see that awful thing.

He looked at the walking cane that he had purchased on his way up to Scarborough. It was made from bamboo and it had a brass top. He and a few of the trainees had had a group photo taken with Aidan standing in the middle, his right hand in the pocket of his flying jacket, the left holding on to his cane. Everyone who saw the photograph remarked that he looked dapper or suave with the cane; he very much doubted anyone would say that about the dreaded shoe. He tapped his chin thoughtfully with his fingers. If he could meet Ellie on the farm, there would be no need for the shoe; in fact, it would just get filthy dirty and be more of a hindrance than a help. But what if she said no? What if she was so used to city life, going to dances, the cinema and such, that she didn't want to go back to Oxton?

He stared miserably down at the page before him, then cursed inwardly. This was all a pipe dream! For all he knew Ellie might have a boyfriend. He was sure she would not be short of suitors; she might even have plans for marriage and a life with someone who could offer a better future than a farmer. For no matter how he looked at it, he knew he was destined to take over Springdale. His parents would not be able to tend the animals or the land as the years went by, and besides, he loved farming as much as he loved flying, although for the time being flying was his priority.

Before the war, he had envisaged renovating the old barn in the back meadow. It wouldn't take much doing either, he considered: the roof needed some TLC and of course glass would need to be put in the windows, but it already had a water supply, and was not as far from the main road as Springdale itself. It would make a perfect home for newly-weds, intent on bringing up a family. He imagined himself and Ellie there, Ellie by the sink or, more likely, ankle deep in mud herding the cattle back to their meadow. He smiled; that was better! Ellie loved the animals and would want to get stuck in to the farming side of things, and he imagined their children would be the same.

He cast his eyes to the ceiling, and tried to shake the thoughts from his mind. It did no good to daydream about a future that was far from certain, certainly not when they were so many miles apart.

He picked up a piece of paper and looked around for his pencil. He would write back to Ellie and fill her in on his news, not that there was much, and suggest a meeting, but only if their paths crossed. Ellie might well be leading a new life, with a boyfriend whom Aidan knew nothing about, but he did not need to hear that news just yet, so he would leave things be and see what came along.

When reveille sounded, the girls from Ellie's barracks were up betimes and out on the yard before any other. Corporal Caldecott looked pleased, although slightly suspicious to see such an early, well-turned-out section standing in front of her.

Ellie tried to keep a smile from forming on her lips. She was very proud of her section, which had empathised with the corporal and deemed it their duty to make her life a little easier. Marching around the yard, Ellie noticed that other sections kept glancing in their direction, and by the time parade was over all eyes were on Section B, who ripped off a textbook salute in perfect unison. When the command came to fall out. Evie was one of the first to come over, her face full of suspicion.

'What's got into you lot? Bit eager, aren't you? Tilly told me about Caldecott's kid and if that's what's made you turn into a bunch of robots then I think you're overdoin' it a bit.'

Ellie grinned. 'Were we really that different from yesterday?'

Evie's brows rose towards her hairline. 'You know damned well you were.' She eyed her shrewdly. 'What're you after?'

Still grinning, Ellie shook her head. 'Just because we're enthusiastic doesn't mean to say we're after anything. Not everyone expects to gain something from their actions, you know. Personally speakin' I'm glad to be home. I am a Liverpool lass, after all.'

Evie sniffed primly. 'If you don't want to tell me then you don't have to, but it's not fair on the rest of us, you creepin' round her like that. She's goin' to expect it from all of us.'

Ellie's grin disappeared, to be replaced by an irritable frown. 'We are not creepin' around anyone! For heaven's sake, Evie, don't you feel sorry for her at all? Or is it really all about you?'

Evie shook her head reprovingly. 'Not at all, but you won't find me schmoozin' up to anyone for extra favours.'

Ellie fought the desire to say 'That's not what I've heard' and said instead, 'Is that all? Can I go now?'

Evie relaxed a little. 'Have you heard off that mate of yours, that pilot chap?'

'Not since telling him that we were going to be coming back to Liverpool. Why?'

'Just wondered. Do you reckon you'll meet up with him now you're fully trained?'

Ellie tried to keep the smile from her lips. She had never met anyone as eager as Evie to find herself a mate she considered worthy. She crossed her fingers behind her back. 'I promise that if I ever meet him and you're in the vicinity I'll introduce you, although I don't think he'll be your type.'

Evie furrowed her brow. 'Why not? I thought you said he was training to be a pilot?'

Ellie let a giggle escape. 'I did, and he is, but … oh, never mind. If I don't see you before, good luck for tonight.'

Still looking confused, Evie shrugged. She had no idea what the silly girl was on about or why she found the whole thing so amusing. She supposed it must be the lack of breeding. People from the slums weren't likely to be intelligent or come from good stock, unlike herself, but rather than get into a debate with someone who, in her opinion, was only half cooked she replied, 'The same to you,' before wandering off to join the rest of her section.

Gwen jogged up behind Ellie. 'Fancy a stroll round the camp? Kill a bit of time before we go on duty?' She nodded in the direction of the medical unit. 'I've never been prodded about so much in all my life as when I joined up. What about you?'

Ellie gave a mirthless laugh. 'We didn't have no money growing up, certainly not enough to spend on doctors and dentists and the like. The only time we ever got a doctor out was when me mam was really ill, and even though he did help a little at the beginning, in the end there was nothing he could do. I'm not sayin' they're no good, just that they're not miracle workers.'

Gwen looked shyly at Ellie. 'Your poor mam. You must miss her an awful lot.'

Ellie nodded. 'Being in the ATS helps, because they keep you busy so you don't have time to sit and dwell on things. She died around this time last year, so it's still quite raw, if you know what I mean.' She gave Gwen a determined smile. 'She always wanted me to complete my School Certificate, and to get a "proper job", not to spend my life cleaning and washing for other people the way she did. But things changed when she fell ill, and when she died I left school and took on all her work so I could pay the bills. I know being in

199

the ATS probably isn't what she had in mind for me, but I still think she'd be proud of me if she could see how I've coped since she's gone. First workin' on the farm, then joining the ATS.' She stopped speaking as Evie walked past.

Gwen rolled her eyes. 'That reminds me, what did she collar you for just now?'

'She's been asking about Aidan again. I told her I'd introduce them.' As the words left her lips, Ellie felt an unpleasant lurch in her stomach.

Gwen chuckled. 'Poor Aidan. Why would you do that to him?'

Ellie shrugged. 'I just wanted to stop her pestering. Besides, the likelihood of them ever being in the same vicinity is pretty remote. If I meet Aidan it'll probably be at his parents' farm or somewhere close to where he's stationed. You don't think I was wrong to make her think there was a chance of them meeting, do you?'

Gwen shook her head decidedly. 'Nope. It's her own fault for pestering all the time. Besides, she'll have found some poor bugger and tied him down before she's ever likely to set eyes on your Aidan, by which time it will be too late.'

Later, back in the Nissen hut, Ellie drew her diary out from underneath her pillow and turned to the correct date. Smoothing down the page with the tips of her fingers, she placed the nib of her pencil to the paper and started to write. *So here we are at last! Tonight is our first night on duty. I don't know how the others feel but I'm filled with mixed emotions. I'm a little daunted at the idea of working the night shift, but I suppose we've all got to start somewhere. Fingers crossed for a peaceful night.*

Despite what she had written in her diary, however, deep down she had visions of grandeur. How she and the rest of her section would make the history books, as the ones who saved Liverpool from the biggest air raid the country had seen to date. She could see it now: the bell would ring out, sounding the alarm that the city was under attack; the spotter would scan the skies for the enemy and shout out the position of the squadron coming towards them. There would be ... oh, seven planes flying in single file within their sights, all enemy, all Heinkels. Ellie herself, being on the height-finder, would look through the binoculars and get the first plane in view before calling out the coordinates to the girls on the predictors, who would, in turn, line up the planes and call out the information. There would be a repetition of the figures, the large shells would be placed in the gun, and the call of 'On target' would go up before each shell was fired. She could see the German planes, one by one, being shot down before they reached the city, ensuring that not one single Liverpudlian was hurt as the planes either exploded over the sea or came hurtling down, great plumes of smoke streaking behind them, until they too disappeared beneath the waves.Then there would be wave after wave of bombers, and her section would destroy them all. They would go into the city the next day, so that she might show her friends the sights and sounds of Liverpool, and, being in ATS uniform, they would be recognised as the conquering heroes who had saved the city from damnation. The newspaper stand would

201

scream the headline, *Local girl saves Liverpool and destroys three quarters of the Luftwaffe*. There would be hearty handshakes, slaps on the back, and drinks all round. Sighing happily at the thought, she looked at the top of the page before replacing the diary underneath her pillow. The date, she was sure, would remain etched on her mind for the rest of her life. It was the first of May, 1941.

Ellie looked at the scene below her. Everyone was in position, all eyes on the aircraft that were steadily droning their way across the sky. She watched the two women on the height-finder. One of them, she knew, was herself. She listened to the information being yelled out.

'One zero five and a three zero.'

'Range, one one two and a three one, kept on target.'

'One one two and a three on target and a three one kept on target.'

'Engage.'

'Fifteen two hundred … fire.'

'Fifteen two hundred; set.'

'Fifteen two hundred, two tonner … fire!'

It seemed odd to hear her voice from outside her own body as she continued to shout out orders. She appeared so calm, concentrating solely on the job in hand. She did not turn away from her position, not even for a second, and yet here she was, all alone, high above herself, watching her section putting all they had learned into practice against the enemy for the very first time.

The German bombers were not far from her now. They appeared to be flying at high altitude, and she smiled: the ack-acks might not be able to reach them at such a height, but neither could the bombers be sure of hitting their targets. She watched them droning their way towards Liverpool; they reminded her of mosquitoes on a hot summer night.

Something caught her attention, and turning her head she saw a lone bomber coming in from a different angle. It seemed odd that this one pilot was not in formation with the rest of his squadron. The plane was so close now that she could see the German pilot staring straight ahead, apparently unaware that he was being watched. She was near enough to peer into the cockpit, and she saw a photograph of a young woman, her dark hair curled back from her face. She appeared to be holding some sort of bundle. Ellie looked hard at the picture and realised that the bundle was a baby wrapped tightly in a blanket, no more than a few months old. A small child with pigtails, wearing a frock that was far too big for her, clutched her mother's knees. The pilot's family, Ellie concluded. Yet how could people as cruel and evil as the Luftwaffe have family?

She jumped slightly as the pilot raised his hand, gesturing to one of his crew members and jabbing a frantic finger in Ellie's direction. She could see that he was shouting, and a face appeared at the window behind him, its owner speaking reassuringly to him and waving a dismissive hand towards the window. The pilot was still clearly terrified, so Ellie did something that she had not done since she was a small child. Placing her thumbs in her ears she waggled her hands and stuck her tongue out. She saw a drop of sweat trickle down the side of his face. Slowly, he turned towards her. His eyes rounded as their eyes met and Ellie shook her head disapprovingly. This proved too much for the pilot, who pulled hard back on the stick in front of him, sending the bomber into a steep climb. Ellie saw the plane collide with another, and there was a moment's pause before both planes exploded in mid-air. She gasped, and held a hand to her mouth in horror. What had she done?

She blinked as she felt solid ground beneath her feet once more. She was looking through the binoculars and shouting the coordinates of the craft in her sight, hearing her figures being repeated even as she was yelling out the position of the next craft. The procession seemed endless, and with information overriding itself Ellie was surprised that none of the orders got lost in the melee. Pushing all thought of the humanity of her targets aside, she got on with her job.

It had started just before eleven p.m. The alarm bell had sounded and everyone had jumped to attention, all eyes turned towards the heavens where the powerful searchlights criss-crossed the inky dark sky as they searched for the Luftwaffe.

Ellie had expected one or two squadrons, but when the enemy approached their numbers had blotted out the stars, turning the brightly jewelled sky black. She had stared, her mouth dropping open as she and the girl next to her – she could not remember who it was, just the sound of her voice as she read out her figures – had locked the height-finder on to the first target. They had followed it across the sky and called out the information before going on to the next one. Ellie wondered how many planes had escaped being tracked. She knew that even one plane down was a target saved and that the guns helped force the bombers to fly too high to be successful, but even so, the sight of those planes and the noise they made had demonstrated a power which no one had thought possible.

Had she thought the first night to be a baptism of fire, it had been nothing compared to the nights that followed. On the third night there had, she had heard later, been over three hundred German bombers. She did not doubt it, as the sky had seemed to be full of them, the planes swarming across the sky, dropping their bombs indiscriminately on the people of Liverpool far below. Their main targets were the docks and the factories around them, and Ellie could understand this; what she could not understand was the bombing of innocent people's houses, hospitals, churches – nowhere seemed safe, and even though the RAF sent fighter pilots up in support of the ack-ack batteries prevention seemed to be an impossible task. The air raids had continued for the next five nights, although not on the same scale as the night of the third, but the gunners in Ellie's section still remained on tenterhooks, expecting them to come back in force as they had on that dreadful night.

It was the eleventh of May and Liverpool had been given respite from the attacks for the past three nights. 'If they come back and continue in the same number as before we'll be in real trouble. Why d'you reckon they stopped?' she asked Gwen as they sat round the table in the canteen, their eyelids heavy as they tried to get some food into themselves before collapsing into their beds.

'People are saying that Hitler's getting ready to attack Russia, which is bad news for the Russians but good for us. He can't fight on two fronts, so we may get a bit of a break, but how long for is anybody's guess.'

'I was going to go down into the city and see if I could be of any help. Do you fancy coming?' Ellie said, trying to focus on Gwen, who was shaking her head.

'You're goin' nowhere bar your bed, Ellie Lancton, and that's exactly where I'll be goin'. The folk of Liverpool need us protecting the skies, not falling asleep because we've burned the candle at both ends.'

Ellie nodded. 'I suppose you're right. But if we get a bit of rest now, how about tomorrow? I want to see what's been hit. This is my home, don't forget; I want to make sure all my old pals are safe. I thought I could call in on the Winthorpes, and the Murrays too. I haven't heard from Connor or Arla, but I bet they're beside themselves with worry. I'd go and see Aidan's mam and dad as well, only they're too far away, so I thought I'd give Aidan a call instead, you know, just to check ...'

Gwen smiled sympathetically at her. 'I'm lucky that me auntie and uncle are safely tucked away in the Welsh hills.' She looked wistfully at her plate of stew. 'Although they've been setting the mountains alight so's to distract the bombers.' She stopped talking and gently slid the plate of stew out from underneath Ellie's arm. Then, stepping around the table, she gave Ellie's shoulder a gentle shake.

'Wake up, Ellie, you can't sleep here. Let's get you into your bed.'

Ellie's lips moved and her voice came out in a sleepy whisper. 'Range, one one two and a three one, kept on target.'

Gwen's brow furrowed. They had all suffered from the anxiety; even when you went to your bed you couldn't escape the nightmares that followed. The hut had been filled with people crying out in their sleep. Quite often the order to fire escaped a sleeping figure so clearly that several others in the hut fell out of bed as they tried to respond. Everyone was going through the same horror, but for Ellie it was worse. This was her home, the place where she had grown up, the streets that she had walked on her way to school or work or to visit a pal, the church that she had attended with her mother every Sunday. Her friends, her history, her very memories were all under threat, and poor Ellie was helpless to do anything except shout orders to fire guns which boomed into the night sky.

Ellie jerked her head up from table and looked around the dimly lit room. 'What time is it?' she asked, her voice hollow through lack of sleep.

Sliding one of her shoulders underneath Ellie's arm, Gwen helped her friend get to her feet. 'It's time for your bed. Section D's on shift, so you've nothing to worry about.'

Ellie frowned. 'But Tilly and Evie're in Section D. Aren't they tired?'

Gwen held her tongue. Evelyn had supposedly been struck down by some mysterious stomach complaint after the first night of severe bombing. If it had been left to Corporal Caldecott, Gwen thought Evie would have been forced to get out there, stomach complaint or not, but Evie had gone straight to Sergeant Barton, who had insisted she stay in solitary confinement rather than spread the illness. Solitary confinement indeed, Gwen thought bitterly. She had been placed in one of the spare rooms in the sergeant's billeted cottage. Gwen had felt certain that the other girls in her barracks would comment on the matter, but no one seemed willing to raise an objection.

Gwen placed her arm around Ellie's waist and guided her friend to the door. 'We're all tired, chuck, but everyone's got to sleep – even the Germans – so let's get you into bed. It'll all be better for a good night's kip.'

Ellie yawned sleepily. 'A good night's kip? What's one of them? Even if we aren't dragged out of bed by the sirens, you can't relax, not properly. I reckon I'll feel better after I've been to the city. First chance I get I'm going to see what's left of the place … might even pay old Lavender Court a visit.'

Gwen pulled a face. She did not know for sure which areas of the city had been hit, but by all accounts you would be lucky if you did not know someone or somewhere close to your home that had been affected by the raids. If she were any judge, Ellie would be lucky to find her childhood home still standing.

A few days later, the planned visit had been made, and Ellie in particular had been distraught at the sights that met her eyes. A lot of the places she had promised to take the girls on their nights out had gone. Blacklers had been destroyed, leaving a mere shell of a building, as had Lewis's department store. Gwen had linked her arm through Ellie's as her friend pointed out the devastation. She had shaken her head. 'I don't know what to say, Ellie, I really don't,' was all she could manage.

Trying to find their way around a city that had been partially reduced to rubble was difficult, and with no familiar landmarks it was a while before Ellie got her bearings. As she guided her friend in the direction of Lavender Court, the girls found themselves being stopped by civilians who wanted to thank them for preventing the Luftwaffe from totally obliterating the city. They had been surprised, having feared they might get accused of not doing a good enough job, and were both relieved and happy to hear the opposite; pleased also to see that even though the city itself had been badly damaged the people remained in good spirits.

'You got family there?' one man had asked when Ellie had stopped to ask for directions to the courts.

Ellie shook her head. 'No, but up until recently it was my home, and I've still got friends who live there.'

He pulled a face. 'Some of 'em've been hit, but it's hard to tell what's what when you get there. Right bloody mess it is. Don't go enterin' somewhere what's got damaged by the bombs, will you? Even if it is still standin' it don't mean to say it won't come down round yer ears ...' He continued to drone on whilst Ellie scanned her surroundings. She knew which way she was headed; the main question now was which was the safest way to get there. A lot of the roads were blocked by rubble, and the buildings that did remain were, as the man said, unsafe to walk through. He stopped talking and looked at her inquisitively.

'Sorry, what was that?' she said.

'I said to try goin' straight down to the bottom of this 'ere road an' take a left. Some of the buildin's are still standin' down there, so if you're careful you might be able to pick your way round 'em.'

Thanking him for his help, the two girls followed his directions. A journey that would normally have only taken Ellie ten minutes took twice that time as they made their way across the broken city.

Ellie stopped abruptly in front of a pile of rubble. Pointing over the top of the broken bricks, she turned to Gwen. 'It's just over there. We'll have to go round; I don't fancy climbin' this lot, so—' She broke off as a familiar voice hailed her from behind.

'Ellie Lancton! What on earth are you doin' back 'ere? I thought you was off with the ATS …' The speaker paused, eyeing the khaki uniform. 'Don't tell me you were on the ack-acks when all this was goin' on? Blimey, I bet you was scared.' Looking at the bricks on the floor in front of him he pulled a face. 'I'm bloody glad we moved in with the wife's rellies a couple of months ago – I wasn't at the time, mind – else …' He shuddered.

'Mr Rogers!' Ellie said, a feeling of relief sweeping over her at the sight of a familiar face. 'This is a pal of mine, Gwen Jones. We're in the same section, and in answer to your question we arrived the day before the bombing started; in fact our first night's duty was the first night of the bombing.' She glanced at the ruins of the building in front of her. 'I wanted to show Gwen where I used to live, but it's been a bit of an ordeal just to get this far. What's the best way from here?'

The old man removed his cap from his head and gripped the peak firmly between his gnarled fingers. 'Don't you know where you are?'

Ellie frowned. 'I've a rough idea, but to be honest, one pile of rubble looks much like another.' She eyed Mr Rogers cautiously. There was something unnerving about his stance, and he appeared to be worried. Perhaps he was concerned she might ask him to climb over the rubble with her. She tried a different approach. 'Mebbe you can point us in the right direction? I'm sure we'll be able to get there once we know which way to go.'

'You're here,' he said, then, seeing her incomprehension, he continued, 'that is to say, you're home.' One arm leaning heavily on his cane, he waved the other in a sweeping motion at the bombed-out building.

The colour drained from Ellie's cheeks as she cast an eye over the pile of rubble. 'Are you tryin' to tell me that this is Lavender Court?'

Slipping his hand into hers, the old man smiled sympathetically, revealing a set of crooked teeth. 'God love you, queen, I thought you'd realised.' He nodded at the devastation which lay before them. 'This is – was – Lavender Court.'

Ellie rocked on her heels and squeezed his fingers tightly. 'I – I didn't know. I thought it was further on ...' she said, the tears welling up.

He shook her hand gently. 'It's just bricks and mortar, luv. I know it were your home, but when all's said and done ...'

The tears ran silently down her cheeks. 'It was more than just my home, it was the place where I grew up. I lived here with me mam, right up to ...'

211

Mr Rogers lowered his head. 'I can still remember you runnin' round in your nappy. 'Appy little bugger you were.'

Gwen placed her arm round Ellie's shoulders. 'I'm so sorry, cariad. I can't begin to imagine how you must be feeling.'

'It's like losing me mam all over again. It may have been a rotten, dirty, stinking place to live but it's all I had left to remember her by. Now all those memories, everythin', has just gone.'

Mr Rogers stood in front of Ellie and lowered his head to catch her eye. 'You listen to me, Ellie Lancton. You don't need no bricks and mortar to remind you of your mam. You've still got all your memories in that there noggin' of yours. She'll allus be in your thoughts. She were a good 'un, were Millie: always had time for everyone, never turned her back ... and we don't need no stinkin' court to remind us of that.'

Ellie sniffed, a frown wrinkling her brow as another thought crossed her mind. 'You said you didn't live here any more when it was bombed, but what about Mrs B and Mr Turnbull? I know you were all livin' together at one stage.' She turned large hopeful eyes on him. 'Had they moved out too?'

Removing his cap, he scratched the top of his balding head. 'Mr Turnbull moved out a month back, went off to live with his daughter in Scotland ...'

Ellie tried to look into his eyes but found he was avoiding her gaze. 'What about Mrs B? Where was she?' The panic started to rise in her throat, and her next words came out in a hoarse whisper. 'Please don't tell me she was at home.'

He wiped his nose on the back of his hand. 'She was meant to be leavin' to stay with her sister, but she'd had a change of heart. There was just her and Sid here when the bomb fell.'

Ellie hid her face behind her hands. 'She's gone? I'm – yes, I'm glad Sid's dead, but not her. Not Mrs B. You couldn't have wished to meet a kinder, more thoughtful soul.'

Mr Rogers screwed his cap up in his hands, then unscrewed it and placed it firmly back on his head. 'Sid's not dead, queen. He made it out. In fact, they're hailing him as a bit of a hero.'

Ellie interrupted, her face lit up with hope. 'Did he save her? Did he get her out? I know I've said some pretty bad things about him in the past ...'

Mr Rogers laid a restraining hand on her arm. 'Hang on a minute, queen. I never said nothin' about him savin' no one, I just said they hailed him as a bit of a hero.'

Ellie's shoulders sank. 'But if he didn't save anyone, why would they?'

'He tried his best to get her out of the building, but the walls were collapsing around his ears and they got separated,' Mr Rogers began, but Ellie was having none of it.

'You don't believe him, do you? He'd not save his own mother if it meant putting his own life at risk. You don't know him like I do, Mr Rogers; I bet he didn't even try to get her out. Did anyone check to see if she was still alive? Is she still in there?'

Ellie began to climb the rubble, calling out, 'Mrs B! Mrs B! It's me, Ellie. Are you in there?'

'What you doin'?' came a gruff voice from behind them. Turning, Ellie saw a young man in warden's uniform approaching them.

'Is that you, Wally Redfern?'

The warden grinned. 'Sure is.' He wagged a reproving finger. 'Sorry, Ellie, but no one's allowed to go playin' on bombed buildings. There could be anythin' under that lot, unexploded bombs, broken mains ... any number of hidden dangers. You can't stay 'ere, luv. I'm goin' to have to ask you to move on.'

Ellie shook her head. 'Not until I know whether—'

Mr Rogers cut across her. 'They've already taken the body out, Ellie.'

Ellie's lip trembled as she began to make her way back towards the trio. 'I – I didn't realise,' she said, just as her foot slipped down some of the bricks. There was a slight rumble behind her and several more bricks began to tumble from the top of the pile.

'Watch out!' shouted the warden.

Ellie jumped down on to the pavement. 'I'm so sorry, I didn't mean—'

'Did you hear that?' Gwen said suddenly, looking towards the disturbed bricks.

The warden turned pale. 'It weren't a ticking noise, was it?'

Gwen shook her head. 'It sounded like a baby.'

From under the rubble there came a faint cry. Gwen, Ellie and Wally exchanged glances, and the warden nodded slowly. 'Blimey! You're right, that did sound like a baby, but surely to goodness ...'

The sound came again, but stronger this time. Ellie peered at the rubble. 'Hello? Can you hear me? Shout if you can, and we'll try and get you.'

Mr Rogers pointed to where some small stones were trickling down the pile. 'Well I'm blessed.' Ellie looked, and to her amazement a small black fluffy ball poked its head through the rubble.

Leaning forward, Gwen made some encouraging noises as she tried to persuade it to come towards them. They watched its tiny legs wobble while it sought to gain balance on the precarious terrain. Kneeling down beside Gwen, Ellie beckoned. 'Hello, little one! Come here. We'll look after you.'

It turned to face them, eyeing them for a moment or two before leaping across the rubble towards them, mewing as it came.

Ellie scooped the kitten up into her arms and smiled as it pushed its head against her chin. 'You poor little thing, you're skin and bone. How long have you been under that lot?'

Mr Rogers shook his head disbelievingly. 'Wonders will never cease. The mother must've crawled in there to give birth.' Craning his neck, he tried to get a better view of the hole from which the kitten had emerged. 'I reckon this 'un must've got lost or left behind, 'cos I can't hear nowt else, can you?'

Ellie wiped her tear-stained cheeks with the back of her hand. 'No, but we'd best look, don't you think?' She half expected the warden to object, but when the kitten in her arms began to mew loudly a returning chorus came from the top of the pile.

Wally had already placed a tentative foot on the unsteady bricks. 'Sounds like there's a few more in there. I'll take a quick peek inside the hole, see what's what.'

They watched as the warden, arms held out for balance, slipped and stumbled his way towards the hole. He bent down gingerly, and peered into the gloom. When he looked back his face was split by a broad grin. He beckoned to Gwen. 'Can you come and give us a hand, queen? I reckon there's at least another two, only they're not as brave as that one, so I'm goin' to have to reach in.'

Delighted there were more survivors, Gwen picked her way across the bricks. The warden tentatively pushed his hand into the hole and passed her a kitten. 'I can see the mam and one more little 'un. You take this one back to the old feller whilst I get the last one out.'

Obediently, Gwen passed the kitten over to Mr Rogers, who, despite Ellie's warnings, had climbed a little way up the debris. Returning to the warden, she held out eager hands. 'I'm surprised their mam didn't try and fight you off. Perhaps she realises we're tryin' to help them.'

Nodding, the warden held the last kitten out, then peered back into the gloom. Gwen watched as he wormed both hands into the hole. 'C'mon, darlin', come and be with your babbies. We're not goin' to hurt you,' he soothed, his fingertips brushing against the soft fur. He shook his head. 'It's no good, I can't reach her. Lemme get my torch out, see if I can find a better way …' Shining his torch into the hole, he gave a cry of triumph. 'That's better. I can see her properly now. Tek that little 'un down to Ellie and come back here so's you can shine the torch whilst I get a hold of her. She's tucked herself into a corner, probably scared out of her wits.'

Gwen did as she was told then crouched down beside Wally as he located the cat and placed his hands around her, his expression turning from one of delight to one of apprehension. 'What's wrong?' said Gwen.

Shaking his head, he pulled the limp body out into the open air. 'Poor beggar, she must've been half starved before she even give birth. I reckon it were a miracle she managed to do that, given the state of her.' He smoothed the fur down on the lifeless body.

'What's happening?' Ellie called up from below.

'C'mon, we'd best go and explain,' Gwen said. She held out a hand to steady Wally as he descended the loose bricks with his pitiful burden.

One look at the cat was all it took. 'Oh, the poor, poor thing,' Ellie said, her bottom lip beginning to quiver. 'They shouldn't have to suffer because of a world at war. It's not right.' She cuddled the kitten in her arms close to her cheek. 'I know what it's like to lose your mam, but don't you worry. We're goin' to take good care of you.' She looked hopefully at Wally and Mr Rogers. 'Please say you can take at least one of the kittens home with you? I'm sure we can take this one back to the barracks, but there's no way they'll accept three!'

Wally held out his hands to the kitten in Gwen's arms, but Mr Rogers coughed uneasily. 'I'm too old to take on a pet, queen. Besides, it's not my 'ouse. I would otherwise ...'

Wally took the third kitten from him and held one in each hand. 'Me mam loves cats, and black 'uns is meant to be lucky. She'll not say no.'

Ellie grinned. 'You're a star, Walter Redfern, and your mam's an angel!' Standing on tiptoe she kissed his bristly cheek. 'There's not many with a heart as big as yours.' She brushed her lips over the top of the kitten's fluffy head. 'We'd best be off and get this one some milk and summat to eat.' She turned to Mr Rogers. 'Give my best to Mrs Rogers.'

The old man nodded gravely. 'I will. You girls take care of yourselves. It's a dangerous job you're doin' and we're grateful.' He ruffled the top of the little kitten's head. 'Youse a good gel, Ellie Lancton. You've done your mam proud.'

Chapter Eight

'Ellie! How are you? Did you manage to see my parents? Are they all right?' Arla's voice came anxiously down the telephone.

'Yes, they're both fine. A bit shaken, but that's understandable. Your dad said he was one of the people who attended a fire in a house a few streets down from yours. He reckoned the flames were twice as high as the roof. Good job there was no one in when it happened.'

Arla sighed with relief. 'Thank goodness! When I spoke to them they tried to assure me they were both all right, but me mam sounded terrible. I s'pose it's the trauma of all the fires an' that.'

'Everyone's in the same boat, chuck. Even if you haven't been bombed you know someone who has. I thought I'd check on Connor's parents too whilst I was in the city, and even though they never got hit all the glass has come out of their windows so they're all boarded up now. Mrs Murray said it's good at night because they don't have to worry about the blackout blinds, but it's a pain during the day because they have to have the lights on all the time.'

'I can't tell you how good it is to know that you're in Liverpool. I'd have been sick with worry if it weren't for you. Thank you so much for checking on them. I know they're more than capable of looking after themselves, but Dad always says everything's fine even when it isn't, so you can't take his word for anything.' There was a moment's pause before she spoke again, and this time her tone was tentative. 'What's the city like?'

Ellie froze. This was a question she had hoped her friend would not ask.

There was an impatient sigh from the other end of the phone. 'Can you hear me? I said, what's the city like?'

'Surviving,' Ellie said practically. 'A lot's been badly damaged, but they're making the best of things.'

'That's the spirit of Liverpool, that is! God, I miss home. I should be able to get some leave soon. Are you going to be there for a while, do you think?'

Ellie smiled. 'I hope so, but who knows for sure? It'd be great if you could come back. You could come to one of the dances at the camp. It'd be so good to see you after all this time.'

'I'll let you know when—'

'Caller, your time ...' The tinny voice of the operator cut across Arla's words.

Arla sighed impatiently. 'I know, I know, my time is up, please replace the receiver. Ta-ra, Ellie. I'll ask about leave and let you know. Love to all.'

'And you' was all Arla heard before the line went dead. Replacing the receiver, she sat down beside Archie.

He pushed a mug of tea towards her. 'Everythin' all right?'

Arla nodded. 'Yes, although I'll feel a lot better when I've been home for a visit.'

He raised a questioning eyebrow. 'Did you tell her?'

She shook her head. 'No, not over the phone. I told you, I want to see her reaction.'

'She'll be surprised, no doubt about that. I wish I could come with you, but I've not long been back.' He paused. 'Talk about good timing! Any later and I'd've been slap bang in the middle of it all.' Leaning back in his seat, he glanced at the clock that hung above the doorway. 'Drink up, they're showin' *King Kong* in a bit. It's a good 'un is that.'

Arla nodded and raised the mug to her lips. She felt guilty about keeping her friend in the dark; she just hoped that no one spilled the beans before she got a chance to tell her in person.

'It looks fine to me, and if it means you can fly, or walk without problems, I don't see what all the fuss is about,' Connor said plainly. He was turning Aidan's special shoe over and over in his hands.

'*You* try wearing it. The damn thing stands out like a sore thumb. At least when I was limping people assumed that I'd been hurt doing some heroic stunt or other, but with that thing on I just look … look … '

Handing the shoe back to his cousin, Connor arched his brows. 'Like you haven't got a limp?'

'You know damned well what I'm on about, Connor Murray, so stop playin' silly beggars. You saw those Waafs, all doe-eyed and fluttering lashes until

221

they noticed this bloody thing.' He dropped it before kicking it sharply underneath his bed. 'It was a different kettle of fish then, wasn't it? They couldn't get past us quick enough; they didn't even bother to salute.'

Connor averted his gaze to the forsaken shoe that could just be seen poking out from beneath his cousin's bed. He had a very different perspective on the business with the Waafs, and knew the women hadn't ignored Aidan. If anything it was the other way round. As soon as Aidan saw them approaching he hung his head and didn't raise it again until they had passed by. Connor would have said as much, but he was only visiting for the day and could not see the point in causing an argument. He knew that when it came to the shoe, Aidan could be bloody-minded.

If it had been Connor, he would have happily accepted the shoe if it meant he would be taken on as a pilot. As it was, he had to settle for being a gunner. Not that there was anything wrong with that, but he knew it didn't get you the same kind of attention from females as pilot wings did. When he first donned his uniform, the women in the WAAF had regarded him with far more favour than when he had been training as an electrical engineer, but he did not kid himself: when push came to shove a pilot was treated by the women as some kind of god. He sat down on the bed opposite his cousin and tried a different approach. 'I reckon it's all in your imagination. You can hardly see it under your trousers and you know as well as I do that a lot of women can be intimidated by a man with ranking. Besides, you don't have to wear it all the time, just when you're flying. I really don't see why you're lettin' it stop you from seein'—'

Interrupting, Aidan pointed an accusing finger at the shoe. 'I wanted to impress Ellie with my new look, but how can I do that if she sees me with that on?'

Connor wagged a reproving finger at his cousin. 'You know Ellie's not like that. She wouldn't care if you had two peg legs as long as your heart's in the right place.'

Aidan shook his head gloomily. 'I know that what you're saying is right, but you must see that there're hundreds of pilots out there, all decent fellers, all with two legs which work fine, and none of them wearing some stupid, ugly, thick shoe just so that they can fly a kite.'

'But they're not you, are they? If you're not the feller for Ellie it wouldn't matter whether your legs were good or not, so I wouldn't go fussing over summat you can't do nothing about.' Connor's tone was becoming impatient. 'You should try being me, I may have two good legs, but next to you and that uniform of yours I may as well be a ghost!'

Aidan chuckled. 'I reckon the only reason you wanted to become a pilot was so that you could wear the uniform and pull the lasses.'

Connor grinned. 'And I reckon that a good, kind, loving cousin would see fit to lend me that uniform, just so that I could try it out some time.'

'Get out of it!' Aidan spluttered. 'Could you imagine the trouble we'd get into if I let you impersonate a pilot?'

Connor waggled his eyebrows menacingly. 'Not half as much trouble as I could get into with the ladies, given half a chance.'

Aidan eyed his cousin shrewdly. 'Fair enough, but on one condition.'

Connor's jaw dropped and he nodded his head vigorously. 'Anything, you name it.'

Picking up the shoe from under his bed, Aidan held it out to his cousin. 'You have to wear this.'

'Oh, very funny,' Connor said dejectedly. 'Who do you think I am? Cinderella? Just for starters, your feet are smaller than mine, so not only would I be walking with one leg longer than the other, I'd be in excruciating pain. I'd end up looking like Quasimodo, lurching around with me face all twisted up.'

Aidan roared with laughter at the image. 'Don't worry, Connor,' he said as he fought for breath, 'if she's a really nice girl it won't matter what you look like.'

'Bagheera?' Gwen said, her tone incredulous. 'Like out of *The Jungle Book*?'

Nodding, Ellie stroked the top of the kitten's head.

'But Bagheera's a huge panther, and he's ...' Gwen pointed a finger at the kitten sitting on Ellie's lap, 'he's nothing like that. My foot's bigger than him, you can feel his ribs, an' I've seen more fat on a butcher's pencil.'

Ellie shrugged. 'You saw the state of the place he was livin' in. You've got to be a real little fighter to get out of that lot in one piece, and he was the only one who climbed out on his own, so he's an adventurer.'

Gwen sat down beside Ellie. 'My turn,' she said, holding her hands out expectantly.

Ellie scooped Bagheera up and placed him gently on Gwen's lap. When they had brought the kitten back to the barracks both girls had anticipated objections to his presence, if not from the other girls then certainly from Corporal Caldecott, who would have to be consulted on his proposed living quarters – an old cardboard box with a blanket, which would be kept under Ellie's bed – but instead the new arrival had been welcomed with open arms by everyone, apart from Evie.

Having gone over to see why a group of girls had congregated around Ellie and Gwen's beds, Evie had screwed up her nose. 'He stinks of wee. You can't possibly mean to keep him here? Not smelling like that! Look at him, he's practically knockin' on death's door as it is.' She shook her head decidedly. 'Kindest thing you could do is have him put to sleep. Where on earth did you find him, anyway?'

Hoping to appeal to Evie's better nature, Gwen told the story of Ellie's bombed-out home and the rescue of the orphans.

'*Now* it makes sense. Even court kittens are slummy little scrag-ends.' Evie looked disdainfully down her nose at the small ball of fluff. 'Still, at least there's some good news, I suppose.'

Gwen frowned. 'I thought you didn't like him?'

Evie rolled her eyes impatiently. 'I *meant*, that Jerry has started a slum clearance. It's taken them two weeks to do what the government should've done years ago.'

'That was Ellie's home, you heartless bitch!' Gwen said, her temper rising. 'And I'll tell you summat for

225

nowt, I'd rather share this hut with a pee-soaked kitten than I would with you, Evie Maddox. After all, we can always bathe him to get rid of the smell, but when it comes to you—'

'Is there a problem?' Corporal Caldecott's voice broke through the atmosphere like a knife.

Evie smiled maliciously at Gwen. 'I'd call *that* a problem,' she replied, pointing at Bagheera.

The circle of women dissipated like mist on a summer's day, leaving Bagheera curled up on Gwen's knee purring loudly whilst Ellie braced herself for the dressing-down.

'Dear God, where on earth did you find such a squalid-looking creature?'

Taking a deep breath, Ellie tried to keep her explanation as short as she could, finishing with, 'I couldn't just leave him, and Mr Rogers is too old, and the warden took the other two.'

The corporal sat down on the bed opposite them and held out her hands. 'May I?'

Kissing the top of Bagheera's head, Gwen handed the tiny kitten over, adding as she did so, 'We've called him Bagheera, after the black panther in *The Jungle Book*, because he's a fighter.'

Caldecott rolled the kitten gently on to his back and placed a hand on his tummy. To Ellie's dismay, he brought his little back feet up, kicking ferociously, and tired to sink his tiny pin teeth into the back of the corporal's hand. Seeing the smirk of delight on Evie's face, she leaned forward to take the kitten back, apologising profusely as she did so. 'He's never done that before. I'm terribly sorry ...'

226

Caldecott laughed. 'Not to worry, he's only playing.' She glanced at Ellie. 'We used to have cats when I was little. Mine was a tabby called Tigger – of course – and my brother had a black one just like Bagheera, only he was called Sooty.'

Ellie smiled. It was the first time the corporal had ever spoken of her personal life. Caldecott rolled the kitten back on to his tummy and rubbed a finger under his chin. Closing his eyes, Bagheera purred with pleasure. She looked up at Ellie. 'I gather you intend to keep him?'

Ellie looked at her hopefully. 'Yes, but if he really can't stay I thought I could take him to live on my friend's farm. I've got a forty-eight coming up so I could take him with me when I go. But I thought it might be nice to keep him here, for morale.'

'The rats'd have him for breakfast on a farm; he's far too little.' Raising her voice, Caldecott glanced around the barracks. 'I take it there are no objections to Bagheera's remaining here?'

All eyes turned to Evie, who flushed red but shook her head.

'Good!' The corporal turned back to Ellie. 'I'll go to the cookhouse and see if I can get him some cheese and milk, and whilst I'm there I'll ask them if they've got any old roasting trays you can put some earth in for him to use as a sort of potty until he's big enough to venture out.'

A noise escaped Evie's lips, causing Caldecott to look in her direction. 'Did you have something to add, Maddox?'

'Just clearin' my throat,' Evie said sullenly.

227

Handing Bagheera back to Ellie, Caldecott stood up and walked over to Evie. 'Sergeant Barton isn't the only one round here who can make people's lives easy or hard. I wouldn't like to think you'll be making trouble for our new mascot.'

Evie shook her head, but Ellie could see she was seething inside.

'Good!' said the corporal, and turned to leave the room, calling over her shoulder as she did so, 'I'll be back in a bit.'

'She said he's our mascot,' squeaked Gwen. 'There I was thinkin' the poor bugger was in for the high jump, but instead she's made him official, like one of us!'

Evie was eyeing Bagheera disdainfully. She glanced frostily at Ellie. 'Don't let that flea-ridden, smelly creature near me or my things.'

Ellie smiled. It felt good to know that they had an ally in Caldecott. Perhaps Evie would start being a bit nicer now she knew they also had a friend in authority.

Wiggy scanned the letter before him, then handed it back. 'I don't understand.'

Aidan sighed. 'I always thought that if I was going to arrange to meet Ellie I'd have liked it to be back at the farm, just like old times, but according to this she's already there, although I reckon she's probably been and gone and is back in Liverpool by now.'

Wiggy nodded. 'Ah. Did she never tell you she was intending to go back to the farm for a visit?'

Aidan looked awkward. 'She did say she was going, it's just ...'

Wiggy shook his head. 'Pride comes before a fall, pal, and you've shot yerself in the foot. With both barrels, if you want my opinion.'

'Well I don't,' Aidan said sullenly. He looked ruefully at the letter. Wiggy was right: he was making a right mess of things when it came to Ellie. She had written to him several weeks back informing him that she intended to visit the farm later on in the year, and how much she wished he could join her there, and how had he responded?

Dear Ellie, I don't know what it's like on a gun site, but being a flying officer I can't just take off willy-nilly whenever the urge arises, so I'll give it a miss if it's all the same to you ...

He had sounded like a condescending idiot. He looked resignedly at Wiggy. 'I've been a bloody fool. After my last letter, I wouldn't be surprised if she didn't want to have anything to do with me, and what's more I wouldn't blame her, and all because I was worried she might find out about my flying shoe when it's ten to one she already knows.'

Wiggy handed Aidan a blank sheet of thin writing paper. 'Then stop being stupid, apologise, and go from there. She sounds like a good girl does Ellie; she'll come round. Chances are she won't have taken it personally anyway.'

Aidan smoothed the paper out. 'Sounds logical when you say it. Let's hope you're right.'

Wiggy grinned. 'Course I'm right! You mark my words, six months from now you'll be lookin' back at this and wonderin' what all the fuss was about.'

*

Ellie approached the gate that led into the cobbled yard. She had been surprised at how much the smell of the farm had changed. When she had left to join the ATS it had been midwinter and everything was covered in snow or ice, which had dampened the smell of the farmyard, whereas now, in the heat of the summer sun, the smell of manure, pigs, cattle and horses seemed pungent in her nostrils. As she laid a hand on the old wooden five-bar gate that separated the farm from the lane she felt a sense of belonging, and her spirits rose as she heard Lady give out a loud friendly woof as the old collie alerted the family to her presence. Not that anyone ever took much notice when Lady barked, mainly because she would bark at anything that took her fancy, from a crow which had landed on top of one of the chimneys to a rat running along the line of stables.

Ellie felt a sense of awkwardness as she stood waiting for someone to open the door. When she had written to Aidan to let him know that she intended to visit the farm, she had hoped he would try to get some leave so they could meet there, but instead his response had been rather standoffish, as if he thought himself to be too good for her. She began to wonder whether things had changed and she would not be as welcome as she once was; perhaps the Murrays had only agreed she might come and visit out of a sense of duty.

'That you, Ellie?'

'Yes, Auntie Aileen,' Ellie called back through the stout wooden door.

'What the bloomin' heck are you standin' out there for? Come on in, child, you've no need to knock. You're family.'

Ellie smiled. She had been worrying over nothing. As her feet crossed the threshold, she felt as though no time at all had elapsed since she was last there. The fire still burned brightly in the grate, and there was the familiar smell of Auntie Aileen's home-cooked food coming from the Aga. Ellie thought, not for the first time, that even though she had only stayed on the farm for a few months it felt as though she had lived there far longer.

Uncle Kieran instructed her to go and put her things in 'her room', and when she returned Auntie Aileen enveloped her in a warm and friendly hug, whilst planting a kiss on top of her head and telling her to 'sit down and tell us all about it'.

At breakfast the next morning Ellie expected to be introduced to the land girls, and was surprised to find that there were none.

'Some of the old fellers have come out of retirement wanting to do their bit. It seemed logical to have experienced hands working the farm, and it helps the old fellers feel as if they're contributing towards the war effort, so it works out all round,' Uncle Kieran explained as they sat round the table, eating the thick creamy porridge that Auntie Aileen always served up for breakfast. 'They may be riddled with arthritis, but they know what they're doin',' he added, glancing defensively at his wife.

'You just don't like the idea of strangers on the farm, Kieran Murray, so don't go pretendin' otherwise.' She looked enquiringly at Ellie. 'Besides, I don't want to talk about land girls. I want to know if Ellie's seen our Aidan since he started flying them there moths?'

Uncle Kieran cast his eyes to the ceiling. 'Tiger Moths, you silly mare, not moths! How could you expect him to win the war on the back of a moth?'

'*Tiger* Moths,' Mrs Murray corrected.

Ellie shook her head. 'I've not seen anyone from home since I joined up, apart from Arla, of course. I did ask Aidan if we could meet back here, but he couldn't get away.'

Two dimples appeared in Auntie Aileen's large pink cheeks and she clapped her hands together. 'Ah, well, I expect he's very busy. Him and Connor both write regular and I know they're hopin' to end up in the same aircrew. Kieran says he'll take me to see them one day, if they don't have time to come here. I can't wait to see our Aidan in a smart uniform. I expect he'll look a right bobby-dazzler.'

Uncle Kieran winked at Ellie. 'We all know who he gets that off, what d'you reckon, Ellie?'

Giggling, Ellie nodded. '*All* the Murray men look alike if you ask me. It's the black hair and green eyes.'

He gave his wife a satisfied smile. 'See, woman? I'm always tellin' you that you're lucky to have a feller like me.'

Auntie Aileen gestured towards Ellie with the large wooden spoon. 'I reckon our Aidan needs to keep his mind off women and on the job in hand. I told him as much, and he agreed,' she said smugly.

Ellie felt a sense of relief wash over her. Whatever the reason for Aidan's abruptness in his last letter, it was not because he had found himself a girlfriend, so maybe he was telling the truth. Maybe he really was too busy to come to the farm, she thought, and if that's

232

the case it means I'm still in with a chance, only I'd better make my mind up quickly, else my fears really will come true and some other woman will snap him up. A pilot's uniform is like gold dust to some women, especially ones like Evie, and I refuse to lose him to the likes of her just because I can't make my mind up as to whether I just love Aidan or whether I'm *in* love with him.

When breakfast was over Ellie made her way to the milking shed and found the small three-legged stool in the same place as it always was. Pulling it towards her, she tethered Dave and fetched the pail. She wondered whether she had lost the knack, but as the milk squirted into the bottom of the bucket she smiled to herself. She loved her role in the ATS, but she also loved the simplicity of working on the farm. It didn't matter in which order you did your chores, as long as they got done some time during the day. The animals never shouted or ordered you around, which was a far cry from life on a gun site, where shouting and being shouted at was all part of a day's work.

Returning to the farmhouse, Ellie entered the kitchen and all she could smell was the Irish stew that Auntie Aileen had doled out into dishes in readiness for the workers. It was a far cry from the NAAFI, which smelled of disinfectant, food and body sweat. Having washed her hands, she took her place by the table.

'I wish you could come and work in the kitchen for the ATS. I reckon you could teach 'em a thing or two when it comes to cooking,' she said, blowing on a spoonful of stew. 'I know we're all on rations, but I don't think the army cooks have ever heard of salt and pepper.'

The older woman beamed. 'When you're the wife of a farmer you have to make sure the men never go hungry, so you learn a trick or two along the way. I dare say they aren't taught that in the army. I did notice that you seem to've slimmed down since joinin' up.'

Ellie saw Uncle Kieran's eyebrows rise above the top of his newspaper. 'That's more to do wi' growin', though, don't you think?' He brought the pages of the paper together as he looked at Ellie. 'I mean to say, she never 'ad a waist before she left Springdale, nor a bosom neither ...'

'Kieran!' Auntie Aileen shrieked as she flicked the tea towel at him. 'That's not a polite thing to say about a young woman.'

He placed the paper momentarily down on his lap and frowned up at his wife. 'Why not? It's true, and it's only natural. I was just sayin' that I thought the food was goin' to the right places.'

Ellie frowned. Surely she hadn't changed that much? It was girls like Evie, Arla and Gwen who had figures. Ellie was more like a beanstalk, or at least she had been when she first joined the ATS. She looked down towards her plate and realised to her surprise that Uncle Kieran was right. She had formed a bust, albeit a smallish one. She glanced up. 'May I be excused?'

Auntie Aileen slapped Uncle Kieran's arm with the back of her hand. 'See? You've embarrassed the poor girl.' She smiled kindly at Ellie. 'Of course you may, but do come back to finish your plate, won't you?'

Nodding, Ellie climbed the stairs to her room. There was a half-length mirror on the front of the wardrobe, and she examined her reflection. She was wearing an old pair of dungarees that were too big for her, but when she placed her hands on her hips a smile formed on her lips. I *have* got a waist, she thought, turning to look at her profile. The smile widened. And my bust looks bigger here than it does when I look down at myself. Turning from side to side, she marvelled at her reflection. Why hadn't anyone said anything sooner? Surely Uncle Kieran couldn't be the only one to have noticed? Realisation dawned. It had been months since she had seen any of her old friends. But why hadn't she noticed herself? That was an easier question to answer. The only mirrors she ever saw herself in were either the ones above the washbasins in the ablutions or the hand-held one that belonged to Gwen.

She made her way back to the kitchen, where a rather sheepish-looking Uncle Kieran greeted her. 'Sorry if I—'

Ellie held up a hand. 'No need for apologies. It just came as a bit of a shock, because I hadn't noticed myself how much I'd changed until you said.'

He grinned smugly at his wife. 'Told you our Ellie hadn't run off upset because of me.'

'All I can say is you're lucky, Kieran Murray, 'cos if I thought you'd upset our Ellie with your crude talk ...'

Ellie laughed. 'He might be a bit blunt at times, but there's no harm in that.' Scraping the last of the stew from her bowl, she looked towards the Aga. 'I don't s'pose that's apple crumble and custard I can smell, is it?' she asked hopefully.

Uncle Kieran winked at her. 'Aye, it is, and thanks for diggin' me out of the mire.'

Later that evening, as Ellie snuggled down in her small cosy bed, she closed her eyes and listened to the sounds of the farmyard as it settled down for the night. Every now and then one of the cows would call to the bull, who would bellow a response. The pigs snorted and snuffled as they adjusted their sleeping positions in the sties, and the barn owls hooted softly as they glided past her window on silent wings. She wondered what the girls in her barracks would be doing right now, and whether Bagheera was behaving himself. She glanced at the alarm clock on the bedside cabinet and imagined that they would all be in their beds, trying their best to snuggle beneath the itchy blankets whilst not getting stabbed in the back by an errant piece of straw from one of the biscuits. Gwen would be snoring, which would annoy the other girls as there was no one to give the underside of her mattress a good shove, a practice which normally guaranteed an end to the snoring. Ellie smiled. Given a choice between army life and farming life, she would choose farming every time.

Chapter Nine

'Are you sure you don't want to come with me? I don't mind ...' Ellie had begun, but Gwen waved her into silence.

'You haven't seen Arla for ages; you need some alone time to catch up. Besides, if she's here for a week I'm bound to see her at some stage.'

Ellie smiled. 'Too right you will. Can't have me Welsh bezzie not meetin' me Scouse bezzie, can I? Besides, Arla's dying to meet you – and Bagheera, of course.'

Gwen, who was taking her stockings off by the door to the hut, glanced along the row of beds. 'Speakin' of which, I don't s'pose you know where he is?'

Ellie shook her head. 'He didn't get me when I came in, so I'm guessin' he must be further down.'

Taking care to walk down the centre of the hut, Gwen glanced at each bed as she drew level with it. She placed her stockings on her top bunk before heaving herself up. 'What time are you off?'

Ellie glanced at the clock. 'I said I'd meet her in Bumbles at four, so I've got a good hour or so before I have to leave.'

The door to the hut swung open and Sandra Hill, another girl from Section B, came in tentatively. 'Where is he?' she asked, slipping off her shoes.

Gwen shrugged. 'Dunno, but I don't think he's up this end.'

Sandra glanced along the line of beds. 'Oh well, here goes nothin'.' Gripping her shoes and stockings tightly to her chest, she made her way down the length of the room and sat down on her bed, only to jump up with a squeal. 'Little blighter! Gerroff!'

Gwen stifled a giggle. 'You found him, then?'

Sandra unhooked the small kitten's claws from around her ankle and carried him over to Ellie. 'When did Caldecott say he'd grow out of this phase?'

Ellie held up her hands to receive Bagheera, who was looking very pleased with himself. 'She didn't, she just said once we let him go out of the hut he'll have lots of mice and rats to ambush, so he won't need to practise on us any more.'

Sandra rubbed her ankles. 'So why don't we let him out?'

Ellie looked affronted. 'He's still too small. It's a big world out there and he's not used to any of it. What if he gets run over by a truck, or picked on by a dog, or ...'

Sandra eyed Bagheera, who had grown considerably in the past month. 'Then the dog would be in for a shock, wouldn't it?'

Gwen giggled. 'She's got a point, Ellie. Baggy's quite capable of lookin' after himself, even if you can't see it.'

Ellie smoothed her hands over the kitten's back. 'I'll let him out when I've got time to supervise him.

My friend's coming home on leave, Sandra, so I won't be able to do it this week, but I promise I'll do it soon.'

Shaking her head, Sandra headed back to her bed. 'Tomorrow never comes, didn't your mother ever teach you that? There's no time like the present, you should take the bull by the horns and run with it: all old sayings and all very true.'

'Tried that once and it was not a good idea,' Ellie muttered as she continued to stroke the fur on Bagheera's head. 'Try not lookin' so pleased with yourself, Baggy. You're not helpin' matters.'

Gwen raised an eyebrow. 'You're lucky he doesn't attack Evie, because there's no way she'd put up with it.'

Ellie shrugged. 'He may be small, but he recognises evil when he sees it. He knows she'd hit back.'

Watching Bagheera ambush people had become something of a spectator sport. Now whenever one of the girls entered the hut she would almost absentmindedly remove her shoes and stockings before making her way to her bed, or, as some of them had put it, running the gauntlet. As they made their way down the hut, all the other girls would stop what they were doing and watch with interest. It was always entertaining to see one of your roommates leaping around as she tried to remove a furry limpet from her ankle, but never amusing if it was happening to you. He might have been small, but his claws left noticeable nicks in the stockings of anyone indifferent to the idea.

Ellie sighed. 'I will let you out, little fellow, but only when I think you'll be safe.'

Gwen raised her eyebrows. 'I don't think you need to worry about his safety. You called him Bagheera for a reason, don't forget. He's more than capable of looking after himself, no matter what you may think.'

'Archie? As in Archie Byrnes?'

Arla giggled. 'Yup! He said you'd be surprised!'

Ellie stirred the contents of the teapot then poured some into her cup. 'Surprised is a bit of an understatement, especially since you joined the ATS in the hope of marryin' an officer or summat similar. You may as well've saved yourself the bother and stayed back home.' She stared quizzically across the table at her friend. 'You two used to fight like cat and dog. I knew things had improved a bit since you started working together, but I never thought for a minute you'd end up together!'

'I know. Funny how things turn out, isn't it? If you'd told me six months ago that me and Archie would end up as boyfriend and girlfriend I'd've said you was tapped in the 'ead, but now,' she sighed wistfully, 'I couldn't be happier.'

Smiling, Ellie shook her head. 'I reckon he must've cast a spell on you, or given you some sort of love potion. I've never seen such a turnaround.'

Resting her arms on the table, Arla placed her chin in her hand and smiled black at Ellie. 'I gorra admit I'm not sure how it came about meself, only that when you live and work with someone you get to know them really well, and the more I got to know him the more I liked him. He's so different in the army. Back home he was annoyin' and stupid, but now,' she

240

sighed happily, 'he's kind, carin', thoughtful, helpful, and he treats me like I'm the only girl in the world.' Seeing the disbelief on Ellie's face, she chuckled. 'I know how it must seem, Ellie, and I won't deny that I had me sights set a lot higher than Archie, but truth be told, officers don't want to date a private, especially not one from the courts, and now I wouldn't want to date them either. I'm far happier with my own kind. The courts ain't the best place to live, far from it, but there's a lot to be said for the folk what live in 'em.' She took a sip of her tea before continuing. 'But that's enough about Archie an' me. What've you been up to? Have you seen anyone who takes your fancy?'

Ellie shook her head. 'I've been to a few dances, but I've not met anyone who stands out from the crowd.' She regarded Arla with an enquiring eye. 'You don't care what people think, then? About you and Archie gettin' together?'

Arla shook her head. 'Why should I? It's no one's business but mine who I choose to spend time with.' She returned Ellie's questioning look. 'You don't think any less of me, do you?'

'No, of course I don't. I was just a bit surprised, that's all. As you say, it's up to you who you see, and what other people think doesn't matter.' Even as the words left her lips, Ellie knew them to be false. At first, she herself had worried what Arla would think of Aidan when she met him, and that was the reason why she had never mentioned his disability, but now she admitted to herself that if anyone had a problem with Aidan's appearance it was she, Ellie. It wasn't that she minded the way he looked herself, but she was worried about what others might think when they saw him.

She glanced tentatively at Arla. 'D'you remember me tellin' you about Aidan?'

'Of course; how could I not? You banged on about him for ages, although accordin' to you there weren't nowt in it. Why?'

'I never told you about the accident he had when he was a kid, did I? Only it's left him with one leg a bit shorter than the other, so he walks a bit funny, and he uses a cane, like old Mr Rogers in Lavender Court.' Sitting back, she waited for Arla's response.

Confused, Arla leaned forward. 'What's that gorra do with the price of fish? And why are you tellin' me now?'

Ellie shrugged. 'Dunno, really. I s'pose I was worried it might bother you.'

'Why on earth should it bother me?' Arla eyed her friend curiously. 'Does it bother you? But why would it, if you're not inter— Oh.' As the penny dropped, she cocked an eyebrow. 'You *are* interested in him, aren't you? In fact, I'd go one further, I think you really like him, and that's why you talk about him all the time. I *knew* you were keen on him, only you got naggy if I so much as suggested—'

'I didn't get naggy,' Ellie said crossly.

'Of course you didn't, just like you're not gerrin' naggy now.'

Ellie's shoulders relaxed. 'I'm just confused. I don't know what I want, but at the same time I can't stop thinkin' about him.'

'Sounds to me like you really like him. Has he asked you out on a date?'

Ellie shook her head. 'But he asked me not to join the ATS and stay on the farm with him.'

Arla's jaw dropped. 'You didn't tell me that! Crikey, Ellie, he must really like you! Why didn't you say owt?'

Ellie shook her head in shame. 'I don't know. I thought mebbe you'd laugh or tell me I could do better'n a farmer with bad legs.'

'You're blaming me? You're saying it's my fault?' Arla said, her tone unusually brusque. She sat back and shook her head in disbelief. 'My God, you are, aren't you?'

'Not at all. If it's anyone's fault it's mine. But you always said how you wanted the best for me – for both of us – and I thought I might be lettin' you down ...'

Arla sat upright and glared accusingly at Ellie. 'You are! You're blamin' me! Which is a bit rich, 'cos I only wanted the best for you, and if that meant you married a farmer with dodgy legs or a docker wi'out a penny to his name, as long as he loved you to the moon and back then that's what I wanted. So don't you go blamin' me, Ellie Lancton. It's not on!'

Ellie looked pleadingly at her friend. 'Please let's not fight. I haven't seen you for such a long time, and I'm not blamin' you, really. I'm not. There's nowt wrong wi' wantin' the best for your bezzie, and I wanted that too. I'm afraid I've put things awfully badly, and I didn't mean to.'

Arla heaved a sigh. 'I know you didn't, and I suppose I did harp on about marryin' officers and getting out of the courts, so I s'pose I can't blame you for thinkin' I might've scorned your feelin's for Aidan. And if truth be told, back then I might've done, but we've both grown up a lot since then.' She placed a hand over Ellie's and clasped her fingers tightly in her own. 'Let's start again, shall we? Only this time, nothing but the God's honest.'

Ellie nodded thankfully. 'I've been so confused! I don't know whether I love him as a friend or whether I'm in love with him, an' then there's the business of what happened to me mam.'

Arla frowned. 'What did happen to her?'

Ellie took a deep breath. 'I'm the same age me mam was when she met me dad, and by all accounts he promised her the earth, the moon and the stars above. He treated her like a queen and took her to places she'd never been before. He talked of a fairy-tale future where they'd live in a cottage beside the sea and she'd stay at home lookin' after the kids whilst he went out to work.' Picking up the teapot, she lifted the lid and examined the contents. 'But that never happened, did it? He were leadin' her up the garden path just so's he could have his wicked way with her. As soon as he found out she were pregnant he upped and left, leavin' her on her own wi' a babby to bring up.'

Arla frowned. 'What's that gorra do wi' Aidan?'

'What if he does the same to me? He says I could stay at the farm, but what if he changes his mind? What would I do then? With no home to go to, no money behind me and no job?'

Arla nodded. 'Oh, I *see*! But he wouldn't do that, would he? What would be the point?' She paused momentarily. 'Unless …'

This time it was Ellie's turn to frown. 'Unless what?'

Arla pulled a rueful face. 'Unless he just wants you to help him with the farm when his mam and dad get too old to work the land. You did say he wasn't a looker; mebbe he thought he couldn't afford to be picky.'

'Thanks a lot!' said Ellie.

'I don't mean that there's owt wrong wi' you, just … oh, dear, it's not goin' well this, is it?'

Ellie considered. 'You may be right, though. What if he does only want me to help with the farm?'

Arla shook her head. 'Ignore me, Ellie. I don't know Aidan, I've never even met him, an' I shouldn't have said owt.'

Ellie shrugged. 'I've only known him for a few months, so if it comes to that I don't really know him that well either.' She looked expectantly at Arla. 'What should I do?'

'If I were you I'd forget just about everything we've said here today, and go with your heart …' She held up a hand as Ellie started to protest. 'I know that's what your mam did, but you're not your mam, are you? Besides, we've both known Connor for years, and I don't think for one moment that Connor would have taken you to the farm if Aidan was a wrong 'un. Blimey, Ellie, he treats you like a kid sister – me too, come to that – an' he'd not want to see either of us get hurt.'

Ellie still looked doubtful. 'You're right about Connor, but even if Aidan is all he appears to be I don't know whether he feels the same about me. As you say, we've both grown up a lot, and things will've changed for him too.'

'The best thing you could do is meet up with him. That way you can see for yourself whether he still feels the same way about you. It's not easy over the telephone or by letter – which is why I wanted to tell you about Archie and me face to face – so how about givin' him a call and arranging to get together?'

Ellie nodded. 'All right, I will. But not whilst you're in town.'

Arla raised her brow. 'Why not? Don't you think your bezzie'll want to know all the gossip hot off the press?' She glanced at her wristwatch. 'D'you know the number of his NAAFI?'

'Yes, but surely you don't mean I should ring him now? I don't know what to say. I need more time ...'

Arla shook her head chidingly. 'You've wasted too much time as it is. Strike while the iron's hot, that's what I always say. Come with me, my girl. You've a phone call to make.'

'Ellie! What a nice surprise!'

Ellie gulped, her mouth drying up. She stared appealing at Arla, who mouthed, 'How are you?'

'How are you?' Ellie said, twisting the cable to the receiver around her fingers.

'I'm grand. You know I've got my wings, don't you? I'm sure I must've mentioned it.'

Ellie smiled. 'Just a thousand times. You're still enjoying it, then?'

He chuckled down the receiver. 'I love it here in Waddington, and having Connor as my tail-end Charlie is the icing on the cake.' There was an audible pause. 'But why are you ringing? There's nothing wrong, is there?'

The two girls were squashed into the small kiosk and Ellie was holding the phone between them so that they could both hear Aidan's end of the conversation. Again, she looked appealingly at Arla, who mouthed, 'No. When can we meet?'

Ellie nodded. 'No, I just wondered if there was any chance of meeting up. We did say we'd try ...'

'I can do better than try, chuck. Me and Connor'll be coming to RAF Speke sometime in the not too distant future, so we'll definitely be able to see you then.'

Ellie's smile split her face in two. 'That's wonderful. Make sure you let me know when, won't you? At least that way I can try to get some leave, or arrange to be around, or ...'

He chuckled again. 'Of course I'll let you know. Couldn't come all the way back there and not see my favourite girl, could I?'

'Ow!' Grinning, Arla had nudged her in the ribs.

'What was that?'

Stifling her giggles, Ellie pushed her friend out of the kiosk. 'Nothing, just hit my elbow on the door. I've got to go, Aidan. Give my love to your parents.'

Outside the kiosk Arla was jiggling excitedly. 'See? That wasn't so hard, was it? I bet you're glad I came home now, aren't you?'

Ellie linked her arm through Arla's. 'I was glad you came back before, although I must admit I am pleased you made me ring him. I don't think I'd have done it otherwise.'

'You must let me know what happens when he comes to Speke. You never know, this time next year you could be gettin' married, you in your uniform an' him in his. I bet you'll make a great-lookin' pair.'

Ellie pictured herself outside the pigsties, dressed in dungarees and wellies, with a small bouquet of lavender in her hands. Next to her stood Aidan in his tatty overalls, his unruly hair blowing across his eyes whilst the vicar read their vows. She giggled.

Gwen waved to Arla, who trotted towards her, holding her cap firmly to her head as a gust of wind tried to remove it.

'Come to say goodbye?'

Arla nodded. 'Where's Ellie? Only I've gorra get a wriggle on. I'm runnin' late after sayin' ta-ra to me mam. I thought she were never goin' to let me go!'

'My aunt was the same last time I went for a visit. She wanted to load me up with bara brith, scones an' Spam sarnies. I didn't want to seem ungrateful but it's not easy carryin' lots of squashy food in a kitbag on a crowded train, but when I mentioned it she just said it all goes down the same way so what does it matter.' She wrinkled her nose. 'Spam and bara brith do not taste good when smudged together.' She pointed towards the officers' mess. 'There she is! She's lookin' for Bagheera. She let him out this mornin' after we'd had brekker, an' we've not seen him since.'

Arla grimaced. 'Oh, heck, he's still quite small so he could've hidden in any number of places. How long has she been looking?'

'Since ten minutes after she let him out.' Gwen sighed. 'She should've done it when he were a bit younger: he wouldn't have felt so brave then, and wouldn't have ventured off so easily. Someone told her to put butter on his paws; said it'd make him come back home.' She glanced at her wristwatch. 'He's been gone for two hours, so I think we can safely say the butter theory is a lot of old hogwash.'

Arla looked back towards the guard's gate. 'I haven't got long before my taxi comes to take me to the station. I must say, I've really enjoyed spending the week with you and Ellie.'

Gwen smiled. 'Thanks, cariad. It's been grand meetin' you too. Ellie suggested we might visit you in Lincoln when we get a bit of leave. You don't mind if I tag along too, do you?'

'Not at all. The more the merrier, an' you'll be able to meet Archie.' A thought occurred to her. 'Speakin' of boyfriends, would you mind keepin' an eye on Ellie and that Aidan if they meet up? Only I don't want to see her gettin' hurt, and whilst he sounds ideal ...' She frowned. 'I dunno, I s'pose I'm just worried he might be too good to be true, and my experience of men with rank is that they tend to think themselves above the rest of us. He may have been shy and reserved on the farm but being a pilot in the RAF will've brought him out of his shell for sure.' She glanced towards the barracks that Gwen shared with Evie. 'Women are ten a penny when it comes to pilots, so he'll have had more than his fair share of bottle-blonde floozies flingin' themselves at him, if you know what I mean.'

Gwen nodded. 'Don't you worry about Ellie. I'll make sure he doesn't get a chance to treat her badly. I don't know her as well as you do, of course, but she has told me some stuff about her life before the war, and I gather it was far from plain sailing, especially when it came to men.'

'She's been through the mill all right. When I learned I was going to Cornwall when she went to Weybourne I must admit I was concerned for her.' Arla patted Gwen's arm in a friendly fashion. 'Now I know she has a pal like you to watch out for her I'll rest a lot easier.'

The girls were interrupted by a yelp of outrage from somewhere near the officers' mess. 'Bagheera!' cried Gwen and Arla simultaneously. Trotting in that direction, they found Ellie on her haunches, carefully unhooking Bagheera from around an officer's thigh.

'I'm so, so sorry,' Ellie babbled as the officer, his face a mask of pain, glared down at her. 'I'm afraid you probably scared him more when you shouted; he must have thought you were angry at him. He's not used to people shouting.'

'What the bloody hell was he doing underneath the damned building in the first place ... Argghh!'

'Try not to shout. He just sinks his claws in tighter if he feels threatened,' Ellie said, the sweat beginning to form on her brow as she started again to unhook Bagheera from the man's uniform trousers.

The officer, who had opened his mouth to protest, appeared to change his mind. He took a few deep breaths before asking in as cool and calm a manner as possible, 'Threatened? How in God's name is he the one who's feeling threatened when he's been clawing his way towards my ... my ...' his mouth tightened, 'the top of my leg!'

Ellie looked up pleadingly. 'I'm sure if you relaxed a little ...' She jerked her head in Arla and Gwen's direction. 'Thank God you're here. Give us a hand, will you? Arla, you grab his back legs and lift them upwards – slowly – and Gwen, could you put your finger in the corner of his mouth?' Fortunately, before either girl could come within reach, for reasons known only to himself Bagheera released his grip on the officer.

Rubbing his leg, the officer glared at Bagheera. 'By rights I could have that thing shot, only I understand he's been good for Corporal Caldecott, got her smiling again.' His glare softened. 'I suggest you give him some sort of training. Next time he might not be so lucky.'

'Thank you, and I'm ever so sorry. I promise I'll keep him under better control. I'm going to put him back in the hut right this minute so he can't come to any more harm,' Ellie told him.

The officer's eyebrows shot toward his hairline. 'I wouldn't worry about him coming to any harm. If anything someone should warn the dogs that there's a lion on the loose.'

Cuddling Bagheera close to her chest, she turned to Arla and Gwen. 'Thanks for coming to my rescue. Let's get him back before he gets up to more mischief.' She started off towards the barracks, then stopped abruptly. 'Gosh, I've just realised: today's the day you're heading back to Lincoln. How long have you got before you leave?'

Arla looked at her wristwatch and grimaced. 'About ten minutes. It would've been longer but you know what me mam's like when it comes to goodbyes.'

Ellie giggled. 'You need a good half-hour and plenty of room for all the extra goodies.'

Arla stroked the top of Bagheera's head. 'How come you let him out? I thought you were waitin till I'd gone back to Lincoln before you let the little feller stretch his legs for the first time?'

Ellie looked round guiltily. 'He peed in Evie's shoe … again.'

Arla emitted a shriek of laughter, then clapped a hand to her mouth. 'Sorry … was she awfully angry?'

Gwen coughed on a giggle. 'She would be if she knew, but luckily I caught the little blighter before he'd finished so the damage wasn't too bad. I jammed a load of toilet paper in there to soak it up then rubbed in some of Ellie's Lily of the Valley talcum powder.' She smiled. 'It smelled quite nice, actually.'

Arla giggled. 'You do know that if she ever finds out, all hell's goin' to break loose?'

'Well, she won't, will she? After all, if she were ever going to notice it would've been this morning, and he won't do it again, because I'm going to make sure he starts going out every day.' Ellie glanced at the ablutions block. 'Although it might be a good idea to see if we can block up some of the holes under the buildings. That way he won't be able to ambush anyone.'

Reaching the gate, Ellie handed Bagheera over to Gwen before embracing Arla. 'I'm going to miss you so much! I promise to come and visit as soon as I get some leave, and I'll let you know what happens with Aidan, of course. Oh, I wish you weren't going!'

'It's been good coming back. I was a bit worried that being in the city after the blitz might dampen my spirits, but after seein' you two, and me mam an' dad, well,

252

it's made me feel more positive about the whole thing. If we can survive that, we can survive anything, am I right? Besides, I didn't want me an' Archie to get married an'—'

'Hold on! What do you mean, get married?' said Ellie, her eyes rounding.

'Don't worry, we've not planned owt, and in fact he's not even asked me yet—'

'But you've thought about it?'

Arla laughed. 'Doesn't every girl? When they meet the right one?'

Ellie took Bagheera back from Gwen and smoothed down the fur on top of his head. 'So you think he's the one, then?'

Arla shook her head. 'I don't think he's the one, I know he is. I've loved being home, really I have, but I've been missing Archie like you wouldn't believe.' A smile formed on her lips. 'You'd think I'd be glad to get away from him for a bit, but it's quite the opposite. I wish he could've come home with me.'

A car pulled up behind them and sounded its horn. Turning, Arla waved at the driver. 'It's my taxi come to take me to the station.' Placing her kitbag on the ground, she embraced Ellie and Gwen. 'Gosh, I'm goin' to miss you two! You come over and see me as soon as you can, promise?'

Ellie nodded. 'Wild horses won't stop me. Make sure you ring to let us know you arrived safely the minute you get back. Even if I'm on duty someone'll take a message.'

Getting out of the driver's door, the man picked up the large kitbag with a grunt and put it in the boot of the car. 'Sorry to break things up, ladies, but if you've gorra be at Lime Street ...'

Sinking into the back seat, Arla wound down the window. 'Take care of each other, and remember, first bit of leave ...'

Ellie and Gwen waved until the car was out of sight. 'One down, two to go,' said Gwen, linking Ellie's free arm.

'Two to go? Oh, you mean the boys.' Ellie's stomach lurched unpleasantly at the words. 'I know Aidan said they were coming our way on some kind of business, but he didn't say when. It could be months yet, which I s'pose could be a good thing, as I'd have plenty of time to work out what I want to say to him.' She kissed the top of Bagheera's head. 'Then again, I reckon when push comes to shove and I'm standing in front of him, whatever I've decided to say will disappear from my head.'

'Don't start worryin' over stuff that hasn't happened yet. We'll come up with a foolproof plan. Besides, I'll be with you for moral support – give you a bit of a nudge when needed, that kind of thing.'

Ellie smiled gratefully. 'Ta, chuck. It's good to know I'll have you with me.'

'That's the spirit! With the two of us together, the boy doesn't stand a chance. It'll give me a good excuse to give him the once-over an' all, see what all the fuss is about.'

Ellie chuckled. Even though she had told Gwen that Aidan was not particularly good-looking, she felt sure that Gwen had not believed her. 'Don't be expectin' Cary Grant, because I've already told you Aidan's not like that.'

'You seem awful worried that he's goin' to be snared by the likes of Evie, so there must be summat about him which you find irresistible.'

An image of Aidan flashed into Ellie's mind. His dark curly hair flopped over one eye as he grinned at her through the straggly beard that grew in patches around his cheeks and chin. Dressed in his tattered old farming clothes, he leaned against his cane. She turned to Gwen. 'Wait and see! Now, how about we take this little fellow back to the hut and go for a cup of tea?'

Tilly collected her letters from the board and examined the writing. One was from her parents, the other, if she was any judge, from her Auntie Margot. One of these days, she thought, I'll get myself a boyfriend, and when I do he'll write to me every day and tell me all about his exciting life, and his letters will not contain stories about Dad's gout. Placing her finger inside her parents' envelope she pulled it open, and was in the process of removing the letter when a pair of hands landed heavily on her shoulders. Tilly squealed, only to be hushed into silence by an impatient Evie.

'You'll never guess what I just heard in the canteen,' she said.

Tilly shrugged the other girl's hands off her shoulders. 'You shouldn't go jumpin' on people from behind like that. You're lucky I never gave you a good wallop!'

Evie rolled her eyes. 'Stop making such a fuss.' She linked her arm with Tilly's. 'So?'

'So what?' Tilly said, her patience beginning to wane. If Evie was excited about something she would bet her last penny that someone else would be suffering as a result.

'Don't you want to know the gossip?'

'Not particularly, but I dare say that won't stop you.'

Pulling her friend to a halt, Evie frowned. 'What's up with you?'

'Nowt, 'cept I've had enough of you creatin' trouble. The girls in our barracks have started avoidin' me, and I think it's because I hang around with you all the time. I'm not sayin' I don't want to be your pal, I just wish you'd leave folk alone, that's all.'

Evie narrowed her eyes. 'Shows what you know then, doesn't it? Because I've not done a damn thing, apart from overhear a conversation—'

'You mean you've been eavesdropping?'

'No! Blimey, you've got it in for me today, haven't you? I'm not sure I should tell you if you're going to be rude. I can't help it if people can't keep their voices down, can I?'

Believing she may have done Evie an injustice, Tilly apologised. 'Sorry. It's just … oh, never mind. Go on, what did you hear?'

Evie's pout was replaced with a malicious grin. 'That girl from the slums, Ellie, her pal is coming over to stay for a bit, the one who's a pilot.'

Tilly frowned. 'Why's that so exciting? He's comin' to see her, not you.'

'That's what he thinks at the moment, certainly, but by the time I've finished it'll be me he spends most of his time with.'

'How do you work that one out? He doesn't even know who you are,' Tilly said, although she suspected the answer would be one that involved Evie's causing upset.

'Not yet he doesn't, but he will, and I'm goin' to make sure I have his undivided attention whilst she's out of the way.'

'How? You can't control Ellie, and she's not goin' to listen to you if you tell her to leave the two of you alone.'

'I won't have to. She'll get out of the way all of her own accord.'

Tilly's eyes narrowed as she studied Evie's smug expression. 'Why would she want to leave you alone with her pal?'

Evie's grin widened. 'She won't want to leave me alone with him, she just won't have any choice.'

Tilly folded her arms. 'What are you going to do?'

'I've got several plans up my sleeve, don't you worry, but I'll tell you this: it'll be me that ends up with him, you mark my words.'

'And why do you want him in particular? You've never even seen him. Yes, you're after a pilot, but let's face it, that probably goes for half the WAAF. I know you, Evie Maddox, so come on, spill the beans. Why do you want to be with someone you've never even met?'

Evie avoided Tilly's gaze. 'Because his family's got land, but mainly because Lancton seems to think he's someone special, and no matter what she says I reckon she's got the hots for him. And after all she's done to me I think she deserves to be taken down a peg or two.'

Tilly stopped abruptly. 'Sorry, but I think I must be missing something. I thought you were the one who started it all. Wasn't it you who began mouthing off before they'd even spoken to you?'

Evie continued walking. 'You're missing the point. I was more than happy to let bygones be bygones until she got that little mate of hers to start spreading rumours about me behind my back.'

Tilly shook her head. 'It'll end in tears, you mark my words.'

Evie turned to face her. 'You're right there, only they won't be mine.'

Jogging to catch up, Tilly wondered yet again why Evie had to go out of her way to be so mean to everyone. She had the kind of figure most women would give their right arm for, and her naturally blonde hair fell in a bob of beautiful sleek curls. Long thick lashes surrounded wide blue eyes, and her lips were a perfect cupid's bow. With looks like that she could have any man she wanted, and did, yet she still felt it necessary to upset just about every other women she came in contact with. But everybody says that war changes folk, thought Tilly, so maybe it'll change Evie. After all, it must be very tiring to be constantly battling with everyone around you.

Chapter Ten

'For goodness' sake, Gwen, will you stop pacin' up
and down. You're goin' to wear a hole in the floor!'
Ellie said, as she tried to pin her curly hair into a
bun.

Gwen checked the clock on the wall above the door.
'I want to get goin' before Evie smells a rat.'

Ellie gave up trying to make her hair do as it was
told. 'Here, you have a go. It's too ... oh, I say, aren't
you clever?'

Having successfully pinned Ellie's bun into place,
Gwen gestured towards the door. 'I know they say it's
a lady's prerogative to be late, and I know you don't
want to appear too keen in case he thinks you're
desperate—'

'I'm not desperate,' Ellie interrupted, 'I just wanted
to make sure I looked my best, especially when there's
cats like Evie prowlin' round lookin' for a mate.' She
stopped abruptly. 'Speakin' of which, where's Baggy?'

She took half a pace back before being expertly
fielded by Gwen and steered back in the direction of
the door. 'Stop stalling. He's fast asleep on Caldecott's bed.'

Ellie felt her heart beat faster as they neared the NAAFI. It had been several months since Aidan had told her of his and connor's being sent to Liverpool, and she had used the time to worry over what she would say to him. So far she had come up with nothing.

Entering the NAAFI, she stood on tiptoe to look for her friends. Her eyes scanned the dance floor and the queue for food, and flickered across the tables to the bar, where to her delight she saw Connor sitting on a stool waving at her. Clasping Gwen's hand in hers, she started to tow her friend across the room. 'Connor's sitting by the bar. C'mon, I'll introduce you.' She had let go of Gwen's hand and moved to hug Connor before she realised that she had made a mistake. 'Aidan! But ... you look so ... so ...'

He rubbed his bare chin. 'Different? Well, they weren't too keen on the beard when I joined; said it had to go.'

A voice called out from the crowd and Ellie found herself being hugged by Connor. 'Wotcha! Blimey, you've filled out a bit.'

Ellie blushed. 'I'm not the only one.' She locked eyes with Aidan. 'I thought you were Connor. You look so alike now.'

Connor slapped his cousin on the shoulder. 'Who knew he'd turn out to be such a handsome devil under all that fuzz?'

Grinning, Aidan removed his cap. 'Gave me a bit of a haircut, too.'

Ellie's gaze took in the new Aidan. The once unkempt man was now clean cut and handsome. Standing up from his stool, he embraced her, and Ellie was not surprised to feel the same tingling sensation course down her body as she had when they had ridden through the woods all that time ago.

Releasing Ellie, he held out a hand towards Gwen. 'You must be Gwen. Can I get either of you two ladies a drink?'

Gwen shook his hand. 'Lemonade, please, or squash. Anything'll do.'

Ellie nodded. 'And I'll have whatever you're having.'

Aidan looked down at his small glass of beer. 'Barclays?'

Ellie opened her mouth to reply, but was interrupted by a petite blonde from Section D who was leaning against the bar, her eyes fixed firmly on Aidan. 'Hello! I like Barclays too. You're new here, aren't you? You stayin' long?'

Aidan shook his head. 'Only a week, and I'm afraid we'll be working most of the time we're here.' He smiled at Ellie and patted her on the shoulder. 'But we couldn't come all this way without paying our friends a visit.'

The girl eyed Ellie and Gwen. 'Lucky friends. But if you're here for a week, who knows, we might bump into each other again.' Taking her drink, she headed back towards her mates, all of whom appeared to be taking a keen interest in Aidan and Connor.

'As I was about to say, before we were so rudely interrupted,' Ellie shot a withering glance towards the table of ogling women, 'a glass of Barclays would be lovely.'

Gwen prodded Ellie gently in the back. 'You said you hated beer. Reckoned it made your tummy churn —' she began, only to be interrupted by Ellie's clearing her throat noisily.

She scowled at Gwen. 'That was different. It wasn't Barclays.' She looked across to the small blonde who had spoken to Aidan. 'If she can drink it I'm sure I can.'

The barmaid who had been waiting for them to come to a decision sighed impatiently. 'Do you want it or not?'

'Yes please,' Ellie said, making sure her eyes didn't make contact with Gwen's. The woman swiftly removed the bottle top and poured the beer into a glass before handing it to Ellie, who screwed up her eyes as she lifted it to her lips. Determined to get it over and done with as quickly as possible, she drained half the glass before coming up for air.

Aidan looked expectant. 'Well? Did it pass muster?'

Nodding, Ellie forced a smile. 'Shall we go somewhere a bit quieter, find a table perhaps? They do sandwiches sometimes, if you're hungry?'

Aidan rubbed his stomach. 'You know me, always up for a bit of grub. Lead the way, and make sure you fill me in on all the gossip.'

Standing in the queue, Ellie eyed the other women, all of whom were taking a keen interest in the handsome pilot. Hens, she thought bitterly, they're like a brood of hens clucking and preening themselves. If I want to speak to him on my own I'll have to find a less crowded part of the NAAFI, otherwise I'll find myself fending off rivals all evening. Looking round the room

262

for somewhere suitable, her attention was caught by the door that had just swung open. She rolled her eyes in dismay. It was Evie. Cursing inwardly, Ellie looked towards the front of the queue. With a bit of luck they could get their sandwiches and sit down before the other girl noticed them. She glanced back at Evie, and Aidan followed her gaze.

'Friend of yours?' he said.

Ellie shook her head. 'No!' she said brusquely. Then, seeing the look of surprise on Aidan's face, she lowered her voice. 'She's in my barracks, but she's in a different section – thank God – so we don't have much to do with each other.' She glanced sideways at Aidan, who was watching Evie as she walked towards the bar. 'She's known to be a bit of a man-eater when it comes to rank. The more stripes the better, if you know what I mean.'

Aidan laughed. 'There're plenty of them in the forces.'

Ellie eyed him suspiciously. What did he mean by that? He made it sound as though he had encountered women like Evie before. She looked back to where the other girl had been, only to find that she seemed to have vanished.

'There's Spam, or cheese.'

Ellie frowned. 'Sorry?'

The girl behind the counter folded her arms. 'Spam or cheese?'

Ellie looked from the sandwiches to Aidan. 'One of each? That way we can share.'

'Good idea,' he said. 'Have you seen a space?'

Ellie pointed to a table in the far corner of the room. Taking the lead, she could not shake a niggle in the back of her mind. It wasn't to do with Evie; something else was wrong. She frowned as she tried to trace what it was, and clapped a hand to her mouth. 'Gwen!' She looked wildly around her. 'Where did Gwen go? I completely forgot she'd come in with me ... oh, Aidan, I feel awful. Some kind of friend I am.'

Laughing, he put the plates down on the melamine table top. 'Don't worry. She's a big girl, I'm sure she can look after herself.'

'I know, but I feel awful. I shan't be a mo. I can't believe I was so rude.'

Aidan chuckled. 'Off you go. I'll just sit here and try not to eat these delicious-looking sarnies.'

Ellie trotted off in the direction of the dance floor and was relieved to find Gwen and Connor dancing a hearty foxtrot. Catching Gwen's eye, she mouthed the word sorry before heading back to Aidan.

As she approached their table her heart sank. She could not have been gone for more than a few seconds, yet Evie had managed to hunt Aidan down and was standing chatting to him. Ellie watched Aidan smile pleasantly up at the other girl and crossed her fingers behind her back. Maybe, if I'm really lucky, Aidan'll ask her to leave, tell her that he wants to spend the evening with me. A small groan escaped her lips as Evie pulled out a chair and sat down beside him.

As Ellie took the chair on the other side of Aidan, Evie smiled brightly at her. 'Ah, here she is. I've being keeping an eye on Pilot Officer Murray for you whilst you were gone. You shouldn't leave him on his own like that, Ellie. You know what the girls in our hut are like: once they see a handsome man they're like flies on a hot summer's day.'

'Hmm,' said Ellie. She picked up her beer and was about to take a reluctant sip when she noticed that three more glasses had been placed on the table. She raised a quizzical eyebrow at Aidan, who shook his head.

'Nothing to do with me. Your friend ...' He glanced apologetically at Evie. 'I'm sorry, what did you say your name was?'

'Evelyn, but my friends call me Evie.' The smile she flashed at Ellie revealed a set of impeccable white teeth. 'I never welch on a deal, and I did tell you I'd stand you and Aidan a drink for jumping to the wrong conclusion that time.' She gestured to the glasses. 'And here it is!'

Aidan looked curiously at Ellie, who was looking confused. 'What's all this about jumping to the wrong conclusion, and why am I involved? Not that I'm complaining, mind you; it's not often a beautiful stranger buys me a drink.'

Beautiful! Ellie thought bitterly. I may as well give up now.

'When Ellie said you were coming to visit I assumed you were her boyfriend. Of course, she soon put me straight on that score, but she was pretty miffed, so I offered to buy you both a drink by way of apologising for my mistake.'

Aidan's cheeks flushed pink. 'Oh, right.' He raised his glass. 'Thanks.'

Ellie felt as though she had been hit with a shovel. What on earth had Evie gone and said that for? She had made it sound as if Ellie found the idea of being with Aidan repulsive. She looked at Aidan and wondered how she could rectify the situation. She wanted to say that Evie had lied, or misinterpreted what she had said, but she didn't trust Evie not to make some retort that would make things even worse. She glanced across at Evie and was maddened to see a malicious grin etched on the other girl's face. I was a fool to ever mention Aidan in front of her, Ellie thought bitterly. I should have listened to Gwen and kept my big mouth shut.

Evie raised her glass. 'Cheers!'

Without uttering a word, Ellie took a large swig of the beer that Evie had bought for her, but as soon as the liquid touched her tongue she realised that this was a completely different drink from the one Aidan had bought. If she had found the first beer unpleasant, then this one was completely foul. Rather than spit it out she swallowed, but the liquid burned her throat and she began to choke and splutter.

Evie was grinning gleefully at her.

Ellie scraped her chair back and ran out of the NAAFI. Entering the ablutions at breakneck speed she felt the sick begin to rise in her throat, and hurtling into an empty cubicle she vomited down the toilet.

Gwen, who had seen her friend's flight, rapped on the door with her knuckles. 'Ellie? Is everything all right? Only you left the NAAFI like summat was on fire.'

'It was that stupid drink,' Ellie said miserably. 'And before you say I told you so, I don't mean the one Aidan bought me, but the one Evie bought. I assumed it was

266

Barclays, which is bad enough, but it wasn't. It was vile, and it burned my throat.'

Gwen peeped round the edge of the cubicle door. 'It all tastes nasty if you ask me, although I don't think I've ever heard anyone saying it burned them before. Can I get you anything? A glass of water, perhaps?'

Ellie shook her head, then nodded. 'You can get me my dignity back if you like. I think I left it at the table with Aidan and Evie.'

'Bugger that,' Gwen said firmly. 'You're comin' with me. You can't leave him out there on his own with her, she'll have him for brekker.' A thought struck her. 'You don't s'pose she put summat else in that drink, to make you sick on purpose? That'd explain why it tasted so bad.'

Ellie frowned. 'She'd be taking a bit of a risk. What if Aidan had picked it up instead of me? Besides, what could she put in beer which would make it undrinkable?'

Gwen looked astutely at her friend and tapped the side of her nose with her forefinger. 'People like her would do anythin'.' She turned the cold tap on. 'Wash your mouth out with some water, go back in there and show her she can't get rid of you that easily. I'll be by the dance floor if you need me.'

Ellie smiled gratefully. 'You're a real pal. I feel such a fool for rushing off like that. What must Aidan think?'

Gwen shrugged. 'That you really needed the loo?'

Ellie gave a mirthless laugh. 'He won't be far wrong then, will he?'

Entering the NAAFI once more, Ellie walked over to the table where Aidan was seated and looked shyly at him from under her lashes. 'Sorry for rushing off like that.' She glanced at the empty chair. 'Where did she go?'

Aidan laughed. 'I think I must have some strange effect on women. They can't wait to get away from me.'

Ellie's stomach went into a painful knot. 'I'm sorry, Aidan, but that drink Evie gave me didn't agree with me at all. My tummy's lurchin' summat awful. I think it might be best if I got an early night.'

Aidan looked at her kindly. 'There's no need to apologise, alanna. Tell you what, I'm not much of a one for dances, so how about you and me meet for coffee tomorrow at Bumbles, say ten a.m.?'

Ellie smiled happily. 'Sounds good to me.'

The next morning Ellie was in the ablutions brushing her teeth when Evie walked in behind her. 'Ellie! I'm so glad to see you're feeling better. It was such a shame that you had to rush off last night. Someone said it was because of the beer? I do hope it wasn't my fault; I'd hate to think I'd made you sick.' Her tone oozed with false sympathy. 'Still, every cloud and all that, at least I got to know Aidan a bit better. I must say I think he's a real charmer, and clever to boot. I'm surprised you never found him attractive.'

Ellie shoved her toothbrush back into her small wash bag and looked up at Evie with an air of defiance. 'What beer did you give me? Only I've never tasted one like it before.'

Evie's face was set with a fixed smile. 'It was Barclays.'

'No it wasn't,' snapped Ellie. 'I had Barclays earlier and it tasted nothing like that.'

Evie's eyes narrowed, but the smile remained. 'I hope you're not accusing me of lying, Ellie? I wouldn't do anything to hurt you, you know that.'

'All I know is it tasted different to me, and I think you'd do anything to get your hands on a pilot.' She had turned to leave when Evie held out a hand.

'He asked me out on a date. I said yes, of course. I do hope you don't mind?'

Pushing Evie's hand to one side, Ellie left the ablutions to the sound of Evie's laughter, the tears that brimmed in her eyes beginning to trickle down her hot cheeks. How could he? she thought miserably. Anyone would be better than Evie. Didn't he realise how mean and nasty the other girl could be? Surely he could see that she was only after him so that she could show him off as some sort of prize catch? Remembering her promise to meet him at Bumbles, she decided she would take the opportunity to warn him off the wretched girl.

Bursting into the hut, she rushed over to Gwen, who was reading a copy of *Woman's Own*, and told her friend about her encounter with Evie and her intention to warn Aidan.

Sliding off the top bunk, Gwen shook her head. 'I wouldn't, if I were you. He might think you're interferin' or being nasty, and you've got to remember how charming Evie can be when it comes to men. You're far better off lettin' him find out of his own accord. Besides, you already told him she were only after a feller with stripes – or in his case wings – so he's already got the heads-up.'

Ellie chewed her lip thoughtfully. Was Gwen right? Would Aidan really think of it as interfering or would he see it as it was intended, to stop him from making a mistake? If he did think it was interfering she might be driving him, albeit unintentionally, into Evie's arms. She glanced at Gwen. 'So what do I do? Just leave her to sink her claws in even deeper?'

Gwen pulled a face. 'I don't see that you've got any choice. But if you take my advice, you'll leave well alone. Least said, soonest mended, as the saying goes.'

Ellie sat down on the edge of her bed. 'So I'm supposed to go to Bumbles and not mention Evie?'

'Yup.'

'What if he mentions her to me, asks me about her? What am I meant to say then?'

'As little as possible. He'll soon find out what a nasty little cat she can be.'

Ellie was disappointed. She had wanted an excuse to warn Aidan off the horrid Evie, and Gwen's answer was not the one she had been hoping for. 'What about Baggy? She was horrid to him. Aidan loves animals – he wouldn't like it if he knew how nasty she'd been. I thought you'd be on my side, if only for Baggy's sake.'

Gwen smiled sympathetically. 'I am on your side, that's why I'm tellin' you to let him work it out for himself. He will in the end; they always do, that's why she keeps moving on from one feller to the next. It's not her that dumps them, it's the other way round.'

Ellie drew a small bag of humbugs from her pocket and handed one to Gwen. 'I know you're right, but keeping my mouth shut is going to be hard.' Popping one of the sweets into her mouth she smiled at Gwen. 'Maybe these will help. Thanks for the advice.'

Gwen stowed her humbug into one cheek. 'That's what pals are for. Now off you go and have your cuppa with Aidan.'

Bumbles was a popular haunt and Ellie was not surprised to see that the small café was already crowded. Choosing a seat by the window, she informed the elderly waitress that she would order when her friend arrived. Looking up the tree-lined street, she watched as a strong gust of wind picked up the crisp autumn leaves and sent them swirling down the pavement. A small boy ran past the café window as he tried to snatch a handful of the leaves, and his mother who was trotting along behind him bent down to pick up the school cap that had blown from his head. Ellie thought back to the times when her mother had walked her to school. Ellie would be holding her hand whilst trying to avoid stepping on the cracks between the paving stones, which involved taking giant leaps over some whilst dodging round others. Millie had often complained. 'You'll have me arm out of its socket if you keep leapin' about. It's like trying to walk a hare to school.'

Watching as the mother caught up to her son and the two joined hands, Ellie wondered if the boy ever played the same game.

The bell above the café door rang sharply, making Ellie jump. Glancing up, she saw Aidan closing the door firmly behind him.

He grinned at her. 'Mornin', queen. How's your stomach?'

Ellie groaned. She had been so busy worrying about Evie and Aidan getting together, she had quite forgotten the foul drink. 'Don't mention that awful stuff. I reckon it must've gone off or summat; it really upset my tummy.'

Aidan sat down next to her. 'I must admit we both wondered about that, because mine was okay and so was Evelyn's. I was going to taste yours, but Evie knocked it over by accident. That's why she rushed off, to mop herself down.'

Ellie pursed her lips. She'd bet a pound to a penny that Evie had realised he intended to take a swig and pushed it over before he had the chance, the crafty cow.

Aidan raised his hand to gain the waitress's attention. 'Pot of tea for two and a couple of your lovely scones, please, Clara.'

Ellie was bemused. 'How on earth do you know the waitress? You only arrived the other day.'

Aidan tapped the side of his nose. 'First thing you do when you get to a new station is find out the best caff in the area and make friends with the staff.'

The elderly waitress brought a tray over and began to distribute the cups and plates on to the table. Aidan rubbed his hands together gleefully. 'Just what a feller needs to set him up for the day ahead, this is.' He glanced at Ellie. 'You could march an army on Clara's food. You'd never know rationin' restrictions applied in her kitchen. Tasty, too.'

Clara tutted and shook her head with a wry grin. 'You're a charmer, Aidan Murray, just like your cousin.' She glanced expectantly out of the window. 'He not joinin' you this mornin'?'

Aidan grinned. 'He's still tired after all the dancin' he did last night. He was like Fred Astaire, or at least that's what he keeps tellin' everyone.'

The old lady chuckled as she made her way back to the counter. Ellie looked curiously at Aidan. 'I've been here for a while now, yet I didn't know Clara's name until today. You put me to shame, Aidan Murray. Anyone'd think you'd known her all your life.'

Aidan winked. 'Always important to make friends with the locals, especially when they're the ones providing food.'

Outside, another gust of wind threw a pile of leaves up against the glass, and Ellie nodded towards the window. 'Won't be long till the bad weather sets in ... I hope we have a green Christmas. I don't fancy the idea of being on a battery with a foot of snow on the ground.'

Aidan shrugged. 'Depends on your point of view. Heavy snow means no flying, and that applies to them as well as us; it's a bit of a double-edged sword, I suppose.'

She looked up guiltily. 'I didn't think of that. In that case I'll be keeping my fingers crossed for a white Christmas.'

Aidan was about to take a bite out of his scone when he appeared to remember something. 'We had word today that we're goin' to be headin' back to Waddington sooner than we thought, probably in a few days, so I'm afraid we won't have much time together.'

Ellie's shoulders sank. 'It's not fair. You only just got here, and I miss having my old friends around. You and Connor are so lucky to be working together.'

273

Aidan nodded. 'I must admit, life's a lot more pleasant now that Connor's joined us.' He leaned forward and lowered his voice. 'Don't tell him I said that, though! Speaking of work, I told you about our old bomber, the Blenheim Beauty? Well, the reason we came to Speke was to pick up a new one. It's a Lancaster. Why don't you come and have a look at her? I can't show you around today, because – well, I've got stuff to do – but how about tomorrow? I could pick you up around ten, if you're free, that is?'

Ellie, who had just taken a large bite out of her scone, nodded enthusiastically whilst covering her mouth with her hand so as not to spray him with crumbs. 'I'd *love* to! I've never seen a bomber up close, you know – well, I have a Heinkel, but that doesn't count.'

Aidan's brow furrowed. 'You've seen a Heinkel up close? How come?'

Ellie waved a dismissive hand. 'I've not actually seen one for real. It was a dream, I suppose, but it was incredibly detailed …' She explained her 'encounter' with the Heinkel and its pilot during the May blitz, and how she had realised that even the enemy had families who would grieve for them every bit as much as she grieved for her own mother if anything happened.

Aidan eyed her curiously. 'Wow. It sounds like some kind of out-of-body experience. I've heard of those, but I've never met anyone who's had one. Do you think it could have been that?'

Ellie frowned. 'I really don't know, and perhaps I'll never be sure. I'm just glad it hasn't happened again … fingers crossed,' she added hastily.

Aidan shuddered. 'Real or not, it's jolly unpleasant staring into the eyes of the enemy. I should know – I've done it more than once.'

Ellie reached across the table and took hold of his hand. 'I think you're ever so brave. I'd be terrified if it were me.'

He squeezed her fingers. 'I'd be a liar if I said I wasn't scared, we all are, but in a strange way that's what keeps you going.' He gazed thoughtfully out of the window. 'But let's not talk about it.' Leaning back, he took a swig from his teacup. 'I know you said your old landlord had been bombed out of his premises, but has anyone seen him since? He's not knockin' about the city, is he?'

Ellie shrugged. 'My guess would be that he's either signed on as a docker or joined one of the services.' She gave a mirthless laugh. 'I can't imagine anyone'd take him on, though, unless it was to clean the latrines.'

'Well, if you should bump into him and he starts giving you grief just you let me know. I'm sure I can persuade him to leave you be.'

Ellie smiled. 'Just like your cousin, comin' to a girl's rescue. I'll have had two knights in shining armour then. It's almost worth bumping into Sid.'

Chuckling, Aidan glanced at his watch. 'Damn, I'll have to be off in a mo. Did you say you were all right for tomorrow? I can pick you up from camp, 'cos the crew have got shares in a small motorcar. I kind of hoped you'd say yes, so I already asked them if I could have it in the morning.'

Ellie nodded eagerly. 'I'm on lates all this week, so I'm free for most of the day.' She studied his face. It wasn't just his hair and beard that had changed; his brow had acquired thin lines which made him look more mature. She gazed into his twinkling green eyes and marvelled that the war had not doused the spark that lay deep inside, as it had in so many of the other men she had encountered. Aware that she was staring, she turned her gaze to the crumbs on her plate. 'Those scones were delicious, but I don't reckon they're a patch on your mam's.'

He leaned forward. 'Neither do I, but I'd never admit it to Clara,' he said, his voice just above a whisper. 'She might stop givin' me extra butter and jam if she knew the truth.'

Ellie smiled cheekily. 'Clara's got you bang to rights. You are a charmer, Aidan Murray.'

'You look like the cat that got the cream,' observed Gwen. 'I take it all went well?'

Ellie nodded. 'He didn't make me feel at all embarrassed about my dicky tummy last night, and he's picking me up tomorrow mornin' at ten o'clock to go and see the Lancaster Lass – that's his new bomber.'

Gwen pulled a face. 'Did he mention Evie?'

Ellie pursed her lips. 'Only to say that she knocked my drink over by accident, so I reckon you were right, and she had slipped something into my glass.'

Gwen grimaced. 'Can't say I'm surprised. Did he mention taking her out?'

Ellie shook her head. 'I don't know what she was on about this morning and I don't care. I don't believe Aidan would ever—'

276

Gwen held up a hand. 'Before you go on, she's off to meet him now. In fact, I think she left about five minutes ago.'

Ellie sank into the chair next to Gwen's. 'Are you sure? What exactly did she say?'

'She said he'd told her he was busy this morning but would meet her around eleven thirty.' They both glanced at the clock above the NAAFI door. It was eleven forty.

Deflated, Ellie looked appealingly at Gwen. 'Why didn't he tell me he was meeting her?'

Gwen shrugged. 'Where did he say he was going, after you, I mean?'

Ellie thought back. 'He didn't say exactly, just that he had some stuff to do.'

Gwen shook her head disapprovingly. 'I don't think Evie would like it if she knew that he was referring to her as "stuff".' She eyed Ellie cautiously. 'Are you still going to meet him tomorrow, or ...?'

'I suppose so. It's not as if he's done anything wrong, is it? I just wish he'd told me, but then again, I didn't ask.'

'You feel like you've been betrayed, though, am I right?' Gwen said.

Ellie nodded. 'Only because he never mentioned her, but then I did tell him that we weren't friends, and I suppose I was a little bit uncomplimentary when it came to her relationships with other men, especially those with wings or stripes ...'

'That'll be it then. He hasn't told you because he knows you wouldn't approve, but does that make it feel any better?'

277

'Not really,' said Ellie, 'but it's my fault that he feels he has to keep me in the dark in the first place.' Placing her elbows on the canteen table, she rested her chin in her hands. 'What shall I do? The last thing I want is for Aidan and Evie to get serious about each other.'

'Why? Do you want him for yourself or not? Before he arrived you weren't sure of your feelings towards him. Do you know how you feel now?'

'Not really. I hardly spent more than ten minutes with him last night, and only an hour and a half this morning,' she said.

Gwen looked thoughtful. 'What if it was me who was meeting Aidan? What then? Would you wish us all the luck in the world?'

The question threw Ellie into turmoil, but it did give her the answer. The truth was she was in love with him, but seeing him looking so handsome in his pilot officer's uniform had silenced her. His good looks would attract a lot of women far prettier than she, and Ellie thought she would not stand a chance among them, especially against Evie, who had obviously set her sights firmly on her handsome friend. She would have to be positive that Aidan really wanted her and no one else before she would even consider a relationship. Sighing heavily, she wished he would remain single until she was sure how he felt. She said as much to Gwen, who frowned reprovingly at her.

'That's not fair, Ellie Lancton, and well you know it. Especially for a man in Aidan's line of duty. You can't expect him to dangle on the line whilst you make up your mind. What if you decide in a month or two that you don't want a relationship with him? Better yet, turn it around and see how you would feel if he wanted you to wait indefinitely for him ... would you do it?'

Ellie looked crossly at Gwen. 'I don't expect him to hang around waiting for me. I never said I did.'

Gwen wagged a finger. 'Don't you go getting irritated with me just because you know I'm right. By wanting to destroy his relationship with Evie – that's if they've even got a relationship – you're trying to keep him free for yourself, whether you're willing to admit it or not.'

'I wouldn't purposely set out to make him unhappy. I'd never do that to Aidan, I just don't want to see him make a mistake.'

Gwen raised an eyebrow. 'It's not up to you to decide whether he's making a mistake or not, and even if he is, it's his mistake to make. I know you're scared of getting hurt, and I don't blame you, you've suffered a lot in the past, but that's life. You mustn't be frightened to take a chance in case it all goes pear-shaped.' She gazed sympathetically at Ellie. 'I know you're worried that he won't want you with Evie practically throwin' herself at him, but I'm afraid you're going to have to take a back seat on this one and see what unfolds. But I still think you should meet him tomorrow, because if he does fall for Evie – and I'm not saying he will, but if he does – then he'll need a friend nearby to pick up the pieces, especially if it ends like all the rest of her relationships have.'

Ellie nodded weakly. 'I know you're right, and I'm sorry if I've been acting like a spoiled brat, but losing me mam broke my heart and I'm scared of opening up to him just to have it broken all over again. I almost wish I hadn't got any feelings for him; life would be so much easier. I'm so glad you're here. I'd've made a right mess of things left to me own devices.'

Leaning across the table, Gwen clasped Ellie's hand in her own and gave it a comforting shake. 'I keep tellin' you, that's what friends are for, cariad, to stop each other making a right pig's ear out of life. If the shoe were on the other foot I know you'd do the same for me.'

When they pulled up beside the Lancaster bomber, Ellie's jaw dropped as she took in the immensity of the four huge engines, the vast wingspan and the sheer height of the craft, which towered above the small car. 'It's huge! Surely you don't fly this one?'

Aidan chuckled. 'I don't bloomin' well push it, that's for sure.'

Connor, who had been waiting for them, jogged towards the car and gripped the passenger door handle. 'It's a bit temperamental,' he said, grunting as he pulled and lifted at the same time.

'You were the one who said you could get it fixed,' Aidan said pointedly.

Connor helped Ellie out of her seat. 'I'm too busy wooing the ladies to be messin' round with cars in me spare time.'

Aidan laughed. 'Listen to him! Anyone'd think he was a right little Casanova. Truth is, he's only got one date, and that's by default!'

Ellie frowned. 'What do you mean, by default?'

Aidan grinned as Connor took a playful swipe at him before answering her question. 'Don't go listenin' to him, he's only jealous. Besides, we're not here to talk about my love life. Ellie, this is the Lancaster Lass!'

Ellie automatically looked up at the pilot's seat. 'How do you get in?'

Aidan pointed to a ladder that led into the fuselage. 'Through there, but first we'll show you where our Connor sits. It's quite a squeeze to get into, so you're better off seein' it from the outside.'

Connor had already started to walk to the rear of the plane. He stopped below a huge Perspex dome, out of which guns protruded. Ellie's eyes flickered over the dome. 'Haven't you got any metal to protect you?' she asked incredulously.

Connor shook his head. 'Only the blast door behind me, which is to stop me fallin' out whilst I spin round.' He chuckled at Ellie's shocked expression. 'The turret moves so that I can aim better, and the dome's made of Perspex so that I can see them coming from just about any direction. I wouldn't be able to do that if I was surrounded by metal. Besides, it's quite sturdy stuff, this, you know. It doesn't break easily.'

Aidan pulled her gently by the elbow. 'Come with me, I'll show you where I sit.'

Preceding her up the short ladder, Aidan guided her into the pilot's seat, adding as he did so, 'Don't touch any of the instruments. We don't want to take off, or not just yet at any rate.'

Ellie stared out of the cockpit, then looked at the dials and switches before her. Aidan pointed at two pedals on the floor. 'I steer the plane with those.'

She looked admiringly into their upturned faces. 'I knew you both did a dangerous job, of course I did, but coming here and seeing it first hand gives you a real sense of things. I can see that's it's more than dangerous, it's exciting and complex.'

Aidan's chest swelled with pride. 'All in a day's work,' he said with an air of nonchalance, although the grin on his face didn't fool Ellie, who could tell that her words had thrilled him.

'Have either of your mams ever seen one of these up close?'

Aidan choked. 'Good God, no! And they never will. It'd only give 'em summat else to worry over.'

Ellie nodded. Before today she had only envisaged them high up in the air in a sort of vacuum, but now she could see it all too clearly, and she began to think that she also might have been better off not knowing.

Aidan looked at his watch. 'We'd best be gettin' you back, Ellie. Me and Connor've got a few things to do before our next meeting. Sorry it couldn't have been longer.'

Connor nodded guiltily. 'My fault, I'm afraid: made prior arrangements. But we'll meet up again soon, I promise.'

Lying in her bed later that night, Ellie closed her eyes and tried to think of anything other than the Lancaster Lass going on a mission with a squadron of bombers. But the more she tried to put it out of her mind, the more she found herself thinking of the cockpit where Aidan sat surrounded by instruments, dials and switches, and, worse still, Connor sitting in the rear of the plane, finger on the trigger, ready to shoot down anyone who dared to attack. Slowly, she drifted off into a sleep plagued with nightmares.

Looking into the cockpit of the Lancaster Lass, Ellie watched Aidan. Even with the oxygen mask obscuring most of his face, she would have recognised those sparkling green eyes anywhere. Shouting his name as loudly as she could, she waved an enthusiastic hand, but his gaze remained fixed on the horizon. Failing to gain his attention she looked around her. The sky was empty except for the heavy bomber. Looking below, she saw, thankfully, that there was no sign of an ack-ack battery; neither was the sky lit up by beams from searchlights. We must be above England, she thought with a sense of relief, and then chided herself for feeling scared. You can't get hurt in dreams, you silly girl, so there's no need to be afraid. She made her way to the rear of the plane where she found Connor having an animated conversation with one of the crew over the headset. Retreating, she found a spot from which she could see both Murray men. Aidan was throwing his head back in laughter, much the same as his cousin. After her visit to Speke station earlier that day, she had imagined the men to be serious and fraught with worry whilst up in the air, but seeing them happy and relaxed brought her a sense of relief. She peered at Aidan, who was looking at an instrument in front of him. He started to jab his finger at it in an excited fashion. Ellie frowned. What on earth was he talking about now? Perhaps the dial was broken, but that was no way to fix it, surely? Then, like a radio being switched on, she heard their voices so clearly it sounded as though she were standing next to both of them.

'He's coming in port side. Connor, keep your eyes peeled. Can you see him, Geoff?'

The mid-turret gunner was nodding vigorously. 'I see him, skipper.'

Ellie glanced at Connor, who seemed unperturbed by the frantic communications going on around him. Typical Connor, she thought, cool as a cucumber until the last minute, then bam! It'll be all guns blazing.

Aidan's voice broke the silence once more. 'What is he? Can you see clearly yet? Keep your sights to port, Connor, I think he'll be with you any second now.'

There was a brief pause before Aidan spoke again. 'Connor? Did you hear me?'

Ellie looked towards the rear of the plane, and, seeing the lack of interest on Connor's face, she realised the awful truth. Something must have gone wrong with the headsets, and Connor was unable to hear his cousin's warnings. But surely he could hear everyone shouting? Then she remembered the blast door and very much doubted he would be able to hear anything through the thick metal.

'Messerschmitt!'

Ellie jumped as she heard the bullets streaking towards the fuselage. Geoff opened fire.

She saw Connor jump as the bullets shot across the rear of the plane. Realising they were under attack, he looked frantically around for a sighting, but the Messerschmitt was concentrating on the fuselage. She heard the bullets pelting into the side of the Lancaster Lass, followed by a large explosion. She turned her attention to Connor, who was still waiting for the enemy plane to come within his sights. But it was too late; the Lancaster Lass had suffered too much damage. Ellie heard Aidan's voice instructing the crew to bail out. She looked back at Connor, who was still sitting in his seat, talking desperately into his headset whilst cupping a hand over his earpiece.

Ellie's heart sank as she watched him trying to talk to a crew who had already left the plane. She steered her parachute towards the dome and started to slap her hands against the Perspex.

'Get out! Connor, you've got to get out, everyone's already gone, and you're going to crash! Connor, get out!' Tears streaming down her face, she thumped her fists against the Perspex in unison with the last three words. Her voice was hoarse from screaming, but she knew that Connor could neither hear nor see her. She watched helplessly as he continued to try to make radio contact with the rest of the crew.

She dropped away from the plane with the others, hearing Aidan's screams, clear as a bell, ringing out through the night sky. 'Connor! Get out! Connor!' Everything went black.

Connor's voice broke the darkness. 'That was a lucky escape.'

Ellie saw that he was standing next to her, and in front of them the Lancaster Lass lay in a twisted heap between two wheat fields. Frowning, she looked at Connor. He didn't appear to have a single scratch on him. 'How did you get out? I screamed and shouted, but you never heard me.'

Connor grinned. 'I jumped out when the plane was about eight feet from the ground. I don't know why everyone doesn't do that. It's perfectly safe, you know.'

Standing on tiptoe, Ellie scanned the field for signs of Aidan. 'Did you see where your cousin landed?'

Connor placed an arm around her shoulders. 'His parachute collapsed, so I'm afraid he's a goner. Still, every cloud an' all that, at least you don't have to worry about him getting together with Evelyn now.'

Ellie looked at him, aghast. 'Connor! How could you say something so cruel? I'd never do anything to hurt Aidan, or you for that matter. I don't care who he sees as long as he's safe.'

He glared at her accusingly. 'Me be cruel? You're the one who put up a fuss about them getting together.' He slid his arm from around her shoulders. 'It's a bit late to be changing your mind now. You really should have said something a lot sooner; if you had he might still be with us!'

Ellie stood open-mouthed as she started to protest, but before any words could leave her lips Connor faded from view and a hollow voice spoke from behind her.

Turning quickly, she saw to her relief that it was Aidan. 'Oh, thank goodness!' Throwing her arms around his neck, she tilted her head to look into his face. 'Connor told me you'd not made it. He said ...' She tried to focus as tears blurred her vision. Aidan's eyes were as green as they ever were, but their usual sparkle had gone, leaving them dull and lifeless.

Aidan smiled down at her. 'Connor's only angry because he knows how much you meant to me.'

Stroking her hair back from her face, he said, 'Don't you go worryin' your head none; you've always known what to do for the best. Like the time you left Lavender Court to come to Springdale. You knew that was the best thing to do, just as you knew you had to leave us and join the ATS, even though you were happy on the farm.' He arched his eyebrows. 'So why do you suppose it is that when it came to me, you didn't know what to do for the best? Surely you know whether you love someone or not?'

Ellie looked imploringly into his eyes. 'Please forgive me. I didn't mean to hurt you, and I suppose I've always known deep down. It's just that—'

Aidan looked sharply over his shoulder, as though he had heard something. Following his gaze, she felt a glaring white light pierce her eyes, and she dipped her head on to his chest. She felt Aidan's lips as he gently kissed the top of her forehead. 'Sorry, alanna, but I've got to say goodbye.'

Ellie looked up sharply. 'But you never say that. You always said you hate goodbyes. That's why you say t.t.f.n.'

He frowned uncertainly. 'But what would be the point in that? You only say t.t.f.n. when you intend to return, but I won't be coming back, not now, not ever.' He eyed her sadly. 'Shame it took you so long to work out what you wanted when it came to me. We could've stayed on the farm together for the rest of our lives.'

Darkness enveloped him, and Ellie found herself standing alone. No Connor, no Lancaster Lass, no wheat field, no Aidan. Just darkness.

*

Gwen gently shook Ellie's shoulder. 'Wake up, Ellie, you're having a nightmare. Open your eyes. It's not real, it's just a bad dream.'

When Ellie awoke she found herself surrounded by a group of girls, all in their pyjamas, one of them – Evie, of couse – scowling at her. Evie spoke first.'Mind tellin' me exactly what you mean by shoutin' out my feller's name in your sleep?' she said accusingly.

Ellie felt her cheeks redden as a sea of faces awaited her answer. 'I don't know. I was dreaming, for goodness' sake.'

Evie interrupted haughtily. 'Don't know, or won't say? I don't go round dreaming about other girls' boyfriends.' She ignored a suppressed giggle from the back of the group.

Ellie leaned up on one elbow. 'You can't hold me responsible for shouting stuff out in my sleep. I can't control my dreams!'

'I asked you if you were interested in him and you said no, or was that a lie? Perhaps it's more a case of *he* isn't interested in *you?*'

Ellie's cheeks glowed with humiliation as she heard the other girls murmuring behind Evie. 'This is ridiculous. I wouldn't lie. I – I ...'

'I – I ...' Evie mimicked. Leaning forward, she hissed into Ellie's ear, 'You keep away from him, understand?'

Forgetting her humiliation, Ellie leaned back. 'You can't tell me who I can or can't see, Evelyn Maddox. I've known the Murrays a lot longer than you have, and I have no intention of ignoring either of them just because you say so.' Looking into Evie's startled eyes, she continued, 'And what's more—'

'Oh, shut your cakehole,' said Evie. Stepping back, she looked haughtily at Ellie. 'I don't know why I'm bothered. It's not as if he'd give you a second glance, and as for that foul-smelling, putrid animal you call a cat,' her eyes narrowed maliciously, 'if I get my way – and believe you me, it's only a matter of time – that rancid moggie—'

'You so much as touch Bagheera—' Ellie started, but reveille drowned her words. Sniffing contemptuously, Evie strutted back to her bunk.

'Oh, dear.' Gwen looked anxious. 'Don't let her get to you. She wouldn't dare do anything to Bagheera. He's very popular with the other girls; she'd have a lynch mob on her hands if she did anything silly.'

The small group that had surrounded Ellie's bunk dissipated. Wrapping her greatcoat around her, Gwen retrieved her and Ellie's wash bags. 'You were shouting rather loudly. Can you remember what your nightmare was about?'

'It was the Lancaster Lass. Connor and Aidan died when they got attacked by another plane. I think it was a Messerschmitt, not that that's important … ' She frowned. 'I'm starting to wish they'd never taken me to see her. I'll probably be plagued with nightmares now.'

'So it was nothing to do with you and Aidan gettin' together. Completely the opposite, in fact.' Gwen snorted. 'Bloomin' Evie kickin' up a fuss when she hasn't got all the facts. It's so silly, particularly when she'll probably be seein' someone else this time next week. After all, didn't you say the boys were only goin' to be stayin' for a few more days?'

Ellie nodded. 'It's so frustrating, because I'd already made up my mind to take a step back. Why did I have to go stirrin' things up with some stupid dream?'

'Like you said, you can't control your dreams, and from what you said it were more to do with their new plane than Aidan himself.' She handed Ellie her wash bag. 'Come on, else we'll be late for drill.'

Following in Gwen's wake, Ellie felt her cheeks redden again. Gwen had got hold of the wrong end of the stick, but Ellie had no intention of putting her right. There was no need and besides, as Gwen said, the boys would be gone in less than a week, by which time, by all accounts, Evie and Aidan would be nothing but a distant memory.

Chapter Eleven

Like most people, Ellie enjoyed hearing the odd scrap of gossip, but not when it was about herself. Knowing that Evie would be telling anyone who stopped to listen about her nightmare, she had feared that some of the women might take the other girl's side. She had been pleasantly surprised when she heard first-hand that this was not the case.

'She can't go around telling folk who they can and can't be friends with, especially when it's old pals from before the war,' said one of the spotters in Evelyn's section. 'If she thinks she can stop another girl being friends with someone that she's dating, the rate she goes through 'em none of us would be allowed to speak to any men at all!'

This conversation had taken place as they queued up in the canteen. There had been a general murmur of agreement and Gillian Stokes, a tall brunette with broad shoulders and hips to match, aired her thoughts. 'Not just that, she threatened Baggy, which isn't on. She can't go takin' it out on a poor defenceless animal – not that he's exatly defenceless, but you know what I mean. Just goes to show what kind of girl she is.'

Ellie wished fervently that she could tell Aidan about Evie's outburst, but she feared he would probably laugh it off as 'girls being girls'. It was typical, she thought sullenly, that men could come to blows over the slightest thing, but as soon as two women had a falling-out, it was dismissed as trivial nonsense. That aside, Ellie knew that she could not tell him a half-truth, and if she told him of Evie's threats she would have to tell him about her dream.

Aidan rang her two days before he and Connor were meant to go back to Waddington and asked if she would like to take a trip around the city. She agreed, and made a mental note that she would not spend their last afternoon together discussing Evie.

When the car pulled up beside her where she waited by the camp gate, Ellie immediately noticed Aidan's flustered appearance. On their previous meetings he had always looked smartly turned out, but today his uniform looked skew-whiff, as though it had been thrown on in a hurry. Indeed, he was still adjusting his tie as she walked towards the passenger door.

'Your tie won't settle properly because your top button's not done up. Have you been wearing it like that all day?'

Averting his gaze, Aidan shrugged. 'Must've been. Still, I think I've got it now.' He gripped the handle to the passenger door and heaved it open.

Her eyes flickered over him. 'Didn't you say you were going to be in meetings all morning?'

Nodding, Aidan closed the awkward door, nearly catching his fingers as he did so and cursing softly beneath his breath. Ellie opened her mouth to speak, then shut it abruptly. Sitting forward, she fished underneath her bottom with one hand until her fingers closed around a small cylindrical object, which she held up for closer inspection. Raising her brow, she turned to Aidan. 'Yours?'

Taking the tube of lipstick, he glared at it before throwing it into the glove compartment. 'It must belong to one of the other fellers' girlfriends.'

He clunked the car noisily into gear. Opening the glove compartment again, Ellie withdrew the tube and twisted the bottom, pulling a face at the bright red stick that came into view. 'Bit tacky,' she said, replacing the lid and pushing the tube back into the compartment.

'Like I said, nowt to do with me,' Aidan said shortly.

Ignoring Gwen's advice, she voiced her thoughts. 'I know it's none of my business, but are you courting someone?' Her face flushed with embarrassment as the words left her lips.

Frowning, Aidan glanced briefly at the glove box. 'No, why?'

Ellie felt her heart begin to beat a tattoo. Why had she asked such a silly question? She knew it was none of her business, had even said so, but his response had been to lie to her, which meant their whole friendship would change. With no reply forthcoming, he added, 'Oh, you mean because of the lipstick? As I said, it'll belong to one of the girls that the other fellers are dating. I did tell you that I shared the car with the rest of the crew, didn't I?'

Ellie nodded miserably. She could hardly tell him that the lipstick had nothing to do with it; that she knew he was seeing Evie, because the other girl had told her so. If she did, he would want to know why she had asked a question to which she already knew the answer. Writhing within, Ellie wished fervently that she could turn back the hands of time and stop herself from asking such a foolish question. Now she was stuck for the rest of the afternoon with the man she adored most in the world wishing she was nowhere near him. The silence was deafening and she had to break it.

'I just thought that a handsome young pilot such as yourself would have women queuing up,' she said lamely.

He cocked a brow. 'Wouldn't matter if they were as long as you were at the head of the queue.'

Ellie stared hard out of the car window. How could he tell such a blatant lie? He was treating her like a child, someone to be humoured. Reflecting on the night in the NAAFI when she had drunk the awful beer in order to impress him, Ellie wished that she had stuck to lemonade like Gwen. If she had, she would never have got ill and Evie would never have been alone with him. She imagined the other girl, all sultry and seductive, laughing scornfully at her. She thought back to his unkempt appearance when he had first pulled up. He could only have taken Evie out a couple of times, the last one, judging by the lipstick, only moments before he had called for Ellie, so if his clothes were anything to go by ... Ellie shook her head. She would have expected Evie to act like an alley cat, but surely Aidan was not the sort of man who would bed a woman after only a couple of dates?

She thought back to the day when she had told him she was leaving Springdale Farm and how she had made it clear that she wanted to find her own way in the world before settling down. Perhaps Aidan wanted a woman who had already made her way in life, not a child who was still trying to find it. Once again her thoughts turned to Evie. The girl had certainly dated more than her fair share of men, several of whom must have been older than her, and Ellie felt sure that some of them would want far more from a girl than cuddling in the back row of the cinema. Ellie herself had never so much as kissed a man, and was certainly not ready for that kind of relationship. Had she really expected Aidan to wait around until she was? If he had turned to Evie it was hardly his fault. Ellie was the one who had said she wasn't ready for a relationship, and perhaps he had only denied courting Evie because he wasn't serious about her. Another thought occurred to her. If he really had been with Evie that morning, then why had he only just pulled up in the car? Surely he would've planned to drop her off a bit earlier than he had arranged to meet Ellie, then just wait? Petrol was rationed and could not be wasted on unnecessary journeys. Could he be telling the truth? No one, as far as she knew, had ever seen him and Evie together, and even if he had gone out with her he might have done so only as a friend. Ellie flushed guiltily. She had been very quick to believe Evie over Aidan.

Aidan drew the car to a halt in a lay-by and turned to Ellie. 'Are you all right? Only you look as if you're a million miles away.'

'I'm fine, just a bit tired, that's all. It's been a real whirlwind since you got here. I wish you could stay for longer.'

He brightened. 'You can always come and visit us in Waddington. There're some lovely B and Bs close to the camp. You could bring Gwen with you, but probably not Bagheera. I think they'd draw the line at a cat who thinks he's a sniper.'

Ellie giggled. 'That'd be nice. What's Waddington like?'

Putting the car into gear Aidan pulled back on to the road. 'Quaint is the best way to describe it. The best place for you to stay would be the Horse and Jockey. There're some lovely walks around there, and whenever I have time I often go for a wander.' He sighed wistfully. 'We could go for a walk after brekker, then have lunch at the Jockey; they do a marvellous stew with dumplings.'

Ellie gazed at him as he continued to talk. She had been acting like a complete child over the whole Aidan and Evie business, which just went to prove that she was too young to consider any kind of relationship. Aidan was a pal, and a good one at that, and she would not do anything to jeopardise their friendship.

Happy with the thought that she had made the right decision, Ellie enjoyed the next few hours, and when Aidan took her back to her barracks and leaned across the seat to say goodbye she turned to respond, only to find his lips planted firmly on hers.

Realising that he had meant to kiss her on the cheek Ellie gabbled an excuse. 'Sorry, I thought … that is, I didn't see …'

Aidan brushed his fingers over her cheek reassuringly. 'Don't apologise; I rather enjoyed it. You know I'm no good at goodbyes, so all in all that was a nice surprise.'

Ellie blushed hotly. 'I didn't do it on purpose, Aidan Murray.'

Grinning, he winked cheekily. 'I know, I know, so let's get you out safely before we have another accident.'

Despite her embarrassment, Ellie giggled. She watched as he got out of the car and grasped her door handle in a businesslike fashion. 'I'm going to have to have a word with Connor about fixing this thing. It's a real nuisance,' he said, heaving the door open.

Slamming it shut, he climbed back behind the steering wheel. As he crunched the car into gear he called over his shoulder, 'T.t.f.n., alanna.'

Ellie's tummy lurched unpleasantly. Her dream, came back to her in a flash, and a shudder ran down her spine. In that moment, as she watched him driving away, she made up her mind. She knew what she wanted, and it was Aidan. She would rather run the risk of having her heart broken than never have given things a go. A torrent of mixed emotions rushed through her as she waved him out of sight. There was only one person who could help her now. Ellie headed towards her barracks.

Flinging the door open, she started to remove her shoes and stockings before Gwen called that Bagheera was outside somewhere so it was safe to enter. She skipped across the room and carefully removed a pen and paper from her friend's unresisting hands. 'Sorry if you were in the middle of a letter, but I've got a bit of a problem and I need your help.'

Gwen frowned. 'I take it your meeting with Aidan didn't go too well?'

'We had a lovely time, and he's invited us to go to see him in Waddington when we get some leave.'

'Doesn't sound like a problem to me. So what's up?'

'I've made up my mind about Aidan. I know what I want and it's him.'

Gwen nodded thoughtfully. 'Now I understand. Your problem is Evie.' She puffed her cheeks out. 'Speakin' of which, if I were you I'd keep out of her way, 'cos she's got it into her head that someone's nicked her—'

'Have you ever thought that she might be lying? About her relationship with Aidan, I mean?' Ellie said, unapologetically interrupting her friend mid-sentence.

Gwen shook her head vigorously. 'Why would she?'

'I don't know, but it kind of came up in conversation …' she held her hands up to stop Gwen from butting in, 'not about him seeing Evie, if that's what you're thinking, but about him seeing anyone at all. At first I didn't believe him, but now I'm not so sure.'

Gwen's brow furrowed. 'So you think that she's been lying about the whole thing, and making it up to look as if they're together?' A small grin formed on her lips. 'Little monkey! I still don't get why she'd do it, though. It's not as if she can't get a feller.' Her lips parted as a thought struck her. 'Unless he is in love with you, and he turned her down. If he told her about you mebbe she's done it out of spite. She must know you're not the sort of girl to try to pinch someone else's feller, so she's pretending they're an item so that you'll steer clear and he'll lose you too.' She shook her head reprovingly. 'They do say hell hath no fury like a woman scorned.'

Ellie grinned. 'He told me in the car that even if there was a queue of women lined up for him he wouldn't be interested unless I was at the front of it!'

'You've got to get a message to him before he leaves. Tell him how you feel!' Gwen said, her voice squeaking with excitement.

Ellie nodded. 'He hasn't long gone, and he's not due to leave until tomorrer.' Her shoulders drooped a little. 'But I've got to be on duty in an hour.'

Gwen clicked her fingers. 'Got it! Jonesy said he was goin' into town ...' she looked at the clock on the wall of the hut, 'in about five minutes, I can't remember what for, but I'm sure he'll give you a lift there and back. It's not far out of his way.'

Hugging Gwen, Ellie kissed her on the cheek. 'You're a star. I don't know what I'd do without you.'

Gwen blushed. 'Don't you worry about it – you'd do the same for me. You wait till I see Evie. I'm goin' to tell her that I know no one nicked her lipstick 'cos he never gave it her in the first place and she's making the whole thing up.'

Ellie's face fell. 'What lipstick?'

'The one he supposedly bought her as a leaving present. She said it was—'

Ellie sank on to her bed. 'A red Rimmel stick in a black tube.'

'That's right. How did you know?'

299

Ellie took a deep breath. 'She lost it in his car. I sat on it by accident, but he said it belonged to one of his mates' girlfriends.'

'The lying swine,' Gwen began crossly, but Ellie shook her head.

'At least I found out before rushin' off and makin' a fool of myself. If I've learned anything from me mam it's not to make the same mistake she did.'

Sliding from the top bunk, Gwen placed an arm round her friend's shoulders. 'I'm so sorry, Ellie. I should've said it were a lippy from the start; at least that way you wouldn't have gotten your hopes up.'

Ellie shrugged dismissively. 'It's not your fault; you weren't to know.' She turned towards Gwen, her eyes brimming with tears. 'I just *wish* I'd told him how I felt sooner. That way it'd be me he was givin' lippy to. Not that I'd want lipstick, mind you.' She sniffed. 'Horrible stuff. Makes my lips feel all waxy.' She rested her head against Gwen's shoulder. 'Besides, I'm not ready for that kind of relationship.'

'What kind of relationship?' said Gwen.

Ellie went on to explain Aidan's unkempt appearance and how she suspected he had got dressed in a hurry.

Gwen eyed Ellie sternly. 'What you've got is precious, Ellie. I'm glad to hear you won't give it up willy-nilly, not like her. Crikey, she barely knows him.'

'I must say I was a bit surprised,' Ellie agreed, 'but then maybe that's why all the fellers break it off. Once they got what they wanted, and if Aidan's anything to go by it didn't take them long, they lost interest. She's probably got a right reputation amongst the fellers.'

Gwen's brow rose towards her hairline. 'I should say so, and not a good one either.' She squeezed Ellie's shoulders. 'Like you say, good job you found out the truth before jumping into something you aren't ready for. And if I'm honest, cariad, you're not the sort of girl for him, not if that's what he expects, so it would never have lasted anyway.'

Ellie checked the time. 'Let's go and get a cup of tea and see if they've got any treats in the NAAFI. I could do with a bit of cheerin' up.'

As they stood up to leave Gwen pursed her lips thoughtfully. 'If Evie asks you if you've seen her lippy, what are you goin' to say?'

'I shall deny all knowledge and let her spend all her free time searching for it. Although I'm sure her boy-friend will find a way of getting it back to her before he leaves,' Ellie said tartly.

'Why'd you have to go and threaten the cat? Caldecott warned you she wouldn't stand for no nonsense, and what do you do? Make threats in front of a room full of witnesses.' Tilly scowled at Evie, who seemed quite unperturbed.

'It's not my fault that silly little tart went whinging to Caldecott. Besides, I didn't threaten him directly, did I? And if she had done as she was told and agreed to stay away from my man—'

'She's not one of your maids – not that you have any of them any more – an, you can't go orderin' people around and expect them to obey your every command,' Tilly said, her temper rising as she spoke. She had very much enjoyed being close to home, and was annoyed that her friend's outburst had caused them to be relocated halfway across the country.

'Anyway, it's worked out brilliantly for me. I did worry that our relationship might not survive long distance, but this way we'll be right on his doorstep!' said Evie.

'Oh, well, that's all right then. As long as Evie's happy that's all that counts,' snapped Tilly.

'Don't be such a sourpuss. You know I don't like to see you unhappy, and I'd have thought you'd be grateful to get out of this dump and go somewhere decent for a change!'

'Don't call my home a dump. You live here too, don't forget.'

'Not for long,' Evie snorted. 'When he asks me to marry him ...'

'Someone's counting their chickens. I bet if he found out what you'd done, he'd have a few choice words to say and none of them would be "Will you marry me".'

'Don't you dare go telling tales about me, Tilly Jarvis. It was only a prank, but it might easily get misconstrued.'

Tilly wagged a reproving finger. 'You know damned well that you did it on purpose to get him all to yourself, so don't go pretendin' otherwise.'

Evie pouted. 'Let's not argue. I know what I did might be a little bit naughty, but I'm desperate to get back to where I belong, and surely there's nothing wrong with that? I'm not like the rest of you, I wasn't born to beggary.'

Tilly's eyes rounded. 'Beggary? How *dare*—'

A flushing noise from one of the cubicles interrupted Tilly mid-sentence. Evie's cheeks turned scarlet as the cubicle door swung open and one of the cooks from the canteen emerged. She glanced briefly at the two girls as she washed her hands, but no one said anything until the cook disappeared through the door of the ablutions.

Evie spluttered an apology as Tilly checked the rest of the cubicles. 'I'm so sorry, Tilly, I don't know why I said it, I didn't mean it, honest to God I didn't. I know you're not a beggar, nothing like, so please say you'll accept my apology, I was just angry.'

Striding towards the door of the ablutions, Tilly spoke through pursed lips. 'I have lost countless friends by sticking up for you, Evie Maddox, not to mention the lies I've told to cover your back. I've put up with all your snide comments towards the good people of Liverpool and ignored the mean remarks you make to me, but this is the last straw. Any more tricks like the last one and our friendship is over, and this time I mean it.'

Evie made a sweeping motion with her finger across her chest. 'Cross my heart and hope to die ... I swear I won't cause any more trouble.'

Tilly, looking unconvinced, snubbed Evie's attempt to link arms. 'Time will tell.'

Heading across the yard, Evie allowed herself a half-smile. She knew Tilly would forgive her; she always did. She glanced towards the barracks where she supposed Ellie would be sitting on her bed, an idiotic grin on her face as she stroked the foul-smelling feline. Quickly, she conjured up a more pleasing image of the other girl, her face a picture of misery as Evie announced the date of her wedding. She grinned gleefully. It would serve her right. After all, it was all her fault that Evie and Tilly had been rowing in the first place. How could anyone think Ellie fit to marry an officer? The whole thing was ridiculous. If anything Evie was saving Ellie's face by denying her the opportunity to make a fool of herself. She nodded approvingly. Ellie wouldn't know how to behave at social events; she would probably turn up in a tattered old dress, her curly hair sticking out like a bush, and as for that dreadful accent! It was preposterous to even try to imagine the two of them together. Evie shook her head. Tilly might criticise me for my actions, but it's only because she's never known anything different. Once a Scouser, always a Scouser, and I appreciate that she doesn't know any better, but it's different for me. I want more, and if Tilly had half a brain she would too.

'Married?' Ellie said disbelievingly. 'Who on earth told you that?'

Gwen held out a hand and began ticking the list off on her fingers. 'Mildred who does the orders for the canteen heard it off Bert who brings the supplies, who heard it off Jonesy who heard it off Penny the cook what done the mashed spuds yesterday.'

'But that's ridiculous. They've only been out a couple of times—'

Gwen interrupted. 'That's not all. Accordin' to what Penny heard – she were in the lavvy whilst the row were goin' on – Tilly were accusin' Evie of doin' summat to someone so that she could have Aidan all to herself ...'

'Me!' Ellie squeaked. 'You thought she'd done summat to my drink at the time, didn't you? Evil bloomin' cow.'

'That's not all,' Gwen continued. 'Tilly said their section's bein' moved across the country because Evie had threatened to hurt Baggy, and that's how the argument started.'

Ellie brightened. 'Thank goodness for that. I can't say I'll be sorry to see her go—' Seeing the look of concern on Gwen's face, she stopped short.

'She said summat about how their relationship will be even better now that she's movin' closer to him.'

Ellie's shoulders sagged. 'You mean I've actually driven her into his arms?'

Gwen wagged a reproving finger. 'We've been through this, and we both agreed you're not ready for that sort of relationship.'

'I didn't mean it!' Ellie groaned. 'That's what everyone says when they know they can't have what they want.'

Gwen put a comforting arm round Ellie's shoulders. 'There's no point worryin' over spilt milk. What's done is done.'

'When are they off?'

'A couple of days.' She paused. 'The boys left nearly two months ago. Evie said she worried their relationship might not have lasted long distance, so for all we know things might have started to fizzle out already.'

Ellie shrugged. 'Anything's possible, but it won't make any odds. Once she's in clutching range she'll

305

dig her claws in good and proper, and he'll never get away from her then.'

'They say that absence makes the heart grow fonder, but not if the relationship's suffering after only a couple of months.' Gwen gave Ellie an encouraging smile. 'Chin up. You could be worrying over nowt, we'll just have to wait and see.'

Dear Ellie,

Have I got news for you! Only I'm afraid I can't put it in a letter nor say it over the phone, so you and Gwen are going to have to come for a visit! The only thing I can tell you is that there seems to have been a frightful row between the cow from Cheshire and the farmer. No one knows what it was over, but those who bore witness to her end of the telephone call reckoned she was furious, accused him of avoiding her and demanded he meet her. No one could hear what he said, but they reckon she went scarlet then slammed the receiver down without saying goodbye first.

A smile curled Ellie's lips as she read Arla's epistle. It was mid-July and the brightly burning sun was shining through the window by Ellie's bed. Sitting in her vest and knickers, Ellie periodically fanned herself with the letter. She continued reading.

So I reckon you should strike while the iron's hot. When was the last time you had some leave? As far as I recall you've not had owt since goin' to see Aidan's folks, and that was months ago! Give me a ring or drop me a line when you can arrange something. I'd best be off, I'm on duty in fifteen mins, let's hope for a quiet one! Love, Arla.

The sound of reveille came from outside the hut. Around her, girls were yawning, stretching and jumping noisily out of their beds. Above her, she heard Gwen throw back her sheets before landing on the floor beside Ellie.

'How come you got up so early?' She lowered her voice. 'Baggy hasn't peed in someone's shoe again, has he?'

Ellie giggled. 'No! Blimey, he only did it a couple of times, poor little feller. You know I had that letter from Arla? Well, I didn't have time to read it last night, but …' She held up the paper. 'You sit there and read it whilst I make your bed. That way you won't be late for drill.'

Taking the letter, Gwen's eyes widened whilst she read. Occasionally a stifled giggle could be heard leaving her lips, before she handed the letter back to Ellie.

'So?' Ellie said as she picked up their wash bags. 'D' you fancy a trip to Lincoln?'

'I should say so!' Gwen squealed. 'Oh, Ellie, a real holiday! I've never been away without my folks before. When do we leave?'

Ellie laughed. 'Dunno. We'll have to have a word with Caldecott.'

Gwen clapped a hand to her mouth. 'I've just remembered. Ann from the cookhouse reckons Caldecott's found her kid. Not sure how or when, but it's good news, isn't it?'

Ellie nodded. 'And in more ways than one.'

Gwen frowned. 'How so?'

Ellie grinned. 'Because we're going to ask her for leave, and I should think she's on cloud nine, so no matter what we ask her for the answer will be yes!'

*

Aidan was sitting on the edge of his bed in the small bedroom that he shared with Connor in their billet in RAF Waddington when he heard the door latch lift. Separate billets were a luxury that only aircrew had, and whilst the small stone cottage was not as impressive as the Grand Hotel in Scarborough, it was heaven-sent when compared to the cramped intrusive conditions of a Nissen hut. Smiling, he remembered the day they had first arrived. They had barely put their kit away before someone was knocking on the door. Expecting to find one of the crew on the doorstep, Aidan had been surprised to see the hunched figure of an old woman.

'Hello, dearie. We heard there was a new lot moved in, and we always like to make you boys feel welcome in our village, so I've brought you a pot of rabbit stew, but don't you go askin' where the rabbit come from,' the old woman had said, tapping the side of her nose with a weathered forefinger. 'You boys are doin' a grand service for your country, and don't you think me and the hubby aren't thankful.' She handed him the blackened casserole dish.

'Thank you. Please come in, Mrs ...?'

'Gregson, but you can call me Dolly. I won't come in if you don't mind, but I'd be grateful if you could return the dish. We live in the flat above the post office.'

Carefully lifting the lid, he was treated to the scent of the stew. It smelled delicious. 'Thanks ever so much for this. I'm afraid we're not the best cooks, and though they try their best in the mess ...'

She nodded wisely. 'There's nowt like a proper bit of fresh game with some dumplings to fill a man.'

Now, smearing polish on to his shoes, he grunted a welcome. 'You been out dodgin' bullets?'

Connor hung his jacket on the hook on the door. 'Oh, very droll. If you must know I've been talkin' to Arla, and guess who's coming for a week's visit?'

'Winnie the Pooh,' said Aidan, not looking up from his task.

'Close. It's Ellie and Gwen.'

Aidan looked up. 'Really? When?'

Connor chuckled. 'Thought that might get your attention! In a fortnight. They're goin' to be stopping at the Saracen's Head. I thought we could pay them a visit, take them out and about. What d'you reckon?'

Aidan shrugged nonchalantly. 'See what Ellie thinks, only she's been quite distant with me since Liverpool.'

'That's not like her; normally you can't shut her up. Something must be wrong.' He paused. 'You don't think she's found out about Evie, do you?'

Aidan shook his head dismissively. 'Not a chance. She'd not hold her tongue if she thought something was going on. Besides, all that's in the past now. There's nothing to find out, not any more.'

Connor seemed not to notice that his cousin's cheeks had flushed pink. 'Perhaps she just feels a bit down, you know, having her pals around her one minute then gone the next? I'm sure she'll be happy to see you.'

Aidan regarded his cousin quizzically. 'You write to her, don't you? Have her letters been short, small talk, that sort of thing?'

Connor pulled a face. 'They always have, same as most folk's. You can't say anything too exciting because the censor will only go and chop it out.'

Aidan rubbed his chin thoughtfully. 'She used to write me lengthy letters, though, so summat's changed, and it looks like I'm the one who's caused it, although I haven't got the faintest idea how.'

Connor began to undress. 'Well, I for one am not going to try and suss out the workings of the female mind, not this late in the day. You need a lot more time than that.' Climbing between the sheets, he glanced at Aidan. 'She's always had a soft spot for you. Maybe she hoped you'd ask her to be your belle when you were in Liverpool.'

Having tucked his shoes beneath his bed, Aidan turned off the light by the door then gingerly felt his way back across the room. 'Don't you remember what Evie said about Ellie being offended by the very thought of us being together? Ellie didn't even deny it. So no, I don't think she was disappointed that I didn't ask her to be my belle; if anything I'd think she was relieved.' Climbing into bed, he yawned sleepily. 'I did think that maybe she was upset that we're all in Lincoln – you, me, Archie and Arla – whilst she's stuck in Liverpool, but if that was the case I'm sure she'd have asked to move closer.'

Connor snorted as he tried to stifle his laughter. 'Oh yes, I'm sure the ATS would go for that.' He put on a squeaky voice. 'Excuse me, but I don't like it in Liverpool any more please could I go and join my friends in Lincoln I promise I'll be go— What was that?'

'My sock. If you haven't anything helpful to add to the conversation, you can jolly well go to sleep.' Closing his eyes, he immediately saw Ellie brushing the mud from Spud's thick winter coat, and sighed

310

heavily. What he would give to be back on the farm with Ellie, milking the cows, collecting eggs and sitting down to one of his mother's roast dinners.

'What the hell are they coming here for? I thought I'd seen the back of those two when we left Liverpool!' Evie said, her face turning red.

'They're coming to see Arla: you know, the one that signed up the same day as us? I suppose seeing the Murrays will be an added bonus. I don't see why you're so bothered; it's not as if they've come to see you,' Tilly said matter-of-factly.

Evie scowled. 'Anyway, how do you know what they're up to? Don't tell me you've gone and palled up with that Arla.'

This was the question that Tilly had been dreading. 'I've been writing to them.'

Evie's mouth hung open. 'What? Since when? More to the point, why?'

Tilly shrugged. 'It's nice to stay in touch and keep up with all the news.'

Evie stiffened. 'Do you tell them our news? Or rather, have you told them anything about me and—'

Holding up a hand, Tilly cut her off. 'I haven't mentioned you in any of my letters; I didn't think they'd be interested. So you can put that thought right out of your head.'

Evie relaxed. 'Good! I wouldn't like to think you were gossiping about me with the enemy. It's bad enough that you're fraternising with them.'

'For goodness' sakes, Evie, they are not the enemy. They're just a couple of girls who you don't get on

311

with. If I were to avoid every girl you don't get along with I'd find it impossible to function properly.'

'Oh ha, ha, very funny. It's not my fault all the women are jealous of me. I did try to make friends when I first arrived ...'

Tilly held up a warning finger. 'First thing you did was make snide remarks about Lincoln and the camp. You said it was a hellhole filled to the brim with the dregs of society. If that wasn't enough, you went on to boast about your boyfriend in the RAF, which was a big mistake, especially when you failed to produce him.'

Evie scowled defensively. 'It is a hellhole, but so are all the ATS camps, and as for the remark I made about the dregs of society, you saw those girls.'

'Yes, I did, and there's nothing wrong with any of them.' Tilly turned her face away from Evie and added under her breath, 'And I bet they have boyfriends who exist.'

Unfortunately for Tilly, the latter comment did not go unheard as she had intended.

Evie stamped her foot irritably. 'Tilly Jarvis, you're mean and nasty! That was a rotten thing to say. You know full well I never made him up. I don't know what's got into him since we arrived, but whatever it is it has nothing to do with me.'

'I know and I'm sorry, but you have to remember that I get a lot of the flak when you're horrid to the girls. Besides, that's their words, not mine,' said Tilly.

'I hope you jolly well put them right. Nasty little cats, and there you are telling me I'm the one in the wrong.'

Tilly's body sagged. It was no use trying to explain the error of her ways to Evie. Her friend was completely blind when it came to recognising her own faults. 'I did put them right, but you needn't think the old rumours won't start up again, because they will.' She eyed Evie. 'I know you say you and Sergeant Barton are just good friends, and I hope you're telling the truth. I had a gutful sticking up for you when we did our initial training. You said they were just spiteful rumours, and if you say you're just good friends then I believe you, but some of the girls in Liverpool certainly noticed the two of you seemed closer than perhaps you should ...'

'Then you should have told to them to mind their beeswax, because once again the vixens were jumping to the wrong conclusion!' Evie shook her head chidingly. 'Honestly, Tilly, I thought better of you than to believe idle gossip. The man's married, for goodness' sake.'

'I know,' said Tilly defensively, 'and that's why I need to believe what you say. I would hate to think I was defending a liar.'

Evie flushed angrily. 'Just you take that back, Tilly Jarvis.'

Trying to catch Evie's eye, Tilly noticed how she seemed to be avoiding her gaze. 'I'm sorry for calling you a liar, but—'

Evie, who did not appear interested in further explanations, moved towards the door of the hut. 'Good. Don't do it again.'

Tilly stared at the door that had swung behind her friend. She couldn't even look at me, she thought, nor wait to get away from me. A feeling of dread filled her. I'm sure she's lying, and if she is Sergeant Barton will find his way here somehow, and when he does ... She shook her head. It didn't bear thinking about.

She turned her thoughts to Sergeant Barton's wife. She was a good, kind-hearted woman who always had time for the girls under her husband's command, including Evie. She doesn't deserve this, Tilly thought ruefully. If Evie is still seeing him it'll only be until she doesn't need him any more; then she'll drop him like a hot cake and move on, but what can I do? I can't prove anything, and it's not worth stirring the pot when both of them will certainly deny the accusations. She heaved a sigh. With no proof she had no choice but to let sleeping dogs lie. There was always a chance that her friend was telling the truth and if she was, Tilly would not only have caused untold damage to an otherwise secure marriage, but would have lost her best friend to boot. Tilly made up her mind. For now, she would leave things be, but if she ever found out that Evie had lied to her, then their friendship would be well and truly over.

Ellie and Gwen stood on the crowded platform waiting for the train that would take them on the first part of their journey to Lincoln. 'A whole week!' Gwen breathed; she shaded her eyes from the glare of sunlight penetrating the thick bank of cloud, then cried out with delight as she spied the approaching steam. 'It's here, it's here! Finally, we're off on our hols.' Trying to pick her heavy kitbag up from the floor, she

314

added hastily, 'Come on, Ellie, we want a good seat. Have you got your ticket ready?'

Ellie smiled. Ever since Caldecott had granted their leave all Gwen had done was chatter excitedly about their holiday. Now, hoisting her kitbag over her shoulder, she gripped Ellie firmly by the hand, towed her aboard the waiting train, and marched her down the corridor until they found an empty compartment. 'Window seats! Pass me your bag and I'll push it under the seat with mine, that way we don't have to worry about them falling off the rack and bonking someone on the head,' she said, shoving the bags securely under her seat with her heels.

The compartment soon began to fill up with servicemen and women, and before too long it was standing room only. Outside, the guard blew his whistle and waved his green flag. There was a loud gushing noise as steam hissed between the great wheels, which were squealing as they fought to gain traction on the rails. Leaning her head against the window, Ellie smiled as the rhythmical beat began to pick up speed. She glanced at Gwen, who was beaming with joy, then let the quiet chatter of her fellow travellers wash over her as she gazed out of the window, her mind wandering back to her last telephone call with Arla.

'When you get off the train, ask for directions to the Stonebow. It's like a big archway into the city; everyone knows it. When you go through it you'll see the Saracen's Head on your left. It's a huge building right next to Lidgett's watch shop – you can't miss it. I've booked you a twin room for the week, I hope that's all right. I wish I could be there to meet you off the train, but of course I'm on duty so I won't be able to see you until the next morning, so make sure you're up bright and early, because I'll be knocking on your door ready to go for breakfast.'

Ellie wondered what news Arla had that she could neither write nor tell her over the phone. She hoped it was more details about Aidan and Evie and what appeared to be their diminishing relationship.

When Aidan had left for Waddington, Ellie had decided that she would not waste any more time mooning over a relationship which could never be, and had decided instead to find herself a partner, someone closer to her own age whom she could go to the cinema and dances with. But even though she had not been short of suitors, she had found herself constantly comparing them to Aidan.

'They're like over-excited puppies; that last one was downright sweaty,' she had told Gwen, rubbing the palms of her hands on her khaki skirt. 'He must've put a handful of that dreadful Brylcreem in his hair, too; it was shinier than my shoes, and when he lowered his head I swear I could see my reflection in it!'

Gwen had giggled. 'He seemed nice enough, and he liked you; I saw the smile on his face ...'

Ellie had grimaced. 'So did I, and his teeth were all yellow and crooked, not like Aidan's.'

Gwen had rolled her eyes. 'Aidan, Aidan, Aidan! Don't you think it'd be a lot quicker if you just lined 'em up, so that you can see which of them measures up to Aidan? Not that I think any of them will. You've got rose-coloured specs when it comes to pilot Officer Murray.'

316

Ellie had groaned. 'Don't call him that. I hate hearing that name, it reminds me of her.'

'Forget her, and him. You can't keep mooning over him, Ellie; it's not good for you – or me, come to that – and you've got to learn to move on. I promise you, there is life after Aidan!'

As the train pulled into a small station most of the passengers in the compartment gathered up their belongings and got off the train. Standing up, Ellie opened the top window. 'Bit stuffy in here. Does anyone mind?'

Apart from Gwen the only other passengers were two young Waafs, who shook their heads simultaneously. Sitting down, Ellie stretched her legs out in front of her. 'I hope there's no one else coming in. These carriages aren't meant for large servicemen with huge kitbags.'

The door to their carriage slid open and an old woman entered. She wore a multicoloured headscarf which only half covered her greasy greying hair, and Ellie was just able to make out a pair of small sharp blue eyes peering out of her deeply wrinkled face. She wondered how old she was, and thought she must be getting close to ninety. I've never seen so many wrinkles, she thought, as the woman settled into the empty seat next to Gwen; she reminds me of a walnut. The old woman locked eyes with her, and Ellie, aware that she had been caught staring, was about to turn away when the woman spoke.

'Mornin', lady. Would you like to buy some lucky heather?'

Gwen gave Ellie's shoe a sharp kick and wagged a warning finger that only Ellie could see. Turning her attention to the old woman, she spoke in clipped tones. 'We don't want any heather, lucky or otherwise, thank you very much.'

The wizened woman narrowed her eyes. 'Was I askin' you?'

Ellie cleared her throat. 'Sorry, but I don't want any, though thanks for the offer.'

The woman grinned, revealing her two remaining teeth. ''Tis no matter, child.' She rummaged around in one of her pockets. 'Lucky sixpence?'

Ellie shook her head.

'With the luck my charms will bring you, you'll have more money than you have now.' She nodded encouragingly at Ellie, but Gwen was having none of it.

'If they're that lucky why are you so keen to sell them?' she said pointedly.

The woman's blue eyes stared icily at Gwen. 'Because I like to share the luck around, but if you don't want none then that's your business.' She began to search around in her large knitted bag. Ellie watched as the woman's arthritic fingers, the nails black with dirt, rummaged through the contents. 'Clothes pegs!' she cried triumphantly, flourishing the pegs towards the four girls. 'Everyone needs clothes pegs.'

Frowning, Gwen folded her arms. 'We're in the ATS, and they're in the WAAF. Why on earth would we need clothes pegs? They do our washing for us.'

'Wouldn't know. Never been in the services,' the old woman said. Thrusting the pegs back into her bag, she closed it up and glared out of the window.

Ellie fished around in her purse. 'Is a penny all right, for the heather I mean?'

318

The woman's face lit up with a broad grin and she nodded eagerly. 'Bless you, my child, and don't forget to give it a rub for luck whenever you need it most.'

Avoiding Gwen's reproving stare, Ellie tucked the heather into her purse. If buying a piece of heather really did bring good luck then she needed as much of it as she could lay her hands on.

Shooting a defiant glare at Gwen, the old woman crossed her feet and made herself comfortable. Within minutes a soft snore emanated from her gummy lips. Quietly getting to their feet, the two Waafs took the opportunity to leave the compartment.

'I see they've got some sense,' said Gwen. 'You shouldn't buy anything off women like her, Ellie. It just encourages them. We used to get a lot of 'em where I lived, and whilst some of them are fine the rest can be really nasty, especially if you don't buy anything off them. They stand on your doorstep shouting, cussing and cursing you fit to burn. My uncle always said it's better not to get involved in the first place.'

'She never cursed either of us when we turned her down the first two times, so she's obviously one of the nice ones,' Ellie said matter-of-factly.

Gwen looked accusingly at the old woman and felt positive that she saw the sides of the snoring lips begin to curl into a smile before relaxing again. Leaning back in her seat, she folded her coat into a sort of pillow then placed it between her head and the window. 'I s'pose you could be right.'

With the matter put to rest, Ellie turned her attention to the passing scenery. Two large cobs just like Samson and Hercules were being used to plough a meadow, and watching the magnificent beasts tirelessly pulling the heavy plough reminded Ellie of her days in Springdale. Glancing at her wristwatch, she wondered what the Murrays were doing. It was nearly a quarter past eleven, so Mr Murray and the farmhands would have finished milking long since, the livestock would have been fed and water troughs checked, and any animals which were housed, like pigs and hens, would be getting mucked out. Today was Monday, which was a baking day for Mrs Murray who would be in the kitchen, her apron covered in flour, baking bread and pies. Lunch would probably be cheese, pickles, and any leftovers from the previous evening's meal. Ellie's mouth began to water. Rather than bring sandwiches, which would end up getting squashed in the kitbags, they had decided to buy something at one of the stops. She peered ahead of the train in the hope of seeing a station.

'If you got another one of them pennies I could read your palm and tell you what your future holds.' Ellie jumped at the sound of the woman's voice. She looked across at Gwen and saw that her eyes were tight shut and her lips slightly parted. Quietly, she produced another penny and placed it on the woman's outstretched palm. Hiding the penny in the depths of her skirts, the woman leaned forward eagerly, indicating that Ellie should do the same. She pulled Ellie's hand towards her and started to trace the lines on the palm with one grubby finger.

'You've had a lot of sorrow in your life; I see that clearly by this line 'ere.' She peered closely at Ellie's hand. 'Your mam's gone, but she watches over you, allus has, allus will. That's a mother's love for you; it don't know no boundaries.' She smiled kindly at Ellie, then returned her attention to her palm. 'This'll please your mam. The man you're goin' to visit will end up bein' your hubby, an' you'll 'ave lots of kiddies and live in the country.'

Ellie looked at her own hand. 'Do you see anything else?'

'Yes. Your pal sittin' there – the one what's listenin' but thinks I don't know it – she's goin' to end up with his brother.'

Ellie glanced at Gwen, who had surreptitiously opened one eye, and saw the other girl's cheeks redden. Leaning away from the window, Gwen looked at the old woman through narrowed eyes. 'What a load of old tosh! He hasn't got a brother, so that blows your nonsense out of the water.'

Without replying, the woman turned back to Ellie's hand. 'Whether you believe me or not, I'm tellin' you what I see, and you'd best take heed, because they're both in grave danger.' Releasing her grip on Ellie's fingers, she sat back in her seat.

'Is that it? Can't you tell us—' Ellie began.

'Don't take no notice of her, Ellie, she's makin' it up as she goes along. Aidan hasn't got a brother.' She paused for a moment. 'Has he?'

Ellie shook her head. 'No, but maybe it's not Aidan I'm going to marry.'

Gwen scowled at the old lady. 'You shouldn't be tellin' people a load of mumbo-jumbo just to earn a penny. It's not nice.'

The old woman pulled a face. 'Like I said, I tells what I see.' She looked past Gwen. 'Ah, we're stoppin'.'

Ellie and Gwen looked out of the window. The train was indeed stopping, and seeing a sign for a café Ellie pointed towards it. 'Come on, let's go and get summat to eat. I'm starvin'.'

Gwen hesitated as she remembered the kitbags under her seat. The old woman rolled her eyes. 'You think I'm goin' to nick two honking great big bags full of your tat?'

Gwen bridled. 'My things aren't tatty ...' she began, only to be interrupted by Ellie who had raised a hand.

'Come on, you two, we've still got a while to go before we reach Lincoln. I'd like to finish the journey in peace if it's all the same to you.'

'I'm not the one ...' Gwen began, but Ellie had opened the carriage door.

'You comin' or stayin' here? Only we don't know how much time we've got before the train leaves.'

'You got a good ten minutes at this station,' the woman said knowledgeably. 'I do this route all the time, and the driver always stops for a wiz here.'

'Charming!' Gwen said, before being ushered out of the carriage by Ellie. On the platform she tugged at Ellie's elbow. 'I've gorra go to the lavvy too. Get me any sarnie and a sticky bun, an' a bottle of lemonade.'

By the time Ellie had neared the top of the queue Gwen had returned. Both girls were aware that the guard kept glancing at his wristwatch. 'I hope we manage to get summat before he blows his whistle,' Ellie said, looking back at the train again. 'It's a good job I don't need the loo. But hang on – isn't that the woman from our carriage?'

Gwen turned. 'Bit of luck the train'll leave without her.'

Watching the old woman disappear through the small gate that led from the platform Ellie noticed a small pony just like Spud outside. When he moved off the old lady was sitting on a small cart behind him. Ellie frowned, feeling her stomach lurch. The old woman had not said anything about leaving the train. Whilst she had not had either of the bags with her, something about her departure made Ellie uneasy.

'All I got left is corned beef and tomato, corned beef and pickle, or corned beef and onion.'

Turning, Ellie met the gaze of a middle-aged woman who had a cigarette dangling from the corner of her mouth. 'I'll take one with pickle and one with tomato, a small bottle of lemonade and two sticky buns, please.' She looked back at Gwen and nodded to where the pony had been standing. 'No need to worry about her missing the train. She's just left the station.'

Gwen shrugged. 'Good riddance to bad rubbish, that's what I say. I know she didn't threaten us with curses, but—'

'Sorry for interruptin', but are you talkin' about the old girl who's just left on the pony and cart?' enquired the woman who was selling the food.

Ellie nodded. 'That's the one. Why d'you ask?'

'You didn't leave anything behind in the carriage, did you?'

Gwen shrugged. 'Only our kitbags, but she hasn't taken them. We'd have seen her.'

'Did you have anything valuable in them?'

Gwen's heart sank. 'Me mam's locket. It isn't valuable, it isn't silver or anything like that, and it's broken, but it's valuable to me.'

The woman from the café shook her head in annoyance. 'She won't have had time to check it over. She just takes anything she thinks she can sell later on.'

Clutching the bags of food, Gwen trotted along the platform towards the carriage. 'I told you she was bad news. I knew we shouldn't have trusted her to be alone with our things.' As she entered the carriage she let out a groan of dismay. Peering over Gwen's shoulder Ellie's heart dropped as she surveyed the contents of both kitbags, which were strewn across the floor.

Gwen placed the food on the seats and started to sift through their belongings. 'You never know, she might not have seen it,' she said, her voice tinged with hope. 'She was old, so her eyesight's probably quite poor …' But after every item had been put back into their bags, there was no denying that the locket had gone.

'I'm so sorry, Gwen. I feel awful. I should've listened to you.'

Gwen shrugged. 'Wouldn't have made the slightest difference if you had. She'd have taken it no matter if we'd bought all her pegs and heather and lucky coins and both had our fortunes told. She's a thief, simple as.'

The door to the carriage opened and the guard appeared. 'I just been speakin' to Alice from the caff; she told me about Mary. Did she take owt?'

Gwen nodded. 'My locket. It wasn't valuable but it was the only thing I had left from me mam.'

He shook his head sadly. 'Sorry about that, chuck. I'm afraid there's nowt we can do about it unless we catch her sellin' it somewhere. She'll be long gone by now, and what with her havin' no fixed abode ...'

Gwen smiled resignedly. 'I know, I know, we get them all the time at home. You won't be able to trace her, and even if you did you wouldn't be able to prove that she didn't find it on the floor somewhere. Don't worry, I know you can't do anything to help, but thanks for coming to check on us.'

Nodding grimly, he closed the carriage door with a whoosh.

'What was that?' Ellie said, pointing to a small piece of paper that had whirled into the air. Bending down, she picked it up, turned it carefully over in her fingers, and held it out to Gwen. 'Is that the picture of your mam?'

Peering at the tiny photograph Gwen gave a gasp. 'Ellie Lancton, you're a bloomin' marvel! If I could've chosen what to find this would have been it! I can buy a locket anywhere, but the photo is irreplaceable.' Carefully placing it in her purse, she threw her arms around Ellie and squeezed her tightly. From outside they heard the guard calling out to any passengers still to board.

Several hours and train changes later the girls finally arrived in Lincoln. After asking for directions they soon found themselves at the Stonebow, and walking through the arch Ellie pointed to the large sign on the nearby hotel's façade. 'There it is, just as Arla described.' Inside there was a long passage leading to an ornate staircase. Ellie rang the small silver bell on the counter, and a skinny woman with steel-grey hair pulled into a tight bun poked her head round the door to the office. Smiling brightly, she moved to the counter and peered at them from over the top of her horn-rimmed spectacles.

'Good evening, ladies. May I be of assistance?' She eyed the large kitbags and added, 'If you're booking in I'll ring for one of the boys to carry your luggage up to your room.'

Ellie returned her smile. 'We've reservations under the names Lancton and Jones.' She craned her neck as she watched the woman flicking through the reservations book.

'Ah Yes, here we are.' The woman struck the top of the silver bell smartly and a young boy, not much bigger than the kitbags themselves, appeared behind the counter. He smiled cheerfully at Ellie and Gwen, but when his eyes rested on their luggage his face fell.

'Room four, please, Edward.' The receptionist turned to face them. 'Breakfast is served between six and nine. Here is your room key. I do hope you enjoy your stay.' She handed over a large brass key ring engraved with the hotel's name.

Ellie stepped forward as Edward struggled to pick up one of the bags, but he waved her back politely. "S'all right, miss, I can manage,' he puffed, his cheeks reddening. Gwen, who was also itching to help, stood by wincing as the boy, practically on his knees, placed the bag on his shoulder. Bracing himself, he managed to stand up briefly before toppling over backwards and landing heavily on the bag.

The receptionist opened the hatch on the counter and pulled Edward to his feet. 'For goodness' sake, Edward, stop messing about.' She turned apologetically to the two women. 'I'm so sorry. I hope there was nothing fragile inside.'

Edward pouted indignantly. 'Give me another go. I wasn't ready for it the first time,' he said, but Ellie had already swung the bag into her arms. Leaning down, she ruffled the boy's hair. 'No harm done, and thank you for trying, but I think we'd better take our own bags. We're used to them, you see.'

'Only if you're sure, miss,' said Edward, although Ellie noticed he appeared highly relieved. 'If you'd like to follow me, I'll show you to your room.'

As they left the debriefing room, one of the Waafs handed Aidan a piece of paper. 'Telephone message, sir.'

Aidan's brows rose as he read the note. He grinned at Connor. 'Ellie and Gwen arrived at the Saracen's Head last night, and they want to know if we're free over the next couple of days.'

Connor yawned. 'Sounds good to me, but at the moment all I want is bacon and eggs, followed by a bit of kip in a soft comfortable bed.'

Aidan beamed. 'I'll give them a ring before we call it a night, see if we can arrange something, maybe a walk followed by a spot of lunch?'

'You do that, but in the meantime ...' Connor's nostrils quivered as he inhaled, 'I smell bacon!'

Chapter Twelve

'Married? When and where and why didn't you tell me sooner?'

'He popped the question Saturday night. I'd far rather tell you face to face, and with you arriving in a few days I thought it not too long to wait. As for when, we're still working on the date. Obviously we want as many there as can make it, but with three sisters all in the services it's going to be tough going. As for where, the register office in Brougham Terrace, and therein lies another problem. Mam rang to see when the next available date was and they said it's months away. What with it being summer an' all, they're already chocka with people gettin' wed.'

Ellie beamed. 'I can't believe me bezzie's gettin' married! How did he pop the question? I hope he got down on one knee!'

Arla grinned. 'We'd nipped into the Old Crowne for a nightcap on our way back from the theatre. The place was packed and Archie was having trouble getting served, so when he started to shout I assumed it was to get the barman's attention, but then I realised he was calling for silence. I didn't think anyone would take any notice, but within a moment or two you could've heard a pin drop. Every person in that bar was staring at Archie when from out of nowhere he drops down on one knee and produces a jewellery box. You could've slapped me with a kipper there and then, and when he asked me to marry him ... everyone was staring at me, Ellie, all waiting to hear what I'd say. I'm sure my face was like a beetroot. When I finally found my tongue, of course I said yes, and you should've heard 'em all cheering. The landlord give me an' Archie a free drink to celebrate, then everyone started buyin' us drinks after that. I don't think Archie had to put his hand in his pocket once.' Arla held out her hand so that Ellie and Gwen might admire the silver-banded gemstone. 'It was his nan's. It's real silver.'

Sniffing loudly, Ellie embraced her friend. 'I'm ever so happy for you both. I can't wait to see you ...' she paused, '*are* you havin' a dress?'

Arla shook her head. 'We've decided to get married in uniform, 'cos if it weren't for the ATS we might never have got together.' Taking a large bite of toast, she pushed it into her cheek and continued to talk. 'Have you spoken to the boys?'

Ellie nodded. 'We've not set anything in stone, but they know we're here. Have you heard any more gossip about Aidan and Evie?'

'Nope.' Arla looked around, then spoke quietly. 'Although we do think Evie's seein' someone else in a desperate bid to make Aidan jealous, but I'm not sure I believe it, mainly because the man she's supposedly seeing ... well, let's just say Aidan wouldn't be jealous, especially if he knew the facts. If anything it would make him run for the hills.'

Ellie started to shake her head, then stopped abruptly. Leaning forward, she hissed, 'Not a married man?'

Arla nodded conspiratorially. 'Although I daren't say who, just in case I'm wrong. The repercussions ...'

'I bet it's Sergeant Barton!' said Gwen. 'We thought she was seeing him in training, and remember how she was always wangling favours in Liverpool?' She paused to pat Arla, who had started to choke, on the back. 'Am I right?'

Regaining her composure, Arla stared at Gwen. 'Blimey, you've got no hairs on your tongue, have you? And yes, you're right, but for goodness' sake don't go repeatin' it to no one else. We haven't got any proof. It's just that they've been seen together, and why would he come all the way over here if nothin' were goin' on?'

'Is Aidan seeing anyone else?' Ellie asked.

Arla shrugged. 'Connor's not mentioned owt, and if I'm honest I'd rather keep out of it. If you take my advice you'll ask him directly. I spoke to him last night and he suggested that we pop round for a visit one afternoon.'

Ellie turned to Gwen. 'What do you think?'

Gwen shrugged. 'I'm easy, but I think it would be good if you saw Aidan as soon as possible, grasp the nettle before you change your mind.'

'How about we go for a walk up there tomorrer mornin'?' Arla suggested. 'We can call in on the boys around lunchtime, and if they're free we can go to the Jockey for summat to eat.'

Taking a deep breath, Ellie nodded. 'Sounds like a good idea. As Gwen's already said, the sooner the better, before I get cold feet. Only let's surprise them. That way, if I change my mind ...'

As they approached RAF Waddington, Ellie's nerves started to get the better of her. Her fingers were twisting around themselves and her mind was beginning to race. It's too soon, she thought. I'm not ready. I never should have let the girls persuade me; we should have left it until later in the week. I'd better tell Arla before ... But it was too late. Arla was already chatting to the guard on the gate.

'Wotcha, Benny. Have you seen the boys today? Only I've brought them a couple of surprise visitors.'

'How do, Arla.' Looking past Arla, he waved to Ellie and Gwen. 'Who're these fine-lookin' ladies?'

'These are my pals from Liverpool, Ellie and Gwen. Is it okay for us to go and see the Murrays?'

He opened the gate. 'Course it is. I bet the fellers will be pleased to have a bit of company.'

Walking towards the small stone cottage, Ellie drew her friends to a halt. 'It's not a good time. I think we should go back; my mouth's gone dry.'

Gwen was having none of it. 'Strike while the iron's hot, there's no time like the present ... I can carry on if you like, but you know yourself that you'd only be puttin' off the inevitable.'

Whilst the two girls talked, Arla walked briskly to the cottage door and without pausing rapped a tattoo with the knocker. Ellie's heart raced at the sound of approaching footsteps. Gwen laid a reassuring hand on her shoulder. 'We're with you, cariad. You'll be fine.'

The door was flung open and a rather flustered-looking Connor stood before them. As soon as his eyes met Ellie's his face was wreathed in smiles. 'Thank goodness it's you. Come on in.'

Ellie hesitated. 'Were you expecting someone else? We can always call back if it's inconvenient.'

'No, no, not at all—' he began, only to be interrupted by Gwen.

'Since when did you gain your wings? I didn't know you'd passed muster,' she said curiously.

Standing back, he ushered the girls inside. Aidan, who had been lying on his bed, jumped to his feet and cleared the clothing from the chairs. 'Sorry it's a bit of a mess; we weren't expecting company. Can I offer anyone a drink?'

Her eyes narrowing, Arla folded her arms across her chest. 'Never mind drinks ... Gwen's right, only I know full well you've not been promoted, Connor Murray, so I'm assuming you're wearing your cousin's uniform?' She eyed him accusingly. 'Come on, out with it, but you'd better make sure it's the truth. I'll know if you're tellin' me porkies!'

Connor glanced at Aidan, who held up his hands. 'This is nowt to do with me. I told him it was a bad idea from the start.'

Taking a deep breath, Connor sat down on the end of Aidan's bed. His voice pleading, he smiled sheepishly at the girls. 'First, please don't tell anyone. Aidan and I could get into a lot of trouble if someone found out, and it was never meant to go this far.'

Ellie looked from one to the other, and seeing the grave concern on both faces she nodded. 'You know we'd never tell on you, I'm sure you have your reasons, although I can't think what they could be.'

Connor exhaled. 'It all started that first night when Aidan and me met you two in the NAAFI. I think I'd probably been there for about an hour when Evie came up to me at the bar. She started talking to me right away, and it was as if we'd known each other for years. She was full of smiles, and so friendly we had a rare old time, so much so that we arranged to meet the next day. It was only when she said goodnight and called me Aidan that I realised she'd been thinking I was him the whole evening. I know I should have put her right there and then, but I'd've felt a fool telling her she'd made a mistake.' Connor, his face a picture of guilt, continued to explain himself to his small audience. 'Within minutes of her leaving, Aidan came outside and I told him what had happened. He thought it was hilarious – said something about wondering where she'd disappeared to.Then he told me that she was one of those girls that's only after officers. Of course that was me well and truly out of the running, but then I remembered that I'd arranged to meet her the following day. I asked Aidan what he would do and he said to come clean, turn up and see what happened. If she really liked me it wouldn't matter how many wings I had, and if it did matter, then I was better off without her. But I really liked her, and didn't want to mess things up so soon, so I persuaded him to lend me his uniform just for that one date.'

Arla's mouth twitched with amusement. 'I think we all know where this is going.'

Connor nodded miserably. 'I met her in Aidan's uniform, and we had a wonderful time. I took her to Lyons café for tea, then we went to the cinema and watched *Gone with the Wind*, everything was perfect, and when I asked if she'd like to meet again before I went home, I was delighted when she said yes. I thought she liked me enough not to care about my rank, but Aidan had been talking to some of the fellers on the station and they had warned him about the trail of Evie's men who'd seen the error of their ways. The more we talked the more I realised that the relationship was doomed. I told Aidan that I'd meet her anyway and explain what I'd done, but Aidan was worried that she might be angry that I'd played a trick on her and cause a lot of trouble for us both. He said there was no sense in rocking the boat when we were leaving at the end of the week, so I may as well borrow his uniform for that last meeting and when we left Liverpool I could just let things peter out.'

'Only she got drafted to Lincoln ...' Ellie began, trying to keep the smile from her face.

He nodded miserably. 'I thought I'd got off scot free until she arrived in Waddington. I made lots of excuses, but she wouldn't listen. What's worse, she's turned into a real whinge bag. I tell you something for nothin': once you get past those big blue eyes there's nothing but a thorny nest. Especially for someone like me who hasn't got the money to take her to fancy places.'

'I take it you were on your way to see her just now?' said Gwen, who had been sitting in silent fascination on the end of Connor's bed.

'I thought I'd pop over and tell her I was leaving for Africa and that I had no intention of carrying on a long-distance relationship, but she'd gone into the city with one of her friends.'

Ellie shook her head. 'What a tangled web we weave when first we practise to deceive. Africa indeed! Haven't you learned anything? What if someone sees you around Lincoln, what will you say then?'

'Aha! But this time I'm not lying,' Connor said, with a satisfied grin. 'We really are off to Africa. Not for a while, I admit, but there's no point in carrying on with a—' Seeing Ellie's face, he stopped abruptly. 'Are you all right, Ellie?'

Ellie was staring at Aidan, her eyes rounding. 'But you can't. It's too dangerous. When will you be back?'

Aidan shrugged. 'Depends how long we're needed, but I shouldn't think we'll be back for a year at least. That's why—'

Ellie ran outside.

Aidan gaped at Arla. 'What's up with her?'

Rolling her eyes, she pointed to the door. 'What do you think? She doesn't want you to go, you twerp. Now go after her.'

'Hang on a mo—' Connor began, only to be hushed into silence by the two women.

Cautiously, Aidan peered round the corner of the door. Ellie was leaning against the wall of the cottage, her hands covering her face. Closing the door softly behind him, he put a hand on her shoulder. 'We're not off for a while yet, so we've plenty of time before we need to say t.t.f.n.'

Ellie stared up at him, her face streaked with tears. Pulling a handkerchief from his pocket, he began to gently wipe the tears away, but stopped midway when Ellie placed her hand over his. 'You don't understand. I don't want you to go at all, not ever, I thought you were with Evie, you see ...' Her voice trailed off as she tried to find the words.

Placing a finger under her chin, he looked into her eyes. 'No, I don't understand. I thought you didn't want a relationship with me. You never denied it.'

Ellie sniffed. 'Denied what?'

'When Evie said you were annoyed that she thought we were together.'

Ellie knitted her brows. 'But we weren't together, and the way she put it she made it sound seedy somehow, and that's not how I see you.'

'I should hope not!' He looked into her eyes. 'So are you saying that you wouldn't be utterly repulsed by the thought of us getting together?'

Ellie sniffed as she giggled. 'No, of course I wouldn't, but what about all those beautiful women like Evie who would willingly be seen on your arm?'

'Women like Evie are ten a penny, but I don't want a woman like Evie. You're the one I want.' Smiling into her upturned face, he gently brushed her hair back. 'What I'm trying to say is, will you be my girl?'

Ellie's heart sang. 'Of course I will.'

With a small whoop of joy, he lifted her up and swung her round before gently placing her back down, only before her feet could touch the ground his mouth had met hers and Ellie, who had never been properly kissed before, felt as though she was going to melt into a puddle. His soft lips were gentle yet firm, and his green eyes burned with passion.

There was the sound of someone clearing their throat. It was Connor. 'I'm pleased for you both, of course, and I did try to stop you before you left, but I think you should put on more clothes to go outside than your vest and pants, pal.'

Looking down, Aidan chuckled. 'Blimey! Let's get inside before tongues start wagging.'

With little time to spare before the boys were back on duty, the group headed into Lincoln to celebrate the new relationship between Ellie and Aidan. 'How about we go for a drink in the Wine Vault first, and then a meal in the Saracen's Head?' Aidan said, clutching Ellie's hand tightly in his.

After the Wine Vault Gwen, Arla and Connor had offered to let the other two have some time alone, but Aidan and Ellie had both refused. 'This is the start of our life together, and we want our friends with us to celebrate,' Aidan said as they headed for the Saracen's Head. 'Besides, I'm planning to take Ellie for a look around Lincoln on Thursday, then nip over to Waddington for a meal in the Horse and Jockey, followed by a lazy stroll down by the river.' He looked across at Gwen. 'I hope you don't mind. I'm sure you didn't exactly plan on coming here just to have Ellie whisked away from you.'

'Shows what you know. That was my plan all along.' She winked at Ellie. 'Besides, Arla and Connor will keep me company. I'm sure there's plenty to do in Lincoln. We could go dancing.'

Arla nodded. 'My Archie can come too. That way no one feels left out.'

As they walked through the entrance to the hotel, Gwen pointed to a solitary figure coming down the stairs. 'Blimey. Fancy seein' her here!'

Ellie hastily grasped hold of Gwen's elbow to tow her away before they were spotted by the approaching Evie, but she was too late. 'What the hell are you doing here?' Evie hissed, her face reddening.

A man who had been descending the stairs behind her appeared to change his mind halfway down. Turning, he had started to go back up when Gwen called out, 'Sergeant Barton, what are you doing here?' She looked accusingly at Evie. 'How many more have you got up there?'

Sergeant Barton froze mid-step before changing his mind yet again and heading down once more. Standing beside Evie, he smiled awkwardly. 'Lancton, Jones, what a coincidence this is.'

Evie pointed an accusing finger at Connor. 'Why are you wearing an air gunner's uniform?' Her eyes darted from him to Aidan and back again, and then, her voice sharp, she did not attempt to hide her anger. 'What the hell's going on? And why has he been wearin' your uniform?'

Aidan stepped forward. 'Maybe we should talk about this somewhere a little more private.'

Evie glanced at Aidan's walking cane. 'I couldn't give a rat's behind who hears me. I'm not the one pretending to be someone I'm not.' Her eyes narrowed as

338

she continued. 'I suppose the only way someone like you can get a girl is by pretending to be someone else,' she said in disgust. 'It doesn't take a genius to work out why.'

Ellie's cheeks flushed angrily. 'For your information, I'm with Aidan, and the only reason Connor dressed in his cousin's uniform was because you made a mistake that night in Liverpool. It was you who got them confused. If you'd been interested in more than his wings, you might have realised your error.'

Evie laughed scornfully. 'Well, I sure as hell wouldn't be interested in dating a cripple, wings or not … but either way I won't be made to feel like the one who's in the wrong when he's been impersonating an officer.' She stared accusingly at Aidan. 'And you lent him the uniform to do it.' She folded her arms defiantly. 'The way I see it, it's two birds with one stone, and you're both going to get into a lot of trouble for this. No one makes a fool out of me.'

Gwen nodded. 'If we're talking about honesty, then you've not been entirely honest with Connor either. After all, you got one of your pals to lie and say you were in the city with one of your friends, but you're not, are you? You're in a hotel with Sergeant Barton.' Her eyes met the sergeant's. 'It's been a while since I saw your wife. She's a lovely lady, always very concerned about you. I'll make sure I pay her a visit when I go back, let her know that I've seen you.' Pausing, she peered momentarily at her feet before catching his eye once more. 'I'll tell her we saw you too, Evie. I believe the two of you were quite friendly at one point. I'm sure she'll be pleased to know you're keeping an eye on her husband for her, although she might wonder what you were both doing in the same hotel, coming down from the rooms.' She smiled brightly. 'Still, that's not for me to worry about, is it?'

Evie scowled at Gwen. 'You can tell her what you damn well please … There's nowt wrong with visiting someone who's staying in the hotel on a bit of leave—'

Sergeant Barton, who had gone white, interrupted. 'I'm sure everyone's made a mistake at some time in their lives, and I think it would be best all round if we forgot all about this.' He addressed Connor. 'Let's put it down to a bit of high jinks, shall we? No harm done, after all.'

Evie's face was a picture of fury. She opened her mouth to speak but shut it quickly as the sergeant's complexion went from white to blood red in an instant. He gripped her by the elbow and hissed through gritted teeth, 'If my bloody wife finds out about this, I'm done for. It's her parents' old house we live in, so just you keep your bloody mouth shut, because I can guarantee you one thing: if she makes my life hell I'll do the same to you.'

Snatching her elbow from the sergeant's clasp, Evie glared at the small group. 'Fine! Just you keep your distance, Aidan, or Connor, or whoever the hell you are, and if anyone asks, I dumped you, understand?'

They watched as Sergeant Barton and Evie ascended the stairs once more, bickering as they went.

When they were out of sight, Connor gave a low whistle and clapped a hand on Gwen's back. 'Well done, Gwen! I thought it was going to get nasty for a minute there. How could you be so sure they were together, and what was all that about his wife?'

Gwen smiled absently. 'It's a long story, and right now my heart's racin' fit to burst, so if you don't mind can we go and get some lunch?'

'Fine by me, and after that little performance I'm paying!' He winked at Gwen before adding, 'I'll even stand you a seat in the cinema.'

Tilly shook her head in disbelief. 'You swore to me you were telling the truth, yet here you are, whining that you're the one who's been hurt! And you want me to tell on them?'

'I'd do it for you,' Evie pouted. 'He's made a ruddy fool out of me, and he shouldn't be allowed to get away with it. You should have seen that Ellie, she looked like the cat that got the cream.' She stamped her foot angrily. 'I won't have it, Tilly, I won't have that nasty little slum queen getting the upper hand. If you tell someone you saw Connor in his cousin's uniform they can't do anything to me, or to Sergeant Barton. That way the sergeant and me will come off scot free!'

Tilly stared incredulously at her friend. 'You don't get it, do you? You were the one who made the mistake when you got the two of them confused. I'd wager if it weren't for your rank-eating reputation,' she held up a hand as Evie started to protest, 'they'd never have thought of doing it in the first place. But you, on the other hand, you've always known that Barton was married. Good God, woman, you've even had tea with his wife! Have you no scruples, morals or principles?' She stared into Evie's blank face. 'You haven't, have you? As long as you're all right you couldn't give two hoots about the rest of us! Well, I've had it with you, Evie Maddox. I promised myself that if you were lying our friendship would be over and I meant it. From now on you're on your own, and you can tell Sergeant Barton that if his wife, or anyone else for that matter, ever asks whether there's any truth in the rumours, past or present, I'll be sure to tell her all I know.'

Evie's mouth dropped open. 'But you can't! I'll be ruined! You know you're the only friend I've ever had ...'

Tilly nodded. 'I do, and no matter how hard I've tried to change people's opinions of you, you've always thrown it back in my face. I'm sorry you fell from grace, I know you had a dreadful time of it when your father appeared in the papers, but truth be told, he's the one you should be angry with, not everyone else! I know you love him, and I know you've found it hard, but I can't keep making excuses for you. I'm afraid you've got to grow up, and you won't be able to do that if I keep covering your tracks.'

Evie's eyes narrowed. 'I don't need you, or anyone else for that matter. If I'd known how you felt about Daddy ...'

Tilly shook her head. 'Stop blaming everyone else, Evie Maddox.' She turned to leave the room.

'Where do you think you're going? You can't walk off; you haven't agreed to be my friend again yet. You know you always apologise in the end, so why don't we sort it out now?'

Tilly shook her head, then, without turning, she opened the door to the hut. 'Not this time, Evie. Not this time.'

Ellie listened to the sound of the engine as it puffed its way across the English countryside. She glanced at Gwen, who was snoring softly, her head resting against the shoulder of the Waaf to the right of her. With two hours of their journey left before they reached Liverpool, the other occupants of the compartment were also trying to get some rest.

Placing her coat against the window, Ellie closed her eyes. The past week with Aidan had been blissful, and they had spent their last day exploring the city of Lincoln.

It was on this day that Aidan had chosen to wear his special flying shoe in front of her. He had picked her up outside the Saracen's Head and they had driven into the centre of Lincoln before parking on a side street just off Steep Hill. Having walked to the bottom of the hill, Aidan had raised his brow expectantly.

'Notice anything different?' he said anxiously.

Ellie looked him up and down. 'Nope. Should I?'

He shrugged, then offered her his arm. 'Maybe not yet. I'll ask you again in a moment or two.'

Arm in arm, the two had begun to ascend the hill. When they were halfway up Aidan stopped and pulled her to face him. He was grinning. 'Now do you notice anything?'

Ellie looked at him quizzically. 'Sorry, but no. I'd like to think I'm pretty observant, being on the ack-acks, but—'

Aidan waved his arms up and down. 'No cane!'

'You don't always use a—' Ellie's hand flew to her mouth. 'You're not limping!' Taking a step back, she looked at his legs. 'But how come?'

Lifting the hem of his trouser leg up, he had shown her the shoe. 'It's my flying shoe. I don't normally wear it in public, but it does make walking easier and Steep Hill is a bit of a blighter to go up with a cane.' He gazed lovingly into her eyes. 'You really didn't notice, did you?'

Ellie shook her head. 'Why would I? I'm not in the habit of staring at people's shoes.'

He had started to chuckle, but it soon turned into a belly laugh. 'To think I was so worried as to what you might think when you saw the awful thing, and you never even noticed.'

'I don't see what's so funny, or why you were worried about what I would think about your shoes. I'd rather look at your face than your feet.'

Ellie smiled at the memory. Before she could get another word out, Aidan had put his arms round her waist, pulled her close and kissed her. It had been the start to a perfect day. When they eventually reached the top of Steep Hill, they had wandered around the beautiful cathedral, which Ellie had first mistaken for a castle. They had stopped for lunch at Stokes High Bridge Café before taking a bus into Waddington, where they took a stroll along the riverbank before returning to the Horse and Jockey to have their supper. It was here that Aidan asked Ellie the question that had been uppermost in his thoughts. 'What made you finally make up your mind? About me, I mean?'

Ellie had lowered the forkful of pasty from her lips. 'I always liked you, ever since the day we first met, but when I told you that I needed to find my own way in the world I meant it. My mam was left holding the baby when my dad beggared off. If it wasn't for her I'd have ended up in an orphanage, but she was a strong woman, fiercely independent and a force to be reckoned with. I wanted to be just like her when I grew up – still do – so I was a little disappointed with myself when I had to rely on you and your family to look after me. My mam wouldn't have relied on hand-outs, or anyone else's help; she'd have struggled through somehow.' She raised her brow reflectively. 'Having said that, she would never have got herself in that predicament in the first place, because Sid wouldn't have dared try anything on with her. She'd've had his guts for garters amongst other things if he'd so much as looked at her in the wrong way, and whilst I'll always be grateful to you and your family for helping me out at such short notice, I needed to prove to myself that I was capable of being the same sort of woman as me mam.' She chewed thoughtfully on the pasty before adding, 'Enduring nights like the May blitz showed me that I am that woman. Now do you see?'

Aidan had nodded. 'As far as I can see you've always been that woman, only you couldn't see it.' He held up one hand and started to tick the list off on his fingers. 'You worked two jobs when your mam died, you fought Sid off and escaped to a whole new life where you learned new skills, which you took to like a duck to water, might I add.' He smoothed her cheek with the backs of his fingers. 'You never batted an eye when you realised I was disabled, and you never treated me any differently. It made me realise that I wasn't that different from everyone else, and that's why I went to the town hall day after day until one man saw the same person you did.' He eyed her anxiously. 'Trouble is, when all's said and done and the war is over, I'll go back to being a boring old farmer once more, and after all your adventures I don't know whether you'll find farm life a bit too mundane. I suppose I'm worried that whilst you might have said yes to being a pilot's girl you might have second thoughts when I'm back on the farm shovelling manure for a living.'

She had looked at him in astonishment. 'I would never describe you as boring, and if you must know, I was saying yes to Aidan the farmer, Aidan the pilot and Aidan the man. That do you?'

Leaning across the table, he had cupped her face in his hands and brushed his lips against hers. 'That suits me fine.'

As the train's wheels clickety-clacked along the tracks, Ellie sighed wistfully. Hearing a soft chuckle, she opened one eye.

'Dreamin' o' summat nice, were you, gal?' said one of the men in naval uniform.

Aware that she had been grinning like the Cheshire Cat, Ellie nodded shyly.

'Or perhaps someone,' he said with a wink.

Eyeing the sailor shrewdly, Ellie pulled her ATS cap down over her face, and smiled.

*

'Gwen! You've got to come and read this.' Ellie, flourished a piece of paper at her friend. 'It's from Arla, I got it this morning.'

As Ellie positioned herself cross-legged on the bottom bunk, Gwen nestled beside her. 'What's up?'

'Gossip, and it's hot off the press.'

Several of the women in the surrounding bunks lifted their heads in interest. 'Anyone we know?' said Delilah.

Handing the letter to Gwen, Ellie nodded. 'The letter's from my mate Arla. She's the girl me and Gwen went to see in Lincoln.'

There was an audible gasp from Gwen. 'Blimey! I never saw that coming.'

'What?' said Delilah, who had got up to join them.

'Evie's been taken off the ack-acks and sent to Scotland. Apparently Sergeant Barton arranged for her to be remustered as a clerk,' said Gwen.

Delilah's jaw dropped open. 'Scotland? Surely she could've trained somewhere closer to home?'

'According to Arla, Barton wanted to get rid of her, reckoned she'd been trying to cause trouble between him and his wife.' Ellie glanced knowingly at Gwen.

Delilah pointed an accusing finger at Gwen. 'You knew there'd been rumours, didn't you? When we first got here, I heard you telling Ellie about your initial trainin' an' that.' She pursed her lips. 'No smoke wi'out fire, and I reckon you were right.'

Gwen glanced up from the letter. 'Right or wrong, it makes no difference now, not with Evie out of the picture.'

Delilah nodded grimly. 'She always was trouble, that one; I remember the grief she gave Ellie over that pilot friend of hers. It's about time someone put her in her place.' She giggled. 'Scotland! I bet she was like a bear with a sore head when they told her where she was going! Does she say any more?'

Gwen glanced at Ellie, then shook her head. 'Nothing of interest.' This seemed to satisfy the curiosity of the women around them, who went about their business. Gwen turned her attention back to the last paragraph of Arla's letter.

Fancy asking Tilly to tell on Connor and Aidan. Of all the low-life things to do! Still, it backfired on her good and proper, didn't it? I'd have loved to be a fly on the wall the day Tilly told Barton she wouldn't keep her mouth shut if his wife came asking questions. I bet his face was a picture. She knew he'd try and send her off like he did Evie, so she told him straight that if he even thought about having them posted together she'd be sure to pay his wife a visit before she left!

Gwen glanced around the room, and when she was happy that no one was listening she spoke quietly to Ellie. 'Good for Tilly, that's what I say! Just goes to show that we were right about her from the start. She wasn't such a bad egg after all.'

Ellie nodded. 'It does sound as though she's come out of her shell good and proper since Evie's gone. Arla even invited her to her wedding; it's just a shame she won't be able to make it. I, for one, would have liked to thank her in person for standing up to Evie.'

'Me too, It can't have been easy; they'd been friends for ever such a long time.' Ellie took the letter from Gwen and tucked it back in its envelope. 'She'll make a lot more friends now she hasn't got Evie overshadowing her. Probably be a lot happier, too, so all in all I'd say it's worked out pretty well.'

It was the morning of Archie and Arla's wedding. Ellie, Gwen, Arla and her sisters were squeezed into Arla's old bedroom, each doing the other's hair and chattering excitedly.

'You're going to be married in a couple of hours,' Ellie breathed as she curled the top of Arla's hair into a roll. 'You'll be Mrs Archie Byrnes.'

Gwen gazed wistfully at Arla. 'I wish I was gettin' married, but knowin' my luck I'll be left on the shelf. I'll probably end up like one of them old women that sits in a rockin' chair all day, surrounded by cats.' She pulled a face as the image formed in her mind's eye. 'I can just see me now, Baggy on my knee whilst his little 'uns try to bite my ankles.'

Arla giggled. 'You should've brought him. You could've put him in a penguin suit; he'd look adorable.'

Clipping Arla's hair into place, Ellie stood back to admire her handiwork. 'You're bonkers, both of you.' Holding up a mirror, she showed Arla the back of her hair. 'How's that?'

'Oh, Ellie, it's beautiful. Thanks so much for comin' round early. You've allus been better at doin' hair than me,' said Arla, gently patting the back of her head.

'I'm so glad to be here,' said Ellie. 'I must admit when you told me the date I was a bit worried I might not be able to make it, and I'm thrilled the boys could come before leaving for Africa.'

Looking in the mirror, Arla smiled at Ellie's reflection. 'This'll be you and Aidan one day, but I bet you won't be getting married in uniform, will you?'

Picking up a piece of tissue Ellie, blotted the lipstick her friends had persuaded her to wear. 'Knowing Aidan we'll get married in farm overalls and have a tractor as the wedding car.'

Gwen was dabbing at her uniform with a wet flannel, trying to remove the baked bean juice from her breakfast. 'Not on your nelly! I've seen the way he looks at you: you'll be getting the best he can afford, and to be honest I'm surprised he hasn't asked you already.'

Ellie shrugged. 'We've neither of us mentioned marriage. I think we're still gettin' used to being together. Besides, he'll be off to Africa soon.'

Arla turned to face her. 'You're not suggesting you might change your mind?'

'No, I'm just saying he's going to be far away and anything might happen. I don't want to make the same mistake me mam did and assume everything is coming up roses only to find it goes pear-shaped!'

There was a brief knock on the door. 'Come in!' they chorused.

Arla's mother poked her head round the door. 'Mr Bent has brought your bouquet, love. He got some pink and blue cornflowers; they really are beautiful. Do you want me to keep hold of 'em till you're ready?'

Arla nodded. 'Thanks, Mam.' She turned to Ellie. 'Try to think positive. I know you're a bit superstitious about countin' your chickens an' that, but just because it went wrong for your mam doesn't mean to say it'll be the same for you.'

There came another brief knock on the door, followed by the voice of Arla's father. 'It's time to go, queen.'

The morning after the wedding Ellie and Gwen had arranged to meet Aidan and Connor for an early lunch.

'I'm having haddock and chips,' Connor decided after a quick glance at the menu. 'I'm starving after all that dancing last night. Don't you ever get tired?'

Gwen laughed. 'I think it must have been all the excitement of the wedding. I felt fine at the time but when I woke up this morning my poor feet felt as though I'd spent the entire day square-bashing.'

'It was good fun, though, and Arla looked beautiful. Even Archie scrubbed up well. I thought it was lovely the way everyone saved up their coupons and pitched in with the wedding breakfast,' said Ellie.

'Why do they call it a wedding breakfast when it's served at lunchtime?' Aidan asked. 'They did the same at my cousin Jean's wedding, and I didn't have anything to eat all morning thinking we'd be having breakfast at the wedding.'

'Poor Aidan.' Ellie laughed. 'They call it a wedding breakfast because it's the first meal you eat as a married couple.' She patted his tummy. 'Just you be grateful they didn't get married late in the afternoon.'

A waitress hovered by Aidan's shoulder, her pencil poised on her notepad. 'Are you ready to order?'

'Everyone want tea?' said Ellie, not taking her eyes off the menu.

There was a general murmur of agreement. Gwen put her menu down on the table. 'Sausage roll and peas, please. It's not as if I've gorra watch me figure.'

Connor frowned. 'There's nothing wrong with your figure. I dunno why you women are so obsessed with your weight. Every chap I know would prefer a girl with a bit of meat on her bones who can dance the night away, not faint halfway through 'cos she's half starved.'

Ellie added her menu to the others in the middle of the table. 'I'll have baked beans on toast, please.' She looked across the table to Connor. 'You're not courting anyone, are you, Connor?'

Connor shook his head and was about to reply when a blushing Gwen broke in. 'Is anyone interested in going for a wander around Paddy's Market? I'm not after anything in particular, I just love having a good old nose.'

'Can I order fishcake and chips first?' Aidan said, his tone a touch wounded at the thought he might miss out on a meal.

'Oh, sorry, Aidan. Don't worry, we didn't forget you,' Gwen chuckled.

Ellie smiled at the sudden change in the conversation. She had watched Gwen and Connor dancing at Arla's wedding and had remarked to Aidan how well suited the two were.

'She's all he's talked about since your visit,' said Aidan. 'I was quite surprised, as I didn't think she was his sort, not after Evie; the two are polar opposites. I did mention it to him, but he fobbed me off, saying that they were just pals and he enjoyed her company.'

Ellie had cocked her head on one side as she watched the pair swirl around the floor. 'Maybe he's right, maybe they are just friends. Seems a bit of a shame, though.'

Later that night, when the girls were tucked up in bed, Ellie had prodded the underneath of Gwen's bunk. 'You and Connor had a good time tonight. Everybody thought you were a couple.'

There was a considerable pause before Gwen answered. 'Really? I am surprised. He's awfully good fun and I like him a lot, but I don't think of him that way.'

It was the pause, Ellie thought to herself now; it was too long before she replied.

Connor's voice brought her back to the present. 'I'm up for that. Crikey, I've not been to Paddy's Market for years. You mean the one on Great Homer Street?'

'Here's your tea. I'll bring your food over in a mo.' The waitress started distributing cups and saucers.

Full from their lunch, the four of them headed towards Great Homer Street, where they strolled along the pavement looking at the various stalls. Ellie and Gwen walked on whilst Aidan and Connor stopped to barter over a set of golf clubs, until Ellie spotted a beautifully beaded kiss-lock purse. Picking it up, she looked around for the stallholder.'

'She's just nipped to the lavvy, luv; she won't be long,' the man on the next stall told her. 'I'd serve you meself, but I can see there's no ticket on it.'

'Do you mind if I carry on whilst you wait?' Gwen asked.

'You go ahead. I'm sure she won't be long.'

As Gwen ambled off, Ellie was pleased to see a plump woman hurrying towards her. 'Sorry about that, darlin', but I'm a martyr to me bladder. What can I do for you?'

Holding up the small purse, Ellie noticed that some of the beads were missing and others were decidedly loose, so putting it back down she selected another one similar to the first, but in better condition. 'How much?'

The woman smiled. 'Tell you what, how about I do you a deal on the two? I can see the other one's seen better days, so I'll let you have the two for sixpence.'

'What would I want two purses for?'

'You could give the other one to a pal, or your mam ...'

Ellie laughed. 'Nice try, but I only want the one.'

Shrugging, the woman fished out the ticket that was inside the purse. 'That'll be fourpence ha'penny. You sure you don't want the other one?'

Handing the money over, Ellie shook her head. 'Me mam's dead, so she's not in much need of a purse, and Gwen's already got one.'

Blushing, the woman hastily apologised. 'Sorry, luv. Me and me big mouth. My Bertie allus said I should think before I speak.'

'No harm done.' Looking round the stalls, Ellie could see Aidan and Connor walking towards her with the set of golf clubs, so she smiled a farewell to the woman and went to meet them.

'We wore him down in the end.' Aidan laughed. 'I thought if Connor carried on much longer he was going to start throwing in free golf balls just to get rid of us.'

'Where's Gwen?' said Connor. Hefting the bag on to his shoulder, he pointed a finger past Ellie. 'Forget that. I can see her, and judging by the smile on her face she's bagged herself a bargain.'

Beaming, Gwen held out a necklace. 'What do you think? It's got some feller's picture inside but that should be easy enough to remove.' She handed Ellie the locket.

Ellie carefully clicked the little clasp open, and focused on the picture inside. Looking up sharply, she spoke urgently. 'Who did you get this from?'

'Some old feller. Why?' Gwen was clearly taken aback by her friend's brusque manner.

Ellie handed the locket back. 'Remember when we went to Lavender Court and Mr Rogers told us that Mrs Burgess had been killed in the bombing?' Gwen nodded. 'Well, this is her locket, and the picture is of her husband, Arnie Burgess. She never took it off, so I'd like to know who you bought it from and how they came across it. Can you remember whereabouts they were?'

Gwen looked down the lines of stalls. 'I think so. It was a scruffy-looking man, covered in scars, sort of tucked away between two stalls. He'd not got a table, just an old wooden box.'

As Ellie turned, Connor caught her elbow. 'Hang on a mo. You don't know that her kids didn't sell that locket. It's perfectly possible, you know: times are hard and folk need the money.'

'Very true, but not with his photograph still inside. They'd have taken that out,' said Ellie evenly. 'Besides, I only want to see who sold it to Gwen. Once I've done that I'll make my mind up what to do next.'

Aidan clasped her hand. 'We'll come with you. If this feller has come across it by foul means I don't want you wading in on your own.'

They set off down the long line of stalls, Gwen taking the lead. After a few minutes she turned to Ellie. 'I think we must've gone past him; I'm sure I didn't come this far down. Either that or he's already gone.'

Ellie heard a familiar voice that cut through her body like a knife.

'That'll be sixpence, love, cheap at 'alf the price. This is the only one I got, take it or leave it.'

Ellie glanced at Connor, who had also recognised the voice. He mouthed the word 'Sid', and Ellie nodded. Pulling her cap down, she lowered her eyes to the ground, then glanced sideways to see if she could spy the foul beast of a man. Swivelling round, Gwen looked to where Sid Crowther stood, and turning back she nodded to Ellie.

Aidan pulled gently at Ellie's elbow. 'Not here,' he hissed, taking her to one side. When they were out of earshot Ellie spoke hotly.

'The lying beast of a man! He never tried to save Mrs B, he bloody well robbed her.' Tears trickled down her cheeks. 'And now after all this time, he's making money out of his wicked deed. We need to tell the police. Everyone should see him for what he is: a lying, thieving coward.'

'And they will,' Aidan assured her, 'but we can't take any chances. We've got to make sure he doesn't run off before the scuffers get here. The two of us will keep an eye on him, make sure he doesn't leave.' Turning to Connor, he continued, 'You and Gwen must go and find the nearest scuffer, explain the situation, make sure he understands, then bring him back here.'

Nodding briefly, Connor and Gwen headed off in search of a policeman. Aidan turned back to Ellie. 'Stand here beside me and pretend to be interested in something on one of the stalls. Don't look at him or he might get suspicious.'

Connor and Gwen pushed their way through the crowded pavement until they found a policeman leaning against the wall as he rolled a cigarette. Connor smiled. 'PC Downey!'

Looking up, the man beamed at Connor. 'Bless my soul, if it ain't little Connor Murray. Blimey, you in the RAF now, are ya?' Glancing at Gwen, he added, 'Got yourself a pretty young woman too, I see.'

Connor waved a hand. 'I'm afraid I'm not here for a chat.' He went on to explain about the locket and Sid Crowther, and was pleased when the man tucked his cigarette into his top pocket and straightened his jacket.

'You are sure it's him, are you? Only no one's seen hide nor hair of him since the bombing.'

Connor nodded. 'He's covered in scars, but even so it's him all right. Come and see for yourself.'

The constable shook his head gravely. 'Lead the way, young Connor. If what you say is true and that locket

357

belonged to Mrs Burgess, then Sid Crowther's got a lot of explaining to do.'

An approaching policeman overheard Sid's name being mentioned and cut in.

'Sid Crowther, did you say? I thought that old git had long gone. Don't tell me he's still knocking about. What's he done this time?'

Back at the market, Ellie must have looked at the same wrench fifteen times before the stallholder eventually approached her. 'D'you know what that's for, love? Only you seem a bit distracted.'

She looked up from the wrench in her hands. 'What? Oh yes, sorry, I'm trying to make my mind up.'

A couple of stalls up from Sid's was a woman selling all manner of ladies' items. 'Perhaps we'd better go up there. It'd look more natural if you were looking at women's wear rather than spanners,' said Aidan.

As they passed Sid, Ellie could not resist the urge to look at him, and was horrified when their eyes locked.

'You!' Sid growled. 'I thought I'd seen the back of you a long time ago, you thievin' little tart.'

Fixing Sid with a steely glare, she eyed the network of scars on his face, and the patch that covered one eye. 'I see the bomb improved your looks. Tell me something, do you know what a thief is? I do. It's someone who takes lockets from around a dead person's neck – that's if Mrs Burgess was dead when you took her jewellery. Or perhaps you just left her for dead?'

Leaping to his feet, he grabbed the black cloth containing his wares and stuffed it into his pocket.

'No you don't!' Aidan shouted.

Eyeing Aidan's walking cane, Sid laughed scornfully. 'Who the bloody hell's going to stop me?' As he made to push past Ellie, Aidan took a step forward, and raising his cane brought it round in a sweeping motion. The hooked handle caught Sid's ankle and sent him crashing to the floor. Landing heavily on top of him, Aidan twisted his arm up behind his back. 'Ellie is neither a thief nor a tart. You, on the other hand, are in it up to your neck.'

'Well, well, well, it really is you, Sid. Still up to your old tricks, I see.' Leaning down, PC Downey swiftly cuffed Sid, who was trying to scramble to his feet. The constable turned to Gwen. 'This the feller what sold you the locket, love?'

Gwen nodded. The policeman held the locket in front of Sid's good eye. 'Recognise this?'

Sid glared menacingly at Gwen. 'Never seen it before in my life.'

PC Downey lowered his voice. 'Only the picture inside is of Arnie Burgess. He were a family friend was Arnie; his missis, too. She wore this necklace all her life, never took it off ... So how come it ended up in your possession?'

Sid's face contorted as he struggled in the policeman's firm grip. 'It's got nowt to do wi' me. I never seen it before in my life. She's a bloody liar, that's what she is.'

A small crowd had started to form and one of the women stepped forward, holding a hand out to the constable. 'May I?'

Nodding, he handed her the locket. Clicking it open, she nodded her head. 'She's not lyin'. You tried to sell me this locket no more than half an hour ago. I told you I didn't want a locket with somebody else's picture in it. Especially not some old feller. My 'Arold'd think I were 'avin' an affair!'

Gripping him by the collar, PC Downey slid a hand into Sid's pocket. 'Let's see what else you have for sale, shall we?'

Trying to duck out of his grasp, Sid began to shout and swear, but nothing he could say or do was going to stop the inevitable. The policeman pulled out the piece of linen that contained Sid's wares and passed it over to the other constable, instructing him to look through the contents. Ellie let out a cry.

'That's her wedding ring; I'd recognise it anywhere. It's made up of a band of tiny forget-me-knots, and if you look closely their names and the date of their wedding are inscribed on the inside!'

Bellowing with rage, Sid lunged at Ellie, only to be hauled back by his captors. Ellie was too angry to cry. Instead she fixed Sid with a look of pure hatred. 'You didn't even try to save her, did you? Was she …?'

Sid spat on the ground. 'Why would I put my life in danger for some old biddy who owed me rent? I lost everything in that bombing, or doesn't that matter?'

It was all too much. Ellie brought her hand round hard against Sid's face with such force that they both cried out.

'Brutality! You all saw that! They allowed her to attack me—' His last words were lost in a yelp of pain as PC Downey yanked on the cuffs.

'Time to go, Sid, 'cos when word gets round that you robbed a dying woman instead of trying to save her like you told everyone you did we'll have a lynch mob on our hands, and even though I'm sworn to protect you I won't be able to do a damned thing to stop them.' He glared at Sid from the corner of his eye. 'God help me, Sid Crowther, but I'll be damned if I'll be caught in the crossfire trying to save the likes of you from this lot.'

Sid eyed the sea of angry faces. 'Lies,' he mumbled, but he no longer fought as the constable led him away.

Ellie turned to Aidan, her eyes brimming with tears. 'Do you think he did leave her to die?'

Holding her in his arms, he pressed her cheek close to his chest and kissed the top of her head. 'Try not to think about it, alanna. We'll never know the truth, so no good can come from dwelling on it.'

Lifting her head from his chest, she looked into the warmth of his gaze and murmured, 'Thank you for stopping him getting away. I couldn't have done it without you.'

Smoothing her hair down, he smiled reassuringly. 'I'll always be here for you when you need me, Ellie, don't ever forget that.'

Connor cleared his throat. 'Can we get a shuffle on? Only I want to see if I can find a golf bag.'

Ellie started to giggle. 'You and your golf clubs! If you'd been here five minutes earlier you could've used one of them to pan Sid out.'

Aidan chuckled. 'He'd have more chance of hittin' Sid than he has of hitting a golf ball.'

The change in conversation was just what they needed, and it was a happy group that made their way round the rest of the market, although word soon spread and no matter which stall they visited the owner had already heard of the heroic arrest. Connor even got a half-priced golfing bag from their good deed. But even through the smiles, Ellie could not break her thoughts away from the fact that the boys would be leaving for Lincoln in a few hours, and in a few days they would be off to Africa.

As the two men made their way towards the Lancaster Lass, Connor glanced at his cousin. 'I hope you're not goin' to be moping the whole time we're in Africa. I was looking forward to visiting the pyramids, so cheer up, for goodness' sake.'

Aidan forced a smile. 'It's all right for you. You haven't got a woman like Ellie waitin' for you.'

Connor rolled his eyes. 'Thanks a lot, pal, remind me again how I've lucked out in love for the whole of the war so far.' He wiggled his eyebrows. 'Although I might have women throwin' themselves at me in Egypt. The lads have come back with some blindin' stories about mysterious eastern temptresses with silky black hair, seductive dark eyes and' – he waved his hands in the air – 'curves in all the right places.'

Aidan arched an eyebrow. 'So you're not even slightly interested in Gwen?'

'Nothing's changed since the last time you brought her name up. I've always thought of her as Ellie's mate.'

'Connor Murray, all I hear from you is talk about dating different women but you never actually do anything about it. I've not seen you with any other girl than Evie, and what a disaster that turned out to

362

be.' Reaching the Lancaster Lass, Aidan made his way to the front of the craft. 'Why don't you put your money where your mouth is and ask the best woman you've met so far out on a date? Because from where I'm standing you two are a perfect match.'

Connor shrugged. 'Maybe, maybe not, but either way it's a bit late to be thinking thoughts like that. I'll ask her when I get back, that's if I haven't found the next Mrs Murray in Egypt, of course.'

Aidan rolled his eyes. 'God give me strength!'

Arla smiled as she handed Ellie's letter to Archie. 'She's spoken to the scuffer what arrested that toerag Sid Crowther. He said Sid's given them a full confession about robbing poor old Mrs Burgess, but says she was dead at the time and that he only did it because she owed him rent, but Ellie says they found a load of jewellery and black market stuff in the room what he's renting down by the docks, so it's not just her stuff he's in the mire over, it's all the other bits too.'

Archie raised his brow as his eyes scanned the letter before him. 'If I had my way the bugger'd swing for all the hurt he's caused over the years.'

Arla laughed mirthlessly. 'They won't do that, not just for some nicked stuff, and they can't prove he left her for dead neither. But I reckon they'll make an example of him, so with a bit of luck he'll go away for a long time, and as Ellie said, when he does get out everyone in Liverpool will know what he did. So if he has any sense at all he'll leave Liverpool for ever, otherwise the locals will succeed where the hangman failed!'

Chapter Thirteen

Dear Ellie,

When we first arrived the fellers said it'd take us a while to get used to the heat. Well it's been a whole year and it's still as unbearably hot as it was the day we flew in.

Bursting through the door to the hut, Gwen stamped her feet loudly on the floor. 'Blimey, if this weather carries on for much longer we're going to need a dinghy to get to the battery.' She glanced at the epistle in Ellie's hands. 'Lover boy?'

Ellie nodded. 'If you mean Aidan, then yes.'

Shaking the rain from her shoes, Gwen sat down on the bed beside her. 'Why, how many other lovers does the lady have lined up?' She dodged Ellie's outstretched palm and continued. 'Cheer up, cariad, a few more months and it'll be Christmas. I know it's not the same in wartime, but at least it's a bit of a break in the routine.'

Ellie nodded. 'I wonder what Aidan and Connor will do this year? I know they were lucky enough to have some leave last year so they went to Egypt and saw the pyramids and relaxed by the pool, but I can't see them having the same type of luck two years in a row.'

Gwen smiled wistfully. 'What I'd give to be lying by a swimming pool in the sun right now, glass of wine in one hand and—'

'Connor in the other?' Ellie said with a chuckle.

Gwen giggled. 'I don't know what it is, but ever since he left for Africa I've seen him in a whole new light.'

'It's because he's so far away. They say absence makes the heart grow fonder and they're right. Mind you, it's only what the rest of us have been saying for ages.'

Gwen raised her brow. 'And what's that, Mrs Clever Clogs?'

'That you and Connor make a perfect couple.'

Bagheera jumped down from the corporal's bed and strolled over to Gwen and Ellie. Jumping lightly on to Gwen's knee, he kneaded her lap before settling down to sleep. Gwen tickled him between his ears. 'The trouble is, I can't get the image of Evie out of my mind. She might be horrible on the inside but she comes in a beautiful package, and that's what Connor was first drawn to, isn't it? Only I don't look anything like her, and whilst we may get on well as friends, I don't think I'm his type.'

Ellie shook her head. 'Didn't you learn anything from me and Aidan?'

Gwen methodically smoothed the cat's fur. 'But when push came to shove Aidan wasn't interested in her, was he?'

Ellie chewed her lip thoughtfully. 'Who knows what would have happened if she had pursued Aidan the way she did Connor? Besides, after a healthy dose of

Evie, I don't think pouting blue-eyed blondes are Connor's type any more.'

'What does any of it matter anyway? With Connor so far away it's all pie in the sky.' Gwen glanced out of the hut window. 'If this rain keeps up we'll have a pool of our own, which would be grand if we weren't at the beginning of winter.'

Leaning over, Ellie stroked the back of Bagheera's head. 'When this war is over I reckon we should all go to Seaforth Sands for a little holiday. It might not have pyramids but it does have a beautiful sandy beach. We can make some really big sandcastles and pretend we're in Egypt.'

Raising his head, the black cat yawned. 'According to Connor, cats are sacred animals in Egypt.' Gwen tickled him under his chin. 'They'd love you out there, probably make you into some kind of god.'

Ellie laughed. 'If they treat their cats like gods they must be better behaved than him. The little blighter slept on my uniform last night, and when I got up this mornin' it was covered in fur. It took me ages to pick it all off, then to top it off I caught him playing hunting games with one of my stockings. I'm just lucky I managed to get it off him before he laddered them again.'

Gwen grinned. 'He would be Bagheera, the God of Mischief!'

Nearly two years had passed since they had last seen the Murray boys and a lot had changed in that time. With fewer air raids the men and women on the ack-ack batteries were no longer required in such large numbers, and whilst a few remained a lot had chosen to remuster, including Ellie and Gwen, who had decided to try their luck at driving.

'I learned to drive a tractor on our farm,' Gwen had said as the army truck bumped its way along the small lane that led them to their new barracks. 'We'll be learning to drive everything here, and we'll get to go all over Britain. It's going to be more exciting than sitting around night after night.'

The girls had been sent to train in the wilds of North Wales, where they learned to drive just about every vehicle the army had to offer, and after three arduous months, when they had passed all the tests, they were thrilled to learn that they would be staying at the same camp not far from London.

'We'll get to see Buckingham Palace, St Paul's Cathedral, and the Tower of London,' Gwen had enthused. 'This beats sitting around waiting to be shot at any day of the week.'

Ellie had laughed. 'I think just about anything beats that, but I know what you mean. I always wanted to go to London ever since I was a little girl. I used to practise my curtsey in case I bumped into the King, but we couldn't afford the train fare.'

'Join the army and see the world. Well, London at any rate,' Gwen had chuckled.

It had been on one of these jaunts that they had bumped into Sally, Arla's eldest sister. Gwen and Ellie had been having their photograph taken on the steps to St Paul's Cathedral when someone hailed them.

'Coo-ee! Ellie, Gwen ...'

Recovering her uncle's Leica camera from the passer-by, Gwen waved at Sally.

'Hello, cariad. What on earth are you doing here?'

Grinning, Sally approached. 'I'm based in Biggin Hill, so it's not too far away. You?'

'We're staying in a billet not ten minutes' drive from there. Have been for the last six months,' said Ellie.

'Fancy that! All this time and we've only been a stone's throw apart, yet where do we see each other?'

Ellie laughed. 'Because we're drivers now, we're normally off in the wilds of Scotland, or windy Wales. It's very rare we're in our barracks.'

'Not that we do anything when we get there,' Gwen added bitterly, 'save wait for whoever we're driving to come out of some endless meeting.'

'Or pick up a document, turn round and drive all the way back,' Ellie agreed.

That had been some months back, and right now Ellie was indeed waiting for the officer she was chauffeuring to come out of his meeting. She drummed her fingers on the steering wheel as she glanced at her wristwatch. Three hours! She'd be lucky to get home before midnight if it went on much longer.

She jumped as she accidentally leaned against the car horn. She looked up anxiously, expecting to see an angry officer peering from the door of the office, and was relieved to see she had not disturbed them. Leaning back, she wondered whether Gwen's car had made it back from Scotland in one piece. The last time her friend had undergone the arduous journey, the officer she was driving had complained bitterly upon his arrival back in London.

'Damned near knocked me teeth out. Didn't anybody tell you that you should avoid potholes, not aim for the damned things!' he had said, slamming the door so hard the glass in the windshield had vibrated.

Gwen had marched into the NAAFI and asked for the biggest slice of anything they had left. She had addressed the room in general. 'They give you a car with no suspension, then ask you to take some fat old bugger across the moorland in the dark. How the hell was I meant to see the potholes?'

Now, seeing the door to the office open, Ellie got out of her seat and made her way to the front of the car. Some of the vehicles she had driven had had downright vicious starting handles that would either try to wrench themselves out of your grip or spin off, catching you across the kneecaps. It was the one part of driving that she truly hated; the Morris 8 that she was currently driving was the only car she had ever driven which behaved itself on start-up. Slotting the handle into place she wound it round a few times with ease and smiled as the engine roared into life.

Getting back into the car, Ellie turned to the officer. 'Ready to go, sir?'

He nodded wearily. 'I don't mind telling you that when this is all over I'm not getting out of my bed for a week.'

Knowing better than to ask him what had gone on in the meeting, Ellie acknowledged his comment with a small nod before cranking the car into gear and setting off on the long journey.

Keeping the ride as smooth as possible so that the officer could get some well-deserved rest, Ellie turned her thoughts to Aidan and the rest of the crew of the Lancaster Lass. They had returned from Africa in preparation for the D-Day landings and Ellie had hoped that she might bump into them on her travels, but so far she'd had no such luck. So near yet so far away, she thought miserably. They may as well have stayed in Africa.

Glancing in the rear-view mirror, she could see that the officer had tipped his cap over his eyes, and judging by the gap between his lips he was already asleep. With no hope of a natter to pass the time, she turned her thoughts to the last letter she had received from Aidan before he had returned home.

I can't tell you how much I've missed a proper cup of English tea! Funny, because I wouldn't have said I was much of a tea drinker before going to Africa, but I am now. I must get through gallons of the stuff! They don't do proper sausages either, and as for the bacon, I've thinner soles on my boots! We've visited a couple of cafés but they serve some really weird food out here, and I'm not a fan. Connor on the other hand would eat anything if it had enough salt and pepper.

Giggling at the memory, Ellie's eyes flicked to the rear-view mirror again. The officer slumbered on. The first telephone conversation she had had with Aidan after he arrived back in Waddington had been filled with mixed emotions. On the one hand she was thrilled to have him back, but on the other, she knew he was only home so that he and his crew might take part in the biggest sortie to date.

'No one knows exactly what's going on, it's got to be the best kept secret ever, but we do know that we've all got a part to play and that it's going to happen fairly soon.' His voice had been full of enthusiasm.

'I wish we could meet up, even if it was just for a day, but all leave has been cancelled until further notice,' Ellie had said miserably. 'I don't understand how you've come back to England for the big push, yet Arla and Archie's section are meant to be going to France! Surely they'd be more use here when Hitler launches his revenge?'

'It's hard to say. I suppose you just have to have faith that they know what they're doing. After all, we're just the puppets in this whole affair; it's those in power who control the strings. I'm just grateful to be back. Pyramids and camels are fascinating, but that's only when you're on leave. The rest of the time it's dust, rocks, cactus plants and sand. Give me the green grass of home any day of the week.'

Ellie had smiled. Some of his letters had spoken of swimming pools, blue seas and extravagant statues, and it all sounded very glamorous; so much so, in fact, that she had feared he might prefer being out there and choose to stay.

Reaching the main road that would take her most of the way back to London, Ellie cracked the window of the car open so that the cool night breeze might help her to stay awake. She would be on this particular stretch of road for the next few hours and had travelled it so often she knew it like the back of her hand.

She flicked the wipers on as light rain peppered the windscreen; shifting in her seat she tried to get a little more comfortable, but not too comfortable. There had been more than one occasion when an exhausted driver had rested their eyes for just a moment only to find themselves swerving off the road. Determined not to be one of them, she focused on the strip of road that stretched endlessly before her.

Aidan lay in his bed listening to the soft snores coming from Connor's side of the room and smiled in the darkness. It was the day before the big push and RAF Waddington was awash with excitement. The heavy bomber squadrons had spent hours in the debriefing room running through the plans for the next day.

'We will of course go through all of this before the start of operations tomorrow, but I think it goes without saying that this is going to be the biggest operation of the war so far, and, if we're successful, will be a huge turning point.' The officer surveyed the room before continuing. 'Without bomber command this operation cannot succeed, so remember that when you're up there.'

Reaching out to the chair beside his bed, Aidan fumbled in the top pocket of his flying jacket. His fingers closed round a small golden ring, and he turned it over in his fingers.

The whole time they had been in Africa all he could think of was Ellie and how he planned to propose to her the first time they met again. Some of the men in his squadron had bought their girlfriends 'gold' jewellery from a small shop in the kasbah, but after a while it had proved to be only gold-coloured, and the wearer soon found that her finger had turned an awful shade of green.

Connor had thought Aidan foolish for even contemplating buying a ring which could possibly turn his fiancée's finger green, but Aidan had made sure the shop he had purchased the ring from was reputable. The ring had not been cheap, and he had taken to carrying it everywhere he went. Not that he would admit it to Connor, but having the ring in his pocket made him feel closer to Ellie, and he had made a pact with himself that he would never let it out of his possession until the day he could slip it on to her finger.

His mind wandered back to the forthcoming operation. If the decoys worked and the enemy went to the Pas-de-Calais the operation had a greater chance of success, but if the bluff didn't work ... He tried to put the thought out of his mind. Slipping the ring on and off his finger, he daydreamed of the proposal that he had been planning. He would take Ellie somewhere special for the day, maybe Buckingham Palace or perhaps somewhere in the Lincolnshire countryside, and when the time was right he would get down on one knee and ask for her hand in marriage. He pictured Ellie in his mind's eye; she would be wearing a frock so white that the sun would shine through the layers of material, making her look like an angel, and her beautiful copper hair would be loose around her shoulders.

Placing the ring safely back in the pocket of his flying jacket, he pulled the covers up around his ears and closed his eyes. The next day would be here all too soon, and he and his crew needed as much rest as they could get. He listened to Connor, who was turning over with a snort. How his cousin could sleep with so much going on was beyond him, yet there he lay as if he hadn't a care in the world. Closing his eyes, Aidan thought of Springdale Farm and the small barn that he intended to convert for himself and Ellie to live in once they were married. In his mind he went through the building, room by room, noting the work to be done. Slowly, he drifted to sleep.

Ellie crossed the yard at a run, her greatcoat billowing around her, holding her wash bag over her head as she tried to keep the rain from soaking her to the skin. Bursting through the door to their hut, she heard the inevitable cry of 'Shut that door'. Removing her shoes and coat, she tiptoed across the hut, threw the bed-covers back and climbed between the sheets.

She prodded the underneath of Gwen's bed. 'Blimey, it's blowing a gale out there, and the rain's comin' at you sideways. Good job the boys aren't flyin' tonight. I bet they wish they'd stayed in Africa.'

Gwen looked out of the window into the darkness beyond and nodded. 'Connor used to write that he was looking forward to feeling the rain on his face.' She flicked over to the next page of the magazine she was reading. 'I told him if that was the case he'd be happy as Larry when he got home and I was right, 'cos all it's done is rain.'

Bringing the covers up around her ears, Ellie snuggled down as best she could. 'I don't know how much sleep I'm going to get knowing that they're doing this big push thing tomorrow. I wonder when we'll know whether it's been a success?'

Gwen, who was engrossed in her magazine, gave a half-hearted 'Mmm hmm' of agreement.

Lying back in her bed, Ellie's thoughts turned to the conversation she had had with Arla earlier that morning. She had known that there was a chance her friend might be posted overseas but she had hoped it would come to nothing, and as Arla revealed the news her heart had sunk.

'Do you have to go?' she had said, trying to keep her tone even.

'There's no way I'm letting Archie go over there without me! I've heard stories about them French women, and they ain't gettin' their hands on my bit of Scouse!' Arla had said defensively.

Ellie could not help but giggle. It was typical of Arla to be more worried about some French floozy stealing Archie than she was about confronting the enemy. Closing her eyes, she listened to the rain drumming on the roof.

Heading towards the Lancaster Lass for what was to be their biggest sortie to date, the crew's spirits were high.

'Jerry's in for a nasty surprise and not before time!' said Geoff as they began to climb the ladder into the fuselage of the plane. 'I've never seen it so busy. I hope they've got plenty of bacon ready for when we get back; it's going to take more than one pig to feed this lot.'

Standing on the Alsan toilet, Connor swivelled round to face the rear of the plane. 'I think we're all with you on that one. Just be grateful we're not in Africa. They try their best but no one makes a bacon butty like the Brits!'

Going through the pre-flight checks, Aidan peered out into the bleak night sky. His heart raced with the anticipation of the operation that lay ahead of them.

He knew the role the Lancaster Lass was to play would be crucial to its success, and the responsibility was starting to weigh heavily on his shoulders. He tried to shake the ifs and buts from his mind. Positive thinking was required in circumstances like these. He smiled as he heard the engine choke then splutter before roaring into life. Nothing could go wrong. They knew their instructions inside out, and had done this particular route many times in the past. It's just another day in the office, no different from any other sortie, except you'll have more company on this one. A *lot* more company, he assured himself. As he waited for clearance to take off, he listened to the general chitchat from the rest of his crew as they discussed their plans for the following day.

Taff, the Lancaster Lass's bomb aimer, talked excitedly about his decision to ask his girlfriend of three months to be his wife. 'That bloody Yank what's the AG on Old Harry's been sniffin' round her, the cheeky beggar, offerin' her choccies and stockings. Well, he can jolly well sling his hook.'

'You don't think she's interested, do you?' came a voice from the rear of the fuselage.

Taff shrugged. 'I bloomin' well hope not. What the hell am I meant to do with this ring otherwise?'

'If I were her I'd pick chocolates and stockings over you any day of the week,' Aidan laughed, before stopping short. Holding up a hand, he nodded, then addressed his crew. 'Buckle up, boys, we're off.'

Ellie awoke to the excited chatter of the girls in her section.

'It's on the news,' Sandra told Gwen. 'They reckon the bluff worked – whatever it was – and they've taken Jerry by surprise.'

Glancing at her watch, Ellie swung her legs out of bed. 'Why didn't someone wake me? Have I missed brekker?'

A pair of stockinged feet appeared over the side of the bunk, closely followed by the rest of Gwen. 'Firstly, we didn't wake you because you got in so late; secondly, even if you have missed brekker, there's always toast.'

Ellie hastily threw her greatcoat over her shoulders. 'Have you heard anything from the boys?'

Gwen shook her head. 'From what we know the bombers are back and forth, so they could be anywhere. The only thing we've been told is that everything's going to plan so far.'

The Lancaster Lass had completed her part of the operation and her crew were in high spirits as they headed for home.

'I never seen a sight like that in all my time in the RAF,' said Geoff. 'How many of us were there, d'you think? It wouldn't surprise me if it was in the thousands.'

Aidan nodded his agreement. 'We've certainly given Jerry something to think about. Remember we were told that if this sortie was a success it could be the turning point in the war, and after what we've seen today I reckon they were right.'

Connor joined in the conversation. 'Where's their defence? Serve 'em bloody right, if you ask me. With a bit of luck I can't see the war goin' on for much longer. What do you think, Aidan?'

'It's still early days. I reckon we'll know a lot more this time tomorrow, but if I were to make a guess, then I'd agree with you. After today Jerry's days are numbered.'

Geoff scanned the skies around them. 'I wonder where all their fighter pilots are? You'd think they'd have at least tried to stop us.'

Connor grimaced. 'That's why we caught 'em by surprise, so's they wouldn't get a chance to scramble. After all the damage their bombers've done us, it's about time they got a taste of their own medicine.'

Aidan glanced at his watch. 'Shouldn't be too long now, boys, and we'll be back home. It's plain sailing from here on in.'

Leaning back in his seat, Connor made himself comfortable. 'I hope we're one of the first to get back – that way there'll still be plenty of bacon left.'

'It's like Piccadilly Circus out there. I've never seen owt like it—'

'Shhh!' came the collective response from the crowd gathered around the wireless in the NAAFI.

Gwen beckoned Ellie to join her. 'Just gettin' the latest updates.'

Nodding, Ellie clutched Gwen as they listened to the news. The whole of the NAAFI had fallen silent as they listened to the broadcaster. When he finished, a huge cheer went up.

'It's the same everywhere you go,' breathed Ellie. 'Everyone's talking about it. They reckon the end's in sight; it really does look as if we're going to win and we've got our boys in bomber command to thank for a lot of it.' She was grinning from ear to ear. 'I've always been proud of Aidan and Connor but now everyone's going to see them for the heroes they are.'

'I don't suppose you've heard anything from them?' Gwen said, raising a hopeful eyebrow.

Ellie shook her head. 'No, and I don't expect to, not until tomorrow, if not the day after. I expect they'll be straight to their beds as soon as they're back from their sortie, so's they can be fresh for the next lot.' She smiled reassuringly at Gwen. 'Knowing that they're up there with lots of other bombers makes me feel a little better. It's different when there's just a few of them, and by all accounts they've really caught Jerry on the hop, so I think the odds of anything happening to them must be much less than normal, don't you think?'

Gwen mulled this thought over for a moment or two before answering. 'I think you're right, but the pessimistic part of me thinks of Sod's Law! I can't help it, I'm quite cynical when it comes to stuff like that.'

'Good job one of us has got some faith, then!'

'It's all right for you. That woman said your hubby was going to be fine, but she didn't say his brother, the one I'm supposed to end up with, is going to survive the "grave danger" she talked about. Just my luck, that is.'

'But Connor's not your boyfriend, is he?'

Frowning, Gwen shook her head. 'Course not, but if it comes to that he's not Aidan's brother either.'

379

'But you could see how she'd get the two ...' She eyed Gwen accusingly. 'Hold on a mo, I thought you said you didn't believe in all that tosh? Changed your mind, have you?'

Gwen shook her head. 'No, it's just ... oh, I dunno, I've got a really bad feeling. But never mind that. What were you starting to say?'

'I was saying that you could see how she'd get the two confused. They do look awfully alike – even Evie thought they were the same person. Heck, she even dated the wrong man.' Ellie laughed. 'So if she couldn't tell them apart and her prediction about Aidan is right, then Connor must be safe too, because he's neither Aidan's brother nor your boyfriend. Well, not yet at any rate.'

Gwen turned the idea over in her mind. 'By Jove, I think you're on to something there. She can't have it both ways.'

'That's the spirit!' said Ellie. 'So it's not all doom and gloom; far from it, in fact. And now that we've got that sorted, how about going out for a fish supper to celebrate the good news about the war and the boys?'

Gwen stood up and rubbed her tummy. 'Sounds good to me. I don't know about you, but all that thinking's made me hungry. I'm famished!'

Breathing heavily, Aidan shouted above the sound of gunfire. 'Where the bloody hell did he come from? Is he on his own?'

The lone Messerschmitt had come as a complete surprise. Believing they were home free, the crew of the

Lancaster Lass had been flabbergasted when the German fighter loomed into view.

Aidan twisted round in his seat, desperate to see their attacker. 'Where's he gone? Can anyone see him?'

He was answered by the sound of bullets being fired by Geoff, the mid-turret gunner. 'Port side, port side ... damn, I've lost him. It's all this thick cloud.'

Connor's voice came over the radio. 'Is he on his own?'

Geoff shrugged. 'Dunno. I've not seen any more, but—'

He was interrupted by the sound of gunfire coming from Connor's turret. 'Bloody hell, he nearly hit us. He must think he's one of them kamikaze pilots—' The radio went silent as Connor's guns sent out another torrent of bullets. 'He's not goin' to give up. We're goin' to have to down him before—'

Confusion followed in the next few seconds as Geoff, Taff, Connor and Aidan all tried to relay as much information to each other as they could.

After the frantic warnings, an eerie silence fell on the Lancaster Lass. The German plane appeared to have vanished. Each man held his breath as he scanned the sky, desperate for a glimpse of the aircraft. After a minute or two, Aidan began to relax a little, figuring that the other plane had either lost them or run low on fuel and turned back.

Connor broke the silence. 'He's gone. I reckon he must've been returning from a mission when he saw us and thought he'd have a bash.' He whistled under his breath. 'Just as well, 'cos he was a determined little blighter, wasn't he?'

Aidan, who had deliberately taken the Lancaster Lass into a bank of cloud in the hope of losing the Messerschmitt, smiled at the success of his ruse.

Connor stared into the thick blanket of black cloud. He peered harder. The cloud looked as though it was swirling, almost as if a storm was brewing. He had opened his mouth to warn his cousin when he saw the propellers of the enemy plane breaking through the cloud, and before he could speak it had opened fire again. His finger on the trigger, Connor shouted a warning into his radio. 'Bloody hell. He's back, and he's heading straight for us. Aidan, I think he's going to hit us ...'

Aidan plunged the plane into a steep dive as he tried in vain to lose the German fighter, but it was no use. The Lancaster Lass was too big to outmanoeuvre the smaller plane. He shouted out to Geoff. 'Can you see what's going on? Have you got him in your sights?'

Geoff's voice was frantic. 'I can just about see him, but he's not in my range; it looks as if he's trying to take Connor out first.'

Aidan shouted over the radio. 'Connor, what's going on? Tell me what I can do to help.'

For a brief moment no one could hear anything other than the melee of firing bullets, then from out of the darkness there came nothing but silence, broken only by a whoop of joy from Geoff. 'Got him! He bloody got the bastard! Well done, Connor, but try not to leave it till the last minute next time, there's a good fellow. I don't need that kind of excitement at my age.'

Aidan jubilantly punched the air. 'The Murray boys strike again! Well done, Connor! What happened to the Messerschmitt?'

'Connor must've hit a fuel line or summat, 'cos it exploded then spiralled towards the sea.'

A cheer echoed through the Lancaster Lass. 'Always said you had our backs, didn't you, but I have to agree with Geoff: try not to leave it so long next time.' Aidan tapped the side of his earpiece. 'Did you hear me, coz?' The airwaves remained silent. Aidan turned to the wireless operator. 'Go and take a gander, Ginge. We must've lost radio contact, but best to make sure.'

Ginge pulled back the wooden doors that led to the rear gunner's turret. Shuffling down the small space, he peered through the small glass window of the blast doors. Connor was slumped forward, his arms crossed over the top of his guns. Ginge banged on the blast door to get his attention, but Connor failed to respond, and looking towards the dome Ginge could see that the Perspex was peppered with bullet holes. His heart sinking, he yelled back to Aidan, 'Skip, he's been hit, I don't know how badly. I can't open the blast doors. How far away are we from Waddington?'

Aidan looked at his fuel gauge and swallowed hard. 'Too far, and not just for Connor, either. We're losing fuel fast; the bastard must've hit a line. Get back here and find the nearest base that can take a heavy bomber. When you do, radio and tell them we want permission for an emergency landing.'

Aidan's world played out in slow motion as he listened to Ginge relaying the information. 'They said to go to Biggin Hill. It's the nearest one to us with a hospital.'

Nodding, Aidan set his course. Then, swallowing hard, he asked the question uppermost in his thoughts. 'Is he breathing?'

There was a brief pause. 'I don't know. The doors are stuck fast, but when I called out he never moved.'

The day had been hectic, to say the least, and up in the control tower of RAF Biggin Hill things were about to get a whole lot worse. Sally Winthorpe had taken a telephone call from RAF Waddington warning them to get ready for what could be an emergency landing by a Lancaster bomber. Listening to the pilot of the stricken aircraft describing what had happened, Sally's heart sank.

'I recognise that voice. Is that you, Aidan Murray?'

There was a moment's pause. 'Yes. Who's that?'

'Sally Winthorpe. We met at my sister's wedding. Arla Winthorpe, or should I say Byrnes?'

Aidan spoke urgently. 'Sal! Of all the luck! Do you know which billet Ellie and Gwen are in?'

'Yes, but what on earth has that got to do with things?' There was no reply. 'Aidan?'

'We're losing a lot of fuel because we think he hit one of the lines. I should have enough to reach you, but touching down could be a bit iffy, which is why they told you to make preparations for an emergency landing.'

'But you are going to be okay, aren't you? I mean, if it's just a question of fuel …'

'We don't know if there's any other damage, but even if there isn't, landing a heavy bomber with not enough fuel to reverse the engines could lead to a crash landing, and that's why I want you to get Ellie and Gwen.' There was a brief pause before he added, 'It may be the last time I get to speak to her.'

Desperately scribbling the address of Ellie's billet on to a piece of paper, Sally handed it to another Waaf and pointed meaningfully towards the door. As the Waaf ran off, the paper clutched in her hand, Sally spoke to Aidan. 'I've sent someone to get her. Waddington said your rear gunner had been hit. That's our Connor, isn't it?'

Another pause. 'Yes. We can't tell how badly; the blast doors are jammed.'

Sally wanted to cry, to pretend that none of this was happening, but she couldn't, because they needed her help. The countless hours of training for situations just like this came to her aid. 'Are the rest of the crew all right?'

'Yes, although I don't fancy our chances much if we have to land without enough fuel to brake properly.'

The door opened behind her, and a Waaf appeared in its aperture. She nodded meaningfully at Sally before disappearing back outside.

Pulling her jacket straight and clearing her throat, Sally spoke in clipped tones. 'PA473, we have the all-clear for landing.'

'Roger that,' said Aidan.

Sally's face remained impassive as she raised a fore-finger to her eye and caught the tear before it fell. 'Good luck, and Aidan...?'

'Yes?'

'I'll let you know as soon as Ellie gets here.'

*

Ellie woke up with a start. Gwen was shaking her by the shoulder and looking earnestly into her face. 'Wake up, Ellie, it's important! Oh, you're awake.'

Sitting up on one elbow Ellie looked blearily around the dark billet. A woman whom Ellie had never seen before was standing by the doorway to the small cottage.

Ellie yawned. 'Who's she?'

'Get dressed, Ellie. We've got to get to Biggin Hill.' Gwen turned to the woman by the door. 'We'll be right with you.'

Handing Ellie her clothes, Gwen explained that the woman was a driver from RAF Biggin Hill who'd been sent to fetch Ellie and Gwen because the Lancaster Lass had been damaged in battle. 'I don't know exactly how bad things are, but Aidan asked that you be sent for.'

Pulling the sleeve of her jacket over her arm, Ellie looked beseechingly at Gwen. 'They are going to be all right, though?'

Gwen avoided Ellie's gaze. 'I'm sure they will, cariad. Aidan's one of the best pilots in the RAF.'

Running out to the car, the girls climbed in. Ellie stared at Gwen. 'There's summat you're not telling me. What is it? And don't you even think about fibbing, Gwen Jones.'

Turning away to hide her tears, Gwen spoke quietly. 'It's Connor. He's been hit, but they won't know how badly until they land. They can't get to him because the blast door's stuck.'

Ellie slipped her hand into Gwen's. 'He'll be fine. He's probably ...' Unable to say another word, she fought to stop the tears from forming.

The journey from their billet to the RAF station could not have taken more than ten minutes, but to Ellie it seemed like an eternity. As they approached, the guard opened the gate. Ellie looked into his face as they drove past. He had given a small nod, but his expression was grave.

Reaching the bottom of the control tower, Ellie and Gwen leapt out of the car and raced up the steps to Sally, who was waiting at the top. 'Quickly. We're ready for you, and Aidan knows you're here.'

Hurrying towards the front of the tower, Ellie was aware of the sombre atmosphere. The controller jumped out of her seat and handed her the microphone, giving her an encouraging nod.

Her heart pounding, she spoke into the microphone. 'Aidan? Is that you?'

'Ellie! I can't tell you how good it is to hear your voice.'

Ellie looked round the room at the worried faces. 'They said that Connor's been hit. Is he still stuck in the turret?'

There was a pause. 'Yes, love. The door's locked from the inside, you see ...'

Never taking her eyes off the horizon, Ellie felt the tears trickling down her cheeks. 'I've got Gwen with me, but she can't talk to him, can she?'

She heard Aidan swallow. 'No. I think he might be asleep.'

Ellie screwed up her eyes at the sound of Gwen crying softly behind her.

Aidan's voice came over the radio. 'We've not got much fuel left, alanna, so it'll be a pretty rough landing.' He paused. 'There's something I've been meaning to ask you ever since we got back from Africa, only I wanted to do it in person … I had it all planned, you see, but I think it might be best if I asked you now.' He cleared his throat, and when he spoke next Ellie detected a faint tremor in his voice. 'Ellie Lancton, will you marry me?'

Taking great care to control her emotions, Ellie spoke as softly as she could. 'Yes, my darling man, of course I'll marry you.' Peering into the distance, she could just make out the silhouette of the Lancaster Lass. 'I see you, Aidan.'

'I see you, alanna.' Ellie could hear the splutter of engines as they started to die.

The controller silently held out her hand for the microphone. Handing it over without protest, Ellie saw that the other woman's cheeks were stained with tears.

'PA473, this is RAF Biggin Hill, we have you in sight.' Her lip quivered as she tried to smile reassuringly at Ellie. 'We're ready when you are.'

'Roger that. Ellie, I know you're still there. I just wanted to say I love you, alanna. T.t.f.n.'

Leaning towards the microphone, Ellie smiled through her tears. 'I love you too, Aidan … Aidan?'

In the distance Aidan could see the fire engines and ambulances standing by. 'Good luck, everyone.' There was a general murmur of voices wishing the same back, and as the tail wheel touched the ground they heard another engine splutter as it died. Thrusting the two remaining engines into reverse, he prayed he had enough fuel left to stop him leaving the end of the runway. The engines roared as they tried to slow the heavy bomber down, and Aidan frowned. An odd smell had entered the plane. Not fuel, not oil ... it was more floral. He tried to place the scent and was surprised when he realised it smelled the same as the small bags his mam used to put into the wardrobes and drawers. She claimed it deterred moths and insects, but Aidan had always worried that the smell might penetrate his clothes and people would accuse him of wearing perfume.

'I'm a farmer, Mother. I'm meant to smell of horse sweat and manure, not bloody lavender,' he would say.

Aidan tapped the fuel gauge. The tanks were empty; he was trying to stop the Lancaster on fumes alone. Seeing the end of the runway drawing ever nearer, he knew that if he didn't stop soon he would crash into the soft ground of the fields and the plane could tip or even break up. Keeping his eyes fixed on the horizon, he said a small prayer, and noted, as he did so, that the smell of lavender grew ever stronger.

Ellie and Gwen were about to race down the runway towards the ambulance when Sally ordered them to stop.

'I know you want to make sure they're all right, but you'll only hold things up. Come with me and I'll drive you to the hospital where they'll be taking Connor.'

True to her word, Sally got them to the hospital before the ambulance had arrived. Inside, Ellie and Gwen hovered by the doors whilst Sally went to find out what was happening. After ten minutes or so she re-joined them.

'They've managed to land, but they're having trouble getting Connor out. Something must've jammed inside the turret.'

Staring into space, Gwen cleared her throat. 'He's not awake yet? You'd think with all the noise and palaver he'd have woken up by now.' She turned to Ellie, her eyes brimming with tears. 'This can't be happening. That women said ... But he's not my boyfriend ...'

Sally and Ellie exchanged worried glances. 'Maybe he got knocked unconscious ...' Ellie was beginning, when they heard the ambulance arrive.

Aidan had hammered on the blast doors until, with a loud click, they had slid back; inside he bent over his cousin and undid the harness which had been holding him in place. Swivelling the chair round, he managed to catch Connor as his body fell forward. Aidan could see that his cousin's chest was covered in blood, and knew there was no time for emotion; Connor needed help and he needed it quickly. Pulling his cousin down the narrow passage, he spoke through gritted teeth. 'Please don't die, Connor. I need you to be my best man at the wedding. You can't die on me, mate.'

Ginge and Geoff helped carry Connor out of the belly of the plane and into the waiting ambulance, where the nurses instantly began to work on their patient. Aidan looked into the faces of his crew, and saw that their eyes were round with fear as they took in the extent of their rear gunner's injuries. His voice came out in a whisper. 'It's bad, isn't it? I mean really bad.'

Ginge nervously ran his fingers through his hair. 'It doesn't look good, but I heard one of the nurses say she found a pulse, so he's got a chance, hasn't he? And you don't get to survive all those years as a rear gunner unless you've a whole heap of luck on your side, not to mention a fighting spirit.'

Aidan clapped a hand on Ginge's shoulder. 'You're right. He's a Murray, and we don't roll over for anybody.' He climbed into the back of the ambulance. 'Tell Waddington what's happened. Tell them how he saved us, that if he hadn't shot that Messerschmitt down we'd be the ones in the briny deep. Tell them he's a bally hero.'

Ellie turned as Aidan burst through the doors, his face grey, his eyes hollow, and enveloped her in his arms. His voice was a hoarse whisper. 'Ellie darling, I'm so glad they sent for you.' Looking past Ellie, he beckoned Gwen over and pulled her into their embrace. 'They've taken him straight into surgery. We won't know any more until we hear from the doctors, but they did say one of the bullets had hit an artery, so he's lost an awful lot of blood.' He glanced at the ceiling, his eyes blinking as he banished the tears. 'I thought we were going to lose him. I still don't know if he's going to be all right ...'

Gwen sat down on one of the benches that lined the corridor. 'He can't die, not yet. I haven't told him how much I like him. I was hoping ... ' She looked beseechingly into Aidan's eyes. 'He's not my boyfriend yet, so he has to get better.'

Aidan frowned, but before he could say anything Ellie waved a dismissive hand. 'It's a long story. I'll explain later.'

Sitting next to Gwen, Aidan opened his hand to reveal a thin silver chain. 'He knew how disappointed you were when you had to give the locket that Sid Crowther stole back to the police, so he bought you this when we were in Africa. It fell out of his flying jacket when they got him ready for surgery.'

Gwen picked the chain up and opened the tiny locket. 'He's put a picture of himself in one half.' Giggling through her tears, she held it up so that Aidan and Ellie might see. 'Typical Connor ...' Her voice tailed off as she fingered the delicate necklace.

As Ellie laid a reassuring hand on Aidan's shoulder, he flinched under her touch. Glancing at her fingertips, her eyes rounded. 'You're bleeding.' She took a closer look at his shoulder, then let out a squeal. 'You've been hit. There's a hole in your jacket ...'

He shook his head. 'Don't fuss. It's nowt to worry about, not when we've got Connor in there ...'

She stared at him disbelievingly. 'You knew? Aidan, how could you be so silly? You've got a bullet in your shoulder, you're sitting in the middle of a hospital, and you never thought to mention it to anyone?'

'I didn't know, not until I tried to move our Connor. It was only then that I realised summat was wrong.' He rubbed his fingers over his forehead. 'Compared to what our Connor's goin' through in there, this is nowt, so please don't make a fuss, Ellie. Not until we know Connor's all right.'

Ellie's lip trembled. 'But you've been shot. You're bleeding, and you might get an infection. Why can't you let me at least tell one of the nurses? They can take a look at the wound, get you cleaned up ...'

Aidan shook his head. 'Not until I know what's happening to Connor. Once they know I've been shot they'll want to take me away, and I couldn't bear not knowin' what was goin' on. I want to be here when they come out of that room.'

The theatre door opened and the large-bosomed matron bustled over. 'I take it you're Mr Murray's cousin?' Without waiting for a reply, she continued, 'He's lost a lot of blood and he needs a transfusion. We'll need to make sure you're the same blood type, but hopefully, as you're family ... I take it you've no objection?'

Aidan shook his head. 'Can't you tell us anything else? About his condition, I mean?'

She smiled sympathetically. 'They've managed to stop the bleeding, but there's been an awful lot of damage to one of his lungs and they've had to remove half of it, so even if he does pull through he'll have a long road to recovery.'

'You said "even if he does pull through",' said Gwen. 'Do you think there's a chance he might not?'

'We're doing the best we can, but it would be wrong for me to give false hope.'

Ellie was looking earnestly at Aidan, who nodded reluctantly. 'You asked if Aidan could give blood, but he can't because he's been shot too.'

The matron looked from Ellie to Aidan. 'Please tell me this young lady has got it wrong.'

Getting to his feet, Aidan indicated the bullet wound on the top of his shoulder. 'It's nowt ...' he began, then sat down abruptly. He clamped a hand to his forehead. 'Sorry about that. I came over all queer just then.'

The matron shook her head disapprovingly. 'When will you boys learn? You sit here as though nothing's wrong and let infection take over.' She glanced at Ellie. 'Stay with him and make sure he doesn't move. I'll fetch a wheelchair.'

Gwen spoke up. 'What about Connor's blood transfusion? You can't just let him lie there.'

The matron nodded. 'I take it you're willing to step up to the plate?'

In answer to the question Gwen rolled up her sleeve.

'Come with me. I'll take you to the nurse in charge, then I'll get a wheelchair and come back for this young man.'

Aidan and Ellie watched as Gwen and the matron disappeared through a set of doors.

Ellie linked her arm through Aidan's and placed her head against his uninjured shoulder. 'I know you're worried about Connor, we all are, but you're no good to him wounded.'

When Aidan spoke next his voice was hoarse. 'You've no need to tell me that. Right now my cousin needs me more than ever before, and I can't do a single thing to help him.'

Sitting up, Ellie cupped his chin in her hands and locked her eyes on his. 'You can't blame yourself for that. It's not your fault you got shot.'

The sparkle in Aidan's eye disappeared under the tears which brimmed on his lower lids. He blinked, and a tear dropped on to his cheek. 'I know it's not, but it doesn't change the outcome, does it? All I want to do is make him better. I'd do anything for that boy.'

Ellie lowered her head. 'I know,' she said, her voice barely above a whisper. She raised her gaze to meet his and her eyes too shone with tears. 'You're more like brothers than cousin.'

The matron approached with the wheelchair. 'Come along, young man, let's get you into theatre.'

'Theatre? You mean he'll have to have an operation? Can't you take it out with some tweezers or something, the way they do in the movies?'

Shaking her head, the matron chuckled. 'Don't go believing everything you see in the cinema, dear. When it comes to bullets nothing's as simple as it may seem.'

As she helped Aidan into the chair he looked at her hopefully. 'Was Gwen a match? For Connor, I mean?'

The matron nodded. 'We've got some of your crew in there too, so your cousin's got plenty of volunteers.'

Aidan smiled. 'He's a good lad is our Connor. You will do everything you can for him, won't you?'

She nodded. 'Just you concentrate on yourself for a bit. With luck you'll only need a local, and you'll be right as rain in no time.'

In the early hours of the morning they were finally allowed to see Connor. 'He's very weak, but if you promise me you'll not stay more than a minute or two, and that you won't try to wake him up or get him to speak to you, then I'll let you in.' The matron held out a warning hand as Gwen and Ellie stood up. 'Before you enter you must remember that he's on a ventilator to help his breathing. It looks scary but it should only be temporary, so try not to worry.'

Ellie wheeled Aidan up beside Connor's bed. Aidan smiled. 'He looks so much better now the colour's coming back to his face and all the blood's gone from his chest.'

Stepping forward, Gwen brushed his fringe away from his brow. 'I'm wearing the locket you bought me, cariad, and I think it's beautiful. I'll always treasure it.'

Ellie slipped her arm into the crook of Gwen's. 'He looks so peaceful, not at all aware or worried.'

Nodding, Gwen gently kissed his forehead. 'Just you make sure you get well soon, Connor Murray. I'm going to need you as my escort to Ellie and Aidan's wedding.'

'That's right, pal. You're to be my best man, so just you listen to Gwen here and get better soon.'

Ellie stroked the back of his hand. 'We'll come and see you every day, won't we, Gwen?'

'Just you try and stop us.'

The door opened behind them and the matron looked in. 'Sorry, folks, but that's enough. We don't want to exhaust him.'

Gwen touched her fingers to Connor's hand. 'See you soon, cariad.'

'Any news?'

Gwen shook her head. 'Still the same, I did ask why he hadn't woken up yet but I got the same old reply: it's his body's way of saying it needs the rest.' She leaned against the car door.

Ellie gave her friend a reassuring nod. 'And they're right. I'm sure it's nothing more than that. The nurses did say that his pulse, blood pressure and everything else were all good; if it was anything sinister we would've known by now.' She smiled shrewdly. 'Especially you, Gwen Jones. I've hardly seen you this past week. If you're not on duty you're with Connor, which is all very well, but you need your rest too, you know. You won't be any good to him when he wakes up if you're half asleep.'

'I doze on and off at the hospital, so I'm not doing too badly.' She looked shyly at Ellie. 'Before Aidan went back to Waddington I expected Connor to wake up whenever he spoke, but when he left I began to hope that it might be my voice that wakes him. I know it sounds silly, but I'd like to be the first one he sees.'

Ellie smiled. 'I don't think it sounds silly at all. I'd be the same if it was Aidan, but you can't sit with him for twenty-four hours a day, so try to go a little easier on yourself.'

Going round to the passenger door, Gwen opened it and sat down in the seat next to Ellie. 'I can't; my head won't let me. I feel like a cat on a hot tin roof, and I'm scared that if I'm not there beside him he might never wake up. As soon as he's conscious, I'll know I can rest easy.'

Ellie held Gwen's hand and spoke reassuringly. 'Gwen, darling, I had no idea that was what you were thinking, but you mustn't be so hard on yourself. Whether Connor wakes up or not won't be determined by your presence, so although I'll not deny it's good for him to hear a familiar, friendly voice, you don't have to always be by his side.'

Gwen smiled appreciatively. 'I know, and of course you're right, but no matter what anyone says I'm determined to be with him as much as I can.' Glancing at her wristwatch, she sighed. 'Well, I'm going to have to say ta-ra for a bit. I've got to take Fatso to a meeting.'

Ellie choked on a giggle. 'If Major Gregson ever hears you callin' him that ...'

Gwen smiled brightly. 'He won't, will he, 'cos he's always got his head stuffed into a bowl full of summat or other. Besides, it's not my fault he bounces round in the back of that car like a rubber ball. I've complained about that dratted suspension over and over, but they won't do owt because he's the only one it affects.'

Ellie shook her head. 'Gwen Jones, you do have a way with words.'

Gwen pouted. 'If only that were true. I've asked Connor over and over to wake up, told him how much we miss him, how much he's wanted. I've begged and pleaded, but his eyes don't even flicker.'

Ellie wrinkled her brow. 'Perhaps you're goin' down the wrong path.' She tapped her lips thoughtfully. 'Have you tried mentioning food? That normally works with the Murray men. Or perhaps the time you went dancing in Lincoln? He loves dancing.'

Leaning across the car, Gwen pecked Ellie on the cheek. 'That's an idea. I'll try it tonight and see what happens.' She got out of the car, but before she shut the door she said, 'I wonder if they'd let me take a plate of bacon in? Aidan said it's his favourite.'

Ellie laughed. 'Anything's worth a go. Good luck, chuck.'

Chapter Fourteen

The world washed around Connor. Voices, some unknown, some familiar, came and went as he lay in a state of dreams. He wondered whether he was still trapped inside the Lancaster Lass, but as he could neither see nor feel the world around him it was impossible to know for sure. He had tried to cry out, to gain the attention of the voices, but he was too weak to make himself heard.

He turned his thoughts back to the attack. The last thing he remembered was having his finger squeezed on to the trigger with such force that he feared it might break under the pressure. He saw the Messerschmitt coming towards them and the pilot looking into his eyes, clearly signalling his intent to be the sole survivor. Connor had stared back with the same steely determination. There was only going to be one winner.

So who had been the victor? He tried hard to remember, but found that the only memory he had was of the German pilot hurtling towards him. He felt an icy chill. If he could not remember destroying the enemy, then surely there was only one answer. He must have lost the battle, and not only him, but all of the crew of the Lancaster Lass. Tears pricked his eyes. It explained why he could neither see nor feel anything. Then one of the voices came back, bringing with it an image of a small silver locket.

He and Aidan had gone to the kasbah in search of presents to take home. Aidan had bought his parents two small ornaments, a sphinx and a pyramid. Connor had chosen a beautifully embroidered shawl for his mother and an Egyptian hookah for his father.

Aidan had pointed accusingly at the water pipe. 'Who's that for?'

'Dad,' Connor had said with a grin.

'But your dad doesn't smoke. What's he meant to do with it?'

Connor clutched the hookah defensively. 'It's a talking point. He'll be able to tell all his friends he's got one.'

'How the hell do you intend to get it home? Ten to one says it'll be in smithereens before we get back to Waddington.'

'If it is it'll be your fault, 'cos you're the one in control of take-off and landing.' Connor sniffed. He had peered at Aidan's ornaments. 'You're just jealous 'cos mine's bigger than yours.'

Chuckling, Aidan had shaken his head. 'We'll see. Have you finished here, only I wanted to see if I could find a ring for Ellie.'

Not wanting to admit that he had no desire to cart the hookah around the Kasbah, Connor had shrugged nonchalantly. 'I don't mind takin' a wander.' He paused briefly before adding, 'What kind of ring?'

'The sort of ring you can propose with, or, if it looks like she's not keen, pass off as a really expensive gift.' He chuckled.

Readjusting the hookah in his arms, Connor grinned. 'Blimey, you have got it bad, haven't you?' He glanced around the various shops. 'Young Geoff got his mam some earrings from Bajocchi which looked all right to me. Why don't you try there?' he said, jerking his head in the direction of the jewellers.

Some twenty minutes later the Murrays emerged from the shop. Aidan, having bought Ellie a thin gold band set with what the man claimed was a topaz, was already agonising about whether it would be the right size.

'You can always have it sized when we get home,' Connor had said reassuringly. 'What did you think of the locket I got for Gwen? Do you think she'll like it?'

Aidan cocked an eyebrow. 'I should think she'll love it; my question is why did you buy it for her? I know she was disappointed when she had to give Mrs Burgess's locket back, but what's that got to do with you?'

Connor shrugged. 'I felt sorry for her. I know she can't afford to buy summat like this, not the prices they charge back home, so I thought why not? Besides, I like Gwen, and depending on how she reacts to the necklace I thought I might see if she fancied going out with me to the cinema or summat similar when we get back.'

Now, Connor came to the realisation that he would never know whether Gwen would have accepted his gift. Come to that, she would never know he had bought the necklace in the first place. Lying in the darkness, he thought of the lives that would be affected because he had not managed to shoot the other plane down. He felt a tear trickle down the side of his cheek.

From out of the gloom he heard the voice which had reminded him of the necklace. 'Connor, can you hear me, cariad? I've been talking to Ellie and she suggested that we might go dancing again, you know, like the time we were in Lincoln? And Arla's wedding? You enjoyed that, didn't you? There's lots of excellent dance halls in London ... Connor?'

Feeling the cold air against his wet cheek he tried to reach out with his hand, but it would not move. I have to make it move, he thought determinedly, because if I can move my hand then I can move my arm, and if I can move my arm then I can move my legs, and if I can move them ... I can dance.

The voice came back, stronger this time. 'Nurse! Come quickly! I think he's trying to move. I think ...'

Connor's eyes slit open. At first he could only see blurred objects passing before him, but as he fought to focus, his eyes opened further, and he felt the warmth of a woman's hand holding his own. He tried turning his head to see who it was, but there was no need: the woman had released his hand and was smoothing the hair from his brow. He frowned as he tried to focus on something swinging in front of him. It was like a pendulum. He thought he recognised it, but he could not be sure. Frustration getting the better of him, Connor focused all his attention on seeing what was before him, and like a fog lifting his vision returned. Gwen stood over him, a broad smile on her face and the locket he had brought back from Africa hanging from her neck. He smiled weakly.

Taking his hand again, she raised his knuckles to her lips and kissed them softly. 'Welcome back, cariad.'

Thunder boomed in the distance and the lights in the stone cottage flickered ominously. Looking up from the paper in his hand, Aidan waited for the lights to come back on before returning to his mother's letter.

My darling boy, Trying to stop that cousin of yours from doing chores around the farm is an impossible task! I've told him over and over that the only reason the doctors sent him to Springdale in the first place was because they thought the fresh air and absence of the stress of service life would make it the ideal place for him to recuperate.

But you know what your cousin's like. He just can't keep still, and how we're meant to keep him away from the stress of service life when his pals keep writing to him is anybody's guess.

The only respite we've had was when Gwen came to visit. She's such a lovely, sensible girl; what's more, she's the only one he'd listen to, and now she's gone we're having to keep our eyes in the back of our heads just to keep an eye on the bugger. He might drive me potty, but I'm not half going to miss him when he goes back to Waddington in a couple of weeks' time.

Aidan grinned. Connor was a doer, and standing by whilst others did all the work was never going to happen. He had said as much to Ellie.

'I'm surprised he stayed in hospital for as long as he did. Mind you, he was practically in a coma for the first week so he didn't have much choice. If it hadn't been for Gwen spending every spare moment with him I

403

sometimes wonder whether he'd have recovered as quickly as he did. I just wish we could've stayed longer. It felt as though we'd deserted him.'

Ellie had wound her finger around the telephone cord. 'Time stands still for no man, and they needed you back at Waddington. I visited Connor as much as I could, but they had me up and down the country like a yo-yo. Mind you, you're right about Gwen bringing him out of that deep sleep, or whatever it was.'

Gwen and Connor had been nigh on inseparable ever since the day he woke up, so Aidan had not been too surprised when his cousin telephoned him one night.

'I know you're probably goin' to crow over it, but what you said about me an' Gwen makin' a perfect couple was right. We've decided to give it a go.'

There was an audible pause on Aidan's end of the line, which Connor filled. 'I know full well you heard that, and you're trying your best not to gloat, so I'll say it for you. Told you so. There, that make things easier for you?'

Aidan chuckled. 'Just a bit, although of course I wouldn't dream of gloating, or saying I told you so.'

'Which you just did,' said Connor. 'Well, you've every right; I just wish we'd listened sooner. Not that we're in a hurry or anything like that, so don't get your hopes up for a double wedding!'

Now Aidan's eyes fell to the sentence where his mother spoke of Connor's returning to light duties. Aidan could not wait for the day when he would see his cousin back at RAF Waddington. He knew that with the damage to Connor's lung they would never fly together again, but it would still be good to see him round and about. His thoughts turned to Connor's replacement. Jimmy, a young lad from Dundee whose given name was Eric, was keen-eyed and willing, but no matter how hard he tried Aidan never felt as comfortable with Jimmy in his crew as he had when Connor had been watching their backs.

'It was like having eyes in the back of my head when Connor was with me; we always knew what the other was thinking,' Aidan had explained to Ellie after his first flight with the new crew member. 'Jimmy's a grand chap, but every time we go up it feels as if I'm flying blind, with no clue as to what's going on behind me. I know it's not his fault, but he'll never replace Connor, and I don't feel as safe as I did when Connor had my back.'

He glanced down at the letter and continued to read.

I still don't think they should have sent you all back out. You know how I believe in omens, and the fact that you made it down in one piece should be enough to make the RAF realise that you shouldn't be asked to do any more operations. You'd worked as a team for a long time, and putting someone new into the mix is never a good idea. I know you can't and won't ask to be relieved from flying duties, I just wish this damned war would come to an end, so that I can have you back home where you belong. And I don't think they should be sending Connor back to Waddington. They should send him home where he can drive his mother insane with his constant flouting of the rules!

Folding the letter, Aidan walked over to the window and looked out at the thick bank of black cloud. He had forbidden anyone to tell his mother that he had also been shot the night they landed in Biggin Hill.

'But she's your mother!' Ellie had said, her voice racked with guilt. 'If anyone should know surely it should be her?'

'Have you any idea what she'd do if she found out I'd been shot as well as our Connor?'

'Be concerned?'

'She'd be on the phone begging my superiors not to let me back in the Lancaster Lass, and she'd plague me to distraction with phone calls and letters. I've enough to worry about when I'm up there without her making things worse.'

'I know how she feels. You were lucky to escape the last attack, and the crash landing, but what if you're not so lucky third time round? what if you get shot again?'

Trying to reassure someone over the telephone when they're hundreds of miles away was a hard task, but Aidan had done his best.

'We're winning, Ellie. Day by day we're taking back more land, and driving the Hun back to his homeland. I can't give up now, and I know you don't want me to, not really. Besides, I've got to do it for Connor. He laid his life on the line keeping the rest of us safe, and I know he'd give anything to be back in his turret doing his bit.'

She sighed heavily. 'If you really don't want me to mention it to your mother then I promise I won't.'

'That's my girl.' He changed the subject in a bid to brighten the mood. 'Have you heard from Arla and Archie? Have they mastered the lingo yet?'

Ellie had chuckled as she relayed Arla's last epistle. 'She thought they ate snails because food was so scarce. She said she couldn't believe it when they told her they were a normal part of the French diet. She reckons that's why they smother everything in garlic, so that it tastes better.'

The door to the cottage opened and Ginge peered through the aperture. 'They reckon the storm's goin' to pass before we take off. You ready for debriefing?'

Nodding, Aidan began to make his way to the door before doubling back and opening the little drawer that served as his bedside cabinet. As his fingers closed over the matchbox he remembered the conversation he'd had with Ellie the morning after arriving in Biggin Hill.

'It's a funny thing, but the last thing I remember before landing was an overpowering scent of Lavendar. I wasn't the only one who could smell it – we all could.'

Ellie's mouth had dropped open. 'Lavender was my mother's favourite flower. She used to get those little cushions with it inside and stick them in our clothes drawer to make the clothes smell nice. I know you don't believe in luck or superstition or anything like that, but I reckon she was with you last night, keeping you all safe.'

Before he had left Biggin Hill, she had handed him a sprig of lavender. 'Promise me you'll take it with you every time you fly?'

He had looked around for something to keep the delicate flower from being crushed. He picked up one of the matchboxes from the tortoise stove and gave it an experimental shake before pushing it open and taking out the two remaining matches. He put the sprig inside the empty box and tucked it into the top pocket of his flying jacket. Leaning forward, he whispered, 'I promise,' and kissed her softly on the lips.

Now, Aidan placed the matchbox in his top pocket and fastened the flap. Superstition or not, he was not going to take any chances. Passing the bed which used to be Connor's, he picked up his walking cane and made his way to the debriefing room.

Arla waved to the postman as he reached the top of the lane. 'Bonjour, Monsieur Bouchet.'

Without dismounting he produced a letter from his satchel. 'Bonjour! Juste celui aujourd'hui.'

Arla grinned. 'Just the one today?'

He gave her a small round of applause. 'Very good! Your French is improving every time we meet.'

Taking the letter, she gave a small curtsy. 'Merci, but it will be a long time before I'm fluent.'

His brow furrowed. 'Fluent?'

Arla tapped the envelope against her chin. 'Oh cripes, let me see … parler naturel?'

'Ahh, courant, I think you mean courant.'

Arla nodded. 'Shall I see you tomorrow, or will it be Leo?'

'It will be me. Leo has gone to visit his family.' Pushing his foot down on to the pedal he called out over his shoulder, 'Au revoir.'

Within weeks of the VE day celebrations Arla and Archie had been demobbed and decided that rather than go straight home they would make the most of their time in France by purchasing two bicycles and stopping off in B and Bs or, when money began to run short, offering labour in exchange for their keep, which was how they had stumbled across their present accommodation.

They had been cycling through Bordeaux when they had come across a sign at the end of a long driveway asking for help with the grape harvest.

'What d'you reckon?' Archie said, pointing down the winding drive where a large house was just visible amongst the trees.

Arla shrugged. 'Worth a try, but it could be an old sign.'

Turning his bicycle in the direction of the driveway he beckoned her to follow him. 'Only one way to find out!'

Looking at the old house, Arla thought it must be deserted. 'Look at all those windows, and not one of 'em isn't caked in cobwebs or dust.' She glanced at Archie and shuddered. 'Do you think something awful might have happened to the owner? Some of these places were under German occupation— ' She stopped speaking as the handle to the front door bobbed and weaved as if someone on the other side was trying to get it open. A croaky voice called out, 'Pousser!'

Arla and Archie exchanged glances. 'Your French is better than mine,' Archie said.

'Anglais? Push!'

They pushed the door with one accord and found on the other side a small Frenchman with a balding head, who judging by his stance was suffering with crippling arthritis.

Monsieur Dubois welcomed Archie and Arla with open arms, and after some false starts they soon worked out that his house had indeed been under German occupation, his wife Louise had died some eighteen months back and their only son, Antoine, had been killed whilst serving his country. Monsieur Dubois was unable to cope on his own, and with the Germans now gone the family vineyard had fallen into decline. Originally Arla and Archie had only planned to stay for a few days before moving on, but after seeing the problems the old man was having, Arla suggested that they might see if they could make it a more permanent arrangement.

'We've nothing to go back for except our families, but other than that neither of us has a job, let alone a home to go to. I know we could live with our parents, but it's hardly the life of a married couple, is it? Why don't we put it to Monsier Dubois and see what he thinks? I can't see him turning us down. He's already said he'd be lost without us, he can hardly walk let alone pick the grapes, and I love it here and I know you do too. Can't we at least ask him what he thinks?'

Archie nodded. 'But don't get upset if he turns us down. It must have been hard enough having to ask strangers for help without having them move in.'

When they had approached the old man with their proposal they had expected some deliberation as he considered the idea. What they had not expected were tears.

'You 'ave been delivered to me by the angels; I knew it to be so when you came to my 'ouse. I could not 'ave asked for better than you and your good 'usband. Between you, you have breathed new life into the vineyard as well as the 'ouse. My poor sweet Louise would 'ave been so upset to see 'ow 'er beautiful 'ome had turned into a 'ouse with no soul, but thanks to you, Arla, it is a 'appy 'ome once more.'

That had been months ago, and things could not have worked out better. Arla took care of the house and the kitchen garden whilst Archie tended the vines under the watchful eye of Monsier Dubois, who taught him how to recognise and cure diseases which left untreated could wipe out the entire vintage.

Now, making her way into the kitchen, she sat down at the table and started to read her letter.

Dear Arla, Good news! Aidan is to be demobbed in April next year, so we're having the wedding on 15 June, same day as Mam's birthday. Connor's going to be Aidan's best man, and I want you to be my maid of honour. Gwen's already agreed to be a bridesmaid so it would make the wedding complete if you were to say yes!

I must admit I was a little worried that you might be on grape-stamping duties around that time of year, but Aidan says you don't harvest grapes until later on, so no excuses!

Because I have no one to give me away, Uncle Kieran said he'd do the honours. I must admit I choked up when he suggested it. They're such a lovely family, and I know Mam would have been thrilled. Do have a word with Archie and let me know asap whether you can make it or not, won't you?

The barn's coming on slowly, and Uncle Kieran reckons it'll be ready for us to move into by the time we're married.

Aidan wants to do the fireplace himself. I can't think why, but he's insisting we work around it. You know what men are like!

Gwen and Connor have been talking about marriage. The distance is getting to Gwen and she misses him dreadfully. It won't be long until she's passed her clerical course so she'll start looking for a job in Liverpool soon. As for Connor, he's left the electrical engineering programme; reckons it reminded him too much of when he first joined the RAF. He's starting an apprenticeship in car mechanics any day now.

Arla jumped as the door to the kitchen opened. Archie strode across the room and leaned down to kiss her cheek. 'How's my best girl?'

Arla held the letter up for him to read. 'Looks like we're off to a wedding!'

'June next year, eh?' He said after a moment. 'Are you going to tell her that she'll have to make room for three of us?'

'I'm not telling her anything just yet. You know what the doctor said: best not to tell folk until I'm three months along.'

Archie sagged. 'All this waitin' will be the death of me! I feel like I'm goin' to burst I'm that happy, an all I want to do is shout it from the rooftops! Have from the moment we found out.'

Arla giggled. 'Your time will come, Archie Byrnes, but until then you've got to keep mum, ha ha.' She placed a hand on her stomach. 'Goodness only knows I'll find it hard enough writing to Ellie without letting it slip that she's going to be an auntie in seven months' time.'

'I must admit, I always thought you had a gob like the Mersey, but you've proved me wrong these past few weeks.' He dodged the back of Arla's hand. 'I'm sure Monsieur Dubois's gettin' a bit suspicious, though – I caught him giving you a very funny look the other day.'

'Archie Byrnes, stop teasin',' said Arla. 'It's not good for me in my condition.'

Sitting in the chair beside hers, Archie took her hands and kissed her knuckles. 'In your condition! Me mam's gonna flip when she finds out.'

Arla grimaced. 'So's mine. It's going to be her first grandchild and we're living in a different country.'

'No kid of mine's goin' to grow up in the courts.' He jerked his head in the direction of the window. 'Fresh air and freedom to run around: what more could you ask for?'

Remembering how she had once wanted to marry an officer, she looked into his dancing blue eyes. 'All the time I was searching for my knight in shinin' armour to take me away from the courts and there you were, right under my very nose all along.'

Ellie smiled at her reflection. The war might have been over for a whole year, but money was still tight. Her wedding dress had belonged to Connor's mother, and after a lot of adjusting they had got it to fit perfectly. Swaying her hips from side to side, she admired the way the floor-length skirt swirled around her. She ran a finger over the delicate pearl buttons which adorned each sleeve and noted with satisfaction how small her waist looked in the A-line dress.

Gwen and Arla had worn different suits of palest blue, which they had bought from Paddy's Market, and together the three women had looked captivating.

Aidan, Connor and Archie had all worn their service uniform and Ellie's bouquet had been a mixture of wild lavender – in memory of her mother – and gypsophila.

Aidan's father had wanted to hold the wedding reception at the farm, but Auntie Aileen had flat out refused.

'Give him an inch and he'll take a mile. Before you know it you'll be getting married in the cowshed and havin' your weddin' breakfast in with the pigs. I know we can't afford a big church weddin' but there's nowt wrong wi' the register office and Connor's mam knows the landlady of the Throstle's Nest on the Scottie Road. She said she'll do us a good deal if we go there.'

Ellie smiled. The wedding had been perfect. Uncle Kieran had given her away, and Gwen's uncle had taken the photographs. The wedding breakfast had been a finger buffet and Auntie Aileen had made a beautiful three-tiered fruitcake.

Now, with their guests singing 'You'll Never Walk Alone' at the tops of their voices to the accompaniment of Uncle Kieran on the piano, Ellie had nipped into one of the pub's spare rooms so that she might get changed before she and Aidan left for their honeymoon. Stepping out of the dress, she placed it on the padded clothes hanger and hung it up on the picture rail before pulling her going-away suit out of the leather suitcase. As she smoothed down the creases she was interrupted by a knock at the door.

'Who is it?'

'It's me, Arla. I've got Gwen and Tilly with me. Can we come in?'

'Hang on, I locked it,' she said, her voice muffled as she pulled the jacket over her head before running to open the door.

'We're looking for somewhere a bit quieter so's little George can get some kip,' said Arla as she desperately tried to soothe the squawking bundle. 'What time's your train to Holyhead?'

Ellie glanced at the dainty watch on her wrist, a wedding present from Aidan. 'Couple of hours yet, which is just as well, because I've got something I need to do first. Would you mind holding the fort whilst I'm gone? If anyone asks, tell them I've stepped out for some fresh air and I'll be back in a bit.'

'Do you want one of us to come with you?' Gwen asked cautiously.

Ellie smiled reassuringly at their worried expressions. 'No thanks. I'd rather be on my own. I promise I won't be long.' She picked up her bouquet.

'I hope you're not going to throw that yet! I was hoping to be the one who caught it,' said Tilly, much to their amusement.

Pulling out a single sprig to keep, Ellie threw the bouquet towards Tilly, who caught it in one hand. 'But that's—'

'I threw it, you caught it, don't quibble. You might not have been so lucky down there with all those man-hungry singletons!'

*

Ellie stood before the small pile of rubble, a tear dropping from the tip of her nose to the dusty pavement below. She knew that coming here was important. It would be the last time she ever would; the only thing she hadn't known was what she would do when she got here.

Since her mother was buried in Walton Cemetery some might have argued that she should have gone there, but to Ellie Lavender Court was the only place she had ever lived whilst her mother was alive. All her memories of her mother were here, yet with most of the debris cleared away there were only a few loose bricks left to mark the spot where her home once stood. Closing her eyes, she envisaged the courts as they once were. Dirty, smelly, friendly, familiar and, more important, home. She could see her mother standing beside the small stove, her hands black with the few pieces of coal she had managed to buy, her brow smeared grey where she had wiped it with the back of her wrist. Her beautiful blue eyes smiled kindly at Ellie as she welcomed her home from school.

'Come in, alanna. It's tatties and beans for us teas, then I've got to go to Mr Wong's to do a spot of ironin', but you can come with me if you like, keep me company and help me fold the sheets.' Ellie could hear her voice as clearly as if she was standing next to her.

Too painful to watch, the vision faded, and bending down Ellie brushed dust off one of the few remaining bricks, whispering, 'I wish you could see me, Mam. I've grown into the sort of woman you would have been proud of, and my hubby's a kind, hard-working man who loves me with all his heart. He's the sort of man you would've chosen for me. His family have taken me in as their own and they're good, kind-hearted, honest folk, who'll make the most wonderful grandparents.' Her bottom lip quivered as a smile spread across her face. 'You would've made a brilliant Nana or Gran.' Taking out a handkerchief, she dabbed her eyes. 'I wish you could see me I wish you were here. I miss you so much.'

A hand touched her shoulder, making her jump. 'I thought I might find you here,' said Aidan as he slid a hand round her waist and pulled her close.

Resting her head against his chest, she looked at the remains of her former home. 'What do you think they'll do with this lot? I can't see them rebuilding the courts as they used to be.'

Aidan shook his head. 'I know the courts were your home, alanna, but most folk will be glad to see the back of them.'

Ellie nodded. 'Next time I come I suppose all this will be gone, won't it? No more Lavender Court, not even a hint of it.'

Aidan kissed the top of her head. 'I'm afraid so. Once they rebuild, you'll not be able to tell what once stood here.'

'My home,' Ellie said, her voice barely a whisper.

Turning her to face him, Aidan gazed lovingly into her eyes. 'You're starting the next path on your journey, only this time you won't be alone, you'll be with me, and we'll walk it together. Starting with our honeymoon in Wales, albeit a short one, but it's still a holiday

417

and one I'm very much looking forward to. So come on, Mrs Murray, dry your eyes.'

Nodding, Ellie entwined her fingers in his. 'You're right. That's why I had to come, so that I could bid a final farewell to Lavender Court.' She stopped speaking as Aidan bent down to pick up one of the bricks.

Smiling, he weighed the brick in his hand. 'It doesn't have to be final.'

Ellie's brow furrowed. 'What d'you mean it doesn't have to be final? And what on earth do you want that for?'

Holding the brick up, he smiled at her. 'It's a piece of Lavender Court, isn't it?'

She sighed impatiently. 'Yes?'

'We'll take it back with us—'

Ellie interrupted before he could continue. 'Aidan Murray, if you think I'm going to have it on the mantelpiece like some sort of awful ornament—'

'Not on, in.' He grinned. 'I haven't quite finished the fireplace, and this can be one of the bricks I use. We'll make sure it goes in the middle, so that it's in the heart of the fireplace, the heart of our home.'

Ellie's lips curved into a smile. 'So I'll have a piece of Lavender Court in the heart of my new home, is that what you're sayin'?'

Aidan nodded. 'So you see, you needn't say farewell to Lavender Court because you're taking a piece of it back with you to your new home, your new life, and when we have children you can tell them where the brick came from.'

Standing on tiptoe Ellie kissed her new husband. 'I wish my mam could've met you, Aidan Murray.'

He stroked her cheek with the back of his fingers. 'If you were right about the scent of lavender when we crash-landed at Biggin Hill, then she's not only met me, but saved me too.'

She gazed deep into his twinkling eyes. 'I love you, Aidan Murray.'

Bending down, he swept her off her feet and into his arms and kissed her gently. 'I love you too, Mrs Murray – always have and always will.'

READ ON FOR BONUS CONTENT

Dear Reader,

When I think back to what inspired us to write *A Mother's Love*, I believe it all stemmed from a conversation Mum and I had many moons ago about the poverty in Liverpool during the Second World War, and the type of people who would have lived in the court housing during that time. I felt it a dreadful shame that such a big part of Liverpool was no longer in existence for others to see, but then mum told me about the Museum of Liverpool and the replica they had made of one of the courts. Needless to say it wasn't long before we paid a visit to the museum, and when we arrived we were not disappointed! The museum have done a marvellous job of recreating such a historic part of Liverpool in such a small space, and they really captured the look and feel of the court housing as it must have been; from the dirty windows to the dark courtyard and outside toilets complete with sound effects! You get a real feel for how hard life must have been for those poor people and it makes one wonder what life must have been like for those also suffering the loss of a loved one and finding themselves unable to pay their way and the consequences therein.

Writing *A Mother's Love* was quite an emotional experience for us, especially when you consider how tough it must have been for a fifteen-year-old girl who had lost her family, home and money all within a matter of weeks. I learned a lot about life and love in a war-torn city, with no one but your friends to turn to.

I hope you enjoyed reading it as much as we enjoyed writing it.

All the best,

Holly Flynn x

LAVENDER GIFT BAG

All those of a certain age will remember the small lavender cushions you used to find stuffed into the back of an old chest of drawers. Mum had them, as did my grandparents. The trouble was I never used to leave them in the drawers, as I'd rather use them as pillows for my dolls – although I don't think mum minded much.

To Ellie, the scent of lavender brought back memories of her mother and the good times in her life. I hope making these gift bags bring back your treasured memories of days gone by too.

All the best,

Holly Flynn x

LAVENDER GIFT
BAG GUIDE

WHAT YOU WILL NEED

- Dried Lavender
- Dried Rice
- A fabric of choice
- Thread, pins, tape measure and scissors

1. Prepare your dried lavender filling; take two parts lavender and add one part dried rice.

2. Cut out two rectangles of woven fabric approximately 12cm x 6cm each (cotton works best).

3. Pin the rectangles right sides together and then sew a running stitch along the edges with a 1cm seam allowance. Remember to leave a gap at one corner.

4. Clip the corners with scissors and turn inside out, using a pin to tease out the corners. The patterned side of the fabric should now be on the outside.

5. Fill your bag with your filling, do not overfill.

6. Sew the opening closed.

7. Enjoy your lavender bag!

READ ON FOR AN
EXTRACT FROM

THE
CUCKOO
CHILD

March 1928

'Dot! Aw, c'mon, Dot, I knows you're there!'

The shout came clearly to Dot's ears, echoing slightly through the tin lid of the dustbin in which she was hiding. She could tell that Fizz was in the jigger which ran along behind these yards, but she could also tell that he hadn't got a clue as to where she was. How could he? Everyone was scared of old Rathbone, the butcher, in whose bin she thought she crouched, so the last place Fizz would think of looking would be in Rathbone's yard. She had only gone in there herself because she knew Fizz was hot on her heels.

She cocked her head, listening intently, and heard the patter of Fizz's plimsolls as he trotted along the jigger. She grinned delightedly, hugging herself at the success of her ploy. She had climbed over the wall which separated the yard from the jigger and had dropped down on to the weedy paving stones, meaning to find somewhere to hide, expecting to see a shed or a handcart, or even a pile of old boxes. Instead, she had seen three large galvanised dustbins. She had raised the lid of the foremost of these and had realised at once that it would make an excellent hiding place – if one was not too fussy, that was. But now that she was in the yard, she did not have much choice. Both the other bins were full to bursting, their lids not fitting properly over the mess of refuse within, but the third bin was almost empty. Then, whilst she had hesitated, she had heard a voice, sounding as though it came from the vicinity of Mr Rathbone's back door. It was unbelievably bad luck in one way, because she had thought that the butcher, if this was his bin, would be safely ensconced in his flat above the shop, but it appeared she was wrong.

So she had hopped into the bin, pulled the lid into position as silently as she could, and now waited in the noisome dark for silence to come once more. Then, and only then, would she get out of the bin, scramble over the wall and make for 'home' which, in this particular game of relievio, was the yard of the Old Campfield public house.

Unfortunately, as the sound of Fizz's flapping plimsolls faded, Dot heard the back door of the shop squeak open and footsteps entering the yard. She felt the hair rise up on the back of her neck; oh, Gawd, if old Rathbone caught her here there would be hell to pay. He hated kids and had a sharp way with them. When Dot's Aunt Myrtle sent her to get the messages, she never bought meat off old Rathbone if she could possibly help it, even though he was the nearest butcher to Lavender Court. Aunt Myrtle said he gave short weight on the cheaper cuts and his better stuff was too expensive, but Dot would not have gone to him in any case. She hated his big square red face, the large yellow teeth which showed on the rare occasions when he smiled, and the mean little eyes, almost hidden in rolls of fat. He was spiteful, too; he would deliberately bang your parcel of meat down on your fingers if you were unwise enough to have a hand on the counter, and if you dared ask for a free bone, or a bit of suet for a pudding, he had been known to grab a child by the shoulders and run them out of the shop, saying as he did so that he weren't a charitable institution and didn't mean to keep bleedin' slummies in luxury, not he.

However, the footsteps stopped just short of the dustbins and Dot heard someone inhale deeply, and then begin to speak. 'Ker-rist, that were a narrow squeak, me old pal. Still, it were a bloody good haul; the best so far, I reckon. We can't do nothing immediate, of course, 'cos the scuffers will be turnin' over every fence for miles around – every known villain, too – but they ain't likely to come to a butcher's shop in search of a grosh of jewellery.' Dot, listening intently, was pretty sure that the speaker was Mr Rathbone himself – so she had been right, this was his yard – and crouched even lower in the bin. 'Yeah, I reckon we done pretty well for ourselves.'

'Keep yer voice down,' his companion urged. It was a thin, whiny voice, one which Dot did not recognise, but she could imagine the owner. He would be small, skinny and weaselly, with watery eyes and a loose slobbery mouth. In her mind, she could see him clearly: thinning hair, a pink and whiffling nose, and a tiny, sandy moustache. But now the butcher was speaking again.

'Don't be such a fool; who's to hear me? All the other shopkeepers will be in their flats and not hovering about in their yards.' Nevertheless, he dropped his voice. 'No, we're safe enough here, and we can't talk in the flat. It's sheer rotten luck that me old mam came calling. I can't get shot of her before ten or so, or she'll get suspicious. She's not seen you, since she came in through the shop, and that's just as well an' all! She's a rare gossip, so I don't tell her that I've got me fingers in more'n one pie. You know women; she'd blab to some pal or other, an' our goose 'ud be cooked. No, this is strictly between you an' me, Ollie old pal. We both teks the risk an' we teks a half share in the profits an' all. That's what we agreed, ain't it?'

'Oh aye, I reckon you're right; least said, soonest mended,' the whiner called Ollie said. 'How soon will it be safe to sell 'em on, d'you suppose?'

'If I could take 'em to London, like I means to do, mebbe we'd get away wi' a few weeks,' the butcher said reflectively. 'But mebbe longer if the old feller croaks; you're a might too handy wi' that stick o' yours, Ollie. There was no need to hit him twice, you know.'

The other man gave a whicker of laughter. 'I 'ardly touched 'im,' he protested. 'Skull like bloody paper, that one, but he were comin' round afore we were out the door. You don't want to worry about him; he'll be tellin' everyone how he scared us off before we'd found the safe.'

'I reckon you're right,' the butcher said grudgingly. 'Tell you what, though, we'll have to get rid o' that emerald necklace. It's been the centrepiece of that window ever since I can remember, so everyone who's ever glanced into the shop will reck-ernise it at once. Besides, it's gorra be paste; stands to reason. If it were real it 'ud be worth a king's ransom an' no insurance company would cover it. I didn't mean to tek it, but then I didn't expect the old feller to pop up from behind the counter like a bleedin' jack-in-the-box. I shoved the rings, the gold chains and the earrings an' that into me pockets when he started to speak and the bleedin' necklace must ha' got snagged on somethin' in me hand, so I just shovelled the whole lot away an' legged it.'

'Yeah, I reckon you're right,' Ollie said, after a thought-ful moment. 'Pity, 'cos it 'ud look good on any woman's neck – 'twouldn't matter if it were paste. I don't see why we need to tek the other stuff to London, when there's fences a lot nearer home, but s'pose you took the necklace down there, though? It 'ud be worth a few quid, I reckon.'

'Didn't you hear what I said?' the butcher snapped, almost crossly. 'Wharr'ave you got for a brain, Ollie? Lard? The scuffers will issue a description of everything we took an' the only thing which really stands out is that bleedin' necklace. Diamond rings, gold chains an' fancy earrings are common to every jeweller in the land, pretty well. Give 'em six months an' they'll sell like hot cakes an' not a question asked. I know what you mean, but we might as well write "robbers" on our foreheads in red ink as try to sell the emerald necklace. It's gorra go, and it's gorra go tonight. And I ain't doin' nothin' clever, like takin' it down to the Mersey, 'cos if I did, some interferin' scuffer would either stop me on the way an' search me pockets, or some kid might fish it out o' the mud an' run after me to tell me I'd dropped it.'

'I could take it,' the other said eagerly. 'No scuffer 'ud stop me.'

But the butcher cut across this remark, his voice menacing. 'No you don't, Ollie my son. It ain't that I don't trust you, but wharrever we do, we'll do together. This is goin' in the dustbin. Tomorrer's collection day, and when I dumps the old newspapers in the mornin' I'll put a match to the bin an' the whole lot will go up like a bonfire on Guy Fawkes night. I'll be in the shop early, afore anyone else is about, an' after the fire in the bin has died down I'll rake through the ashes, make sure there's nothin' left to give us away.'

Dot's skin crawled with apprehension, but she stayed still as death; they were, after all, the width of the yard away, which she judged to be about twenty feet. It was only when she heard footsteps coming across the yard towards her, and realised that the butcher must mean to jettison the necklace right away, that she was unable to prevent herself making a quick, involuntary movement, ducking even lower in the bin so that her elbow struck the side with a soft – though quite painful – clunk.

The footsteps stopped abruptly. 'What were that?' the man called Ollie asked suspiciously. 'I reckon someone's hiding behind them bins, for all you said—'

'No one but a midget could hide behind them bins. It were likely a bleedin' rat,' the butcher said dismissively. And as if to prove him right, there was a scuffling, a muffled squeak, and then the butcher's voice, triumphant. 'Told you so. Them bleedin' rats is everywhere. Bloody things is a menace to a butcher. I've had the Public Health round many a time, sayin' me premises ain't clean, but if I gets cats in they grumble about them an' all.' The footsteps began to approach the bin once more, but even as he lifted the lid from Dot's hiding place the butcher continued his grumbling monologue. 'They marches in an' out of me shop as if they owned the place; and them rats is strong too. They shove the lids off the bins an' go rootin' round inside, makin' a terrible mess. Looks like I'll have to borrow a couple o' terriers off mad old Jumbo, what keeps the second-hand bookshop further up Heyworth. They're a mangy-looking lot but they can clear a nest of rats in five minutes flat.'

The bin lid clattered back on even as Dot felt something cold and slithery fall down the front of her ragged dress. Fortunately, her gasp was muffled by the closing lid and she realised, with great relief, that the men had turned away from the bins and were returning to the back door of the shop.

'We'll 'ave a quick bevvy in the back of the shop, then you'd best be on your way, 'cos it's better if we ain't seen together tonight,' the butcher decided. 'We'll meet Saturday night in the Elephant, on the corner of Stonewall Street, but for now I'll open a couple o' bottles o' Guinness, then we'll split. I don't want me mam pokin' her nose in an' askin' questions about what I've been doin', because you know—'

The back door shut quietly, cutting the sentence in half, but it was a good ten minutes later before Dot dared to so much as move in her smelly prison. Until then, she continued to crouch in the bin, going over what she had heard. There had been a jewel robbery – that was plain enough. The robbers had taken the necklace by mistake and meant to destroy it in the morning; that was clear, too. What was not so clear was how the man called Ollie would leave the premises. Dot remembered that there was a door in the butcher's back wall leading into the jigger, to which Mr Rathbone held the key. The sensible thing, she realised, would be for the man to leave by that route, and you never knew when that would be, so it behoved her to get out of the bin – and the butcher's yard – in the quickest possible time.

READ IT NOW

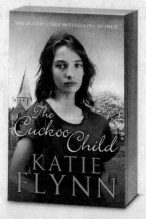

It takes courage to overcome the odds...

Liverpool, 1928: Abandoned by her mother at a very young age, Dot McCann lives a lonely life with her distant aunt and uncle. A cuckoo in the nest, she spends her days trying to keep out of trouble.

When Dot overhears a conversation whilst playing in the street, her life changes for ever. What she discovers could send one man to prison and another to the gallows. In a desperate attempt to right a wrong, Dot teams up with runaway orphan Corky, Emma, a local jeweller whose shop has been burgled, and Nick, a handsome young reporter investigating the crime.

But Dot and Emma have been recognised and they soon find themselves in very real danger. Will they uncover the truth before it's too late?

AVAILABLE IN PAPERBACK AND E-BOOK

Enjoy the best of the

KATIE FLYNN

Springtime Collection

Katie Flynn
The Top Ten *Sunday Times* Bestselling author
Alone and far from home...
Sunshine and Shadows

KATIE FLYNN
SUNDAY TIMES bestselling author of LITTLE GIRL LOST
FORGOTTEN DREAMS

Katie Flynn
The Top Ten *Sunday Times* Bestselling Author
A Mother's Hope

Katie Flynn
The Top Ten *Sunday Times* Bestselling Author
He saved her life. Will he win her heart?
The Liverpool Rose

Katie Flynn
The Top Ten *Sunday Times* Bestselling Author
Darkest Before Dawn

KATIE
FLYNN

If you want to continue to hear from the
Flynn family, and to receive the latest news about
new Katie Flynn books and competitions,
sign up to the Katie Flynn newsletter.

Join today by visiting
www.penguin.co.uk/katieflynnnewsletter